Faraway Hill: Book Two

Gold Editon

This book is a work of fiction. Names, characters, places and incidents are either the products of the author's imagination or are used fictionally.

Any resemblance of any of these fictional characters to an actual person (living or deceased) is entirely coincidental.

ISBN 978-0-9963134-2-1

Dedicated to the good people of a great state who host my silly story and to the pioneers of early television who had to make it all up as they went along.

AUTHOR'S INTRODUCTION

Welcome to the middle part of the *Faraway Hill* trilogy, as the saga of Karen St. John and the Hallorans continue.

As a returning reader, you know that the trilogy is a re-invention of network elevision's first soap opera. Someone asked me recently if the Karen St. John that appeared on TV in 1946 is anything like my Karen St. John. The answer is simple: no.

While few details of TV's "Faraway Hill" are known, it likely relied on a formula common to radio soaps: a well-meaning, generally upright heroine who gets entangled in various dramas. Soaps (especially radio soaps) were targeted to housewives and this gave listeners women to admire or at least to like. This formula was also used in some of the first daytime television sudsers. I didn't want to travel down that well-worn road. My feeling is that by making Karen not a paragon of virtue but a psychopath with a continually twisting view of logic and morals made for a much more interesting and compelling character.

I am also asked if the Faraway Hill I describe in the trilogy is based on a real town. The answer to this question might be: almost.

The truth is that I have been envisioning part of the Warner Brothers Ranch. This studio back lot, built in the 1930s by Columbia Pictures, has a "small town" theme location that has been used for decades, from movie serials to hit movies like "Pleasantville." Its most famous feature is the fountain in the town square. It was at this fountain that Samantha told Darren he'd be a father on "Bewitched"; John Adams, Ben Franklin and Richard Henry Lee sang and danced in the film version of the musical "1776" and the cast of "Friends" got soaked as part of that show's opening titles.

And, of course, people always wonder who will end up with whom; will anyone learn that it was Karen who killed Lewis Halloran and not Munroe Gale; when will Mark Bradley return to further collect on his blackmail, etc. The most immediate questions often involve the first book's cliffhanger: who got shot, who pulled the trigger and will someone die from the incident?

Turn the page and find out.

James A. Richards, author
Faraway Hill

EPISODE ONE

One by one, the darkening clouds gather. By early evening, they have become a quilt of gray and black. The blanket covers everything, from the farms near the Quebec border to the rugged beauty of the White Mountains and the breathtaking Hampton Beach. Thick and heavy drops fall on Manchester's nearly empty streets and sidewalks. The few signs of life come mostly from the glow of street lamps.

Mabel Baxter is trying to stay dry. She is standing alone at a bus stop on Elm Street waiting for her ride home. A stocky woman in her late forties, Mabel is wrapped in her rubber rain coat and holding a big golf umbrella. It has been a long day. Mabel is the assistant manager of a boutique on Merrimack Street. A delayed shipment of merchandise finally came in today. She and an associate had to work late getting them inventoried for the all-important Christmas season. It was exhausting, tedious work and she is anxious to get home.

From the bus stop, Mabel can see the Verizon Arena a couple of blocks away. Its quiet there tonight, but the Monarchs have a big game tomorrow. She isn't much of a hockey fan, but her husband has season tickets. When there is a concert or a game the arena is lit as bright as a star. Tonight it is nearly as dark as the sky.

Across from her is Veterans Memorial Park. People come to the park for all sorts of festivals and concerts. The four acres can fill quickly on some days, like when a popular local band performs on the covered stage. Normally it would be empty on a rainy night like this one. But Mabel can see a man strolling up to the park's centerpiece fountain. He stands there, wearing a long dark coat and holding an umbrella, staring at the Civil War statute. *How weird*, she thinks.

Another man strolls toward the fountain, dressed in a hooded coat, trying to look casual. She can't see many details through the rain but the two men shake hands. They are too far away for Mabel to know what they are talking about, but the meeting alone is strange. It makes her a little scared. *Where is that damned bus?*

The rain starts to fall a little faster and the wind blows a little harder. The two men seemed to have agreed on something and walk toward Elm Street. Mabel pretends not to notice them.

Then she hears the shot.

One of the men falls into the other's arms. Mabel turns to see a third man at the far end of Veterans Park run off. *Oh, my God!* One of the men cradles the other in his arms, looking around in panic. He sees Mabel. "Help me!" he screams. She pulls out her cell phone but is frustrated to see the battery is dead. *Damn!* Frightened, Mabel is about to run across the street when her bus finally appears. At the moment the door opens she says to the driver, "That man, in the park over there, he's been shot!"

****

One shot should do it. If she aims just right, Ann can pick off the head of John Halloran.

This is what it's like, spending most of your days and nights in the same two rooms: you point your imaginary gun at different sites in town --- like the famous statue in Faraway Hill's main square --- just to relieve the tedium.

The rainy weather makes it tricky, but Ann's certain she could still hit her mark. *What a scandal,* she thinks to herself. *That would be a fucking big deal.* But, then, her whole life these days is one big scandal.

Ann Halloran, the unwanted bastard child, is alone in her two-room suite at the far end of the big old mansion. Last Thanksgiving she was living on a struggling farm, dating a hunk named Mark Bradley and wishing for a better life. She was Ann Gale then: a nobody that nobody important or interesting wanted to know. Now she is Ann Halloran, a somebody almost everyone talks about.

"Everyone" seems to include the man who calls her "New Hampshire's most fascinating woman." It happened last night, at the party the Hallorans threw for state's most famous artist. Agnes Gabler is a wonderful and colorful woman who just turned 95. Ann planned to keep to herself. But that one man sought her out. Senator Richard Davis is old enough to be her father. He is handsome an sophisticated. He works in Washington. He has powerful friends in Concord. He has seen the world. Yet, he spent the evening with her, talking about things big and small, and seemed to really enjoy it.

A knock on the door and one of the maids enters. She is bringing the hot cocoa Ann requested. Sometimes living in this house is a little like an extended stay hotel, complete with room service. The woman smiles, leaves the mug, and quietly departs.

The Halloran is mansion very different from the farmhouse. It is large and spacious and elegant. Yet it sometimes seems to have shrunk her world. Ann promised Julie that she'd avoid the main areas of the house. Being here is too upsetting for the Hallorans. Ann is a living, breathing reminder of a tragedy that rocked this family. So when she is home, Ann spends nearly all of her time in these rooms. Servants bring her what she needs. The satellite TV, high speed internet and private phone connect her with the rest of the world. But make no mistake: Ann is being punished for something someone else did.

Shit, it's not as if I haven't suffered, too. After marrying Mark, Ann discovered that he was earning extra money prostituting himself to other men. She kicked him out of her life and he has since disappeared. Then Ann learned that her father wasn't the town drunk Munroe Gale, but instead it was New Hampshire's wealthiest man, Lewis Halloran. She and the rest of the world made that discovery only after Munroe killed Lewis and then himself.

The irony is that Ann spent her whole life wishing to live in the world of the rich and glamorous. Now that she lives in that world the rich and glamorous don't want her. At least, the Hallorans don't.

This leaves her, all alone, looking out her window, trying to find a new imaginary target in the rain.

****

We must look like a painting. Julie Halloran is sitting on a little settee in the nursery with her husband's loving arm around her. Cradled in her own arms is her little boy, taking his last meal of the day. This is a moment she'd like to savor, the kind of moment someone should photograph. Even with Julie's leg in a cast, they must look like the ideal young family. *If only,* she almost says out loud.

The baby finishes his nursing and, with a cute little yawn, John Benjamin Halloran closes his eyes.

"He's likely out for the night," the new nanny, Maggie, advises in her strong Irish accent. She has had the job for only a couple of days, but already Julie likes her. Even so, she is reluctant to put her son back in the crib. They feel like a real family, all three of them, as they sit together. But hovering at the back of her mind is something that has been worrying her: last night, at the big party, she saw her husband passionately kissing his best friend.

His best friend. She is still processing the scene. It was counter to everything she has known about Greg. He was a ladies man in college; he'd even hooked up with a waitress in Manchester a few times before they were engaged. Julie knows all of this. Nor does he act like any of the gay men she has known. Certainly Julie has never seen him look at another man the way she has seen him notice other women. Jack is the same way. *Could they be bisexual?* That would explain a lot.

Maggie gently lifts John from his mother's arms and puts him back in the crib. The new parents wish her a good night. The couple walks across Center Hall to the three-room Master Suite and enter its large, oval parlor. Greg has to help her; Julie's leg is still in a cast from the fall she took on the night John was born. The medication makes her groggy. Looking at her husband, Julie can see a warm, loving smile. *He really likes being a dad.* But she can't shake the image of his kissing another man. Julie isn't sure she can or should avoid the subject much longer. "My parents invited us over for Thanksgiving," she says, releasing him to pick up her crutch. "I think it would be good for them, especially Dad." Julie's father has been going through a tough time. His law partner ran off with most of the firm's money earlier this year. Ben has been fighting to keep the firm afloat ever since.

"I think that's a great idea. My family doesn't do much for Thanksgiving; that's what Christmas is for."

"Your Aunt Joan told me that at breakfast." Several Halloran family members had come to the mansion for Gabler's party. They left this morning. "I'm sure Aunt Karen will be there too. She told me yesterday that she's buying a second home here in Faraway Hill."

"That's great. Do you think it'll be okay if I ask Jack? He and a friend are staying in Manchester. I don't think they have any plans." Greg is casual about the request. *He acts as if nothing happened.* Julie doesn't say anything at first, and just leans on the crutch. But his question touches something in her, something that pushes aside the confusion and leaves only the hurt and the anger. Finally, without looking at him, she responds quietly but firmly: "No, I don't want him there."

"I don't understand."

"I don't want Jack Campbell for Thanksgiving."

"But I thought you liked Jack; Why not?"

"Because," now she looks directly into Greg's eyes and says in a steady, resolute way, "I don't want to sit next to the man you're fucking."

Greg is stunned. He stands there looking pained and dazed, as if someone has just punched him in the gut. Julie can see what he's thinking; it's written on his face: *how does she know?*

"I'm sorry, did I get it wrong? Is *he* doing the fucking?" She wants to be angrier. Julie wants to scream at him or hit him with the crutch or break something. But the meds sap her energy. She can only use her words. "I'm never quite sure how it is when two guys get together."

Again, he just stands there.

"Oh, come off it Greg, just admit it. I saw you kissing him last night. Holy shit, there were three hundred people downstairs and the two of you were in the hall necking like teenagers!"

"I'm . . . I'm sorry." *At least he has the sense to look ashamed and embarrassed,* Julie thinks, *and maybe he is, but I don't give a fuck right now.* "Well, it's big of you to say it. Damn, I am your *wife*; we haven't been married a year and I just gave birth to your son!"

Greg just surrenders. "Julie, I don't know what to say," he responds softly. But she won't give up: meds or not, Julie Halloran wants answers from her husband.

"Let's start with this: What are you, gay, bi, what?"

"I'm bisexual."

He says the words so simply and directly that she knows he has thought about this in the past. For Greg, his sexuality is a long-settled issue; but not for her. "So there have been other men as well as other women?"

"In prep school there were some guys; in college it was mostly women." Before last night, Greg having sex with other men would never have occurred to her. Now he is confessing it. *This is fucking unbelievable.* But Julie is too drowsy to scream. Instead, she asks calmly, "why the hell didn't you tell me before?"

"Because I didn't think it would matter."

"That is an asinine thing to say; of course it matters!" The meds are really starting to kick in. But she needs to get through this. The crutch is literally the only thing keeping her standing. "Well, believe it or not, I could deal with my husband having that kind of past. Hell, this New Hampshire, we have gays and bis and whatevers all over the place; but like *hell* if I will accept a husband who fucks around on me!"

"I have not been fucking around on you!"

"Do you love him? Jack, do you love him? Do you love me?"

Greg hesitates for a moment, a very brief one, and then answers, "Yes."

"Yes to what?"

"I guess . . . yes to both. I love you both and . . . I just don't know what to do about it."

She can see that. *He looks so lost, like a scared little boy.* If Greg was someone other than her cheating husband, Julie might be sympathetic. But he is and she isn't. "So have you been cheating on me since the wedding? When Jack 'comforted' you after your father's death was it in *our* bed?"

"No, no, sweetheart that's not how it is! I *have* been faithful. I love you and haven't touched anyone else since the wedding. I mean, not until . . ." he stops, catching himself before revealing something he knows he shouldn't. But she knows how that sentence should end. It is something Julie has sensed for awhile: "until your last trip to Atlanta."

"Yes," he answers with a quiet shame in his voice. Julie doesn't have to ask why. Ever since they discovered that her best friend is Greg's illegitimate half-sister their marriage has struggled. For months he and the rest of the Halloran family fought Ann, who was determined to become a Halloran in her own right. Julie regularly found herself in the middle. Throughout these past several months, the newlyweds argued over Ann or tried to ignore Ann or simply felt the pressure of Ann.

"So, let me get this straight --- if I can use that word --- at the very moment I was fighting morning sickness and trying to move your bastard sister into the mansion, you were fucking Jack Campbell in Atlanta."

Greg just nods.

"That's it; you're not going to say anything more?"

"All I can say Julie is that I am really sorry and I do, I really do, love you."

"But you love him, too."

"Yes."

The meds are finally starting to win out. She won't be able to stay awake much longer, but Julie needs to make something clear first. "There are no words --- I mean it, Greg --- *no words* to tell you how much you've hurt me. You need to make some decisions. And so do I, because even if you choose me, I'm might not choose you. I don't know yet; this is all so fucking weird." She pushes herself past the meds long enough to stare right into his eyes. "But one thing I am sure of: you are *not* sleeping in my bed tonight." She points to the suite's other bedroom, the one of the other side of the oval parlor. It hasn't been used much for the last couple of years. "In fact, you are sleeping there until *I* decide otherwise."

With that, Julie hobbles into their bedroom and slams the door closed, leaving Greg alone in the parlor, feeling guilty and ashamed. On the other side of the door, Julie doesn't bother to undress. She just drops her crutch to the floor, climbs into bed and succumbs to the medicine, crying herself to sleep.

****

A few miles south of Faraway Hill, a cute little boy with bright eyes and mischievous grin places a blue 4 card on top of the green 4. With a triumphant smile he cries, "uno!"

Jack Campbell smiles back at his son. The kid is just five years old and already he's a master player. Jack saw the Uno deck in a store window this afternoon while they strolled down Elm Street. He thought he'd teach the boy to play. Now it seems the boy, also named Jack, is teaching him a thing or two.

"When is Poppa coming back?" The three of them are staying in a pair of suites at the Radisson Hotel in downtown Manchester. The rooms are nice, spacious and comfortable: Jack is staying in one while Little Jack and his other father, Joe Westbrook, have the other.

"Soon," Jack answers. Joe asked for some alone time. It didn't take a genius to figure out what why. Jack knows that look well and he saw it often while in college: a mixture of loneliness and horniness that all men get from time to time. It just seems odd to him that Joe would experience it. After all, Joseph Westbrook was born Jacqueline Westbrook: she had a sex change after giving birth to their son. Jack has never known a woman to get that horny. Joe did hint recently that he would welcome a night with Jack. But he couldn't see himself fucking Joe, after having had him as Jackie. It would be just too weird --- *and my life has become weird enough.*

"Your turn," the boy says pointing to the cards. The kid doesn't know about the reassignment surgery; he was too young. Nor does he know yet that Jack is his father. The two only met recently when a desperate Joe came to him seeking help from his dangerous stepfather. The old man is angry and embarrassed at having a "freak" in the family.

The kid impatiently taps his finger of the table. "Uncle Jack, I *said* it's your turn." The kid is really into the game.

"So it is," Jack puts the deck together and starts shuffling for another round when his cell rings. The number can only mean one person: Melvin Waite. *It's about time I heard from you, asshole.* The balding, middle aged attorney has been blackmailing him for a year. Finally, with Greg Halloran's help, Jack found the papers in Lewis Halloran's study that Mel wants. He can exchange them for some incriminating photos of Jack hooking up with Mel's young nephew. But the papers reveal information for a secret bank account --- it seems that Mel was also blackmailing the late textile tycoon. Jack has been thinking about his options ever since.

"I'll be right back."

"Okay," Little Jack sighs, unhappy at the delay. He starts shuffling the deck on his own in a way that would make a harden Vegas dealer proud. Jack takes his cell and steps into the bedroom, closing the door so he can speak more freely. "What is it Mel?"

There is no greeting or pleasantries. Jack hates Mel and Mel hates him. "You got it, faggot?"

Jack's in no mood for the lawyer's shit. "Don't you *ever* call me that again --- especially now."

"What the fuck are you talking about?" Jack can almost see Mel's face through the phone. "Shit, I told you not to do that!"

Jack chuckles. *I got him*, he thinks. "Yeah, well, I was never very good at instructions, especially ones coming from assholes like you."

"Don't play with me kid, or your old man will find out his beloved son is a fruity fudge packer."

"Guess what Mel: now that I know about the ten million, I'm not all that concerned about my dad disinheriting me."

Mel pretends to laugh. It sounds very fake. The more Jack talks to him, the less like a lawyer the man sounds. Right now he could pass for a third rate pimp trying to protect his turf. "I warn you, fag: without my password, those papers are worthless. Just turn them over to me and all will be fine."

"How about a new deal, Mel: you give me the password, I'll give you the papers and we split the money right down the middle."

Jack can hear a crash through the phone; Mel apparently threw something out of anger. "Bullshit! I didn't give up my life and career for a fucker like you to walk away with my money." *His money? Isn't it really the Hallorans'?* Jack is grateful that Greg isn't asking for it back. Mel should be, too.

"Think about it, dude" Jack advises him and claps his phone shut.

✳✳✳✳

Eve King fights the urge to throw the phone against the wall. *Is this what it's going to be like from now on?* "Damn you Karen," she yells. "This is too risky." *Calm down,* Eve tells herself, *calm down.* She and her husband Ben were hoping for some quiet time. Too much has been going on too fast; the worst being her sister's surprise decision to buy a house in Faraway Hill. She has been worrying about it every since. So instead of enjoying a restful night in their Colonial

Revival, Eve has called Karen to scream, to beg --- to do whatever it takes --- to change Karen's mind.

"I don't see what you are so upset about," Karen answers with her studied elegance. Her style comes from growing up watching movies, patterning herself more and more on women like Lana Turner. But she can't fool Eve, who imagines Karen on the other end smiling that scary smile of hers. "All I want is to have a second home near my family. I'll still be spending most of the year in New York."

Eve doesn't believe a word. "What if Julie finds out the truth? What do you think will happen?" She glances across the living room to see her husband, watching the early evening news.

"And what if she does? I *am* her mother, after all."

"No Karen, you were *never* her mother. I am the one who changed her diapers and taught her how to read. I'm the one who explained about sex and help her study for the LSAT. All you've ever been is the cool aunt who goes to parties at the Guggenheim and sends expensive birthday presents."

"There is no reason to be upset, Eve. I don't plan to tell her anything."

Eve is tired of the argument. She knows that there is no reasoning with her sister once her strange mind is made up. So they say their goodbyes and Eve slams the handset onto the receiver. "Damn her to hell."

Ben doesn't say anything. He doesn't have to. They've been over this before. Besides, he is still worried about losing his law practice. Eve just plops onto the sofa next to him. Ben wraps an arm around her and pulls her close.

"This just in," the Boston anchor interrupts their moment. "United States Senator Russell Brooks has died of an apparent heart attack at his home in Concord. The senior senator from New Hampshire had served 22 years in the United States Senate and was a key vote in several important issues. The state's junior senator, Richard Davis, has released a statement calling Senator Brooks 'one of the finest people to ever serve New Hampshire and the United States. A good friend and a great public servant; he will be missed.' Again, Senator Russell Brooks is dead at the age of 70."

"Well," says Ben. "Everyone saw that coming, what his heart condition and all." The Kings have met both Brooks and Davis several times over the years; most recently they saw Senator Davis at Agnes Gabler's big birthday bash at the Halloran mansion. "Did you see how much time Davis was spending with Ann?

"No," Eve sighs. "I spent the night keeping an eye on Karen."

The phone rings. They consider ignoring it. But Eve notices an odd number on the Caller ID and picks up. "Hello?"

A police officer is on the other end. Not one from Faraway Hill, but an officer in Manchester. "What happened? When?" Ben turns to see a concerned look on her face. "Yes, thank you, we'll be there as soon as we can." She hangs up.

"What is it?"

"It's about Barry," Barry Studer is the hot young lawyer in Ben's office who has been trying to drum up new business to keep the firm alive. Sometimes his demeanor and his methods have been grating; he is definitely a kid who tries way too hard.

"What about Barry?"

"He was shot while in Veterans Park. He's at Elliot Hospital right now."

****

Its raining harder now; Joe can barely seen anything out the window.

The Manchester Police officer questioning him is polite and professional. He is also young and damned cute. Joe wishes he could remember the man's name. They are sitting in a little corner of Elliott Hospital, not far from the emergency room. Wet, cold and scared, Joe is wrapped in a blanket. The officer is taking notes. "How well do you know the victim?"

"We just met tonight."

The officer raises an eyebrow. It actually makes him cuter. "You met tonight --- in the park?"

Joe considers coming up with some sort of cover story but decides against it. He and his son have been running from Joe's stepfather and his goon for months. But neither knows they are in New Hampshire. *Whoever fired the gun must have been aiming at the other guy.* He realizes that the truth is the best choice, no matter how embarrassing. "It was . . . it was a hook-up. We found each other on Craig's List. All I know is his name is Barry."

The officer nods. He isn't judging Joe, which is pretty cool of him. "We found his wallet. The man's name is Barry Studer. Apparently he is a lawyer here in Manchester."

"I didn't know that." Suddenly Joe remembers the officer's name: Aaron Tracey. Even his name is cute.

"Where are you from, Mr. Westbrook?" It is a measure of how good Joe's surgeon is that most people cannot tell that he used to be a she. "Los Angeles," Joe answers cautiously. "My son and I are staying with a friend at the Radisson."

"Have you any idea why anyone would want to harm Mr. Studer?" They traded pictures online. As far as Joe is concerned, he was just a hot looking top who wanted to get off quick. Joe hasn't been with anyone in months and really craved someone --- trannies get horny, too --- especially since Jack turned him down.

"I honestly don't know. The plan was to meet at the park and then go to a restaurant or someplace to talk some more. We were to decided if --- and what --- to do after that."

Cute cop Aaron writes this down.

"It's safer, you know," Joe defends himself, "to meet in public first." At least, usually it is. *Shit, who expects to be shot at while meeting his trick?* It was one of the scariest moments of his life. Joe is grateful for the bus driver and lady who ran to their aid.

They continue with the interview until the officer is satisfied. Joe can return to his hotel, but cannot leave New Hampshire without telling the police first. He wonders if Barry will be alright. But mostly he worries about what he'll tell Jack and their son.

****

Shit, shit shit. That's all a soaking wet Michael Bickel can say. *Shit, shit, shit.* He's never fucked up a hit before, especially not an easy mark like Jackie Westbrook. He drives around Manchester, drying to dry off and calm down. It doesn't work. So, instead, he returns to the Radisson, to sit in lobby with their complimentary coffee, to think about what to do next and keep an eye on the door. He has a paper, today's *Union Leader*, to hide his face if needed. Sure enough, the freak walks in: wet from the rain and a scared look on his/her face but very much alive.

Shit.

He watches from behind the paper, as the girl-boy makes her way to the elevator, oblivious to the man who tried to kill her less than two hours ago. She is returning to her son and the guy helping them. It was a weird coincidence, in a series of weird things that they are all staying in the same hotel.

Mike has always wondered what the kid thinks of his "poppa". Its hard enough dealing with a real father; it must be strange has hell to deal with a freak like

Westbrook. Michael Bickel loved and hated his own dad at the same. The dude ran off when he was a kid and rarely visited. It left him, a poor black boy growing up in South Central Los Angeles with no real role model. Certainly his choices were limited: become an alcoholic drifter like his father, a slut like his mother, or get a job with the neighbor who drove the cool car. He chose the neighbor. His being a drug pusher and hit man wasn't a bad thing, just a fact of life. It gave Mike a reason to run from the cops, something he and the other black kids had to do anyway. The man became another father to love and hate. He gave the boy lots of great advice. One of them was, "stay cool and you stay in control." That guidance has really helped over the years.

But tonight he forgot the lesson and is paying for it. Big time.

That dumb ass old man. He shouldn't have let Joseph Bologna push him. The boss' people have been tracking the trannie and her son for months. He's been sent on plenty of quick plane trips to different cities to take her out, only to have the freak give him the slip. But while in New Hampshire to confront his errant wife, Mike stumbled onto the boy-girl in Manchester. "Get rid of the freak, now!" ordered a frustrated Bologna. When Mike saw her/him walk alone into Veterans Park, he saw his chance --- and then fucked it up. *So much for staying cool.*

Shit!

****

It's nice to see rain again. Living in California, Vivian missed the change of seasons. That's one of the wonderful things about New Hampshire. Here, spring is unquestionably spring and there is no doubt when its winter. It is never that way in Los Angeles.

She also missed the small things, the little things, like cleaning up after dinner. Her first husband enjoyed doing the dishes together. It kept the evening alive a little longer. Her second husband, Mike, hated it. Now she and Lorene use the dishwasher, but the feeling is the same. "Is that the last of it?"

Lorene steps into the dining room. "No, we forgot a plate." She returns with the errant dish. "Don't forget, you promised to call Sofia."

She hasn't forgotten. If there is one thing Vivian does miss about LA, its spending time with her neighbor. That dear, sweet old lady was her only refuge. Mike always gets mean when he drinks. That's when he's at his scariest and most unpredictable. It took Vivian all the courage she could muster to leave him, and even then she wouldn't have been able to without Lorene paying for the plane ticket.

Lorene's late husband drank, too, but he just became very sad and withdrawn. They don't talk much about Munroe or any of the other men in their lives. They don't have to; both women know it all. Besides, those marriages seem in the distant past.

Vivian glances at the kitchen clock realizes that, despite being three hours behind, Sofia will be going to bed soon. She likes to get as much sleep as she can. So, Lorene takes her lover's hand in hers for the short walk to the living room. They do that a lot, holding hands. Soon the people of Faraway Hill are sure to notice and start gossiping. But neither cares; they are too much in love.

Lorene picks up the needlepoint she's been working on for the last few days and settles into a comfortable armchair. Vivian dials California. These calls used to make her nervous, but they have become routine and even a little boring: Sofia seldom has much news.

It always takes a few rings before the old woman picks up the phone. Sofia Rodriquez is in her 80s, very frail and moves slowly.

"Oh, Vivian, I am so glad that you called," the fear so clear and undeniable in Sofia's voice that Vivian knows immediately what has happened. "Mike found out, didn't he?" Lorene's head shoots up when she hears that.

"I am so very sorry. I didn't tell him, I swear."

"How did he find out?"

"My son got me that caller ID thing and Mike saw the number."

"If you had my number, why didn't you call to tell me?"

"He deleted it, so I had to wait for you to call back."

Oh my God, he's on his way. The fear, the terror, grips her. Vivian knew she should have bought a gun, but let Lorene talk her out of it.

"I am so sorry," Sofia says, sounding guilty as well as afraid.

"That's . . . that's okay. It'll be alright. I'll call you again in a few days." Vivian hangs up the phone and turns to see Lorene, looking worried.

"He knows" She explains, her body shaking and her voice cracking. "My God, he knows where I am."

EPISODE TWO

Dark and dreary and depressing; that's the view from Karen St. John's window. It's as if all of Manchester has gone into mourning for no one in particular. Just hours ago the Merrimack River sparkled in the brilliant sunlight. No more. She'd forgotten how changeable New Hampshire's weather can be, especially in autumn.

No doubt some people are using the evening rain to catch up on their reading or simply veg out in front of the TV. Neither appeals to her. Karen just got off the phone with her sister, who begged and pleaded she not buy the house in Faraway Hill. But it's too late; the deal is done. The papers have been signed. The check has been deposited.

Karen St. John never expected to be moving back to Faraway Hill. She was certain that her life would forever be in Boston or New York. She'd still be in Manhattan if not for one important thing: *my little girl needs me.*

She turns away from the window and pours herself some red wine. It came from the hotel. It's a good but unremarkable vintage. When she settles into the new house, Karen will have bottles from her late husband's collection sent in from his wine cellar. But for an evening of quite reflection, this will do.

Karen sits on the sofa to take a sip and browse through a portfolio of photos of her new home. It is such a classic New England house that it has her thinking back to all of the people and places that meant so much to her growing up in rural New Hampshire. There was the little ice cream shop in Keane and the trips to maple festivals. A sweet elderly woman used to baby-sit the girls and tell them charming little stories. A cute boy named Nathan used to tease the sisters like he was their little brother. But the most important person was a thoughtful, eccentric and sometimes boisterous man she called Daddy.

One plus one equals two. They cannot equal anything else. That simple equation was the first lesson in logic two girls learned from their father. The second thing Professor Reginald Scott taught little Eve and Karen is that the equation can also be misleading: one plus one may equal two, but exactly do "one" and "two" mean?

It was the kind of creative thinking that intrigued young Karen but her sister found boring and silly. Eve used to roll her eyes when their father went on and on about all the various dimensions of logic and philosophy. He loved moral riddles. Such as: if logic is so valued, why must it be so cold? After all, logic dictates that if someone irredeemable harms you, then getting rid of them is necessary. But is it right?

Reginald's beautiful brogue always added depth and meaning to whatever subject he discussed. It didn't matter if it was Plato or chocolate pudding; it was a simple joy just to hear him speak. When he died suddenly, his wife and daughters could feel his absence in ways that cannot be described. They couldn't stay in Keane, where he taught, and moved to Faraway Hill. Throughout the years, his ideas and his words remained at Karen's core even as she struggles to understand them.

She turns the pages of the portfolio, just as her mind turns the pages of time. The house Karen bought in Faraway Hill is a beautiful, Victorian-style built at the turn of the last century. It has a wonderful wrap-around porch and lots of stain glass. She remembers marveling at it growing up, considering it second only to the Halloran mansion for its grace and beauty. The house has had many incarnations, including as a bed-and-breakfast. For that reason, there are almost as many bathrooms as there are bedrooms and the house has a master suite. The price was certainly right, especially for a woman of Karen St. John's means.

The Faraway Hill years were not particularly good ones. Her mother battled depression and alcoholism. Eve escaped through her studies while Karen found safety in watching great old movies. Women like Bette Davis and Lana Turner enthralled her, instilling in her the wish to live the kind of glamorous life not possible in a small town.

Karen Scott first faced a dilemma --- the kind of moral and philosophical question Daddy talked about --- was as a young woman just out of high school and it came in the form of Alexander Mundy.

Alex Mundy was handsome and charming. He played rugby. He knew about wine. He knew about art. He was one of Lewis Halloran's closest friends. And he got her pregnant. It ironically happened the same night Lewis got Lorene Graves pregnant. But while Lewis wanted his child --- and was prevented by his family and his fiancé --- Alex refused to have anything to do with them. He accused Karen of sleeping with someone else. Lewis backed him up. It was devastating. Karen was forced to turn her daughter, Julie, over to Eve and her new husband. From that moment on, she could be nothing more than cool, rarely seen Aunt Karen to her own little girl.

It still makes her angry. There are times when the fury is so strong she can barely contain it. What makes matter worse is that Alex has disappeared. No one knows where he is or what he is doing. She stops for a moment and takes some deep breaths. *Just relax, just relax.*

There were other hard lessons. Many people, especially men could not be trusted. They lie and lie often. This was true in college and in life. So she applied daddy's lessons her own way. This has aided her career in public relations, where she climbed the professional ladder however she need to: sometimes with hard work, sometimes with inside information, sometimes undermining a rival --- and sometimes in bed. The methods were as logical as one-plus-one. But always with the grace, charm and sophistication of the movies stars she adored. As she got better at it, fewer and fewer people got suspicious.

During all those years, Karen's daughter grew up calling another woman mother. Karen's own mother would lose her fight against alcohol, and only Eve was at her bedside during those last moments.

In her new life in Boston, Karen found that she could get away with almost anything, as long as she planned carefully. She would study a problem from every possible angle. Daddy would have been impressed. When one of her lovers deceived her, she remained calm and controlled. Retribution was anonymous and from a distance. It worked. No one ever knew. No one but Karen.

Her biggest break came on a business trip to New York City. There she met financier Martin St. John. Already married with two grown children, Martin was frustrated with his wife and their life together. Karen soon became his mistress. She kept her eye out for opportunities. When she learned of Laura St. John's many health issues, it was easy for Karen to make her death seem natural. Of course, it wasn't.

This was Karen Scott's first murder. Two years later Karen and Martin were married.

Planning and executing Laura's death was nerve-wracking. But Karen found that getting away with murder was the most empowering experience of her life. It proved that seeing things from every angle with careful consideration will make almost anything possible.

Karen closes the portfolio and sets it on the table. She savors another sip of wine and stretches out on the sofa, eyes closed to all but her memories. Even now, she smiles with satisfaction at how she rid herself of Laura and the others. Daddy's logic works.

Martin's grown children hate their stepmother. Both of them are about Karen's age. Fortunately, Jeffrey opted for a new life in England. But Madeline is another matter.

Karen's husband was very wealthy, very connected and very old. As much as she relished the power and privileges of being Mrs. St. John, she still craved a passion Martin couldn't provide. Lovers were risky; so she scoured the web and found a handsome young man using the moniker Johnny X. But with her resources, it wasn't hard to learn that his real name is Mark Bradley. Ironically, many of his clients were some of Martin's friends and associates. Mark typically serviced men (they paid better) than women, but he was happy to have the socialite on his roster. Against her better judgment, Karen developed a crush on him. Mark found her feelings to be restrictive and crushing. At one point she offered to support him completely if he gave up his other clients. He refused. "I'm your escort," he'd insist over and over after taking her cash. "I'm not your lover or your boyfriend or anything else."

Martin found out. It happened shortly after encountering Lilly Halloran again, who was attending the same Manhattan fundraiser as the St. Johns. They hadn't spoken or seen each other since Karen left New Hampshire. For years, she kept on eye on developments with the Hallorans, hoping for a chance at revenge. Alexander Mundy disappeared long ago; no one seems to know where. Lewis and Lilly, it was often said, were unhappy. Their son spent most of his time at boarding schools and they never had another child. Lilly had developed a heart condition that required daily medication. Martin had a similar disease. An opportunity provided itself at the party, when Karen was able to discretely replace some of the pills in Lilly's bottle with tainted ones. All Karen would have to do is wait however many daily doses until Lilly took a wrong pill. That happened two weeks later in Faraway Hill when Lilly Halloran suddenly died of a heart attack. No one questioned it; there was no reason to.

Using her father's lessons, Karen St. John had mastered the craft of murder.

Shortly after Lilly left New York, Martin confronted Karen with information about Mark. She panicked: a scandalous divorce could ruin her. Martin got revenge on Mark by threatening first his clients and then the hustler himself. Mark eventually fled. It wasn't until much later that she discovered him in Faraway Hill, where Mark had married Lewis' illegitimate daughter while selling himself on the side. The irony still makes her laugh: Mark ended up in her hometown merely by accident.

Martin remained a scary problem. But Karen realized that she could be rid of him the same way she got revenge on Lilly. A few days after a particularly emotional show down, Martin died of a heart attack. He had taken one of the tainted pills. Madeline St. John voiced suspicion of her stepmother, but no one would believe her: Karen was visiting friends in Boston at the time. Besides, it was well known that Martin had heart problems.

There remained only two people left for Karen's vengeance: Alex Mundy and Lewis Halloran.

Lewis was in good health; it was impossible to achieve his death the same way Karen got rid of Lilly and Martin. She needed another way. Once again, Daddy's lessons --- combined with good timing --- came to her rescue. Julie announced that she was marrying Lewis' son Greg and wanted her beloved aunt at the wedding. Karen knew about Munroe Gale, the man who raised Ann as his own child. It wasn't hard to murder Lewis and frame Munroe. She knew that Faraway Hill's lazy and incompetent sheriff would be easy to fool, and he was.

But Daddy's logic didn't work all that well this time. No, the Halloran family resented Ann and blamed her for Munroe's "crime". It caused a rift between Greg and Julie that reached crises when Greg renewed his affair with another man. Karen learned all of this from phone conversations with Julie and a private investigator looking into Greg's past.

Now, sitting in her suite and enjoying her wine, Karen St. John must once again look to Daddy for inspiration. She must decided what to do to make things right again for her little girl. Killing Greg or Ann or both are definite possibilities. But getting away with murder can be tricky, even for a skilled killer like Karen.

So, she will do what she knows Daddy would advise: she will wait and watch and look for opportunities. And she'll do it from her wonderful new home in Faraway Hill.

****

For the second time in less than a week, Ben and Eve King rush to Elliot Hospital.

All during the rainy drive from Faraway Hill to Manchester the same questions keep going through their minds: *who would shoot Barry? Why would anyone shoot him? Why hasn't his family been called? Will he die?* The nurse couldn't give them any information on the phone. It wasn't until they arrived at the handsome, century-old Victorian building did they get the good news that Barry will be alright. "The wound isn't serious," explained the charming young doctor whose name Eve didn't catch. "He'll be able to go home tomorrow."

They are directed to his room, where they hear someone snoring even before they reach the door. It's Barry's roommate, on the other side of a thin curtain, a sleeping unseen chainsaw. He looks up at them, an odd expression on his face. "Hi, thanks for coming."

Eve steps over to the bed and takes his hand in hers as only a mother can. "We came as soon as we could. What happened?"

"It was weird; somebody shot me while I was in Veterans Park." *He looks so exhausted,* she thinks. *As if the weight of the world has been pressing down and finally given up.*

"We heard that from the doctor," Ben says. "But we don't understand why. Do you know who did it?"

Barry shakes his head. "Nope, no clue; the guy ran off. The only witness was this lady at the bus stop. But she was too far away to see his face. The police are pretty frustrated. They think it may have been random. You know, some crazy guy."

"But why were you in the park on a night like this," Eve wants to know. "I mean, the Christmas events haven't started and the weather is awful."

Now the odd expression on Barry's face changes to something more recognizable, a mixture of shame and embarrassment. As a mother, she has seen it many times before. "I . . . I was there to meet somebody."

"Who?"

"I'm sorry, Eve, but I'd rather not say. It was . . . a dude I met online."

"Online? You mean for . . ." Ben stops himself; he seems to know what the young man is about to say, although what is lost on her. "For sex?"

"Ben!"

"I'm sorry, Eve, but that's what happened, isn't it Barry?"

Barry looks away to stare out a window whose view is blurred by the rain. "Yes," he answers quietly. "I was meeting another guy."

"I never knew you were gay."

"I'm not Ben; at least, I don't think I am. I never did anything like that before, I swear. But my girlfriend left me, the business is shitty, I have no family here, few friends and . . . and I guess I needed *someone*."

"That's okay," Eve reassures him. "A lot of people get curious." It's the only thing she can think of to say.

"She's right, Barry, don't be embarrassed. Besides, maybe the gunman was aiming at the other man."

"The cops don't think so. He's visiting from out of town. Nobody here knows him." Barry turns from the window to look at Ben. "I am going back to Iowa tomorrow after checking out. I was going for Thanksgiving anyway, you know, but . . . I'm sorry, Ben, but I may not come back."

"Look, Barry, your personal life is your own --- "

"It's not that. It's just . . . we both know the firm is going under. I don't blame you. That asshole Mel Waite did it. But Iowa is where my family is. I may not like them but they're all I've got. And there are firms in Dubuque looking."

"Are you sure about this? Don't you want to think about it some more?"

"I've been thinking about it long enough. This . . . this thing tonight pretty much finalized everything for me."

There is little Ben can say, so he just nods. But Eve knows that, inside, he thinks *that's the end of my firm.*

****

Greg Halloran did not sleep well. All through the night he kept dozing off and having the same nightmare over and over, reliving the painful confrontation with his wife. The details are stunning. Every part of the searing episode, from sharing their son in the nursery to the angry look on her face, are told repeatedly and clearly. Each time she said "I don't want to have dinner with the man you're fucking," Greg would jolt awake. When morning finally comes, all of the sheets and blankets have been kicked to the floor. He just lies there, naked but for his briefs, watching the sun rise through the window.

There is a slight knock on the bedroom door. *Could it be Julie? Is she willing to forgive me? Is she willing to talk?* Last night she ordered him into the master suite's empty bedroom. She stayed in their bedroom across the parlor. "Come in."

Frederick, the family's aging butler, opens the door slightly to peer inside. "Good morning, sir," he says gently. "I apologize for the early hour."

"That's okay," Greg sighs with disappointment. It makes sense that she wouldn't forgive him right away. Granted, he *did* promise Jack that they'd be together again after the baby was born. Still, hurting the woman he loves is the last thing Greg wants. Seeing the pain and anger in her face has given him second thoughts about Jack.

"Mrs. Halloran asked me to move your things right away."

"My things?"

Greg can now see Frederick carrying some of his suits. "Yes, sir; she asked that I bring your clothes in here rather than have one of the maids do it. She feels that this would be . . . more discreet." Greg simply nods without saying anything. Instead he lies on the bed, emotionally drained, watching the butler go back and forth. It's a sad sight. Eventually Greg rises. He can't stay here feeling miserable all day. That's what the office is for.

Walking over to the window he hopes to see something, anything, that will pick up his spirits. But he doesn't find it. The garden that wraps three sides of the house provides a brilliant rainbow of colors much of the year; but not late fall. All Greg can see are bare branches and bits of frost on the ground. Through the naked trees he can see the old red brick building that used to house the estate's staff. His mother began repairing it the year she died, updating the electrical and plumbing and replacing the roof. But it is still empty; a reminder of an age before today's common conveniences when big houses needed lots of people to do all the mundane chores that life requires.

For Greg Halloran, life requires he make a decision. Choosing Jack means divorce, scandal and possibly losing his son. Choosing Julie means never seeing Jack again, always wondering what their life together could be like --- something that will probably lead to bitterness and resentment. He told her the truth last night that he loves them both. But Julie made it clear: he cannot have them both.

Frederick brings in the last of his clothes, nearly tripping over a blanket lying in a heap on the floor. It occurs to Greg that Julie's attempts at discretion won't go very far: servants like to gossip. The moment a maid comes into the master suite for routine cleaning will be the moment word gets out. Having Frederick moves his clothes only delays the inevitable. After putting some socks into a drawer, the butler asks about breakfast.

"No thanks, I'm not hungry."

The butler picks up the blanket and puts it on the bed. "I'm sorry about that Frederick; it's been a tough night."

"That is quite alright, sir."

"Where is Mrs. Halloran right now?"

"She is in the nursery with the baby."

Greg puts on his robe, walks through the parlor and into Center Hall. The door to the nursery is shut. He feels oddly compelled to knock before entering. Julie is sitting on a chair next to the crib nursing their little boy. It's a beautiful sight, even with the cast on her leg. The crutch leans against the nearby changing table. Julie looks up to him but doesn't say anything; she doesn't even smile.

"Good morning," he says, trying to make the best of the situation. But Julie just nods. "Did you sleep well?"

"Yes; the meds took care of that."

Greg is hesitant to step any closer. The tension-filled air is dark and heavy and thick. Only their son seems to provide some light. Greg never thought he could love someone or something so much. He'd take the boy into his arms this very minute; but he knows that might lead to a confrontation. Instead, the new father comments that "he looks so peaceful, so happy."

"Well, that's the look of innocence."

The remark was is as direct and painful as a slap across his face. *I deserve that.* "I'm . . . going to get ready for work."

Again, Julie says nothing. She just lets him walk alone back to his own room. It is only a few steps away, but it seems like miles as the same question goes through Greg's mind: *what the hell do I do now?*

****

What a shitty day. What a fucking shitty day this is.

Ben King is sitting alone in his office on the 17th floor of Brady-Sullivan Plaza. When Ben and his partner relocated their firm years ago from a small storefront, it was a major accomplishment. They, their wives and their growing staff toasted with Champaign. Today Mel is divorced and has absconded with most of the firm's money. Ben has let go nearly all of the employees. Now he is losing Barry Studer. So, here he sits, just before Thanksgiving, all alone in a big fancy suite he won't be able to pay for.

"Hello?" a voice calls from the reception area. *Who could that be today of all days?* Ben steps out of his office to see, standing at the vacant receptionist's desk, Senator Richard Davis.

"Hello Senator, this is quite a surprise."

Davis smiles the warm, confident smile of a politician who understands the power of a warm, confident smile. "Happy Thanksgiving."

"Thank you; and the same to you." As depressed as he is, Ben appreciates the visit of such an important man.

"Are you busy?"

Ben laughs. "Look around you, Senator. I have all the time in the world."

"I know that things have been . . . a challenge for you this past year." Again, he smiles that smile. "But I think I can give you one hell of a Christmas present."

What the hell can that be? Ben escorts Richard into his office where they sit together on the leather sofa. The senator declines the offer of some coffee and instead gets right down to business. "I've just come from a meeting in Concord. We were discussing the unfortunate passing of my colleague."

"Everyone will miss Senator Brooks. He did a lot for this state."

"That he did; but the governor knows he needs to appoint a replacement immediately, especially if the party wants to retain the seat in next year's election."

Ben is hardly in a position to make a donation, and tactfully says so. But the senator shakes his head. "I don't think you understand: the governor doesn't want a donation. The governor wants to appoint *you*."

"*Me?*" The thought of a political career has never entered Ben's mind; not once. He loves the law too much and spending time with Eve at their home in Faraway Hill. Besides, there are other issues to consider. "Senator . . . you know that my firm has been struggling since my partner . . ."

Davis raises his hand to stop him. "Of course I do; everyone in New Hampshire does. But everyone also knows that you did nothing wrong. Mel Waite is the scandal here, not Ben King."

"Well . . . okay," Ben says, not sure how to take that statement. "But why me? I don't have any political experience. I'm not all that important."

Now it is Richard Davis' turn to laugh. "Of course you are! You have been a part of several key committees in both Manchester and Concord. Your wife works at a prominent bank where one of her clients is Agnes Gabler. Your son-in-law is the richest man in New Hampshire. You are a respected lawyer who has been honored twice by the state bar association. You've even had some op-eds in the *Union Leader*."

"They weren't much."

"But they tell us that you are the ideal Democrat to hold and keep this seat: a social progressive who also embraces the independent, Libertarian spirit that is very New Hampshire."

Ben looks around his office and the remains of a once prosperous law firm. The offer is tempting, especially since he really hasn't any other options. Of course, taking the seat would mean spending a lot of time in Washington. Eve may not like that. She is very comfortable with their life in Faraway Hill and her career in Manchester. But then, Washington isn't so far away: maybe something can be worked out. But another concern crossed his mind: "isn't the term up next year? I've never run a campaign before. Won't I have to start that at the same time?"

Davis nods. "Yes, there is no getting around that. But the state party chair and I can help you with everything from staffing to fundraising. Fortunately, you are well respected in this city --- and as every politician knows: if you win Manchester, you win New Hampshire."

Nevertheless, Ben still needs to talk it over with Eve. "Sit down with you wife," he advises. "Talk to her about it. But the governor wants to make the announcement as soon as possible so that Brooks' replacement can be sworn in for the January session --- and he expects you to say yes."

With that, Richard Davis shakes his hand as Ben escorts him out the door, leaving him to think: *Maybe this isn't such a shitty day after all.*

****

This is one shitty day. Greg sits in his office, watching the bad news unfold on TV. He switches between CNN and CNBC and sees the same troubling news: a nation-wide strike is planned in Thailand to protest a political stalemate in the parliament. CNN seems to get the most recent reports:

> "The king, who has been out of the country seeking medical treatment, is expected to return within the next few days. He is considered the most respected person in Thailand, but has had a history of giving the politicians a chance to resolve a crisis before he himself steps in. In any event, a nation-wide strike would be a hit to every major company --- including U.S. firms with substantial investments in Thailand."

Investments like the big textile mill Greg's father acquired before his death. This same mill --- which has the potential to make huge profits for the family company --- has also been a management headache. There were times when he should have gone to handle matters personally but couldn't leave the country because of Julie's pregnancy. Now it looks like there won't be a mill to manage --- and the black ink will quickly turn into blood red.

"Mr. Halloran, would you like me to call everyone in?" Most of the staff took the day off to prepare for Thanksgiving. Greg and his secretary are among the few who showed up.

"No, don't bother; there isn't much anyone can do anyway."

She nods and leaves him alone to stare at the screen. *Could things get any worse?* Suddenly, Greg's cell rings. It's Jack. *I guess I can't avoid him.*

"Hey dude, how are things?" Jack's upbeat voice really contrasts with Greg's mood.

Greg glances to this morning's *Union Leader* sitting on his desk. "They are what they are," he says with a sigh. "Did you see that there was a shooting last night near your hotel?"

"I know; weird, huh? I thought Joe might know something --- he was out for awhile last night --- but I guess not. He said he doesn't." For some reason, the article declines to name any of the people involved. Besides, Jack has some great news: "I think I've found a way to get rid of that SOB and my Dad at the same time." Jack fills Greg in about the deal he has proposed to Mel Waite that will end both the blackmail and Jack's financial dependence on his troublesome father.

"Are you sure this is all okay, dude? I mean, technically we are dealing with Halloran money." Greg should probably insist on getting the money back, especially with what he sees on TV. But doing so would just result in a lot of questions. *Besides, if I have to break up with him . . .*

"No, you keep it; explaining to the family where the money came from would be too complicated." He has no idea what Mel was blackmailing the old man over and doesn't really care as long as the fucker is out of everyone's life.

"It's a ton of money."

"I know."

"Are you alright? You don't sound good."

"I didn't get much sleep last night." He takes a deep breath and says straight out what he needs to tell him: "Julie knows about us."

A stunned silence; finally through the phone Greg hears, "Holy shit! Are you okay? Did you tell her?"

"Not exactly; she saw us kissing the night of the party."

"Fuck!"

The two of them become quiet, both knowing the next question. Jack eventually asks it: "so what does this mean?" Greg can hear the worry in his voice. Jack is obviously afraid of losing him again. He responds softly with a simple, "I don't know."

More silence, more pain. *How can I give him up?* But that is the price Julie demands. And he will probably need to pay it to keep his son.

"Greg, I'm sorry --- we need to talk about all of this --- but I have to go home for Thanksgiving. I can't get out of it. I'm leaving really early in the morning."

"Okay, I understand." He's spending the day with Julie's parents so they won't be able to get together anyway. Greg nearly says "I love you" but instead he just mutters "bye" and claps the phone shut. *Yes,* he thinks watching the bad news unfold a world a way, *this is one shitty day.*

****

Eve King loves to cook big meals, especially Thanksgiving. It doesn't happen often, with her busy schedule. She finds joy and satisfaction in the whole process. From selecting the turkey to kneading the pie dough, everything about it is therapeutic. A welcome break from the stresses of the office.

When the newlyweds remodeled the house, the kitchen was a major focus. It was originally a bland, utilitarian room with cheap metal cabinets that had sometime in the past replaced the original wood. Eve remembers the tacky avocado colored appliances. They redesigned it with big family gatherings in mind. The custom-made cabinetry includes an island where, as a little girl, Julie used to sit on a stool and chat with her mother about anything and everything. She misses those days. Sometimes Ben or Julie would often wander in to find Eve singing to no one in particular, even while stuffing the turkey.

But things are a little different this Thanksgiving.

Ben came home last night and told her that he is being asked to complete Russell Brooks' last year in the U.S. Senate. Taking the seat will upend their lives. It means Ben will need to spend most of the week in Washington and a lot of the rest of the time raising funds and campaigning for the next election. "It's just too much," she told him.

"But, Eve, my firm is dead," he pleaded. "Only the Halloran account is keeping things going. I need to do *something* with my life --- and this is a great opportunity."

She understands that. With Barry Studer gone, the firm won't last much longer. Eve feels sorry for the confused young man. Ben was able to arrange to keep his name out of the papers. Eventually the news will get out. But by then Barry will be home in Iowa and few people will still be interested.

Eve also has another worry: Julie.

"What the hell does Julie have to do with it?"

"Oh, come on Ben! We're living in the age of tabloids, blogs and 24-hour news channels. Don't you think some reporter won't dig up the truth?"

"We both know the odds of that are really small."

He may be right. But with Karen buying a house in town, Eve has become very sensitive to the risks. They debated the issue for hours, but she eventually agreed. This is what they do, what they have done for over twenty years: if one of them really wants to do something, the other supports it. But that doesn't mean Eve has to like it or that she doesn't have to worry. And she is still worrying, even as she cooks her big meal.

The kids arrive on time. Greg sits in the living room with his father-in-law to watch football. It's obvious that Greg really isn't into it, but he seems to know enough about the sport to play along. Julie comes into the kitchen to spend time with her mother. She is still using the crutch. "I wish you had brought Johnny."

"I know Mom, but that would have meant bringing all that baby stuff with us. Besides, the nanny doesn't celebrate Thanksgiving --- she's from Ireland --- so I don't have to worry about leaving him."

Julie seems odd to Eve, as if she is distracted by something. The kids also act strange around each other. It is hard for Eve to pin down. *Maybe they had a fight.* She's about to ask Julie when Karen arrives with her usual flourish. For the rest of the day, Eve's sister takes the spotlight. They hear a story about meeting a Saudi prince and another about a grand party at Lincoln Center. There is not time to talk to anyone else about anything else. Eve nearly grumbles hearing Karen go on and on about her plans for the new house. *Why the hell does she have to do this?*

Ben finally makes his big announcement when dinner is served. He had waited all day, but Karen's domination of the party kept getting in the way. Everyone congratulates him; Julie is especially excited. Eve offers a calm, supportive smile hiding her true feelings. Hiding from everyone but Karen, who seems to read her mind, and gives her an odd smile.

✷✷✷✷

Ann Halloran remains impressed with all the changes made to the Gale farm. Growing up the house always seemed about to fall apart. But since inheriting money from Lewis Halloran, her mother has renovated and redecorated everything.

The mood is also different. In those days, holidays were only happy if Munroe wasn't drinking. There was never a way of being sure when you woke up Thanksgiving or Christmas or Easter morning. Sober, Munroe was loving and gentle and a joy to be around. Drunk, he was morose and sullen and lonely. Today there are smiles all around.

They are eating in the dining room, a space never used while Ann was growing up. There wasn't even a table back then. Now it's decorated in the warm, welcoming and sophisticated earth tones found in other parts of the house. Lorene and Vivian are charming together, and Ann finds herself liking them as a couple. But every so often . . . it's hard to pin down, yet she can sense something is wrong. It is as if they are expecting bad news on the phone or an unwelcome visitor at the door.

The conversation stays clear of anything unpleasant. They talk about the food or the weather. Nothing about husbands or men; and considering their histories, that's probably a good thing. Yet, Ann finds herself thinking about Richards Davis. Older, handsome and worldly; she is still amazed at his interest . . . and even more amazed at hers.

Then it happens: the phone rings and the two older women visibly jump. *What is going on with them?* Vivian gingerly picks up the receiver, hears a voice that frightens her, and she slams it down.

"Vivian," Ann asks, "what's wrong?"

Lorene and her lover exchange a strange look. "Is it that the crank caller again?" Lorene asks in a way that sounds a little rehearsed. Vivian says that it is. When Ann suggests calling the police, the two dismiss the idea. But they appear relieved as if something terrible has been gotten out of the way and the rest of the day is more relaxed. Ann decides not to pursue the subject, but still she wonders and she worries.

****

JD's Tavern serves one of the biggest Thanksgiving buffets Joe Westbrook has ever seen. Every conceivable holiday dish --- from the required turkey to at least two dozen different sides --- is on display. Desserts are exhibited on three big, round tables.

His son Jack keeps fidgeting. Every so often Joe has to give him a warning look while filling their plates. It isn't easy. The restaurant is surprisingly crowded. Not only are there hotel guests at JD's, but apparently a number of locals come here for their holiday meal.

One of these people, obviously staying at the Radisson, keeps trying to talk him up. She is some blonde former party girl named Denise who makes one embarrassing pass after another. She even follows him to the different buffet tables. When Joe was a woman he never would be so crass. Subtly was Jackie's style. This girl has none of it. Finally he gets so fed up that he leans in to whisper sweetly, "you're real cute and all but I prefer guys with big dicks."

At their table, Jack devours the turkey. "Slow down," his father/mother insists. Then Joe looks up to see a surprise: in walks in that cute police offer Aaron Tracey. On his arm is an equally attractive woman, a brunette with shoulder length hair and a friendly smile. Aaron notices him and waves. Joe finds himself waving back.

"Hello Mr. Westbrook."

"Hello Lieutenant," Joe responds hoping against hope that the girl is his sister. *Oh, please let her be his sister.*

"Please, call me Aaron. This is my girlfriend Chloe Thompson." *Fuck, there goes that fantasy.*

"Nice to meet you, Chloe; I'm Joe and this is my son, Jack."

Somehow Joe ends up inviting the couple to sit with them and, oddly enough, it feels comfortable. As if they had known each other one time but haven't seen one another in years. It is strange but welcoming. And surprising: at one point Aaron admits to having a gay sister living with her wife and kids in Boston. "We're having Christmas with them," Chloe adds as if it is the most natural thing in the world. *Maybe it is these days,* Joe thinks, and it makes him again consider making New Hampshire a permanent home.

****

Wealth can be seen at every corner in every town throughout Westchester County. This is where New York City's old money elite have lived for generations. The Rockefellers' massive 3,400-acre estate, Kykuit, is located in Pocantico Hills. Bill and Hilary Clinton live in Chappaqua. The Astors and Vanderbilts had "country estates" in Scarborough.

John and Elizabeth Campbell live in Briarcliff Manor. Theirs is a large house not far from Long Hill Road. Home is a cape cod, strangely out of place among the colonials and Georgians that dot the neighborhood. It is here they raised their two sons. Jack hates this house. Every step is a painful reminder of a strict man never satisfied with his kids or his wife. He avoids coming here as much as possible; but holidays are a requirement for the Campbells. Jack has no choice but to leave Joe and their son in Manchester and hope that they will be okay.

The house has always had an odd, faux quality that seems even more artificial to him compared with the truly historic Halloran mansion. It was built by Jack's grandfather in this town of privilege as part of his campaign for legitimacy and acceptance. *His* father --- Jack's great-grandfather --- started out as one of many Scottish immigrants trying to make it in the New World. A tavern keeper, he stumbled onto a way of making a lot of money by buying property in Manhattan and Brooklyn cheaply during the Great Depression. To call the man a slum lord would be an insult to slum lords. When he died, Grandpa Campbell began to reinvent the family. First he sold off most of the holdings to invest in more glamorous building developments. Then he converted to Catholicism, mostly to use the Church as an entry into a better level of society. Finally, he built this house.

Grandpa may have taken his religion lightly, but not so his son. Jack's father could put the Pope to shame. He forced his kids to go to mass regularly and Catholic schools until finally they had enough. Both boys also learned to keep certain things from their parents. It was safer. Now, as one of his sons arrives the other greets him. "Dude," Nick says nervously at the door. "You gotta go."

"What the hell are you talking about?" Jack spent a fortune on last-minute tickets to fly in from Manchester. He wants to get the day over with.

"He knows, Jack, he knows . . . Dad knows all about you and those other guys."

Stunned, Jack just stares at his little brother as two frightening words come screaming through his mind: *holy shit.*

EPISODE THREE

Jack Campbell has never considered himself to be a lonely person. He has never really understood loneliness. Ever since he was a little boy, he has been the most popular dude in any room. It didn't matter if it was kindergarten or a college frat, people have always gravitated toward him. Jack hadn't really encountered loneliness, true loneliness, until he met Greg Halloran.

Now he understands.

His first reaction to loneliness was not to be alone. This is why Jack Campbell is waking up in bed with someone he doesn't know. Make that *two* someones he doesn't know: a boy and girl --- two college kids around twenty --- he had picked up in a bar last night.

Jack didn't stay for Thanksgiving dinner. Nick tried to hustle him out to avoid a scene, but it didn't work. The old man insisted on seeing him. Even on his death bed, with nurses surrounding him and tubes connected to him, John Campbell is a formidable presence --- and a little scary. But Jack managed to hold his own with him. The two had a loud, painful argument throwing out words like "faggot" and "bastard" and "fuck you." All this time Nick tried to run interference and their mother sat in a corner crying. Eventually, Jack's dad made it clear that he is being disinherited and banned from the house --- and family --- forever. "I never want to see your fucking, faggoty face again," were his dad's last words.

All alone and feeling all alone, he grabbed the train to New York. This is where he finds himself now, naked in a Brooklyn studio with two anonymous lovers.

Jack considers his bedmates as they slumber peacefully, one on either side of him. They are not quite up to his usual standards. The guy is cute, but on the thin side with no muscle definition. An earring is the kid's attempt to be cool. He is an awkward bridge between boyhood and manhood. The girl is rather chunky, with dyed red hair. Her tits are her best quality, big and round. These are suburban kids living a cushy-style of bohemia in Williamsburg who decided not to go home for Thanksgiving. That must have pissed off their parents, who are surely paying the bills.

Hooking up with them was a mistake. But Jack feels so lost: his family disowning him, Jackie becoming Joe --- and likelihood of losing Greg.

The girl snores a little. He remembers making the couple's fantasies come true in a single night: the boy watched Jack fuck his girlfriend, the girl watched him fuck her boyfriend. The night's highlight was a triple, with Jack fucking the boy as he fucked her. He hasn't done anything like this since college. As mistakes go, it was a fun one. The boy came just after he had. *That was cool.*

But his problems, and his loneliness, haven't gone away.

Jack rises carefully so as not to wake the kids. The tiny, sparsely furnished studio has little beyond a mattress on the floor and a computer in the corner. Clothes are scattered everywhere. Drunkenness, loneliness and horniness don't encourage neatness. It takes Jack, nude, some time to gather up his things and dress. Before he leaves, he looks back to see the boy stretch awake and give him a thumbs-up.

****

Michael Bickel doesn't feel lonely. He feels angry and frustrated. Ever since the botched shooting --- something he was pressured into against his better judgment --- he's had to keep a low profile. Part of his frustration is in knowing that not only is Mike's target still alive, but she is sleeping peacefully in the same hotel.

Only the cheap scotch he bought seems to help.

The press isn't mentioning any names and what little Mike has picked up indicates that the police are confused. Instead of investigating Vincent Bologna's mutilated stepdaughter, they are focusing on the local guy who took the bullet. *I suppose that makes sense,* he muses, *after all it must look like he was the target.*

Thanksgiving was not fun. Normally, he'd be watching football while his wife cooked the turkey. Sometimes friends would come over, but it would usually be just the two of them. Of course Vivian would inevitably say something shitty making him slap her. But that never bothered him much: a man needs to keep his woman in line. Knowing that she is only a few miles away just adds to his frustration. *That bitch needs to learn her lesson.*

Mike was going to have his holiday dinner in the Radisson's restaurant, until he found the freak and her son there. They were sitting with another couple. It took him a moment to realize that the man is a local cop he'd seen walking around Manchester. *Shit.* Ever since then, he rarely leaves his room, except for trips to the liquor store. It's too risky to be seen around town much.

Vincent Bologna has called him several times, insisting that Mike carry out his task. But the old man doesn't seem to understand that rushing things is what has caused the current problem. "I need that bitch out of my life," he growled to Mike in their last conversation.

So, Michael Bickel stays in his hotel room, drinking scotch and grousing about the women who bring hell to his life . . . and wondering how to fix things once and for all.

****

Greg feels all alone in the world. The office is closed for the holiday weekend. He hasn't heard a word from Jack. There is nothing much for him to do this Friday morning. Worst of all, Julie has barely spoken to him since last night.

Last night: that awful, painful ride home. Faraway Hill is a small town. The Kings live only a few minutes away. But the drive seemed like it took hours. Julie laid it out on the line. "I don't know what the hell will happen with you and me, but I'll be damned if I'm going to let you screw up my Dad's new career."

The charge surprised him. He likes Ben. "Honey, I would never do anything --- "

"You don't think having his son-in-law involved in a gay sex scandal won't fuck things up for him?"

He didn't respond. They both remained quiet until reaching the mansion. Julie is hurt and angry and she has every right to be. He feels guilty because he *is* guilty. He is guilty of lying and cheating and loving someone who is not his wife.

John was asleep when they came home and Ann --- if she was there --- remained out of sight. When Greg woke up this morning, Frederick told him that Julie went shopping with her mother and that Ann is spending the weekend in Concord. The butler doesn't know why Ann is in Concord, but that doesn't matter much to Greg.

Instead he spends some time with his son. It feels good to hold him, to see his peaceful face and big bright eyes. Julie is right to say John's face is the face of innocence. It's so beautiful, so wonderful. *When did my own innocence end?* Was it during his parent's first real fight when, like all children, he blamed himself? Was it when he was shipped off to boarding school and forced to be older than his years? Was it the time a schoolmate named Andy goaded him into playing a life-changing game of truth or dare? Whenever it was and whatever it was, Greg is no innocent child. He can only hope his son can stay innocent awhile longer.

Throughout much of the day, Greg and the nanny take turns holding John or feeding John or changing his diapers. It feels good. Greg wonders whether his own father did these things but doubts it. Lewis Halloran kept a distance from his son until those last few months of his life.

John sleeps a lot, leaving his dad some free time in the afternoon. Greg goes downstairs to the study, the very room where Munroe Gale committed his crime. It had been kept locked and off-limits to everyone until recently, when he and Jack came in to get the papers Mel Waite is blackmailing his lover for. The staff has since cleaned up the room and replaced the desk chair. Still, Greg can feel his father's presence, a man who began reaching out when the old farmer got his revenge. Now Greg has to live without his father --- and with the annoying, asinine girl Munroe raised.

Out in Grand Hall, he can hear Frederick meeting with the decorating team. Every year, the same family firm comes in Thanksgiving weekend to deck out the house for the Christmas holiday. Hallorans do not hang ornaments; they hire people to hang ornaments. In the past, Greg's mother Lilly supervised. She liked to be in charge. Over the last few years, Mom also hosted an annual fundraiser called the Icicle Ball to benefit the Currier Museum. Since her sudden death, the butler has had to coordinate the holiday trim by himself. There has been no ball for a second year.

Greg pulls out his cell phone to call Jack, but all he gets is voicemail. He then calls the hotel, but Joe tells him he hasn't heard anything either. "Its Thanksgiving, dude, he's probably tied up with the family." Joe sounds so much like one of the guys that Greg has to remind himself that he was once a she. *Maybe Joe's right; maybe Jack is busy with his ailing father or bratty brother.*

But all this still leaves Greg feeling very alone.

****

No one seems lonely at the Mall of New Hampshire. It's the day after Thanksgiving and the mall looks like the busiest place on earth --- or at least in the state. The stores are packed, from Macy's to Sears to Penny's and all the little shops in between. Everyone is in pairs or groups. They are laughing and having a good time while recorded carols play overhead and Santa greets kids in the food court. Yet, Julie Halloran feels alone.

Alone in a mass of people.

Julie and Eve are among the earliest shoppers. She feels separate from everyone in the world, even her mother. She also feels awkward hobbling along with her crutch until Eve jokes "I think it's great; we can use it thin out the crowd." Julie laughs, truly laughs, for the first time in days.

"I'm glad to see that. You and Greg seemed . . . well, a little off yesterday. Is everything okay?"

"Oh sure, Mom," Julie assures her. "We've just been exhausted what with the Gabler party, and the baby and all. Everything sort of hit us at once." She manages to say this with the right amount of conviction. Eve appears to buy it. Julie would love to have someone to talk to about Greg and Jack, but the only person she feels comfortable confiding in isn't with them. "I wish Aunt Karen could have come with us today. She's always fun to shop with."

"I think we'll do fine without her."

Julie can hear the jealousy in her mother's voice. The two sisters have always had a complicated relationship. Remembering this gives her second thoughts about confiding in her aunt; *maybe I shouldn't, it'll just make things more complicated.* But it makes her feel even more alone in world.

They stop to admire some of the items in Christopher & Banks' windows when two ladies emerge from the store: Lorene Gale and an attractive middle age black woman. Julie has seen them in passing but this is the first time that they have come face to face.

"Hello, Lorene," Eve says; "happy Thanksgiving."

Lorene smiles; no --- more than that --- Lorene is *beaming*. "Thank you, Eve." The woman looks happier than Julie has ever seen. "Do you remember Vivian?"

"Of course; I thought you looked familiar. What has it been, twenty years?"

"Something like that," the black woman answers with a warm and gracious smile. Julie notices how close she and Lorene stand next to each other; they are practically holding hands. She has seen them like this as they walk around Faraway Hill's town square or outside her shop in downtown Manchester. There have been rumors about the two of them for weeks. She has meant to ask Ann about it, but Julie is still upset with her.

"Julie, this is Vivian Stevens. She and her husband used to work on the Gale farm."

"I doubt if you remember," Vivian explains, "you were so very young at the time. Just like Annie."

A couple of the shopkeepers in Faraway Hill mentioned that to Julie, but no one seems to know the full story. The only thing anyone knows is that after Vivian's husband died and Munroe returned from a particularly bad bender, Vivian suddenly disappeared. "I've seen you around town Mrs. Stevens, with Mrs. Gale. I'm sorry; I've been meaning to say hello."

"Have you moved back to Faraway Hill permanently?" Eve asks.

"Yes --- and its Mrs. Bickel now --- although you are both welcome to call me Vivian." The woman has a natural friendliness that Julie finds very appealing.

"I've been meaning to say hi too," Eve apologies, "but things have been crazy. Lorene and I have spoken a few times on the phone. She told me you were in town but I didn't know you married again."

"Oh, yes, "Vivian responds with an odd look. "But we're separated now."

"I'm sorry to hear that," Eve says. *Marriages end, but that doesn't mean life does.* Maybe there is a lesson for her in Vivian starting her life over. But Julie doesn't want to begin fresh; *I want the man I married.* Unfortunately another man wants him too.

The four women trade a few more pleasantries before going their separate ways. When Vivian and Lorene are out of earshot, Eve asks her daughter "Do you know about them?"

"No, Mom; I've just heard rumors." It's unlike Eve to be interested in gossip; whatever it is must be pretty interesting. "What is it?"

"Well, apparently they are a couple now."

Julie stops. Christmas shopping can wait. "A couple, you mean --- "

"Yes."

Ann's mother is in love with a woman? "Wow; I never would have expected that."

"Actually, I'm not all that surprised."

Julie gently pulls her mother away from the crowd so they can whisper in confidence at the entry of a vacant store. "What do you mean?"

"Well, I've known Lorene for years. She has never been the type of person who can be alone. That I think that's the real reason she stayed with Munroe. Vivian . . . Vivian is comfortable."

Streams of people walk past them in both directions, oblivious in their holiday revelry. "But that's companionship, what about . . . well, sex?"

"What about it?"

Julie can't comprehend being intimate with another woman. She has only been interested in men, and is sure she always will. "Mom, are you saying they're *lovers?*"

"I think so."

"Holy shit --- I never would have expected that."

"Julie," her mother says with an understanding smile. "There are certain things I have learned over the years. One of them is that sexuality is a lot more fluid that we often think. Something happened very recently to someone I know that reminded me of that."

"Who?" *She can't possibly mean Greg; no one else knows about him.*

Eve shakes her head. "I promised I wouldn't tell. Now let's do some serious shopping. I have a grandson to spoil this Christmas."

****

Ann Halloran expected to be alone Thanksgiving weekend. Her mother and Vivian invited her go shopping, but Ann has no interest in dealing with the crowds. Being New Hampshire's most notorious woman has its limits.

She was preparing for a long, lonely weekend when she got a surprise call from Richard Davis. The handsome older man sweetly invited her to "see Concord with a hometown boy." Ann has only been to the state capital on school field trips. But, more important, is the wonderful gentleman who wants to spend time *with* her, not spend time gossiping *about* her. Despite (or maybe because) of his age, Richard is becoming more and more attractive. He reminds her of those older movies stars. Men like Cary Grant or John Forsythe who seemed to actually become more handsome and more interesting with the arrival of wrinkles and gray hair.

Richard starts their day with a drive around town. Concord is actually a small city, about half the size of Manchester. Yet, in many ways its more "New Englandy". Some of the state's oldest homes, dating to the revolution, are located at the northern end of Main Street. History is everywhere. The State House was constructed about the same time as the Halloran mansion and is the oldest legislative building in the country. As they drive by the capital, Richard mentions in passing that Ben King will be appointed as the newest senator from New Hampshire. *That's news to me.* "When did all this happen?" *No one tells me anything.* She lives down the hall from Greg and Julie and they've haven't mentioned it. But then, that's probably to be expected. *I* <u>*am*</u> *the unwanted bastard, after all.*

"Just the other day; I imagine he told the family at Thanksgiving dinner."

Ann finds it hard to believe that Ben King would give up his law practice. True, it has been barely hanging on, but it's been his life for twenty years. *Julie should have told me; damn it all to hell, they need start treating me like family too.*

"Are you alright?"

"Sure," Ann takes a deep breath. *Fuck, I need to calm down.* She smiles at him and says, "I'm having a great time."

The tour continues as Richard points out sites, historic places like the Eagle Hotel, Phoenix Hall and the home of Franklin Pierce --- the only U.S. President to come from New Hampshire. But this is a little too touristy for her; Ann wants to do some shopping. With a grin, Richard brings her to some of the stores on North Main Street. She finds some nice things at the Fabulous Looks Boutique that her mother will like and even a few things for Vivian. *She is family now, I suppose.* The League of New Hampshire Craftsmen Store has a lot of fun things. All of the items are handmade by the league's members. Ann especially likes this year's ornament --- the league does an official one every year --- a small star made of clear glass.

A special treat is the Granite State Candy Shoppe on Warren Street, where chocolates have been made by hand since the 1920s. This store is crowded, but Ann manages to pick up a few things. Richard and the owner a chat a bit; it seems that everyone in Concord knows him. He tells her that it is his tradition to buy custom made Christmas gifts from Granite every year for his senate colleagues.

But the most impressive part of the day is when Richard takes her to dinner at the Common Man. A state-wide chain, Common Man restaurants can be found throughout New Hampshire, from the Manchester Airport up the interstate to Lincoln. But the one in Concord is different. Located inside a renovated Howard Johnson's, the restaurant's décor isn't much different from the rest of the chain. What strikes Ann is the number of familiar faces. Whether they are at the bar or sitting at a table, she can recognize politicians and business people, the very faces she often sees on TV or the front page of the *Union Leader*. Some were even at Agnes Gabler's recent birthday party at the Halloran mansion.

Richard stops at various tables where he exchanges greetings and introduces Ann to each famous person. He seems to know everyone and knows something about everyone. She is impressed: a professional politician practicing his profession with polish. These same important people treat her as someone important, as if Ann has been a Halloran her whole life. A prominent business man brags about doing business with "your father," meaning Lewis and not Munroe. One woman, possibly the state's most successful author since the scandalous Grace Metalious, treats Ann as a celebrity in her own right. "You must come to Concord more often," she encourages her. "It's *much* classier than most people realize." The table hopping continues. State politicians, bloggers, journalists, even a couple of actors home from a Broadway tour. They all know Richard Davis. And now they know Ann Halloran.

Richard once called her "New Hampshire's most fascinating woman" and these people seem to agree.

Ann has never felt less alone in her life.

****

Julie still feels alone. Despite spending the day with her mother in a crowded mall, she continues to feel isolated. Eve can no doubt sense something's wrong, even on the drive back to the Halloran mansion. But Julie manages to deflect her with the subject of Lorene Gale's surprising new relationship. *I wonder if Ann knows.*

Eve pulls up under the portico where one of the maids helps with the bags. Julie can't carry anything and use the crutch at the same time. "I'm sorry that I can't come in," her mother apologizes. "But we have the senator's funeral on Sunday and the press announcement on Monday and --- "

"Mom, it's okay. I've got help here." She reassures Eve that she and Greg will make it both events to support her dad. "He can count on us." They exchange quick kisses and Eve drives off.

The maid struggles to carry all the bags inside. "My, you've had quite a day, Mrs. Halloran." There are a lot of people to shop for, a list bigger than Julie has ever had before. In addition to her parents, friends and aunt she now has scores of in-laws, household staff and Greg. She smiles ruefully to herself, *what do you buy a cheating husband?*

Usually, the Halloran mansion is so big it can easily make someone feel lost in a sea of antiques. But not today. The butler is busy working with a group installing holiday decor in nearly every room on the first floor. Even the Christmas Trees --- there are several of them --- are being trimmed by professionals. This is one of those times where the house feels less like a family homestead than it does a museum.

Seeing these people so busy makes Julie feel a little guilty. After all, she *is* supposed to be the mistress of the manor. With everything that has been going on --- the Ann crisis, the pregnancy, running her store, the cast on her leg, Thanksgiving, Greg and her Dad --- Julie has left nearly everything regarding the house to Frederick. She feels bad about this. He is not a young man and he is doing a big job.

Julie hobbles down Grand Hall navigating her way through groups of people hanging this or arranging that. Walking past the study she can see a pair of decorators installing a single Canadian Pine garland along the far wall. For months since his father's death, Greg refused to let anyone --- not even Frederick --- into that room. Julie hinted from time to time that maybe her husband should rethink that. None of it worked. But one visit by Jack Campbell and Greg unlocks the door himself. *Shit, that more than anything else should tell me where I stand.*

The maid follows her up the tricky marble Grand Staircase to the suites on the second floor. The door to the nursery is open. Julie can see Greg inside with the nanny, changing Johnny's diapers. It is a wonderful, loving vision of father and son together. *He seems to be getting the hang of that.* Greg looks up to see her in the hall and smiles cautiously. Oddly enough, she finds herself smiling back. *Why can't I hate him?* Julie is angry at him, to be sure, but isn't it normal to hate your husband after he cheats on you?

So, without saying a word, Julie and the maid step into the master suite and the bedroom that she now has all to herself.

****

Loneliness is not something Karen St. John is accustomed to. Ever since she was a little girl in little Keane, she has sought out the spotlight and the applause. Karen *must* be the star --- and she usually is. Loneliness, for her, is something to avoid at all costs.

Today is no exception in the form on her interior decorator: a short fey man in his 50s who is practically worshipping at her feet. He excitedly drove in from Boston to help the New York socialite turn her new country home in Faraway Hill into something a little more sophisticated.

"I can see replacing all of this silly, flowery wallpaper with bright, brilliant solids," Eduardo says with a flourish. Eduardo is not his real name. Eduardo isn't even Hispanic or Italian. Eduardo was born Bernard Brannon in South Boston. But Bernie, like Karen Scott, dreamed of a more glamorous life. He found it as Eduardo.

"Oh, good," Karen responds with a smile. "The house is too . . . quaint for me." The previous owners filled the house with faux Early American pieces to create a look much too common for an uncommon woman.

"I understand, Mrs. St. John," Eduardo drools. "And with your budget, we'll be able to do *wonders* with this place."

"How soon?"

"The sketches will be ready by the end of next week. I think we can get this place into shape in no time at all."

"Good," Karen responds with a smile. The sooner the house is ready, the sooner she can protect her little girl.

✳✳✳✳

When Richard Davis invited Ann to his home, he described it as "a simple farmhouse." She expected nothing more than a much nicer version of what she grew up with. But as Richard drives her down Borough Road, the house she sees is nothing like the Gale farm. It's huge. Although not as big as the Halloran mansion, the Davis family homestead is a farmhouse on steroids. A big, colonial structure first built by his grandfather, the house has been remodeled and expanded several times. There is no farm anymore, but surrounding the house are five acres of trees and flower bushes that must create a magnificent sight each spring. The house even has a name, The Four Corners.

His tour of Four Corners is almost as fascinating as the Halloran tours she took during Julie's wedding. The place is a welcoming hodgepodge. Like the Halloran estate, there are many antiques. But mixed in are things that any family might collect or save. Richard points out heirlooms, gifts from his late wife and items gathered from his travels --- and, to his joy, a misshapen ceramic mug made by his daughter in the fourth grade. The Halloran mansion is designed to impress visitors; Four Corners is designed to be a home.

Another difference: Four Corners has only one full-time servant. There are part-time maids and a gardener, but the only in-home staff is a charming elderly woman named Gertrude. This grandmotherly lady cooks the pot roast and mash potatoes herself and serves them dinner in the dining room without any of the fancy pomp of the Hallorans. Their meal is a nice, relaxing reflection on the day. They laugh and share stories. Richard tells her about places in Washington. Ann describes her few happy childhood memories, like visits to Hampton Beach and Rye.

Once dinner is over and Gertrude wishes them a good evening, Richard gently takes Ann into his arms. He surprises her with the best, most sensuous kiss of her life. *Wow.* He then asks, in the most gentlemanly way imaginable, "Would you like to spend the night?" Ann answers by placing her lips against his and accepts Richard's tongue for another amazing kiss.

Richard guides her up the stairs. Ann doesn't bother to admire the four poster bed or the silk damask on the walls. Instead, she allows him to undress her, softly licking or kissing every piece of skin as it is exposed. This is a man who knows what he is doing, who understands how to caress a breast and suckle a nipple.

She finds her reaction to his body odd. Richard lacks the firmness and muscle definition of her former lovers, all of whom were much younger. There have only been a few, of course, but her ex-husband Mark had a magnificently chiseled physique. Richard is nothing like that. His skin is pale and wrinkled; his stomach is flabby and his chest hair is all gray. Yet, none of this seems to matter. Instead she marvels at his touch. This is not a man who is merely experienced --- like Mark --- but a man who is seasoned. Richard Davis truly understands woman's body.

When Richard places his tongue against her labia, the act sends shock waves right to her soul. No one has ever made Ann feel this way; no one. When Richard enters her, his penis seems to fit perfectly almost as if it were tailor made just for Ann. His orgasm happens fairly quickly. But unlike the boys she was with in college --- who, at this point, would just as soon pull out and go to sleep --- Richard keeps going. Each thrust brings her closer and closer to that peak. But it's when he licks her earlobe and whispers, "you are the sexiest woman in the world" that Ann cums, something that has rarely happened with anyone else. The boys never knew how to do that, only Mark --- and now Richard. Yet, even afterward, as she catches her breath, he remains hard and inside her. Ann wraps her legs around him to hold him there for as long as possible.

****

Joe Westbrook is feeling a special kind of loneliness: the kind that calls for adult companionship. As much as he loves his little boy, sometimes a man --- even a man who was once a woman --- needs a man to talk to. There is only so much intelligent conversation a seven-year-old can manage.

He tries calling Jack's cell a few times but only reaches voicemail. On a hunch, he now tries the SoHo loft. After a few rings, a strange and barely audible voice answers. "Hello?"

"Jack, Jack is that you?"

The other voice clears his throat. "Yeah, who is this?" Joe can hear him better now.

"It's Joe. Are you alright dude?"

"Ah . . . yeah, sure; just getting over the holiday shit." *He doesn't sound alright. He sounds hung over.* "How are you? How's Little Jack?"

The boy is sitting in the living room of their little suite eating a room service lunch of burger and fries. True Southern Californians, neither he nor Joe have any winter coats so they are spending the cold, snowy day inside. "Fine, but that friend of yours --- Greg Halloran --- has called looking for you. When are you coming back to Manchester?"

"Don't know; just give me a couple of days."

Something's wrong, I can sense it; something bad. Joe steps into the bedroom for some privacy. "What's going on?"

"Nothing. Everything. Look, don't worry; I'll explain everything when I get back." Joe fights the urge to ask for more. *I suppose he'll tell me when he's ready.* "Well, okay, but just so you know, I've started apartment hunting."

"In Manchester," Jack asks surprised. "Why there?"

"Because, dude, I can't raise my son and keep running at the same time. I have to make a stand for Jack's sake. Besides, I am so far away now I think that I can convince the old man to leave us alone."

"Are you sure about that?"

No, Joe thinks, *I am not sure.* "What else can I do? Move to another country? I can't do that to Jack or my mom."

"But are you sure about Manchester? I mean, dude, you're a big city person. Can you live in a small burgh?"

"This place isn't that small," Joe shrugs to no one who can see him. "Boston is close. Besides, I've been checking things out and the cost of living here is pretty reasonable. I can really stretch my trust fund income a lot farther here than I could in LA."

"Okay . . . if that's what you want."

There are moments when Joe still feels like Jackie. This is one of them. Just like in the old days, she can sense something is wrong with Jack and wants to wrap her protective arms around him. But the moment passes and Joe feels like Joe again, and dudes generally don't do that sort of thing for other dudes. "Come back soon, will you?"

✵✵✵✵

Feeling tired and lonely, Julie Halloran cannot sleep. The doctor told her she can stop taking the pain medication, but that may have been the one thing helping her rest. There is a problem, a big problem, one that keeps her mind from shutting down. It is getting close to Midnight and everyone else in the mansion retired hours ago leaving Julie all alone.

She is sitting in the family room all by herself, channel surfing. Normally she'd be upstairs in the master suite's parlor to be near Johnny, but that would also mean being near Greg. Julie needs to take a break from playing "the good wife". It's exhausting to play dutiful and supportive when all she wants to do is smack her husband. And she needs to do it again tomorrow at Senator Russell Brooks' funeral.

Thanksgiving weekend TV doesn't offer much to interest Julie. There are holiday -theme documentaries on the History Channel and silly chick flicks on Lifetime. Repeats dominate the broadcast networks including a two-month old episode of "Saturday Night Live" that was barely funny the first time it aired. Pushing the up button on the remote over and over again results in nonsense after nonsense. The reality shows annoy her the most. Soon she comes upon a "Dallas" marathon. The series ended when she was a little girl, but Julie will watch it every so often. The melodrama can be surprisingly engrossing and the changing hair styles fun to watch.

For the next couple of hours, Julie sips her tea as J.R. puts the screws to Cliff time after time. But her mind keeps coming back to Greg and Jack and Johnny. Greg says he loves her; and it galls her that she --- despite his affair with another man --- still loves him. Part of her wants to grab the crutch and hobble up those marble stairs and tell him that all is forgiven. But another part of her warns Julie to stay away. It alerts her of a reality: despite what she told Greg about his making a choice, the decision about their future will really be hers. *He loves us both, but whichever one he chooses he'll always wonder about it. He may even resent it. Can I live with that?* Just as Bobby comes to his family's rescue once again, Julie now understands that she and she alone can resolve things.

There can only be one choice: a divorce.

The epiphany is a heavy weight on Julie's soul. She never anticipated getting a divorce, especially after just a few months of marriage. And a divorce is complicated. First, there is Johnny. Divorcing a Halloran is not like divorcing any ordinary man. There is a family legacy to consider, one that goes back two centuries that her son will inherit. It seems wrong and unfair of her to deny him that just because his father cheated on his mother.

Then there is Julie's father. He is starting a new career, one that is very public and easily affected by scandal. Julie wasn't kidding when she warned Greg to behave. A divorce now will certainly hurt her dad --- especially when the reason gets out.

Finally, there is the biggest and hardest complication of all: *can I really give him up?* Julie already misses him lying next to her, sharing meals with her, making love to her. It has been a tough year, but despite their arguments over Ann they have felt like a team. *Maybe it's true: maybe if Ann hadn't moved into the house,*

Greg and Jack wouldn't have hooked up again. Maybe; but she'll never know for sure; and it doesn't matter anyway.

So, she lies down on the couch, watching the travails of Southfork through watery eyes and mulls over her situation. Slowly an idea starts to form, an idea inspired by Miss Ellie's advice, an idea that might just work --- if she can figure out the details.

****

Korean War veteran, businessman and United States senator, the world says goodbye to Russell Brooks.

Ben King and a group of dignitaries have gathered at the New Hampshire State Veterans Cemetery. About five miles north of Concord, this is where many New Englanders inter the men and women who have served their country. Russell Brooks receives the full treatment, from the drive past the famous Circle of Flags, to a visit by the Vice President (who reads a special message from the President) to the honor guard.

The ceremony concludes as mourners huddle in the cold to watch the casket lowered into the ground. Some of the biggest names in the state are here for a solemn farewell. But for all the dignity and formality of the day, there is a bit of color: the surprising presence of Ann Halloran. She is Senator Richard Davis' guest to the funeral. No one, including Ben, expected to see her here. Ann is still a bit too scandalous to go anywhere without attracting attention. Certainly Greg and Julie (who looks like she hasn't had much sleep) are not happy. Eve is among those surprised at seeing Ann, and asks her husband with a whisper, "why is she here --- with *him*?" Ben can only shrug. He has no idea.

The service over, everyone takes turns consoling the widow. The woman looks quite frail herself, battling the cancer that will surely take her life. *They need to get her inside; it's too cold for her.* Fortunately, the staff immediately escorts everyone back to the warmth of the chapel. On their way, Ben notices his daughter and son-in-law chatting intensely with the governor.

"I detest funerals," Agnes Gabler says with a wry smile as she joins Ben and Eve on the chilly stroll. Arguably New Hampshire's most famous living artist, this 95 -year-year old is a surprisingly energetic lady. "Supposedly, funerals are meant for the people left behind. If that's true, then Americans are shitty at it. We should learn from the Irish: don't cry --- get drunk!"

"And definitely *not* out in the cold," Eve adds with a laugh.

"You said it sister," Agnes gives an exaggerated shiver. She is actually wearing a very thick coat. Gesturing toward Ann and Richard, Agnes asks "How did *that* happen?"

"We were wondering ourselves," Eve replies. Ann and the senator are at the rear of the parade of mourners. "I know they spent some time together at your birthday party, but I never expected anything like this."

Just as they reach the chapel door, Agnes' daughter Scarlet steps up to share some pleasantries and then insist on taking her mother home. "I may be 95," the woman argues, "but I'm no china doll." Nevertheless, the Kings says their goodbyes and watch the two head to the parking lot. The sight is a touching one, watching a middle aged woman caring for her elderly mother. Their fame doesn't matter; at this moment they are like any other family.

Ben and Eve follow the other mourners into the chapel. A worried Greg hangs back to talk to the governor some more. Once inside, Ben takes a moment to admire the big windows beaming sunshine into the large space. The State Veterans Cemetery is a relatively new facility and he has never been inside before. He was too involved in the memorial service to pay much attention to it earlier.

The Kings have some brief conversations with the other mourners as they prepare to leave. Most have already heard about Ben's appointment --- Richard's staff leaked it yesterday --- but the unspoken subject of the day is Ann. People hint about her with phrases like "the unusual guest list" and "I was surprised by all who came."

Julie enters alone and joins her parents. *She seems to be getting the hang of that crutch,* her father thinks. *Although that heavy coat of hers doesn't seem to be helping.* She also looks upset.

"Mom, Dad, you won't believe this! The state is reviewing the way Faraway Hill handled Lewis' murder investigation."

Ben and Eve are shocked. "I don't understand," asks her father. The investigation into Lewis Halloran's death was wrapped up months ago. Faraway Hill's sheriff confirmed that farmer Munro Gale killed the millionaire before committing suicide. "Why?"

"I don't know, Dad, but Greg is really upset and I don't blame him. I certainly don't want to relive *that* nightmare." Julie glances back at the door to see Ann and Richard hold hands like high school sweethearts as they enter the chapel. "Wow, when did *that* happen?"

"That seems to be the question of the day."

"Well, Mom, leave it to Ann to upstage a U.S. senator at his own funeral."

"Why do they want to reopen the investigation?"

"I don't know, Dad. The governor says their not reopening it, just reviewing how Sheriff Reynolds and the Faraway Hill Police handled it. Apparently, the State Police were supposed to be called in but Sheriff Reynolds insisted on running the show himself. I guess Concord thinks he screwed up."

"Well," Ben sighs, "I never liked Reynolds. But it seems like a pretty open and shut case. Munroe *did* confess."

Greg and the governor are still outside. Nearly all of the other guests have left. Ann is practically giggling as Richard walks her over to them. "Well, Ben, are you ready for tomorrow's big announcement?"

"Yes, I am although it seems unnecessary. Everyone already knows."

"It's important to give the press a heads up on things. You'll learn that in time." With a smile and a wink, he guides Ann out the door and to his car. *Richard likes the attention,* Ben reflects, *almost as much as Ann.*

Hopefully tomorrow morning, the attention will be on me.

****

The sun has disappeared, enveloped into the night sky.

With larger flakes following smaller ones, snow begins to fall on Faraway Hill as the little town ends its Sunday. The shops have closed and the street lamps automatically light. A soft white carpet covers the streets and sidewalks. The famous statue of John Halloran is wrapped in a perfectly tailored blanket.

Mike Bickel leads himself on a personal tour as he drives around the town square. *Why would anyone live here? They don't got shit.* He has been drinking heavily for days. The old man has been calling repeatedly about the job at hand. Having botched the hit, Mike has started ducking his calls; too frustrated and angry and drunk.

In the distance is the big fancy house where those Hallorans live. A local guidebook says that it was designed to look the White House. Mike can barely see the resemblance and doesn't care anyway. There is another house that interests him, the house where his wayward wife is hiding. The house where this man will teach his woman a lesson she won't ever forget.

That house is on a farm only a few minutes from the town square. It is still and quiet. Only a few lights are on. Mike slowly guides the rental car up the driveway. He doesn't want anyone to know he has arrived. Not yet, anyway.

He carefully gets out of the car. The liquor makes him unsteady; the pistol nearly falls to the ground. He needs to do this right.

Cautiously, unsteadily, he makes his way to the house. Through a window he can see Vivian. She and the white woman are hanging ornaments on a Christmas tree. They are smiling and happy. *It's time to make the bitch pay.*

EPISODE FOUR

With larger flakes following smaller ones, snow begins to fall on Faraway Hill.
It's Sunday night. Church has been over for hours, the shops have closed and the
street lamps automatically light. A soft white carpet covers the sidewalks. The
famous statue of John Halloran is wrapped in a perfectly tailored blanket
of snow.

At the edge of town, two middle age women are enjoying the peace and warmth
of their little home. A holiday CD plays instrumental carols as they put up a
brand new artificial tree and bring the boxes of trim down from the attic. It has
long been a Gale family tradition to put up the Christmas decorations during
Thanksgiving Weekend.

"I remember this one," Vivian remarks. "You bought it when Annie was born,
didn't you?"

Lorene steps over a box of garland to see her lover gingerly hold a pearl-white
glass ornament with a year hand painted on it. "Oh, yes," she explains. "Actually
Munroe bought it for Ann's first Christmas." Despite his death and the house's
remodeling, there are still echoes of Munroe Gale surrounding them. Lorene
decided long ago not to fight it, even as she now shares her life and her bed with
Vivian. His photo even remains on mantle. Besides, not all of the memories are
bad. Whenever Munroe was sober he was very sweet and loving. She misses that
part of him. "He was trying so hard back then to be a good husband and father."

Another photo on the mantle is more recent. It's of Vivian and Lorene together,
smiling on a summer day. Vivian's return has made Lorene happier than at any
other time in her life. No one, not Lewis Halloran nor Munroe Gale, ever loved
her as Vivian does. Even the townspeople have notice and responded to it. From
shopkeepers to the mailman, everyone in Faraway Hill has shown the couple a
wonderful amount of kindness and support. The elderly woman at the dollar store
called them "sweet".

Without warning, every light and every appliance suddenly shuts down throwing
the entire house into darkness. "Did we blow a fuse?" asks Lorene. But before
Vivian can answer, there is loud frightening bang against the living room door.
Bang, bang, bang! "I know you are in there bitch!" The angry voice is
painfully familiar.

"Oh, my God, Lorene, it's him!"

The two panicked women frantically try to navigate in the dark, tripping over
boxes and chairs. Something glass falls to the floor and shatters. Lorene reaches
the phone, but finds the line is dead. "We need one of the cells."

"My purse," Vivian responds desperately, her heart pounding like a drum. "Where is my purse?" She now wishes she had bought a gun. It was something they talked about, but Lorene found the idea too scary.

Bang! Bang! Bang!

"You left it in the kitchen."

Holding hands --- more for emotional support than anything else --- they manage to find the kitchen. Vivian's purse is setting on the counter.

Bang! Bang! Bang! "Where the fuck are you, woman! I know you in there!"

Vivian nervously flips the phone open and dials 911. She can tell just hearing him that Mike is drunk. He has been like this before. The bruises take a long time to heal.

Crash!

The county service answers. Vivian tries to stay calm and gives them the address. It isn't easy; they can hear Mike break more glass in a window not far away. He is coming. He is coming soon. "Please hurry," Vivian begs into the phone. Hard angry footfalls land heavily on the living room floor. *Dear God,* Lorene begs rather than prays, *please help us.*

****

The house is so quiet. The decorators left hours ago, the holiday trim nearly finished. The servants have retired for the evening. Johnny is asleep in his crib. All of this leaves Greg Halloran alone in his bedroom. He is in his robe, eyes aimed straight above him, staring at nothing and thinking about everything: his marriage, his son, his lover, his business and the now having to relive his father's murder.

Someone raps lightly on his door. "Come in." Julie, wearing her own robe and leaning on the crutch, opens the door but doesn't come inside. *I wonder how long it took before my parents had separate bedrooms.* "Hi, is everything okay? Is Johnny?"

"He's fine," she answers. "I just wanted to say how sorry I am about the state investigation." They didn't talk about it on the ride home. They don't talk much anymore.

"Thanks."

"I know you don't want to relive that. I don't either."

"Julie, please . . ."

She raises a hand to stop him. "Don't make promises you can't keep. Anyway, with Johnny needing us and Dad starting this new career, we are going to have to stick to the status quo for awhile. I can't stop you from seeing Jack. But I expect you to be discrete."

She is so calm about it. "Julie, I never wanted things to be like this."

"I know; but it is. And we can't change it. Anyway, the press conference is tomorrow. We can't be late." Nothing more is said. Julie leaves him as she found him, lying on the bed staring at nothing and thinking about everything.

****

When Peter Brandt suddenly called Ann to say "your mother needs you right away," more was said in the tone of his voice than in his words: something terrible has happened.

Faraway Hill is small enough so that everything is near to everything else. It only takes her a few minutes to get from the mansion to the family farm. There are three police cars, an ambulance and various officers milling in and around the house. *What the hell happened?* Getting out her car, Ann faces the bitter cold and wishes she had grabbed a warmer coat. Peter sees her at the door and walks over to her.

"What's going on? Is my mother alright?" The last time she got this kind of emergency call, Munroe had committed suicide. Finding him slumped in his chair traumatized Lorene.

"Your mom's okay; they're both upstairs and they're both safe." Peter points toward a snow covered tractor parked near the house. A black man is laying face down on the ground, dead, drops of blood dark red against the white snow.

"Oh, my God . . . who is that?"

"Apparently its Vivian Bickel's estranged husband. He broke into the house and started to threaten them. He was chasing them around the house and drove them outside, which where we found them. He had pulled out a gun, and we were forced to fire."

"Holy shit!" She remembers her mother explaining about Vivian's husband. *"Her new husband isn't very nice," she said without going into much detail. "In fact, he is in business with some terrible man out in California. Vivian needed to get away from him and I needed to have someone in my life."* But "isn't very nice" was certainly no hint to this kind of brutality.

Another man, in a parka but clearly not a policeman steps appears. He had been around back. Carrying a toolbox he tells Peter that the electricity has been restored. "It looks like he just cut the wires. It was an easy fix."

"He cut the power? Why Peter, to terrorize them?"

Peter nods. "The sheriff is inside now. It looks pretty clear cut, but I am sure he'll want to speak to you." Ann nods and allows Peter to escort her into the house. The kitchen, dining room and living room are all in shambles. Lorene was so very proud of her redecoration; now much of it is in ruin. A window in the living room is broken, with boxes of Christmas decoration scattered about. Sitting a little too comfortably in a chair is Sheriff George Reynolds. Fat with graying hair, he has all the arrogance of a man who knows that his position in this world is secure. He waves Peter away. Ann has never liked Reynolds. Actually, she doesn't know anyone who likes him. But he runs unopposed every election, so every election he wins.

"How is my mother?"

"The paramedics are upstairs with them. She and her . . . lady friend are being checked over." He says "lady friend" with a grimace. Ann can't tell if Reynolds disapproves of Vivian because she's black, her mother's lesbian lover or both. "You'll be able to see her in a few minutes."

"What happened?"

"This colored --- er, this man --- broke into the house. We found his ID. His name is Michael Bickel. According to your mother's 'friend' he's her husband. I guess he's beaten her before. She left him over the summer to come back here."

"I know some of that. I mean, that she left him. I didn't know about the abuse --- or expect this."

Reynolds nods. He seems more interested in wrapping things up than anything else. He doesn't bother to ask her anything more and allows her to climb the stairs. There she meets with two paramedics. They advise her that, apart from some bruises, the two women appear to be in shock. Ann can see Lorene and Vivian, still shivering from their harrowing experience, lying on the bed comforting each other. She says nothing to either woman. Instead, Ann simply kisses her mother on the cheek, pulls up a chair and sits next to them.

****

It is Monday morning and Mel Waite has had enough. "That damned faggot better call me soon" he says to no one since there is no one else in the room. He is staying at a cheap motel along the highway. Jack Campbell has been avoiding his calls since before Thanksgiving.

The holiday was no fun for him. He couldn't call his family or leave the motel. His meal was a frozen TV dinner he micro-waved in the room. It didn't cook all the way through; the turkey could have been eaten like a popsicle. It just added to his pissy mood.

Flipping the channels, he comes to a Boston station's morning newscast. One of the few good things about this motel is its cable selection. Without it, he'd be even more stir crazy. The anchor is one of those annoyingly perky young women who seem to have no accent. *Where do they get these people?* "Ironically, this incident took place on the same farm where owner Munroe Gale poisoned himself earlier this year. As you may remember, Gale had confessed to murdering textile heir Lewis Halloran."

Well, I'll be damned. The screen is filled with video taken at the Gale farm in Faraway Hill. No body is shown, only the place in the snow where the assailant fell.

"In other New Hampshire news, a press conference will begin shortly at the state capitol building in Concord where the governor is expected to announce that he is appointing Manchester attorney Benjamin King to the U.S. Senate seat left vacant by the death of Senator Russell Brooks." There had been leaks about the appointment all weekend. At least Ben's life is coming together. *Now if I could just get that faggot to come through.*

Mel picks up the disposal cell phone and dials Jack Campbell. Again.

****

Jack checks his cell phone; it's another call from Mel Waite. He sends it to voicemail like all the others. *Bastard.*

He's rarely up this early. But knowing his father, Jack has surely lost his job at the family firm. It seemed best to pack up his office before anyone else arrived. The last thing Jack needs is the humiliation of an audience watching him get disinherited. But it doesn't matter: soon he'll be splitting $10 million with Mel Waite and Jack will finally be a man in charge of his own life. At least, sharing the cash was the plan. But that painful night with his dad, coupled with Mel's blackmail, has gotten Jack to consider a new option: *maybe I'll keep it all.* Unfortunately, the papers lack a crucial bit of information: the password to activate the electronic transfer. Mel has that. But there may be a way around it, and Jack's old friend Eddie Grant is the one person who can help.

That is, if Eddie ever arrives. *Where the fuck is he?* Jack is sitting impatiently, on the sofa in his loft drinking his third cup of coffee and staring at the "Today Show." They exchanged texts last night and Eddie agreed to come over first thing in the morning. He is anxious to hear what he wants to hear.

On the screen Matt Lauer interviews some political expert on Ben King's appointment to the U.S. Senate. The press conference will happen soon. It adds to Jack's worries about a future with Greg. A gay scandal involving his son-in-law could hurt the man's career --- creating another reason for Greg to stay with his wife.

The intercom sounds. Jack walks over to the door to buzz Eddie in. *This is it.* It only takes a few minutes before he hears a knock on the door. Opening it, Eddie greets him with a smile. *Damn he looks good.* The two were on-and-off fuck buddies during college, but they have barely spoken since. "Hey dude," Eddie says sauntering into the loft, checking out the space along the way. A champion swimmer, his body is lithe and his movements elegantly controlled. "Cool; I always wanted a place like this. But Judy insisted on that fucking house in Jersey. I hate it."

Like I care. He wants to know about the account, not Eddie's wife. Jack had hooked up with her once, before she met Eddie. Judy was cold a bitch in bed as she was everywhere else. If Eddie hadn't knocked her up, they wouldn't be together. "That's too bad," Jack guides him to the sofa where they sit, the papers right in front of them. "Look, I've got a favor to ask you --- ".

Eddie won't him finish; instead he grabs Jack by the back of his head and pushes their lips together. *Holy shit.* It never occurred to Jack that his bud wanted to hook-up, although he probably should have. The kiss nearly melts him; Eddie was always good with his tongue and oral sex was his favorite in college. Jack presses a hand on the man's chest. *He still works out.* With some effort, he pushes Eddie away. "Dude, I'm sorry, that's not why I asked you here."

"Come on man, I haven't had anything in *months*. Months! Two babies and the wife won't give it up anymore."

"Look, I'm sorry, but I need your help on something. I need you to help me go over some papers. It's about an offshore account and you're an expert on them."

Eddie looks like he's about to punch a hole in the wall behind them. "Holy shit! Is *that* what this is all about? You make me get up early on a Monday morning, clear my schedule and *you don't want to fuck*?"

"I'm sorry, I really am."

"You should be, asshole. We had great times together. I thought you wanted to have a little fun. I sure as hell need it. So much for being buds!" Eddie starts to get up when Jack grabs him by the arm.

"Fine, so you're pissed off. How many times do I have to apologize? I really need you to explain some important financial papers for me. Please, dude, please?"

"What's in it for me?"

"What do you want?" The look on Eddie's face gives him a clear answer.

"Oh, come on, Ed, don't ask me." Jack feels bad enough about fucking the kids in Brooklyn. Now his college pal wants what will likely be the world's most expensive blow job.

"Do it, Jack." Eddie stands up, unbuckles his belt, and lets his pants and briefs slide down. They used to play this game in college: when one wanted a favor from the other, he got on his knees. Receiving the blow job was always kind of kinky, but there were times when giving it was humiliating. "I'm waiting, dude." With a frown, Jack complies, taking Eddie's hard dick into his mouth. It doesn't take long until Jack is swallowing the man's cum. *Wow, I guess it has been awhile for him.* Finished, Jack climbs back onto the sofa as Eddie pulls up his pants. "Thanks, dude, I really needed that. You have no fucking idea."

"You're welcome, now please," Jack picks up the papers from the coffee table. "Take a look. How can I access this account without the password?"

Eddie starts reading the documents. After checking different sections of the dense legalese, he starts to laugh.

"What's so damn funny?" Jack can still taste the man's cum.

"Dude, this account is a fake."

"What!"

"This bank in the Caymans went out of business a year ago --- three months before this account was supposedly created. There's no ten million; there never was."

✱✱✱✱

As a teen, Karen Scott had grown to hate Faraway Hill. It was too small, too rural, too boring for a girl hoping for a more interesting life. Those were bad days, with many of the stores empty and bordered up and the town near death. It was also the place where she was humiliated by Alex Mundy and Lewis Halloran. Everything about the town was dark and depressing.

How times have changed.

This morning Karen St. John is strolling around the main square and marveling at today's Faraway Hill. Every storefront is filled and people are milling about the sidewalks. The buildings have been cleaned up and look very picturesque, with icicles hanging from the eaves and frost on the windows. It is as if Norman Rockwell recreated the town in his signature, idyllic image.

However, sightseeing isn't really on Karen's mind. The *Union Leader* has reported that the state is reviewing the investigation into Lewis Halloran's death. She never expected this development. Karen has counted on Sheriff Reynolds' natural incompetence to protect her. But the state employs professionals and professionals may dig up the truth. Something needs to be done.

Denise made a discrete call to the Faraway Hill Police and learned that Lieutenant Peter Brandt has the day off. Karen is betting that he'll be Christmas shopping today; and sure enough, Peter emerges from one of the boutiques carrying a bag. She takes a moment to study him: young and handsome, with a brilliant smile and great cheekbones. In this way Peter reminds her a little of Mark Bradley. But where Mark is arrogant and manipulative, Peter gives off the vibes of an innocent small town kid comfortable in the small town world.

"Hello Mrs. St. John."

"Good morning, Peter." Karen smiles the smile that has served her well over the years. Charm can be a great tool, if you know how to use it.

"I'm surprised to see you here; I figured you'd be in Concord for your brother-in-law's big announcement." The press conference is going on right now, but Eve made it clear to Karen that she should stay away.

"Politics is not my style." Karen glances past the statue of John Halloran at the changed town. "Faraway Hill is certainly very different from when I was a girl."

"There was this big push about ten years ago to reinvigorate the town. Manchester was starting to grow and the selectmen wanted to take advantage of the new tourist trade."

"The result is breathtaking," Karen says, subtly baiting Peter, hoping to hook him quickly. She needs to reel him in fast. "I hardly recognize the place."

"I'm free today; want the grand tour?" *Bingo.* This may be easier than she expected. Peter offers his arm and they start walking around the square. Every few steps Karen reminisces about a shop or a building and Peter updates her what has happened to it since. At the same time, she deftly leads him into telling her about his life. Karen has learned over the years that all men like to talk about themselves. Peter is handsome, athletic and young and it isn't hard to picture him running the bases when he fondly remembers childhood softball in the town's field. He tells her about his ailing parents, the girls he's dated --- including Ann Gale --- and his work on the force. But Peter's underlying loneliness is very clear. Too many of his friends have moved away and too many relatives have died. Nights are spent alone. His overseas charity work could not fill the void. Karen can also sense a growing interest in the sophisticated, older woman who is showing him attention. *I can do this*, she concludes, *I can have him.* All it will take is a little time and a little flirtation before she has Peter Brandt in her bed and under her control.

"You are a delightful young man," she says in her most suggestive way. "I'd like to spend more time with you."

"I'd like that too, Mrs. St. John."

"That's much too formal --- please call me Karen."

****

Ben King's press conference lasts a mere hour. It wasn't much news as every journalist in the country had the story days ago. He and Eve are now flying to Washington to start his orientation. Julie went home to be with the baby and Greg needed to get back to the office. Here he receives some good news: the Georgia mill's problems are under control and functioning at full capacity. Georgia will allow the Halloran Company to meet its domestic orders. But the mill in Thailand remains a concern.

A text comes in from Jack: "big problem call me." Greg is about to that when his secretary buzzes: Robert Halloran is on the line. *Why is he calling?* Considered in the family to be "the quiet cousin," Robert rarely speaks up or visits or seems to do much of anything beyond his business interests. Greg barely knew he was a guest at either his wedding or his dad's funeral. But Robert is part of the family trust that owns 40% of the company and he personally owns 10%. He may be quiet, but he cannot be ignored.

"Good morning, Robert," Greg tries to sound as cheery as he can. "How are you today?"

"Not well," is the terse reply. *Does this man ever laugh or even smile?* "I've just had a call from an associate in Singapore."

"What about?"

"He has it on good authority that there will be a nation-wide strike in Thailand within days."

Greg tries to reassure him. The Thais are going through one of their periodic political crisis that has paralyzed parliament. The king has stepped in before and is expected to again. The strike is just a threat to get the parties to make a deal. Every analyst from Boston to Washington has told Greg the same thing.

"I hope you are right," Robert says with something close to an emotion. "But I doubt it." The man hangs up without saying anything more. *What an ass.*

****

Ann stands in her mother's living room, exhausted after spending the morning cleaning the mess. Lorene was so proud of the remodeling she had done, turning a depressingly poor farmhouse into a nice middle class home. Now the window is boarded up and the sofa is in shreds. Part of her wants to blame Vivian. After all, she brought the bastard here. But her mother's lover is just as much a victim as Lorene.

Richard is being wonderfully supportive and has called several times to check on the situation. He wanted her to be at the press conference this morning but it was important for Ann to spend the night. That was strange, sleeping in her old bedroom. She hasn't even stepped inside since her doomed marriage to Mark Bradley nearly nine months ago. Spending the night was a little surreal. It is the one room Lorene left untouched. The faded wallpaper, the second hand furniture, even the unicorn painting Peter Brandt won her at the state fair are all in the same place. Yet, she did not belong: it was Ann Halloran sleeping in Ann Gale's bed. In many ways, they seem like different people leading different lives.

Her cell rings, but it's not Richard this time. "Hello Julie."

"Ann, I just saw what happened on the news. How is your mother?"

"Getting some rest. They've both taken some sedatives."

"Is it true that he was Vivian's husband?"

"Yeah, and apparently he's been pretty abusive over the years. But it doesn't matter; he's dead now."

"Is there anything you need?"

"No, I'm almost done with the cleanup. Someone is coming in from Manchester to fix the window."

"When are you coming home?" *Home; does this mean that the Halloran mansion is now truly home?*

"As soon as I know things are okay here."

"Let's talk when you get here, okay?" There is a welcoming sincerity in Julie's voice, a sound that make hers feel good for the first time today. It reminds her of the old days, growing up when Ann had some crisis and needed someone to talk to. Crises were common with Munroe --- and only her best friend seemed to understand. "Sure, when things are settled here."

****

Greg meant to call Jack earlier, but he has had to deal with one distraction after another. It sometimes seems as if no one has the balls to do their job. One of the biggest headaches involved a supplier to the New Hampshire mill. It took three hours to clean up something Greg is sure should have taken five minutes. *Such is life as the boss, I suppose. How did Dad manage to deal with it?* Finally, he manages to make the call. "Hey, dude," Greg sighs, "sorry it took so long. It's been a crazy day."

"Yeah, my day's been strange too." *It must have been;* maybe it's the background noise but even Jack's voice sounds strange. "Jack, where are you?"

"On the train; I'll be in Manchester by the end of the day."

That means they may lose the signal at any moment. Greg decides to get straight to the point: "What's going on? Your text said there is a big problem."

"Well, dude, it's about that account your dad set-up. There is a problem with it; a big one." *Great, just what I need.* It seems the nightmare of Lewis' murder will never end.

"I had Eddie Grant look over the papers. You remember Eddie from NYU, right?" Yes, Greg remembers Eddie. The bastard would never bottom --- even drunk --- and he eventually knocked up some bitchy debutante named Judy Something. "Anyway, he looked them over and you won't believe it: they're a fake."

What the hell is he talking about? "I don't understand."

There is a silent moment as Greg wonders if they've lost the connection. "Sorry, dude," Jack finally answers. "Some people were --- never mind --- anyway,

Eddie says the bank went out of business before the papers were drawn up. It seems your old man was screwing Mel for screwing him."

Greg smiles: *I'll be damned; good for him.*

****

Eve King has never flown in a private plane. She has also never been to Washington. But this is a day of firsts. Senator Richard Davis and the late Senator Russell Brooks' staff are in charge. Greeting them on the plane is Victoria Datillo. She was Brooks' chief of staff and, at Richard's advice, is staying on to help Ben. Victoria is about Eve's age with shoulder-length brown hair and a business-comes-first demeanor. This is a woman who has dedicated her life to her career, and she makes no apologies for it.

So begins a day of meetings, meetings and more meetings. Ben has to attend them all: the senate leaders (who are supposed to be on holiday recess but flew in special), touring the offices, introducing the staff and --- the most exciting moment --- tea at the White House with the President and First Lady. Eve didn't have a chance to explore the executive mansion, but was able to note how different the place is compared to the Halloran estate.

Camera crews follow them from one stop to the next. The stations from Boston are here, of course, to relay the news back home. But all the cable news networks are also present and Eve has even spotted some of the coverage on TVs in a few of the offices they visit. The reporters remind her of her biggest concerned: that someone might dig up the truth about her daughter.

Perhaps the most interesting meeting was with Frank Turner. On the advice of both Richard and Victoria, he has been brought in to run Ben's campaign. Well into his seventies, this wise old man has spent more than half his life in the whirlwinds of New England politics. He has guided more people to seats in state capitals and Washington than anyone else in the Northeast. "Young man," Turner says with great confidence, "you've got all the right ingredients." When Ben tried to humbly disagree, the old man simply laughed.

One key decision remains: where to live in Washington. They will, of course, be keeping their home in Faraway Hill. Ben plans to commute. But he still needs a place in the capital and fast. Victoria advises sharing an apartment with another senator and has the staff working on it.

They are staying at the Hay-Adams. An old world hotel, the Hay-Adams is elegance defined, from the sage green walls to the ornate woodwork. Their junior suite is on the seventh floor facing the H Street side of the building, allowing for magnificent views of the city. Eve can spot Lafayette Square, the Washington Monument and even the White House from their window.

The evening ends with a quiet, casual dinner in the hotel's Off the Record bar. They had considered eating in the Lafayette, but the restaurant seemed too formal after a day filled with formalities. The bar is much more comfortable. It has handsome wood panels and a beautifully carved ceiling. But the walls, in a dark red that approaches burgundy, create a sense of warmth. The chairs are upholstered to match. Eve raises a glass of imported wine. Her fears may remain, but Eve has never been more proud of her husband. "Congratulations, Ben."

"Congratulations to us both."

A clink and a kiss; yes, this has been a special day. The waiter comes by with the menus and he, too, congratulates the new senator from New Hampshire. But he is not the last to do so: Eve sees a woman, dressed very smartly in a business suit, nervously looking at them. *Will it be like this from now on? Will people now gawk at us?* The woman takes a few steps in their direction and stops. Her eyes meet Eve's, leaving her to wonder what is really happening. "Ben, do you know that woman?"

Ben looks up from his menu. The woman stays frozen in place, like some trapped animal unsure of what to do. "Wow, I don't believe it."

"You *do* know her?"

"We dated when I was at Northwestern. Her name is Grace Bradley." He motions to the woman. She takes a deep breath, forces a smile on her face and steps up to the table.

"Hello Ben."

Ben rises to give Grace a quick hug then turns to his wife. "Hello Grace; I can't believe how long it's been! Grace, this is my wife, Eve."

"Hello, Grace." Eve smiles and tries to make the best of an awkward situation. Just why it is awkward is unclear; their marriage is strong enough to survive meeting an ex-girlfriend. "Please join us." Grace hesitantly takes a seat. "Just for a moment; I don't want to ruin your big night. Congratulations, Ben."

"Thanks. So, how have you been? I haven't seen you in, what, over 20 years."

"More like 25. I'm fine. I work here, in the hotel; I'm in charge of housekeeping." She pauses and then carefully adds, "I have a son, Mark."

"That's terrific." Ben responds with a genuine kindness. Somehow, though, Eve suspects that Grace expected something more. "Is he here in Washington?"

"No," she says quietly as if embarrassed. "He's . . . elsewhere." *Why is she acting so strange,* Eve wonders. "Look, I'm sorry to disturb your celebration. How long will you both be here? I'd . . . love to catch up with you Ben."

"We're leaving tomorrow," Ben explains. "But I might have some free time in the morning."

Grace agrees to a time, exchanges a few pleasantries and leaves them alone --- but not before stopping at the Off the Record's entrance to look back at them for a moment. Ben doesn't seem too fazed by the encounter so Eve decides not to pursue it. Still, she wonders, *what is going on with that woman?*

****

There isn't much to do at night in a small town like Faraway Hill. There are a few bars, but they cater mostly to the farm trade where old men with gray hair and beer guts meet to commiserate after a long day. They gather early in the winter months, when there is less to do. Most young people go into Manchester where there are clubs and restaurants and coffee shops that cater to them. But most of Peter's childhood friends have scattered and he hates going to those places alone. Instead, he ends the day lying on his bed staring at the ceiling.

His thoughts tonight are mostly about women. Seeing Ann Gale last night reminded him of high school. She was his first lover and he hers. They were awkward together, but he enjoyed it anyway. It hurt when she dumped him, telling Peter that she wanted someone with more ambition. He loved her so much then. He might still love her. Ironically, Ann ended up marrying a farmhand --- one that turned out to be a male prostitute. There was a brief moment when Peter hoped that she would come back to him. But then everyone discovered that Lewis Halloran is her father. Her ambition to be "somebody" has been realized. He'll never have her again. Realizing this was so painful that he took a leave of absence and left the country.

While in Africa he met another aid worker. She was a pretty young girl from Canada, who was smart and confident and totally uninterested in Peter. It was like a kick in the groin when she used the "you're like a brother" line. So Peter came home and now spends his nights staring at the ceiling. Alone. *I guess I should get use to this,* he has said to himself over and over.

Until tonight.

It surprises him that someone like Karen St. John should be interested in him. She made this especially clear today in their little tour. The age factor is one reason: she is old enough to be his mother. She is also elegant and sophisticated and reminds him of one of the great old time movie stars. She's even kind of sexy, in the way he finds older women like Susan Sarandon sexy. *Maybe,* he wonders, *maybe I should give this a try.*

****

Little white flakes fall from the dark sky. It has been a long, boring day and a boring little motel along the highway. Few people know this place exists. This is why Mel Waite chose it. This is why no one has found him.

Until now.

A simple car as unnoticeable as the motel discretely pulls into the driveway. The man at the wheel is dressed is dark clothes. This is someone who understands the value of discretion. He climbs the stairs quietly and strides silently along the walkway until he reaches the door. All it takes are a couple of quick raps for Mel to open it. There is a surprise look on Mel's face; he seems to be expecting someone else. "Holy shit, are you a cop? You don't look like a cop."

The man pushes Mel into the room. The bed is a mess, the TV is blaring and empty food cartons litter the table and nightstand. The disgraced lawyer has been holed up inside nonstop for days.

"Just who the *fuck* do you think you are?" Mel is trying to sound angry, but it's only fear that the man hears. "Answer me, dammit!"

The man does answer him --- with a bullet to the forehead.

EPISODE FIVE

"This is the worst one yet," Meryl mumbles to no one in particular. Just 19 years old, she has suffered through a string of minimum wage jobs, mostly waiting on tables at cheap restaurants. All were awful. The customers were often old men who'd leer at her or old women who'd treat her like shit. At the last one, groups of college boys would laugh and taunt her. Eventually she broke down in tears and quit.

Now she is working as a motel maid and has come to hate this job too. But Meryl needs money. Her mother is dead and daddy can't work since his accident at the Halloran mill. The government subsidies and company health insurance help, but don't quite cover everything. So Meryl works at whatever job an unskilled teenager can find. Before school or after school, any job is an important as long as it pays.

When this job opened up, Meryl grabbed it. Cleaning rooms at a motel along the highway seemed easy. Little did she know some of the things that happen in these places: married men bringing their girlfriends or hookers; college kids trashing rooms during wild parties. Drug dealers used to come here for their deals until the State Police stepped in. She has heard couples fight, fuck and ignore each other never realizing that the thin walls make nothing truly private.

But the strangest guest is the balding, middle age man in Room 204. Since checking in, he almost never leaves. He is a hermit living in a modern cave equipped with indoor plumbing and cable TV. Every day, Meryl pushes the heavy supply cart up the ramp to the second floor. She must check each room whether or not it's occupied. But she loathes 204. The balding man's room is creepy. There are food cartons and dirty clothes and piles of newspapers and magazine everywhere. The air has a thick, heavy odor. He is never nice and just growls while letting her inside. As quickly as possible, Meryl changes the linen, empties the trash and re-supplies the bathroom. He never tips her and never thanks her. The bald man simply grunts as she leaves.

But dealing with him is part of Meryl's job. So here she is, standing outside 204 and knocking at the door to announce "Housekeeping."

There is no answer. Usually she can hear him fumbling across the room. This morning there is nothing. She knocks again.

"Sir, this is Housekeeping."

Again, silence. *That's odd.* But then, everything about this man is odd. Meryl pulls out her passkey and announces "I'm coming in". Nothing. Opening the door, she gets a surprise: the man is gone along with all his belongings. But the room isn't just empty --- it's clean. It can even be called spotless. Meryl walks around amazed. Along with his belongings, the stale food, magazines and other trash have disappeared. The carpet smells like it's been shampooed and a scent of disinfectant wafts from the bathroom. The bed linen has been stripped right down to the mattress. *Holy shit,* she thinks, *I'm the only one who cleans; what the hell happened?* Then a weird idea hits her: *Did the bald man scrub down his room before skipping out on the bill?*

Whatever happened, it's just as creepy as the man who lived here.

✳✳✳✳

Its time I got back to work. For Julie Halloran this means returning King's Korner. Her little shop in Manchester sells sorts of giftware as well as coffee and pastry from a cozy storefront on Elm Street. She has been too busy the last few weeks with Johnny and her trouble marriage to pay it much attention. But now the all-important Christmas season is underway and if the shop is to survive, she needs to focus.

Unfortunately her leg is still in a cast. *So damned frustrating.* Frederick orders a car and driver. It is the same young man who got Julie to the hospital the night she fell and gave birth. She is glad it's him; a friendly face is welcome considering all that is going on in her life.

Julie has had to leave the store in the care of Mary Armstrong for the last few weeks. A sweet girl, Mary has somehow managed to keep things running while still going to college. She even got the holiday merchandise inventoried and the decorations up. It's the first thing Julie comments on as she enters. "I am very impressed."

"Thanks, Mrs. Halloran," Mary replies with youthful pride. She eagerly points out what she has done with various displays. The girl even made a tree out of green garland strung on a wall. *Clever.* "Sales are pretty good, I think."

Julie looks around approvingly. The place is busier than usual. One of Mary's friends --- Julie still can't remember her name --- is helping out behind the counter; all in all, a good sign for the holiday season. "I'm glad to hear it."

Mary has to move a spinning rack of holiday postcards out the way so that Julie can better navigate. "By the way Mrs. Halloran, how long do you need to wear the cast?"

"Not long; they tell me just after the first of the year."

"Oh, good," Mary replies with a smile. "My cousin broke his leg once and he had to wear a cast for six months. Six months! It was a real bummer for him."

"My fracture isn't that severe."

"Cool; oh, and someone called. I left the message in your office."

Julie thanks the girl and hobbles her way to the back of the store. The note on her desk is from an architect. She spoke with him the other day about some plans he had worked on for Greg's late mother. *I'm surprised to hear from him so soon.* It's also surprising that he picks up the phone himself; Julie expects to reach a secretary.

"Mr. Benedict? It's Julie Halloran."

"Good morning, Mrs. Halloran." Julie remembers him from their meeting: an exuberant man in his forties, Noah Benedict grew up in Boston where he developed a love for older buildings. He was thrilled to hear from the Hallorans again about a project he wanted to see to completion. "I found my copies of the plans and I think they will do nicely for what you want."

"So we can finish turning the old servants' building into a guest house?" It was Lilly Halloran's idea to add more space for guests. Julie is still calling it that; but in reality she has other plans.

"Yes, depending on the condition of the building."

"What do you mean?"

"Well, it's been a couple of years since your mother-in-law hired me. There hasn't been any work done on it since. I'd like to have my contractor check out the space with me. Just to be on the safe side, you understand."

"Of course; how soon can the work start?"

"Well, fortunately all of the exterior and structural work was done then, including the new roof. The remainder is just interior renovations. The winter weather shouldn't slow that down too much. We should be able to start sometime in January or February."

"Good, the sooner the better."

✶✶✶✶

The Mall of New Hampshire is bustling with holiday shoppers. The entire place has been decked out, with the halls and food court practically dripping with seasonal greenery and ornaments so bright and cheerful it is easy to forget they are all made of plastic.

A delighted Little Jack practically skips out of Macy's. His two dads have just bought him his first winter coat and the California boy thinks it's the best thing *ever*. He's anxious to put it on, so they stride to the food court where they can sit and remove all the tags. Joe has bought one too and even he is a little excited. "Neat! Neat! Neat!" Little Jack screams. Both of his fathers smile proudly.

"Uncle Jack, can we build a snowman?" The boy has never seen winter before and he's been talking about it ever since he saw the flakes from the hotel window.

"Sure --- when there is enough snow." There have been flurries on and off for days, but not enough accumulation to make a decent snowman. It makes Jack feel good to buy his son something. His own father never did; the old man left Jack's mother to handle these things. It helps him feel more like a dad.

"Okay young man," Joe says gently but firmly. "Time to get some lunch; what are you in the mood for?"

Looking very cute, the boy scans the food court, judging each option carefully, and spies a Sbarro's. "Pizza!"

Joe chuckles. "Is pizza good for you, too?" he asks Jack.

"Sure; can you guys get it? I need to make a call." Joe takes their son's hand and walks over to the counter. Jack takes out his cell and dials Mel Waite. It's odd that the old man hasn't called yet today. He typically annoys Jack three or four times before Noon. *I wonder how he'll take the news about the fake account.* But the prick doesn't answer. Instead, Jack hears a recorded voice saying that Mel's cell phone is out of service. *What the hell is going on with him?* He ponders what to do next when a soft, sexy and familiar voice interrupts with two words: "hello, Jack."

He looks up to see, standing before him, a disturbing vision from his colorful past. "Denise, what the hell are you doing here?"

Denise Sullivan gives him the same wicked, naughty smile she gives every man. It says that fun is not far off; an invitation that few decline and one that Jack has accepted more than once. She is looking extra hot today, dressed in a white dress so tight it practically caresses her body. Trimmed with faux white fur, it makes her look like a *Playboy* centerfold. From the December issue. "It's nice to see you Jack. Of course, it's *always* nice to see you."

Jack glances behind him to see Joe and their son wait at the counter for their food. The two will be back any minute and Jack has no desire to subject them to Denise. "I asked you: what the fuck are you doing here?"

"I've got a job. I'm the new personal assistant to a very cool, very rich lady. Her name's Karen St. John. Ever hear of her?"

Holy shit; that's just what Greg and I don't need. "I've met her, several times."

"Oh, that's right. Her niece is married to Greg. I miss him --- and you too. You boys and I had a lot of fun together." In college, Denise was always up for a good time. Jack fucked her on several occasions and he knows that Greg hooked up with her at least once. And then, there was a certain party that became so infamous across NYU that it almost made the papers.

"So, tell me Jack, are you two still fuck buddies? I know he's married and all, but --- "

Jack takes another look behind him and sees Joe paying for lunch. They'll be back any minute.

"Afraid your latest boyfriend and his kid will see me? Oh, alright Jack, but first," she leans in and gives him a quick but terrific kiss. *She's still good at that.* "My cell number is the same. Call me."

Denise gives him another wicked smile, turns and slowly walks out of the food court, her tight, sexy ass sashaying with every step. *Fuck.*

****

Frank Turner is a wise old man, small and gnome-like with a mind as bright as his eyes. He is a font of information, whether it is about committees and chairmen or trivia about the capitol. Throughout the morning he peppers valuable political advice with interesting bits about the city. It's like having a private tour guide for all things Washington. Right now, he points Ben to a famous site visible from the suite's window.

"It took almost 40 years to finish the Washington Monument. Money, politics and the Civil War kept getting in the way. My great-grandfather lived here then and he told me all the stories when I was little. That man lived forever. Anyway, for years it was just a stump and looked like it would never be finished. It became a running joke in the city. They finally completed it in the 1880s but if you look closely you can see the different color stone from when they stopping construction and when they picked up again." Ben stares at the monument. He can't see any difference, but is still fascinated by the story.

Eve is out exploring the shops along Dupont Circle this morning as Frank and Ben's chief of staff, Victoria Datillo, take the time to brief him. There is a lot to absorb. "Don't be too overwhelmed," Victoria advises, sitting on the sofa going over some notes. "The staff will help you every step of the way."

Frank nods in agreement. "And it doesn't look like you'll have any challengers in the primary --- no one serious, anyway. The party plans to give you their full support. This means you'll have more time to learn the ropes. The real challenge will be the general in November."

"November," Ben says to no one in particular staring out the window. This new career and the life it offers him seem bigger than he imagined. "I wonder who it'll be."

Victoria starts packing up her briefcase. Their meeting is scheduled to end in a few minutes. "We think the Republicans will put up Adam Newman. Ever hear of him?"

Ben nods; he has been acquainted with the Concord lawyer for years. Adam Newman is smart and charming and principled. Ben liked him the moment they first met. In fact, Ben wonders how can beat a man like that. "Don't worry," Frank says with a wry, wrinkled smile, "you will."

They finally wrap up the meeting; Ben agreed to rendezvous with Eve for lunch before they fly back home. As he escorts them out, Grace Bradley appears at the door. She looks even more nervous than she did last night. "Am I early?"

"No; you're right on time."

Frank and Victoria give him a look mixing concern with curiosity. Ben gestures that all is fine and that they can leave. But once the two of them are alone, Grace doesn't say anything. Instead she paces the room, glancing at the sitting area and the bed as if she has never been in one of the hotel's junior suites before. "Um . . . where is your wife?"

"Out shopping; we leave for New Hampshire later today." *Why is she acting this way? What could possibly be wrong?*

She nods but again says nothing more. Instead, she stops to stare at the carved ceiling above them.

"Grace, please, tell me what's wrong."

She takes a deep breath, summoning all the courage within her. "Ben, I have been trying to find you for years."

"I don't understand." Ben was just expecting them to reminisce, but Grace is so serious it's unnerving.

"When you graduated, you said you were going to Boston." She still has trouble looking directly at him. Instead she walks around the room, gently placing a hand on the bed's upholstered headboard. "You were going to Boston. I looked for you there. For a long time I looked for you there."

What the hell is she talking about? "I did go to Boston. I just didn't stay. I got work in Manchester and bought a house in Faraway Hill."

Grace nods, her whole body shaking with fear.

"Please, Grace, what is bothering you? None of this makes any sense."

She stops at the window but turns her back on the impressive view. For the first time their eyes meet. He can see the tears slowly trickle down her cheek. "I never wanted to tell you this way."

"Grace?"

"When you left, I was pregnant, Ben. I was pregnant. I was carrying your child."

She can't mean that; she can't. But she can and she does; he can see it in her eyes.

"I tried to find you. I did. I called everywhere I could, everyone I could. I even flew to Boston. But you were gone . . . you were gone . . . my son, Mark, is your son; our son. I wanted to tell you right away. I wanted to tell you years ago. I didn't know where you went. I didn't know how to find you."

"Oh, my God . . ." He sits there, trying to absorb the news. *I have a son . . . I have a son.*

"My parents were furious," Grace explains, her voice breaking. "Dad wanted me to have an abortion but I was too scared. They kicked me out. They gave me money and kicked me out."

Oh my God!

"Now he's disappeared. Mark has always been a . . . problem boy. But now I can't find him. I'm scared he's in trouble. He gets in trouble so easily. I don't expect you to be a father to him. I know it's too late for that. But I'm sure he's in trouble, probably serious trouble. Maybe we can find him together. I hope that we can."

My son, I have a son; a son I never met. "Do you . . . do you have a picture?" *I wonder what my son looks like. Is he like me or like my dad?*

Grace nods and opens her purse. She hands him a wallet size photo: Ben King <u>has</u> met him before. *Holy shit!* Although it is a few years old and the young man's hair is a little longer, there is no mistake: her son --- his son --- is Mark Bradley. The same Mark Bradley who married Ann Halloran; the same Mark Bradley who earned money prostituting himself; the same Mark Bradley who skipped town after Munroe Gale's suicide.

****

Joe is worried. Jack is bottling up too much inside himself. Joe knows something terrible happened over Thanksgiving that Jack refused to talk about last night.

He seems better this today, happier and more animated. Spending time shopping with their son improved his spirits considerably. Now he is quiet again. Maybe it was the phone call Jack needed to make, but something is clearly worrying him. Joe has come to learn that one of the drawbacks to being a man is that guys seldom confide in one another the way women do. Of course, a woman will often go too far and whine. It was one of the many things about women that annoyed Jackie. *Still,* he thinks, *there must be a happy medium.*

As the fathers and son arrive at the hotel, Joe can see Lt. Aaron Tracey waiting in the Radisson's lobby. The officer looks as cute as ever; he really knows how to wear a uniform. *Too bad he's straight.* Joe still hasn't told Jack about the shooting in Veteran's Park. It occurs to him that stoically keeping this from Jack is a very guy thing to do --- the same thing Jack is doing with him. *Yes, there has to be a happy medium.*

The officer discretely gestures to him, so Joe makes up an excuse about visiting the gift shop. Jack and their son take the elevator upstairs. Once they are gone, Joe steps over to the lieutenant. "Do you need to see me?"

"Yes, Joe; can we talk in private?" The officer guides him into the bar at JD's Tavern. They haven't seen each other since Joe and Little Jack spent Thanksgiving with Aaron and his girlfriend. It's a slow time of the day; with few people in the restaurant and none at the bar. After ordering some sparkling water and waiting for the bartender to step away, the lieutenant comes straight to the point. "I thought you'd be more comfortable meeting here than at the station. I have some news for you."

"Aaron, has something happened to the other guy?" *I didn't think his wound was serious.* "Is he . . . dead?"

"What? Oh, no, no he's fine. Actually, he's moved out of state; somewhere in the Midwest where he has family. But . . . We have learned more about the shooting. Apparently the other man wasn't the target." He pauses to look Joe right in the eye and says carefully, "you were."

Oh shit, that means . . . "my stepfather?"

Aaron nods. "He hired a hit man named Michael Bickel. But the attempt failed. Do you read the *Union Leader*?"

"Occasionally; I'm new here and being a single parent eats up a lot my time."

"Well, you may be aware of a recent incident at a farm in Faraway Hill. Bickel's estranged wife is living there. He broke in and, well, things got pretty rough. The Faraway Hill Police ended up being called and Bickel was shot to death."

Vincent must be pissed at that, Joe realizes; *he always relied on Bickel and Bickel was considered a pro.* "That's terrible; is everyone alright?"

"Fortunately, but his gun has been tied to the bullet used in Veteran's Park. e know it was him and we know he was in the employ of Vincent Bologna." Aaron pauses, wanting to be cautious and respectful as he asks, "Joe . . . Are you transsexual?"

The guy's done his homework. I'm impressed. "Yes, I was born Jacqueline Westbrook. That's why my stepfather hates me. He thinks I'm a freak and an embarrassment and he wants to be rid of me --- and take my son to be his own."

"I see," Aaron says with a sigh. He takes another drink. Joe feels compelled to add, "the man I'm with --- Jack Campbell --- is my son's father, although Little Jack doesn't know that yet. As far as my son is concerned, I'm his only papa."

Aaron nods. It impresses Joe how cool the officer is about everything. Usually when people learn about the surgery, they freak. Instead, Aaron calmly asks, "What are your plans?"

"Well, I was looking for a place here," Joe shrugs. "It's tough to raise a child and keep running. I'm tired of it. But now . . ."

Aaron places a supportive hand on his shoulder. "I was talking to the chief. The Manchester Police will do what we can to protect you, but you need to understand --- we are a small city with limited resources."

"I understand, Aaron, and I appreciate it." The news about Vincent and Bickel complicates his hopes to find a nice, quiet home in Manchester or even some town nearby. *Now what the hell do I do?*

****

Life is built on routine. This is true for Peter Brandt, whose day begins the way nearly all of his days begin. He gets up early to take care of his mother and father. They are much older than his friends' parents, having married late. Peter was a surprise pregnancy for a couple who assumed having a child was out of reach. The simplest things are becoming harder for them. His mother's arthritis makes it tough for her to cook meals. His dad's weak knees keep him sitting for hours at a time. More and more falls on Peter's shoulders. He makes sure they eat their breakfast and take their medication before the two of them settle in for a full day in front of the TV.

Peter then goes to work at the sheriff's office. Faraway Hill is an oddity in that it has an elected sheriff heading the small police department. This is one of those quirks that date back to colonial times. Faraway Hill has a lot of these oddities, with departments and terms that are considered out of date. It has often been said that the sheriff should be replaced with an appointed police chief. That will probably happen after Sheriff Reynolds retires. He is too well connected in the town to be replaced any other way.

The morning is spent with paperwork. All of Peter's work days start this way. There is always something from last night or the day before that needs to be handled. But his mind keeps wandering back to the same subject, the same person.

After lunch, he makes the usual rounds of the town with a focus on the square. No matter where he stops or whom he speaks to, he can't help thinking about her. Even now, as he stands in the middle of Faraway Hill, eyes affixed on the snow covered statute of John Halloran, he thinks of her. The man looks impressive, solid and determined. A new thought finally occurs to Peter: "I wonder what it takes to start your own town," he says to no one in particular.

"Usually it takes a lot of arrogance," a soft, elegant voice responds. Peter turns to see the person he's been thinking of all day. With a warm smile, he says "hello, Karen."

****

Frustrated with one problem after another, Greg Halloran comes home early. Most of the company is humming along well expect one important area: the situation in Thailand. Each report is more worrisome than the first. A prolonged, nationwide strike there will affect the Halloran mill immediately and put the whole company at risk. But he is helpless to do anything except watch cable news and wait for the latest update.

Jack wants to meet him later, be he needs to shower and change first. Climbing the marble Grand Staircase, he pauses to see Julie in the nursery conferring with the nanny. The bruises have all healed and only the cast is a reminder of her fall. Mrs. Reynolds says something he cannot hear and it makes Julie laugh. It's a nice sight. It makes him want to go into the nursery and pick up his son. He'd like them to be a family again, even for just one brief moment. But Greg knows that is no longer possible. Instead he steps into the master suite and closes the door behind him. To the left of the parlor is his wife's bedroom; his is to the right.

The door opens and Julie, still a little awkward with the crutch, enters. The smile is gone; face now has a determined look. "Please sit down," she tells Greg. "We need to talk."

He selects a chair across from the settee where Julie takes her seat. "Before I begin, please don't interrupt. Let me finish what I need to say."

Greg nods and braces himself for the bad news. *This is it; she is going to leave and take my son with her.*

"I am still very hurt and very angry at you --- again, let me do this --- and while you may not have planned it, there is no changing things. I still love you Greg, but I've come to believe we don't have a future as husband and wife."

Oh shit, oh shit, oh shit.

"But a simple divorce just isn't going to work. If there is one thing I've learned over the past several months is that being married to a Halloran is more complicated than being married to almost anyone else. In some ways, it's a little like being married to royalty or nobility or whatever. There are . . . obligations in a storied family. They can't be ignored. This house, this family, their legacy . . . part of that belongs to my son. To just pick up and leave would be unfair to him."

Where is she going with this?

"Then there is my dad. I told you I didn't want a scandal to hurt his new career. The world finding out that his son-in-law is fucking a man would certainly qualify. I can't do that to him."

Does this mean she is going to stay with me? Will I have to give up Jack?

"So, that has left me to wonder: what do I do? If Johnny and I pack up and leave, would my son resent me? Will reporters find out about your affair? What would my father do? So, I have come up with a plan."

Greg looks at her curiously and asks simply, "a plan?"

"Yes. First, you and I are going to continue to have separate bedrooms. As far as the world knows, we are happily married. But after the election, we will divorce. As part of the settlement, Johnny and I will be moving into the old servants building out back. I've already seen the architect. Fortunately, your mother began work on it before she died. It'll only take a few months before it's habitable. This way, you and I can lead our own lives while sharing our son --- whose connections with the Hallorans will remain secure."

Her plan is ingenious and impressive. *It might just work.*

"I've thought a lot about this. We have to keep up the public pretense until fall. I hope that won't be too difficult for either of us."

She is being so cool about everything. Most women would be interested in getting even with their cheating husband. "I'll do everything I can to make this work, Julie, I mean that."

Julie nods, picks up the crutch and rises. "One more thing: I don't want to see Jack Campbell. Not in this house or anywhere near it. Not while we're still married. If you are going to see him, do it discretely." Then with a determined tone in her voice, Julie adds "I will *not* be publicly humiliated."

"Of course not."

"Good, because if you do --- if that happens --- don't be surprised if you come home to find your wife and your son gone forever."

"I understand."

With that, Julie crutches her way to her own bedroom and closes the door between them.

✸✸✸✸

"Mark Bradley is my son . . . my son with Grace."

Ben and Eve King are back in Faraway Hill, sitting in their living room exhausted from the whirl of the past few days. Ben decided to wait and tell his wife the news in the comfort of their own home, surrounded by the wonderful life they've built together. The family photos on the walls, the mementos on the tables, Ben hopes that all of these things will help cushion the blow. Right now he is waiting for a response. But Eve is saying nothing. There are no tears, no screams. He wasn't quite sure what to expect, but he didn't count on silence. She just stares at him, as if trying to absorb the news. Finally, she asks, "are you sure it's true?"

"Well, it's not like I can have a DNA test or anything," he answers with a sigh. "Not until we find him. But I haven't any reason to think Grace is lying."

"She has plenty of reasons Ben. You're about to become a United States senator. An illegitimate child would make for great blackmail."

Ben shakes his head. He knows Grace better than that. "No, she hasn't asked for anything. That's not the kind of person Grace is. Besides, we both know I've got nothing to give her."

Again, Eve says nothing. This really bothers him. He can't tell what she's thinking. *Is she mad? Is she worried?* She looks around the room, at the home they've built together. Her gaze eventually settles on the mantle. The photos sitting there tell the story of their marriage and their life. It's the picture of Julie, taken just after her tenth birthday that becomes her focus. A tear slowly snakes its way down Eve's cheek. "Well, then, she did it. Someone else did it."

"Sweetheart, what are you talking about?"

Eve manages to stay calm, but she can't stop her eyes from watering. "Grace Bradley gave you the one thing --- the only thing in this world --- that I couldn't: a child of your own."

Ben isn't sure what he can say to that. Instead, he takes his wife into his arms.

****

Julie snuggles under a warm, comfy quilt. The family room is one of the few places in the mansion where one can relax. There are no antiques here. The walls have no rare paintings. The furniture is overstuffed and comfortable. A plasma screen is the major feature. This is Julie's favorite room; where the formalities of being a Halloran are kept at bay.

"You look like you've settled in for the night."

She looks up to see Ann standing at the door, smiling.

"I love this room," Julie replies turning off the TV. "You know, living in this house, well, it sometimes feels like your living in a museum. History just stares right at you from every corner. But here," she gestures around her. "Here, it almost feels like a real home."

Ann is still smiling, but she remains by the door, careful and cautious. "I haven't spent much time anywhere except my suite, but it does seem nice and comfortable in here."

"I'm sorry about that, by the way," Julie answers gently. When Ann moved in a few months ago it was with the understanding that she'd stay to herself. It was meant to keep peace in the family. Julie was very angry at her for a long time. Things are different now.

"That's okay; I understand. My being here . . . well, it causes problems. Everything I do seem to cause problems."

Julie motions to a nearby chair. "You're exaggerating."

"Am I?" Ann sighs and sits. The chair is soft and comfortable. It would be easy to fall asleep in it. "I see everyone's gossiping about me again."

"If you are talking about your mother and Vivian, I don't think you should give a damn what anyone thinks."

Ann shakes her head. "That's not what I mean. Despite the shooting and everything they seem really happy together. In fact, I don't recall ever seeing my mom look better. No, I'm talking about me and Richard."

"Well, everyone was a bit surprised to see you together at the funeral."

"I'm surprised too." To Julie, the smile on Ann's face reminds her of the days when they'd sit in her bedroom discussing the mysteries of boys. "It all started at the Gabler party where we talked and talked. Nobody has every really talked to me in such a long time. Everything just grew from there. I . . . I think I'm falling in love with him. Sure, it's crazy --- he's old enough to be my father --- and we've only known each other a short time. But still . . . ."

"Do you think he loves you?"

Ann pauses for a moment reflecting on all the time they've spend together, holding hands, visiting Concord and making love. "Yes, yes I do."

"Does he treat you right?"

"He treats me like a princess."

Julie smiles; she needs some good news tonight. "Then I don't see a problem. Let them gossip. It's what they do in small towns."

"Thanks," it's also nice that she and Ann can be friends again. All of the tumult of the past year has really put a strain on their relationship.

"So how is being a mom?"

"I love it. He's like a little miracle."

"Greg seems to like being a dad. I saw him leave earlier. Where did he go?"

Julie was with the baby when she heard him leave the house. It isn't hard to guess where he went. "He's out with a friend."

"Jack Campbell?"

"I guess." *Why did she bring him up?* Even as a little girl, Ann was always a little nosy. It made her feel important --- and annoyed the hell out of everyone.

"They seem pretty close." *She knows something;* Julie can sense it.

"They went to college together," Julie answers carefully. "Jack is his best friend."

Ann just nods without saying anything more. *Yes, she knows something. Damn Greg, you've got to do a better job at being discrete for our deal to work.*

****

Greg Halloran's life is finally coming together. Julie's magnanimous offer will allow him to be a father to his son and still be with Jack. *She is so cool, so fucking cool.* The classy way his wife is handling their odd situation reminds him why he fell in love with her, and why part of him still loves her.

After a brief shower, Greg changes into some casual clothes and jumps into his car for the short drive to Manchester. He feels like celebrating --- and there is only one person in only one way he wants to do it.

It has been so long, so damned long. Julie wasn't much interested in sex during the last weeks of her pregnancy. Since giving birth, she has been too upset with him. There has only been Jack. But even he hasn't been available. Tonight will be different.

Greg is nearly whistling as he strides into the Radisson's lobby and toward the elevator. He is oblivious to the curious attention of the guests, including one very elegant lady looking on with amusement. Karen St. John is beginning to sense a new opportunity.

Arriving upstairs, he runs into Joe leaving Jack's suite. They chat a little, the transman telling him about his son and their trip to the mall earlier today. "He's so cute about his first winter jacket and all," Joe says with a proud smile. "But it looks like Little Jack is finally starting to poop out." The two of them are planning to settle in with a room service meal. *Perfect; that means I can have Jack all to myself.*

Closing the door behind him, Greg can hear the shower running. He slips off his clothes and flops naked on the bed --- a smile and a hardening cock ready to greet his lover. When Jack emerges from the bathroom wearing nothing but a robe, he looks surprised and --- for some reason Greg can't quite fathom --- relieved to see him. He tells Jack "you are way over dressed" and the man dutifully drops the robe to the floor and climbs into bed. The two of them kiss deeply, sensually, for what seems like a lifetime. Their hard cocks rub against each other. Greg is amazed at Jack's body. It seems that no matter how much or how little he works out, Jack remains trim and muscular. There have been times in the past when Greg would spend an entire evening just exploring the other man's magnificent build. Tonight as he caresses Jack's tight ass, Greg whispers, "I need to be inside you."

Normally Jack does the topping, but Greg is too horny for anything else. He grabs the lube from the nightstand. Greg then flips the other man on his back and slides himself inside. He pauses, relishing the warmth and grip of Jack's ass. "Do it, lover" Jack insists. Greg begins fucking him harder and harder when, suddenly, Jack shoots cum across his chest. *Wow, that doesn't happen often.* It makes him wonder if Jack is a secret bottom. It only takes Greg a few more thrusts before until he unloads. Exhausted and exhilarated, the two men lay there, Greg still on top and inside Jack. It takes them a little while to catch their breath. Greg, without moving, tells his lover about Julie's deal. Jack is as relieved and happy as he. "That is so cool . . . so damned cool."

The two lovers remain connected together, not knowing and not caring what else is going on in the world. *Nothing can ruin this,* Greg thinks. There is a sense of joy running through him. *My life is finally coming together. Not a damn thing can go wrong now.*

Nothing, that is, except the news from Thailand, news reported everywhere but in their hotel room: a nation-wide strike has been called to protest the lingering political crisis. Every American investment, including the Halloran mill, is shut down. People all across the world are watching, including the elegant lady from the Radisson lobby. Karen St. John is sitting in her own suite, smiling at the CNN reporter, knowing that Daddy's advice is paying off again. The stars are aligning and the opportunity is coming to make things right for her little girl.

EPISODE SIX

Patrick Halloran has been summoned. It is the kind of invitation he is not allowed to decline, not even on a cold winter day.

The black car with tinted windows travels down one winding road after another --- the driver knows the way, but Patrick always gets confused. Each rural road always looks just like another to him. The heavy December snow makes it harder, but even in summer he never could understand the route. Other people seem to have the same experience. At least those willing to talk say that. Plebes are warned in their first year to be careful what they say and to whom --- and to never say anything to outsiders. Unfortunately, both Patrick and his cousin Matthew have made that mistake recently. But in all fairness, how could either of them know that Greg is not one of them? He should be, as Halloran men have been part of the Brothers since there has been a Brothers.

People write books and make movies about the Templars and the Skulls or the Hellfires. They don't dare do any about the Brothers. The lodge, located out in the Massachusetts hinterland, cannot be found on any map. It has no address, no markings. Your car's onboard computer won't know anything about it. Nothing appears on Mapquest. All that Google Earth will show you are the tops of trees. This is a place that does not exist.

The ride takes about two hours. All that Patrick can be certain --- all that any plebe can be certain --- is that the Brothers' lodge is somewhere west of Boston. Most of the trip has to be taken by side roads.

The lodge was constructed in the late 1890s to replace another lodge on the same site. The current building is a huge, handsome gothic stone structure complete with narrow windows and turrets. The place is even larger than it looks as much of it is underground.

No one will tell him what happened to the original building. Plebes are only told what they need to be told. Even his driver, an employee of the Brothers, has barely said a word the entire trip. He is fat and old and stoic and a little scary. The man nearly grunts as he presses each button of the code to open the gate.

Patrick's heavy wool coat barely keeps out the cold as he walks to the big oak doors. Carved above them is the official name, *Sanctus Frater of Thebes*. He is greeted there by another plebe. The kid must be about 18, handsome and well proportioned. The Brothers like their members to be in the best physical shape possible. He is dressed as all plebes are supposed to dress: simple black pants and white, oxford dress shirt. It is a discreet look reflecting the importance of discretion to the Brothers. Patrick is wearing the same thing under his coat.

"Es vos meus frater?" the plebe at the door asks a little awkwardly. His Latin needs some work to get the formal greeting right.

"Eitam," Patrick replies. "Ego sum vestry frater. May Ineo?"

"Vous may penetro frater."

The plebe ushers him into a privileged and exclusive world, where only people of the right pedigree are even welcome. Women are only allowed rarely and for limited, specific reasons. This is a masculine world, one of carved wood paneling, rare artwork, secrets and ceremonies that are strictly male.

Patrick surrenders his coat and cell phone. The kid directs him to one of the many ornate parlors where his much older cousin, Robert Halloran, is waiting. This is a special meeting; one that Patrick hopes will bring good news. Robert is sitting comfortably in a leather armchair, reading today's *New York Times* with a glass of warm brandy on the table. Robert is known within the family as the shy, quiet Halloran. But within the Brothers his voice is loud and strong.

Robert sets his paper aside and gestures his young cousin to the chair facing him. The man rarely ever smiles so it is a surprise to see one today. "I am happy to say that Melvin Waite has been eliminated."

Melvin Waite, one of Uncle Lewis' lawyers, had stumbled across the Brothers' existence a little over a year ago. He began blackmailing Lewis, who turned to his Brothers for help. But before anything could be done, Waite drained his firm's cash reserves and fled the country. A plan was hatched to lure the blackmailer back with a payoff claim. Fake bank documents were even created and hidden in Lewis' study.

"That's terrific." Patrick dares not ask how the man was removed. Plebes are not allowed such information. "I can't believe it took so long."

Robert shrugs. "The asshole was cleverer than we thought. Instead of agreeing to meet with Lewis directly, he tried to get the documents through an intermediary."

"But who could that be? I thought Waite was working alone."

Robert doesn't answer. He just gives Patrick a chastising look. Plebes are supposed to know their place. The man takes a deliberate sip of brandy before responding. "It seems that our cousin Greg has taken a lover --- a male lover --- who himself was open to Waite's blackmail."

I don't believe it: Greg and another man? "May I ask sir, with all due respect, who the man is?"

"Appropriately enough, the best man at his wedding. It seems they were more than just fuck buddies in college."

"Wow." Many of the rituals of the Brothers, especially the initiations, are sexual. They are meant to bind the men together in the most intimate way possible. But a romantic relationship with another man is something Patrick never considered. He certainly never expected it of Greg.

Robert shrugs. "These things happen. At least he had the good sense to sire an heir first. Speaking of fuck buddies, I understand that your final initiation is coming up soon."

"Yes, sir," Patrick responds --- hopefully with the right amount of humility, "just after the first of the year."

"Good . . . Good . . . While I cannot give you any specifics, I can tell you that it is *very* intense. You will be exposing yourself in every way possible --- especially physically."

Patrick has already gone through some of this, and Matthew has just started. The rituals --- scandalous if ever made public --- have been part of the Brothers for two centuries. "I understand sir, and I am looking forward to it."

Robert responds with another of his rare smiles and gestures the young man away. As he recovers his coat and cell from the plebe, Patrick can't help but wonder if there is more to the man's unusual expression of happiness than removing a blackmail threat.

****

With snowflakes gently falling from the sky and colored lights adorning trees and homes and even streets, the Christmas season as returned to New Hampshire.

College students are taking their winter break at the Cannon Mountain Ski Area. Many of them talk about how cool it is to ski on the same slopes as Olympic athlete Bode Miller. Some hope to get a glimpse of him, but few do.

Families from all over New England come to the little town of Jefferson to visit Santa's Village and meet St. Nick himself in the yuletide amusement park. The little ones gleefully feed the reindeer, the slightly older ones scream with delight while riding Rudy's Rapid Transit Coaster. Their parents snap photos and shoot videos, recording moments that will embarrass the kids just a few years from now.

In Portsmouth, local favorite --- and Grammy winner --- Ed Gerhard takes center stage at his annual Christmas Guitar Concert. Visitors to Portsmouth also take part in the annual Candlelight Stroll and enjoy the Snowflake Festival.

Couples huddle together on horse and buggy rides every evening at Charmingfare Farm. Faraway Hill's famous holiday lights brilliantly illuminate the town square where every bush, every tree, every fixture is wired. Tourists come to the town to stay at the B&Bs, shop the little stores and admire the glow around John Halloran's famous statute.

The state's biggest city embraces the season just as enthusiastically. Manchester's street lamps are all decorated. The Palace Theater's annual production of "A Christmas Carol" performs to sold-out audiences. The museums present special programming. Kids skate at the West Side Arena over on Electric Avenue.

Among those getting into the holiday spirit are Joe Westbrook and his young son. Following a suggestion by Aaron Tracey, they have moved into a beautiful old apartment building not far from the Ralph Miller Public Safety Center. The city's police are headquartered in the center and, as Aaron points out, "we can get to you very quickly if something happens" --- like another of Vincent Bologna's men making an unwelcome visit.

Joe fell in love with the apartment instantly. Located on Pennacook Street, it is one of a group of buildings constructed in the early 1900s by a developer named Edwin L. Gresley. The exterior features towering Corinthian columns and elegant balconies; the interiors have wood trim, built-in cabinets and stain glass windows. The rooms are huge and for the first time in over a year, Little Jack has a bedroom of his own. Best of all is the price: this beautiful two bedroom apartment costs less each month than a studio in either New York or Los Angeles. The two of them can live comfortably on the interest from Joe's trust fund.

The trans man and his son are not the only ones making moves. Jack Campbell has rented an apartment in the same building and spends the weeks leading up to Christmas clearing out his New York loft and putting it up for sale. Finances will be tight for him in the meantime, but once the sale happens he'll be flush again. He finally told Joe what happened on Thanksgiving. "Don't worry," his former girlfriend sympathizes. "We'll be your family now."

Family is on the mind of another man. Ben King uses the holiday break to close up his law offices in the Brady-Sullivan Plaza. These are sad moments as he packs away a 20 year career and says farewell to the remaining staff. Adding to the sense of loss is hearing from the FBI that all leads to Melvin Waite have grown cold. Through it all, lurking at the back of his mind, is a family issue that threatens his new career: Mark Bradley. Eve has calmed down and started to accept the situation. They are keeping the news secret, but Ben felt compelled to tell Frank Turner and Victoria Datillo about his son. "We need to find him, fast," the old man advises, "before anyone else can." Victoria has hired a private investigator who has started his search in Boston where Mark once plied his trade. But so far, there has been no luck so he is expected to move on to New York.

Ben and Eve have other family concerns, which also involve moving. During these weeks Karen St. John's new house is redecorated from top to bottom. Gone are the comfortable, small town touches the former owners liked. The home's new look can best be described as country-modern; a style sophisticated enough to entice *Architectural Digest* to take photos for an upcoming issue. All this time Eve worries, "I know that she's up to something" Whenever she questions her sister, Karen responds with a cryptic smile and the words "there is nothing to worry about."

Greg Halloran is worrying, too. There seems to be no end to the crisis in Thailand. Every foreign company is being affected by the strike, including the Halloran mill. As long as the political stalemate exists, millions of dollars will be lost --- and the family fortune is put at risk. "It was Dad who bet on the mill," he commiserates to Jack. "But it looks like I'm the one who's going to be blamed for losing it all." The two of them continue to see each other, being careful to meet only at Jack's new apartment. It is here they talk and make love and hope for a future that looks brighter than the present. Jack also warns his lover about Denise Sullivan. "She could make trouble for us, Greg." The woman knows a lot about them. Julie has alerted her husband about Ann's apparent suspicions and warned him not to blow their plan. "We'll need to figure out how to keep her quiet" but no one is sure how.

Yes, there is no doubt: Christmas has arrived in New Hampshire.

****

The murals that cover Agnes Gabler's fabled sugar house look especially bright and colorful against the drifts of snow surrounding it. The little building, which dates back to the late 1800s, has been renovated and expanded over the years. But it is the way the house reflects the artist's legacy that makes it truly special. Inside, her history is alive in the memorabilia that line the walls and sit on the tables. Photos of Agnes with royalty and presidents, movie stars and rockers are scattered about as casually as another woman might have pictures of her grandchildren.

Eve King is here to discuss Agnes' investments and finances with the artist and her daughter. This is a meeting that happens at least once a month. But worries about her own family are not far from her mind, and Eve is sure she is telegraphing these fears. The two ladies are polite enough not to say anything right away. Scarlet is especially tactful, but her mother is a different matter. When Scarlet leaves them alone to enjoy their tea --- something that has become a tradition with each visit --- Eve is faced with Agnes' insistent question: "what is wrong?"

"Nothing," Eve answers carefully, taking a sip of her tea. "Everything is fine."

The old woman rolls her eyes. "Don't hand me that bullshit. I can see it in your eyes. Listen to me: I'm 95 and heard it all. Nothing can surprise me anymore. And if you're afraid I'm going to tell anyone --- well, young lady, do you think I could live this long if *I didn't know how to keep a secret?*" That and her wink cause Eve to laugh. Agnes gently touches her hand and says with a mother's gentleness, "tell me what's wrong."

Eve hesitates; she has kept these secrets and fears so long it is hard to let them go, hard to trust anyone with them. But over the last few months these two women have grown close. They laugh and share stories. Eve had begun to see the artist as a second, better mother. Agnes is so very different from the woman Eve and Karen grew up with. Frannie Scott was prim and proper, concerned with how she looked and what people thought. A professor's wife, Mother enjoyed the prestige that position offered her at a small college town. Frannie was a mass of insecurities hidden beneath a glossy layer. But that protective shell shattered with her husband's death. Then her unmarried daughter's pregnancy weakened her fragile ego. Eve found herself the unwilling head of the family, caring for a dying mother, trying to control a troublesome sister and raising her illegitimate niece.

Agnes is very different from Frannie. For her, small town New Hampshire is the beginning of the world, not the world itself. She knows who she is and likes who she is. That confidence, along with Eve's need to have *someone* to confide in, has her revealing all: Karen and Julie, Ben and Mark. Agnes just sits there silently listening to it all, hearing the pain and the anger and the fear in Eve's voice. Finally there is nothing left for Eve to say except a weary "I don't know what the hell to do."

"There is nothing you can do."

Eve stubbornly refuses to believe her. She has always been able to fix a problem. At work, at home, it doesn't matter. "That can't be true; I have to be able to *do* something."

"Like what? You have no control over what your sister will tell Julie --- or even *if* she'll tell Julie. From what you tell me, Karen lives in her own little world."

Eve stifles a laugh. "That's for sure; when we were little I teased her about 'Karenland' like she had a bizarre theme park in her head. But living with us in Faraway Hill . . . I know she's going to tell Julie the truth. It's just a matter of time."

"But hasn't it always been just a matter of time?"

"What do you mean? If Karen stayed in New York, then Julie would never know." *After all, that was the plan. That was the fix to a problem.*

"Not necessarily; remember Jack Nicholson."

That came from nowhere; what the hell is she talking about? "Jack Nicholson? Do you know him?"

"Not really; we've met a few times. But you do know his story, right?"

Eve shakes her head. *What story could she mean?*

"Jack was illegitimate, just like Julie. And just like Julie, he was raised by a relative who told him he was her child. That relative was Jack's grandmother, and he grew up thinking that his mother was his sister."

Holy shit! "I never heard that."

Agnes smiles. "It's true. He found out as an adult when some reporter called him. Of course, Jack being Jack, he found a way to handle the news. So don't underestimate you daughter --- and make no mistake: Karen may have given birth to her, but <u>Julie is yours</u>."

"I know; I've always felt that way. And I hope your right." Maybe Julie will be able to hand the news when the time comes. "But what about Mark?"

"There is still no proof that he's Ben's son --- and even if he is, there is no reason to think that will change anything. Mark may not want to be part of your family. In fact, what I've read about him and heard about him, he'll probably just keep doing what he's been doing and to hell with everyone else."

Eve looks into Agnes' warm, aging and wise eyes and is grateful to have her as a friend. *She may be right; I hope that she's right.* But it's going to be hard to sit by and wait. Especially since she's sure Karen is ready to do something.

****

Karen St. John is ready.

She is currently sitting in Halloran Enterprise's reception area. Their offices, in the Millyard, have a cool, modern, industrial look with exposed brick and girders and pipes. The walls are decorated with photos and architectural drawings of the Halloran mills that once employed thousands in the state. Only one remains now, the mill in Faraway Hill.

Being here, right now, is Step 1. *Step 1,* she thinks with a smile a chuckle, *how Daddy would love this.*

Greg's secretary has graciously brought her a cup of tea. It has no real taste --- its little more than warm water --- but still welcome on a cold December day. "I'm sorry for the delay, Mrs. St. John," She says, "but he had a last minute call he needed to take."

"That's quite alright; I can wait." Karen wonders if the call is from the troubled mill in Thailand or from his troubled male lover. *It doesn't really matter*, she thinks sipping her warm water. *Either works for me.* A copy of this morning's *Union Leader* is sitting on the table in front of her. She opens the first section to find the story she expects. There it is, half way inside: the state is closing its review into how the Faraway Hill authorities handled Lewis Halloran's death. They've chastised the sheriff, but came to the same conclusion about who pulled the trigger. Peter told her in advance, a few nights ago, at dinner. Courting the young man these past several weeks has certainly paid off. Making love to him has also been a joy. His energy and hard, athletic body more than compensate his lack of expertise. Karen has enjoyed being Peter's sexual tutor. They've tried to be discrete, but people in Faraway Hill are starting to discover their relationship. Such is life in a small town.

"I'm sorry to keep you waiting," Greg greets her with a smile and outstretched hand. "Things have been really crazy around here." *That must mean the call was about the Thai mill.*

"Not to worry; in fact, I think I can help."

Curious, Greg escorts her into what was once Lewis' office. The décor is slightly more traditional than the other rooms. One of the first things Karen notices is the desk. Aside from the stacks of paper there are three photos: one is his wedding with him and Julie looking very happy. Another is a framed snapshot of Johnny, asleep in his crib. But the third is the most interesting: it's of Jack Campbell with the man and little boy she has seen around Manchester. A couple of weeks ago her investigator discover that the man is Jack's transgender former lover, and the child their son. Denise laughed at the news. "That's perfect for Jack! He never could decide if he preferred fucking women or men. Now he has both!"

There is a sofa and two overstuffed chairs opposite the desk. Greg invites her to sit with him. "I was really surprised at your call."

"Well, I think I can help you." Karen reaches into her valise to retrieve the proposal and hands it to him.

"What is this?"

"Well, everyone knows that the Hallorans are among the American companies being hit hard by that strike in Thailand."

"Yes, but I just got a call from my man there. The king and his people are negotiating a settlement among the political parties."

That's great news, Karen smiles to herself, *as long as it doesn't happen too soon.* "I'm glad to hear that. But it's no secret that the Hallorans have some serious cash flow problems because of it. This will help."

Greg skims through the proposal. It lays out how Karen St. John will provide capital to help the company whether the crisis, in exchange for stock. It will change the firm's dynamics by reducing everyone's shares while giving her a 10% stake --- and making her the only non-Halloran among the owners. But it will also resolve the crisis. She can see the look of amazement on his face. "Karen, this is an incredible offer."

I know it is; that's the point. "Does this mean you'll accept?"

"Well . . . I'm not sure," she expected his hesitation. "My aunt and cousins will see their positions in the company decline if I issue you this stock."

"Do you need their permission to issue more stock?"

"Maybe; I'll have to check." *I already have checked, and no you don't.* "But why are you doing this? I mean, don't get me wrong, I am very grateful. But I don't understand."

Karen expected this response, too, and is prepared. She reaches out and takes his hand in hers. "Because we are family, Greg," she lies with her most believable smile. "You know Julie has been like a daughter to me. And you are certainly the closest thing I will have to a son-in-law. Please let me do this. Let me make this a special Christmas present for everyone."

Greg, who is visibly relieved and moved, smiles at her. It is as of Karen's words have lifted the burden of Atlas from his shoulders. *I've almost got him.*

Step 1 is nearly complete.

✱✱✱✱

The restaurant is warm and comfortable. The fireplace is crackling. The holiday trim creates a festive atmosphere. The waitresses are friendly and professional. Famous people come up to their table to greet them. This is the kind of place and the kind of moment that should make Ann Halloran feel like a queen. Instead, she finds herself fiddling with her spoon and glancing anxiously around the room. "Don't be so nervous," Richard assures her. "Trust me, she'll like you."

The two of them are having lunch in Concord at the Common Man. As on their previous visit, the senator stopped at various tables to shake hands and greet notables before taking his seat. Ann is still impressed. This man is important and, by extension, she is becoming important too. Normally, Ann would relish everything but instead the same worry sits front and center in her mind: *how am I going to handle this?*

For Ann is meeting Richard's daughter today.

Rebecca Davis is about Ann's age. She studies in Boston, working toward a master's. But there is little else Ann knows about her. The only photos she has seen are a few around Four Corners of her as a little girl playing the piano, smiling with her mother or sitting on her dad's lap. Meeting his daughter is a big step for them. Ann wonders if they are moving too fast. But Richard insisted and so here they sit going over the menus and trying to make small talk.

After an eternity of waiting, Rebecca arrives. Richard sees her at the entrance and points her out. Young and pretty, with auburn hair and bright smile, Rebecca is dressed in what Ann takes as shabby chic: expensive clothes that rich kids buy to look bohemian. The girl wears it well. She walks up to them with all the confidence of someone who has always been popular wherever she is. *Or, maybe,* Ann realizes, *all of the confidence of a daddy's girl.* Richard gives his daughter a little kiss on the cheek and introduces them. The girl is polite, but Ann immediately senses something: s*he doesn't like me.* Throughout the meal, Rebecca talks about all her life at the Boston Conservatory ("I love the fact that we don't have dorms. I'd hate to live in a dorm! They put us all up in these really cool brownstones") and how she is glad to be home for Christmas. "I could never miss New Hampshire during the holidays," she practically giggles. "I mean, there is just no place in the world like it."

"I agree," Ann responds trying to be pleasant and noticing Richard looking on proudly. "New Hampshire is special." *He doesn't get it.* But Ann does: Rebecca is just like the girls in high school who never understood her or cared about her except for gossip and ridicule. And, like those girls, Rebecca is smart enough not to let a grownup know how she feels.

They say little to each other. What Rebecca does say is often condescending. "Right now, I am in love with Chopin. My piano teacher has got me hooked. Did you know much about classical music Ann?" No, an embarrassed Ann admits, she does not.

The three of them decline dessert and settle on some coffee. They are about to run out of conversation when one of Richard's associates in the State House steps over to politely ask him to meet someone. "He's a real up-and-comer from Sullivan County." Richard politely excuses himself, leaving the two young ladies alone for the first time. Without her father there, Rebecca doesn't bother to hide her dislike. She lets her eyes idly roam the restaurant.

"I'm so glad we got a chance to meet," Ann says knowing that she sounds a little forced. "Your dad just adores you."

Rebecca firmly sets her cup down. "Look, you seem real nice. But I've read all about you."

I figured. Ann was tabloid fodder after Munroe killed Lewis and her true paternity revealed. She spent months hiding in either a hotel room or Julie's condo.

"Don't get me wrong --- I'm an artist I don't normally judge people --- but, well, I really don't see the two of you lasting much longer."

"If it's the age difference," Ann tries to defend herself. "Your father doesn't seem to mind and it means nothing to me."

"Not just that. I mean . . . it does bother me . . . but there is also . . . well, Lewis Halloran's bastard daughter who married a male hooker. Believe me, all of that shit hit the Boston papers; it wasn't just the *Union Leader*. So, please don't take this the wrong way."

Ann tries to hold back her anger. This is actually worse than the girls in school. "I know it wasn't just the *Union Leader*. You're sitting with a woman who made it the *Enquirer*."

"See what I mean? I wasn't trying to offend you." Rebecca takes a deep breath and says with a kinder tone, "I don't want my dad getting hurt. He has been so lonely since mom died and well . . . if you really care about him, please --- *please* --- don't let this go on much longer."

Richard returns before Ann can say anything. Instead, she thinks, *I'm fucked.*

✶✶✶✶

The morning sun streams into Greg Halloran's bedroom, slowing warming him awake. It's Christmas Eve and time for the family to make their annual pilgrimage back to Faraway Hill. Greg used to make this trip himself, coming from boarding school or college. Every December he'd board a train or plane like some tribesman returning to his ancestral homeland for a ritual feast required by the clan. In those days Greg's mother reigned in the house. The mansion was her domain and her son one of many subjects. Last Christmas seemed strange with her gone. This year is the first without his father. His life is changing so fast so soon that maybe, Greg thinks, he should simply embrace the tribe.

There are four available suites and nearly everyone has their traditional choices. Robert, the famously silent one, always takes the one behind the master suite. His bedroom will share a wall with Greg's. Matthew will be taking the one right across from Robert, while Patrick will stay in Greg's old suite next to Matthew. Growing up, Patrick was the only cousin Greg spent much time with during Christmas break. Mostly this is because they are so close in age. But they seldom see each other the rest of the year and had little else in common.

Aunt Joan is the tricky one. She grew up in the suite at the second floor's northeast corner. But to keep peace, Ann was moved in there so she could be as far from Greg as possible. Joan's childhood furniture was moved across the hall where she and her boy toy husband Paul will be sleeping. She is still not happy about it, and grumbled a bit at Julie over Thanksgiving. Ann has been wisely avoiding the family, even at Agnes Gabler's big birthday bash. But Greg noticed the other day that she has bought presents for everyone and put them under the tree. *I hope that doesn't mean what I think it means. If Ann shows up tomorrow to spend Christmas with the family, there will certainly be a nasty scene.*

Traditions are everywhere in a house like this. Every year, the family will gather Christmas morning in the Blue Room to open presents before spending the rest of the day eating and gossiping. But this Christmas will be different. The situation in Thailand means a decision needs to be made --- and, as Greg crawls out of bed, he realizes that the decision he'll be asking for may mean a nasty scene will be inevitable no matter what Ann does.

****

Ann arrives at her mother's home just as fresh flakes tumble down from the sky. The remodeled farmhouse looks almost picturesque amid the snow. The damage done from the Thanksgiving attack has been repaired. *It's a shame the place wasn't this nice when I was growing up.*

Vivian greets her at the door. "Merry Christmas, Annie" she says cheerfully. It's hard not to like this woman. Ann follows her into the living room and sets her gifts under the tree. The smell of fresh baked bread wafts through the house, as does the sound of her mother singing. The kitchen was once her refuge; she used it as a place to escape from a drunken Munroe. But it's different now. Lorene seems to find joy in being there. Or maybe it's the joy of being with Vivian. Ann steps to the threshold and watches her mother at work. "Merry Christmas, Mom."

"Merry Christmas, dear," Lorene beams, the joy not just in her voice but also on her face.

****

"I can't believe how crowded that big house can feel sometimes," Julie says, sitting next to Greg as he steers his car passed Faraway Hill's famous light display. The town square is strung every season, and every season tourists come to see it.

"I know; the place gets like that every year," Greg replies. "I just hope that Ann doesn't crash the gathering tomorrow."

"She's a Halloran now, Greg."

He doesn't answer. Like the rest of the family, he just can't accept that. It's still hard for him to even look at Ann. But he can't avoid her, especially tomorrow. Greg told Julie about Karen's offer. It seems wonderfully generous. Unfortunately, it will mean convening a meeting of the family stockholders on Christmas --- and Ann is one of those stockholders.

"She is, Greg, there is no changing that. Matthew was right." Earlier in the day, his cousin Matthew spoke up. In a bold statement that both stunned and angered his mother, the teen pointed out to everyone at lunch that Ann didn't kill Lewis and is as much a victim of Munroe as any of them. "Maybe," the young man concluded, "we all need to remember that." It was a bit of wisdom from an unexpected source. However, it remains to be seen how many will embrace it.

They arrive at the King family home. Some of the happiest moments of her life happened in this handsome, restored Colonial. They were going to bring Johnny, but he's running a fever and the nanny advised against it. *Mom won't be happy about that.* Julie see Aunt Karen's car parked nearby. *Mom's probably not happy about that, either.*

Greg shuts down the motor. He stays seated a moment and then turns to her and says quietly, "do you hate me?"

What can I say to that? She pauses to think and then answers, "Not like I should."

*****

This is a remarkable day in the two hundred fifty year history of a remarkable clan: the bastard daughter of Lewis Halloran and Lorene Gale is allowed to attend a family event. It is not a warm welcome. There are no hugs, no kisses, not even a handshake. But everyone is civil and Ann wisely keeps her own comments to a minimum. Greg suspects that Julie coached her. Nevertheless, the annual the ritual of opening presents in the oval Blue Room happens as usual. Well, almost as usual. No one bothered to buy Ann a gift --- except for Julie, who gives her a nice watch in both their names. Ann did buy presents for everyone, typically expensive things meant more to impress than anything else. Matthew receives a hideous sweater that she must have gotten at some trendy store. Aunt Joan politely accepts a garish pendant that she'll never wear. Greg and Julie get a pricey, handmade vase that goes with nothing in the house.

Christmas lunch is in the formal dining room. The servants lay out the traditional buffet and then leave to spend the holiday with their own families. Conversations are simple, mostly about catching up. Matthew talks about school. Patrick voices concerns about his mother's health. Aunt Joan regales adventures in the Boston social scene. Her boy toy husband Paul espouses on his latest workout regiment. Robert, true to form, says little. Ann manages to deliver the day's only interesting news, by mentioning her mother's new lesbian relationship. The interest doesn't last very long, though: same-sex couples are hardly a rarity these days, especially in New Hampshire.

Now comes the moment for another historic event. This one makes Greg even more nervous than anything his half-sister could possibly say or do.

They are collected in the Green Room: Robert Halloran, the famously quiet one, is here as chairman of the family trust and its 40% stake in the company. Robert also owns 10% in his own right. So does the much married Joan Halloran Newberry Hamilton Logan Lansing. Patrick is here representing his widowed mother, Katherine, who also owns 10%. And, of course, there is Ann and her 10%. The remaining stock, or 20% of Halloran Enterprises, is Greg's.

Surrounded by damask wallpaper, antique furniture and holiday trim, Greg carefully lays out Karen St. John's offer. The plan will reduce everyone's relative share in the company, but the company will be saved without incurring further debt. Everyone fidgets as he lays out the details. None of them are happy. Eventually, he wraps up the presentation by passing out copies of Karen's formal proposal.

"I don't believe this shit," Robert grumbles. Greg is surprised and Aunt Joan clearly shocked: the quiet Halloran isn't being quiet. "In over two centuries no one outside the family has ever owned a piece of the company. Never."

"You know, Mrs. St. John *is* my wife's aunt."

"Fuck that," Robert rolls his eyes. "She doesn't count."

"Doesn't count?" Patrick responds angrily. "Well, what about my mother? She's not a Halloran, not by blood anyway. And she owns stock."

"That's different. She's a Halloran widow --- and you'll be inheriting the shares." It seems odd and out of character to see the man so forceful. Robert turns to Joan and asks her bluntly, "you're not saying anything. What do you think?"

If there is one person Greg felt sure about is Aunt Joan. She stood by him more than anyone during the Ann issue. She helped plan Dad's funeral. But the look on her face worries him. "I don't like it either," she almost whispers.

Everyone falls into an angry, sullen silence. Greg is about to push his case again when he gets support from an unlikely source. "But," Ann argues, "If it will save the company then I think we should at least consider it." The rest are as shocked as Greg that the bastard farm girl would dare have an opinion, especially one that agrees with his. "I mean, would you rather own 10% of a company that's losing money, or 8% of a company that's making money?"

Joan glares at her, "we have plenty in reserve."

"Wrong," Greg explains. "We *had* plenty in reserve. I just went through that. To survive without an investor means building up more debt --- debt that could become a serious problem very quickly."

Robert glares at him. "You are not to do this."

Greg holds firm. "I'm president of the company, Robert. I don't need your permission to issue the stock."

"Maybe not, but I'm chairman of the family trust, plus my own shares." He stands up, defiant and determined. "All I need is one more vote. So, young man, you do this shitty deal and I'll see to it that a different Halloran runs this company!"

With that, the quiet Halloran becomes quiet again as he silently strides out of the room.

EPISODE SEVEN

"Holy shit, I can't believe it."

Greg and Julie are alone in the master suite's oval parlor. She is relaxing on the settee. Her leg, still in a cast, is resting on an ottoman. Greg is angrily pacing back and forth, telling her what happened downstairs, just moments ago. He looks like he's ready to put his fist through a wall. *So much for Christmas spirit,* she thinks.

"He made one hell of a scene."

"But Aunt Karen is saving the family company, doesn't he get that?"

Greg drops into an armchair, frustrated. "That's not how *he* sees it."

Julie is sick of the damned cast. Her leg gets hot and itchy. Thankfully, it's due to come off in about a week. Pity they can't cut off annoying relatives that easily. "Fuck him, what can he do? I thought he only owns 10% of the company."

"He does, but he also chairs the family trust --- and the trust owns 40%." Julie was sure the family would treat him as a hero. Instead, her husband sits there looking like the victim of a beating. "All he needs to do is convince --- or bully --- one more person to back him."

"I don't get it. In all the time my dad worked for the family, I don't think I've heard Robert say more than three words. He hardly ever leaves California." Julie surprises herself; *after what Greg has done to me, why the hell should I care?* "Now here he is, in Faraway Hill, acting like he's the goddamn family patriarch! I can't believe your Aunt Joan will put up with that."

"Except that she's not happy, either."

"Why, because she doesn't like Aunt Karen?" *A stupid reason, but that would sound like Joan.*

"Maybe; I don't know."

Sitting on a table across the room is a photo taken a few weeks ago, of her and Greg with their son. They look for the entire world like a happy family. It occurs to Julie just why she is so angry: Johnny. She has set aside her pride to accept her husband's gay affair for her son's sake. Now Johnny's legacy is at risk. *The things a mother will do.* "Greg, really, what happens if she doesn't invest?"

"Anything, I guess. It all depends on Thailand. Should the strike continue . . . well, there is only so much we can borrow; an investor would be better."

"What about the American mills?"

"The Faraway Hill mill is small, but profitable. The mill in Georgia is really the cash cow; it makes money despite the management problems. The real estate division is doing fine, but Thailand is a big drain right now. We still have expenses and orders that can't be filled."

"Could you sell the Thai plant?"

"That would still mean a big loss; no one will pay full price with all that uncertainty. Besides, it has the potential to make more money that the other two mills combined. That's why my dad bought it. In a few years, the value of everyone's shares could double."

Greg doesn't say anything else. He looks tired and hurt. Julie has to fight the urge to put her arms around him and say everything is alright. *I have to remember: he's cheating on me, fucking another man. I can't love him anymore. I need to stop.* Greg rises, wishes her a goodnight, and walks to his bedroom door. "Greg?" she says stopping him.

He has that sweet, sad, puppy dog look on his face that makes it still harder for her. *I can't love him anymore . . . but I do.* "Sure, what?"

"Screw Robert; make the deal with Aunt Karen."

****

"Screw you, Robert."

Joan Lansing is trying to stay calm. She is in her own suite just a few feet from Greg and Julie. Actually, *her* suite --- the rooms she grew up in --- is across the hall. As a teen, a professional decorator had created a wonderfully feminine environment that Joan loved. Even with her life in Boston, she always felt safe within those walls. She slept there on every visit, at every holiday and between each marriage. But the rooms were given to Ann a few months ago because it kept her farthest from her half-brother. Joan still resents it. Her beautiful furniture looks out of place in their new surroundings. Things have been changing too much in the past year, and now her cousin wants to change them some more.

"Are you telling me that you want that bitch to own our family company?" Robert is standing at the door. He slammed it behind shut after following her upstairs and entering uninvited and unwelcome. Joan sits in her favorite armchair, a beautiful Victorian piece. As a girl she loved pretending it was a throne. She still does.

"What the hell is it to you? She'll only have 10%."

"You can't stand that woman."

"She's nothing to me," a statement that isn't quite true. Joan likes being the center of attention, but whenever Karen St. John is in the room the spotlight always seems to shift. "Besides, who will run the company after firing Greg? I hardly expect you to give up the quiet life in California for an even quieter one in Faraway Hill. Like hell if I'm going to do it. So, who's left, Patrick? I hardly think so."

Robert grumbles. She's right: he hasn't thought things through.

"Hey, lover, what's with all the yelling?" Standing at the threshold to the bedroom is her latest husband. Wearing nothing but a towel around his waist, Paul's carefully chiseled young body nearly makes her squeal with delight. "I thought we were going to celebrate Christmas our own special way."

Still sitting on her throne, she answers regally, "we will dear; Robert is just leaving."

****

"Screw Robert," Patrick Halloran grumbles to no one. He is sitting all alone in the parlor of another of the mansion's suites. This is where his cousin Greg grew up and some of his personal items are still scattered around the room: graduation photos from prep school and NYU, along with those of then-fiancé Julie and best friend Jack. Mementoes from school projects and a life in New York like an autographed playbook. A tennis trophy sits by itself on one table. Second place, the biggest prize Greg ever won.

Patrick never lived in this house. His father had moved to Hartford when he married. But there were always stories about the famous relatives and their famous guests over the centuries. There were especially tales of the Halloran kids --- Lewis, David and Joan. It was David, the middle child, who was the first to marry, the first to have a child and the first to die. Before that, he loved to tell his son of Lewis' wild parties and Joan sneaking out to meet boys and their parents' exasperation. One of their last conversations had Patrick's father telling him about the Brothers. "All Halloran men have been Brothers. We founded the order. With them, son, you can do anything." Anything, that is, except prevent a drunk from sideswiping your car. Dad was killed instantly. Mom had her stroke only a few weeks later.

A soft, timid knock at the door pulls him back to the present. It opens slightly. "Is it okay if I come in?" Matthew asks.

He's glad it's Matthew. He expected Robert to stop by to pressure him. But Patrick can't see any reason to vote against Greg. "Come on in." The boy's father died when he was very young. Three succeeding stepfathers each tried to be a dad to him one way or another. But the kid has always had the shy, quiet demeanor of a lonely orphan. At least until yesterday, when he surprised everyone by speaking up in Ann's defense.

"Are you okay?"

The kid doesn't look okay. He looks worried. "I just wanted to . . . well, ask you about something?"

"What about?"

The boy gently closes the door behind him. "The Brothers."

Matthew's dad died before he could explain about the society; Patrick had to do it. Since then, the two young men have had only each other to confide in. Patrick invites him to sit down. "Your scared about the initiation rites, aren't you?"

"Yes," the teen nods.

"What level are you at, Level One, right?"

Matthew nods again.

"Trust me, dude, it gets easier to handle over time."

"I guess; but, I mean it wouldn't be so bad if they . . . they weren't so fucking old!"

Patrick laughs. Most of the Brothers are in their 30s and 40s, with a large handful even older. That must seem ancient to an 18-year-old. "I know, but we're Halloran men. It's what we do."

"But Greg is a Halloran and he's not a Brother."

"Yea, I know, but I think Aunt Lilly had something to do with that. I think it's wrong, though; I just don't know what to do about it."

Patrick puts a supportive hand on the boy's shoulder. "Just hang in there, dude. It'll all be worth it in the end."

****

Shawn Martin knows how to be a different person to different people. He learned early, growing up in the immigrant stew of East Boston where every generation brings people from somewhere far away. First it was Irish Canadians, then Russian Jews. Pakistanis and other Asians followed. More recently, people speaking Spanish can now be found strolling along Piers Park. He learned their languages and customs and little quirks. He learned to listen and ask the right questions. He easily becomes whatever and whomever he needs to be to get what he wants --- and what he wants is always what his clients want: information.

Information is the reason he is sitting in the living room of a handsomely renovated Colonial home in the small town of Faraway Hill. It is the day after Christmas and he is here to deliver his preliminary report to Ben and Eve King. The couple sits across from him, each holding a copy while Shawn summarizes for them.

"Mark Bradley moved back to New York immediately after leaving New Hampshire. He took an apartment in Greenwich Village, although it remains unclear how he can afford it. I suspect someone has been paying his rent, it's just a matter of time before I find out who it is."

The Kings remain quiet. Shawn notices the unhappy look on Mrs. King's face. He has seen it before; no woman ever has an easy time accepting her husband's bastard child. It is an expression a client normally has after learning of infidelity. This case is very different, but the look is the same.

"He kept a low profile for months, stripping at some gay clubs to earn cash. It appears that around Halloween he started turning tricks again. His clients aren't anywhere near as rich as before. They were high rollers until he was forced out of the city more than a year ago. All men so far --- although he has had women in the past --- we are just starting to confirm names."

The future senator flips through the pages looking for something in particular but can't seem to find it. Shawn glances at the TV, turned to the Weather Channel but muted for their meeting. The reporter silently points to a storm front heading for New England. "Do we know why he left New York in the first place?" Mr. King asks.

"Page seven."

The couple simultaneously opens to page seven. Mr. King's jaw drops as he reads it; Mrs. King mutters, "Holy shit."

"That is interesting, isn't, ma'am? Mr. St. John discovered his wife paying for Bradley's services and forced him out of town. It got pretty scary for the kid from what I hear."

Mrs. King angrily drops the report on the coffee table with a loud slap. "That damned bitch!" *What is she so pissed off about?* "You don't know, do you, about Martin St. John."

Shawn shakes his head; he hasn't done much research into Bradley's clients.

"Martin St. John was my brother-in-law."

****

Julie Halloran has been to many after-Christmas sales --- but only as a customer. This is her first time on the other side of the counter. All of downtown Manchester is buzzing with shoppers looking for deals. King's Korner is no different. She has never been so busy, being pulled from one patron to another wanting either a fresh cup of coffee or a bigger discount on a travel book. The crutch isn't helping; it makes her feel unnaturally awkward hobbling from one part of the store to another.

Mary Armstrong, the college girl she hired earlier in the year, is like a gift from God. With school out for the holiday, she is committing nearly all her time to the store. "I'm a New Hampshire girl," Julie hears her explain to a customer. "I grew up with storms like that. You'll make it through okay."

The weather is a common topic. A blizzard is being predicted for New Year's Eve, which will certainly affect the city's annual celebrations. WMUR has been running bulletins all day.

"I hope so," the customer, a middle aged woman with a southern accent responds. "My husband and I just moved here from Houston. Goodness, I've never dealt with such weather before! I mean, the summer was delightful but I'm not sure I can handle winter."

Julie laughs to herself. *She'll get used to it; everyone does.* As Mrs. Halloran, Julie is a rich woman now. But she's glad to have kept the store. It connects her to the greater world and keeps her grounded. If she stayed in the Halloran mansion, Julie would never meet the interesting new people coming to the city. Manchester has really grown in the last twenty years with people flocking here from all over.

There are more customers with more questions. Julie answers them quickly and politely. But the cast is so damned tiring. She decides to take a break and sits at a table to take in the view along Elm Street. The city has done a pretty good job keeping the roads clear. The merchants have managed to shovel their sidewalks (although a few could do better). Even with the offices closed, there are still many people out. Among them, at the corner a block away, is Jack Campbell. He is out with another young man and a little boy. Julie has seen them before, usually together. They almost look like a family. *What the hell is going on?* Then another thought hits her, making her smile: *could he be cheating on Greg? Now that would be funny.*

****

Four Corners feels like a real home even to someone who doesn't live there. The knickknacks, family photos and even the worn rugs all create a warm, welcoming atmosphere. This is a place were people really live, where kids used to track mud on the floor and dinner isn't announced by the butler. Strangely, Ann is growing fond of the house. She always dreamed of living the grand life in a mansion like the Halloran's. But sitting here, in the living room with Richard, his arm around her, Ann feels much more comfortable than she has ever felt at the big house. Gertrude left them some freshly brewed tea before going out to do some shopping. They are alone now, talking about the holiday. "It was weird, you know," she says after describing the tension-filled Christmas. "On the one hand they almost treated me like family --- almost, I said, not quite --- and then there was that bombshell about the company."

"Well, sweetheart, it *is* a start and you *are* their family. The Hallorans just need time to accept that."

"That's what Mom and Vivian keep telling me." *I wish every day could be like this.*

Richard gently brushes a lock of hair away from her eyes. Everything about this man touches her on so many levels. *Maybe I _am_ falling in love with him.* "It sounds like you've accepted them as a couple."

"Almost," she answers with a sigh. "It's still a little weird, I mean it's the last thing I ever expected from my mother; and then there is the shooting . . ."

"The man is dead now. He can't hurt them anymore."

"I know, but it just makes me wonder what other baggage Vivian is carrying. Shit, I know they were together years ago, but this whole thing came up as such a surprise --- at least for me."

"Love works that way. It's often a surprise. I woke up one morning and realized that I loved Marsha. We were married a month later." Richard seldom talks about his late wife. Photos of her are scattered throughout the house. Each of them is of the same graceful, gentle looking woman who changed little from a teenager to adulthood.

"That's so romantic."

Richard smiles, "Haven't you ever felt that way about someone?"

"No, not really." Growing up, most of the boys felt she wasn't worth the time. Only Peter Brandt treated her as something special. *But I sure as hell fucked that up.*

"Not even your ex-husband?"

"That ass, I never want to see him again!" Even the mention of Mark Bradley makes her blood pressure rise.

Richard calms her with a soft kiss to her cheek. "That's not what I asked you."

"Oh, I don't know," she answer, taking a deep breath. "Infatuated might be a better word. Mark was strong and sexy and I thought that would be enough. But he lied to me about everything. I can't imagine anything more humiliating than finding out your husband is fucking other men for money. I even had to get tested. Tested! Thank God he didn't give me anything."

Richard pulls her closer. Ann relishes the warmth, the tenderness, in every way he touches her. It is so different from Mark or the other boys she has known. Maybe that's the difference: *maybe I needed a man; a real, seasoned, smart, man.*

"Why don't you do something nice for your mother and her partner? You love her, they love each other; show them you support their relationship."

"Maybe I will."

****

Discretion can be tough in a small town like Faraway Hill. There are whispers at church, suspicious glances at store counters and giggles at the school. Everyone seems to know something about everyone else. One would think Manchester would be different, but even here people talk --- especially about the important people, like Greg Halloran. This is why he has been meeting Jack at his new apartment. But they have been hooking up there so often and spending so much time there that the four walls seem more like prison bars. Finally, Jack insisted that two guys should be able to meet in a restaurant without arousing too much suspicion. "After all," he pointed out, "guys do eat together." Greg relented.

"Hello handsome," Debbie, the sexy waitress at Maxwell's, greets him. She gives Greg one of those smiles that reminds him of the days, before his engagement, when the two of them would have quickies in her apartment. "Your friend is already here."

Greg follows her wonderfully tight ass as it guides him past the restaurant's handsome mahogany walls to a booth where Jack is waiting. Greg sits across from him, still a little nervous about a public meeting and hoping it won't be a problem for Julie. Debbie leaves them with a couple of menus and a wink.

"Relax, dude," Jack assures him. "This should be okay. We talked about it, remember? Buds meeting for lunch. Now, what all happened at Christmas."

Greg spends the next few minutes describing the nightmarish holiday, from everyone's forced politeness with the farm girl to the family turning on him about Karen St. John. It's still stressful to talk about it. Finally, Debbie arrives to take their order. It gives him a moment to take a breath. Once she's gone, Jack discretely places a hand on his, "don't worry dude. They won't fire you. They can't. There's no one else to run the company."

"Yeah, I know: that's what I keep telling myself," Greg answers, and adds without thinking, "even Julie thinks they are being asses."

"You . . . you and Julie talked about this?"

"Sure, right after it happened. We were in our suite. She's being really cool about it; she's being really cool about a lot of things."

Jack nods, uncomfortable with the subject of Julie. *What the hell does he expect? She is my wife, after all. We talk about things.* Besides, there are reasons he fell in love with her, reasons he is still in love with her. One of them is Julie's natural confidence. His wife is the most self-aware woman he has ever known. "She thinks I should go ahead and make the deal with her aunt and damn the family."

"Okay, well, it sounds like a good idea."

"It'll save the company." *He knows this; why the hell do I have to defend myself?*

"Yeah, well," Jack seems to be grasping for a reason to complain, "that also means keeping Denise around. That could make our already weird lives even weirder."

Greg shrugs. Past hook-ups are not likely to be an issue. "So we both fucked Denise. That was a long time ago. You and I, we're back together. Even Julie won't care."

"I suppose your right."

"Besides, most of those stories about her are just bullshit anyway."

Jack doesn't say anything, just takes a sip of his Pellegrino.

"Oh, come on, like the party story. That went around for months. Who will really believe she took on a dozen guys in one night."

"Actually, dude, it was only five."

"Huh?"

"It was only five guys."

"How do you know?"

"Because I was one of them."

Debbie returns with their lunches, causing Jack to drop the story. "You guys let me know if you need anything else, got it?" She winks at Greg again and departs.

"Hey, dude," Jack chuckles, "it was what it was." *In other words, those wild days are over.* "Anyway, I finally sold the condo. I have to go to New York next week to wrap things up." Greg doesn't hear much after that, as Jack goes into detail about the sale. All great can think about is how different and how complicated his life has become. Gone are the fun, wild days of college when all seemed possible. Now his life centers a wife, a son, a lover and an illegitimate sister, family politics --- and the constant need for discretion.

✳✳✳✳

From the diner to the dollar store, everyone in Faraway Hill treats Eve as if she were a celebrity. "We are so excited about Ben," beams the Cora, the aging blue haired druggist. It's a few days since Christmas; the New Year is just around the corner. People are out looking for bargains at the town's many specialty shops. But everywhere, everyone stops Eve to tell them how happy they are.

"Thanks, Cora; I'm very proud of him."

"Oh, I'm sure you are." The woman fills a bag with the little essentials Eve came in for. "Of course, it's been a big year: Julie getting married to the Halloran boy, then having her baby and now your little sister is back in town."

"Yes, a big year." Eve tries to sound happy, but knows it isn't working. Having Karen back is certainly nothing to celebrate --- especially after finding out she was one of Mark's clients.

"She's been gone so long, your sister, Faraway Hill must seem like a completely new place."

"I suppose." Eve wishes she could get out of here, but the old woman loves to gossip too much.

"It's nice to see that young Peter has been . . . helping her get reacquainted with the town."

"Peter, you mean Peter Brandt?" Peter went to school with Ann and Julie. He even dated Ann for awhile. *What is she doing with him?*

"Oh, yes, he has been spending time with her for weeks now." Suddenly Eve starts to understand where Cora is heading. *Oh, shit, she's been seen with him because she's fucking him. That stupid, crazy bitch.* "He's such a nice boy to do that for her."

****

New England says farewell to another year with a regional tradition: the New Year's Eve blizzard. The flakes are light and fluffy in the morning, wafting lazily to the ground. Kids run around the backyard or in the neighborhood park trying catch as many as possible on their tongues. But as the day progress and the sky darkens, the snow becomes thicker and heavier and more numerous. People take refuge in their homes, occasionally peering out a frosty window to see the drifts grow.

From Manchester to Faraway Hill to Concord and beyond, people throughout New Hampshire tune in Channel 9 for the latest update. Tens of thousands of people huddle before their TVs as Mike Haddad presents the current conditions and various bundled-up reporters from various freezing locales tell everyone what everyone already knows: it's snowing outside bringing the world to a screeching halt.

Some, of course, are not bothering with their TVs or the view from the window. Some are unconcerned about the disappearing sidewalks and blocked streets. In cities and towns across the state, they are choosing to experience the storm in more intimate ways.

At the Gale Farm, Lorene finds warmth with her lover. She marvels at the differences and similarities of their bodies. Vivian's breasts are fuller, her nipples dark and sensuous. Lorene loves to lick and suckle them. The two of them will spend hours naked, exploring each other.

Not far away, Peter Brandt also marvels, but at the wonders of Karen St. John. His friends would be mystified as to why a guy in his twenties would be drawn to a woman old enough to be his mother. But Karen is nothing like his or any other mother he knows. Her breasts are not sagging and hair is not graying. But most of all, she is the most skilled lover he has ever had. She knows just how to touch him, what to say to him, how to make him feel. Whether it's licking his cock or taking him inside her, Karen knows what he needs. Peter has fucked quite a few girls in his life, but Karen is his first true woman.

Ann Halloran feels the same way about her lover. A few miles north, in a handsome old Concord farmhouse, she marvels at Richard Davis. But it isn't his body, but his tenderness. Schoolboys played with her, Mark simply fucked her, but Richard makes love.

Greg marvels at Jack's body. They are in Jack's Manchester apartment where he is lying naked on his bed, waiting and watching Jack strip. Ever since their first night together in college, he has loved to roam his hands all over the Jack's soft skill, feeling the hard muscles underneath. Jack has always been the popular one, the jock everyone wants to be like or be with. He always wanted Jack's life, but is willing to settle for Jack's cock inside him.

For many people, there are better ways to spend a snowy night than watching the weather man on TV.

****

Eve King is spending this snowy night watching the weather man on TV.

A few steps away Ben is on the phone, again. He takes a lot of calls these days. Eve has given up trying to keep track of them.

She is reclining on the sofa in her comfortable living room, memories of past winter storms making her smile. There was the first one, when it was just she and Ben. The house hadn't been renovated yet and the only heat in the room came from a roaring fire. The two of them huddled under a pile of blankets, sweetly dreaming of their future. Then there were the winter nights with Julie, roasting marshmallows while her little girl waited impatiently for the morning and the chance to sled across the yard.

Those were simpler times, happier times. A blizzard kept the world and its problems at bay. Tonight is different. Nothing can keep Eve from thinking about her sister, what she did with Mark Bradley and what she is surely doing with

Peter Brandt. It's only a matter of time before Julie finds out the truths, the many truths, about her beloved aunt. *I'll lose my little girl, I just know it.*

Ben hangs up on what Eve hopes will be the last call of the night. But instead of joining her on the sofa, he steps over to the mantle, and stares at Julie and Greg's wedding picture. It is one of many family photos sitting there. A lighted garland, matching their Christmas Tree, gives the display a festive look. Ben doesn't look festive. He looks worried.

"What is it? Did something go wrong in Washington?"

Ben takes a deep breath. "No, sweetheart, that was the private detective. He found out whose paying for Mark's apartment."

"Who, Karen?" it would be just like her.

Ben glances back at the wedding photo. "No, dear . . . it's our son-in-law."

EPISODE EIGHT

21 . . . 22 . . . 23 . . . Mark Bradley is in the final stages of his morning routine, doing 50 hard push-ups. In the nude. He likes to work out naked, to watch his muscles flex in the mirror. Even watching his cock flop against his balls is cool. Mark rises each day with the same motivator: taking care of the merchandise to take care of the customers.

27 . . . 28 . . . 29 . . . 30 . . .

After taking a leak and brushing his teeth, the routine begins with stretching. Then he moves on to some cardio, either the Stairmaster or the treadmill. Four days a week he does crunches, the other three he lifts weights. He finishes with push-ups --- all in the nude.

35 . . . 36 . . . 37 . . . 38 . . .

Over the past several months, Mark has been quietly but steadily rebuilding his client base. Things got even easier once that crazy bitch Karen St. John moved back to Faraway Hill. That news essentially reopened New York for him.

42 . . . 43 . . . 44 . . . 45 . . .

Most of Mark's clients are, once again, older men. They are never exactly a turn-on, but he always finds a way of getting hard. He wishes more of them were younger guys. There are times when he actually misses Greg Halloran, even though Halloran never bottomed for him. His favorite client --- far and away --- is a woman. An actress and former dancer, she keeps in shape despite her 70-something age. She plays a matriarch on one of the soaps, having started with the show from its very beginning four decades ago. She's only needed on the set one or two days a week. So, every Thursday like clockwork, he meets at her Greenwich apartment just a few blocks away. Not only is this woman a good fuck, but she always has great showbiz stories. And she cooks him dinner.

47 . . . 48 . . . 49 . . . 50.

Sweaty, he drops to the floor to catch his breath. Mark tends to push himself too hard. A few minutes later, he steps into a hot shower to wash away all of the sweat. Mark is in the best shape of his life and relishes it. Drying off, he walks back to the living room, picks up the remote and checks on the day's news. This, too, is part of Mark's daily routine. CNN is running yet another story about the strike in Thailand (*who really gives a shit?*). Wrapping a towel around his waist, Mark settles in on the leather sofa.

The anchor switches to a live scene from Washington where the Vice-President is swearing in Benjamin King as the newest senator from New Hampshire.

Standing nearby are familiar faces: Eve King, Greg Halloran and, wearing a leg cast, Julie Halloran. *Damn, Greg has gained weigh and he <u>still</u> looks better than most of the guys I fuck.* The ceremony is still in progress when Mark gets a text: one of his regulars has some free time this afternoon.

Yes, business is definitely picking up.

****

It is a cold, windy, wintry day in the nation's capital. Thousands of people are going to their jobs this morning like they do every morning. This includes those arriving at a sleek, contemporary nine-story structure on Constitution Avenue. This is the Hart Office Building, where 50 United States senators and their staffs work. Every day these men and women enter the marble façade and through the magnificent 90-foot high central atrium passing Alexander Calder's final sculpture, a masterpiece called "Mountains and Clouds".

The freshly inaugurated Senator Benjamin King is now among the Hart's residents. His first duty representing New Hampshire involves a reception in one of the committee rooms, where his daughter and son-in-law toast his accomplishment before flying back home. Other senators shake his hand and wish him well, although a few seem less than genuine in their sentiments. *I guess that's to be expected,* Ben tells himself. *That's the world I'm in now.*

His new career is not the only subject of conversation: so is Richard Davis, who has surprised everyone by bringing Ann Halloran as his date. Guests exchange whispers like "who is she" and "she could be his daughter" and "isn't she the bastard child" and "he brought her to the funeral too." Greg and Julie avoid the couple, saying a quick hello before moving to another part of the room. Eve is especially pissed. After the party winds down --- and their daughter and son-in-law have left --- she says bluntly to her husband "this is *your* day, why the hell did he bring her?" Ben just shrugs; something more important is on his mind.

He now has what used to be Russell Brooks' office with what was Brooks' staff. A few of the aides still have photos of his predecessor sitting on their desks. *It's going to be hard for a lot of them to work with me.* Victoria Datillo escorts the Kings into Ben's private office. Eve was in yesterday, helping him personalize it with paintings and pictures and mementoes. That wise old owl Frank Turner is waiting for them in a big leather chair. Tired and bored, he had left the party about twenty minutes earlier. Frank waves at Victoria with his withered, gray hand and congratulates her: "everything went perfectly young lady. Good work."

"Thank you," she answers with a brisk smile. It's true; the day has gone without a hitch so far and Ben says so. Eve, however, remains disturbingly quiet. He knows she's still upset about the Mark situation. But they can't ignore it much longer. They can't even delay it: Ben's secretary buzzes that Grace Bradley has arrived. Eve grimaces at the news and silently sits in a corner chair. *Is she mad at me, sad, what? I wish like hell she'd talk to me.*

Grace enters looking as worried as a little girl called to the principal's office. "Am I late?"

"No, no," Ben assures her. "You're right on time. Martin should be here at any moment."

The room falls into an awkward silence. Everyone knows what is about to happen but no one wants to talk about it. Victoria has a staffer bring them some tea. Grace stares out the window at the landmarks, speeding traffic and piles of snow. Frank finally breaks in with the news that Republican Adam Newman will probably announce his candidacy within the next month. "We need start fundraising immediately."

Ben nods, and thinks: *and what will happen once people find out my son is a prostitute?* Being a victim of Mel Waite's embezzlement is embarrassing enough. But that news can easily end his new career.

The intercom buzzes again: Shawn Martin has arrived. There was some talk about having this meeting at the house in Faraway Hill, but Grace can't get away from work for more than a few hours. Victoria escorts the detective inside. Ben notices how nondescript the man is; he can easily fit himself into almost any situation. *Maybe that's why he's so damned good.* Martin exchanges greetings and hands out copies of his latest report and everyone takes a seat.

"As you know," Martin begins his presentation, "I met with the senator and his wife over the holidays. There isn't much new. Mark Bradley lived in New York City for about three years before moving to Faraway Hill. During that time, he supported himself rather comfortably as a male escort. Most of his clients were older men, but there were a few women as well. One of them was Karen St. John, Mrs. King's sister."

Eve says nothing, even as everyone glances at her. She is too ashamed.

"However, it appears that Mrs. St. John became somewhat . . . clingy, and then her husband found out. Martin St. John used his considerable clout to drive away all of Bradley's clients. Desperate, he left the state --- presumably to find someplace inconspicuous --- and found it in rural New Hampshire. Why he chose New Hampshire is unknown; perhaps he simple through a dart at a map. Anyway, while there, he took a job at the Gale farm in Faraway Hill and began developing a new, but much smaller, client base."

Ben stops him: "do we know who his clients were?"

"In New York or Faraway Hill?"

"Well, both, but mostly New Hampshire."

"A few, the local sheriff's office was able to identify some after they arrested him. But most hookers are able to keep their clients' names secret. Its one of the first things they learn."

Ben glances at Grace, who just sits there taking it all in, sobs. *This is so damned hard for her.* There is something he needs to know: "was Lewis Halloran one of them?"

Martin shrugs. "His name hasn't appeared anywhere, but a rich, older man would fit Bradley's style. That would certainly explain why Greg Halloran is paying his rent. It keeps Bradley quiet and prevents a scandal. May I continue? Thanks. While working at the farm he dated and married Ann Gale, not telling her about his side career. I suspect she provided him a good cover. Unfortunately for him, it didn't last long. The local officials discovered his activities around the time of Lewis Halloran's murder. At some point he convinced --- maybe blackmailed --- Greg Halloran to pay for his return to Manhattan. He kept a low profile for several months, slowly and quietly building a new client base. That seems to have picked up once Mrs. St. John relocated to Faraway Hill. I suspect he wanted to avoid attracting her and all the problems that would mean. Anyway, ladies and gentlemen, those are the basics. Details are in the report before you. Are there any other questions?"

"I have one." It's the first time Eve has spoken since the party. "Was my sister one of his clients while they were both in Faraway Hill?"

"There is no evidence one way or the other. But we are talking a short time frame, so I doubt it."

No one else has anything more to ask --- or perhaps are too embarrassed to ask --- so after a painfully awkward moment, Victoria thanks Shawn and escorts him out the office. Ben looks first at his wife, who looks angry; to Grace, who looks ashamed; and then to Frank, who has a crinkled smile on his crinkled face. "Don't worry," the old man reassures. "We'll figure this out."

✱✱✱✱

For the first time since before the holiday, Joe Westbrook is able to relax. Jack went to New York to finish the sale of his condo. Little Jack is playing quietly in the living room. The last of the new furniture arrived yesterday. Joe managed to find some great pieces that fit well with the handsome old building. None are antiques, but they have a look and feel that evokes the grandeur and classy

"She and Richard --- what makes you think so?"

"Ann and I had a little talk, before Christmas. Apparently it all started at Agnes' birthday party. They've been seeing each other since."

"Shit."

"Well, love can be a surprising thing." *We've both learned that,* Julie says to herself. It reminds her of something she's been want to ask him. "Speaking of which, I see your boyfriend has a new boyfriend."

Greg looks surprised. *Doesn't he know?*

"Jack. I've seen him, out with another handsome young man. Someone with a little boy."

"Oh," Greg no longer looks surprised. Now he looks awkward. "Well . . . that's complicated."

"Simplify it for me."

"Do you really care?"

Julie shrugs. "I'm curious."

"Well, I guess . . ." he pauses, trying to find the right way to say what he needs to say. "That man isn't . . . he isn't entirely what he seems."

"Oh?" *This should be good.*

"He, um" Greg is actually fidgeting. "He used to be Jack's girlfriend."

"Come again?"

Greg takes a deep breath and comes straight to the point: "His name is Joseph Westbrook --- Joe Westbrook --- but he was born *Jacqueline* Westbrook. Before her sex change, she got pregnant. Jack is the father. He just learned about it a few months ago. Joe and Little Jack have taken an apartment in Manchester."

Julie laughs. She just can't help it. *Damn, I was right: this is good.* A stewardess, sitting at the front of the cabin, looks up from her magazine. Julie calms down. "That's just perfect, Greg. It is. Nobody could make this shit up. What a family you three will make."

She expects Greg to say something. Instead, he just sits there quietly. She knows he's embarrassed but doesn't care. It's just too damned funny. She even starts to giggle again as the plane makes its descent.

****

Unlike Manchester or Concord, little towns like Faraway Hill usually take a long time to clean up after a major storm. The town's services are minimal and there are piles of snow everywhere. The farther away from the town square, the worst it gets. In past years, Munroe and Ann would spend a day hand shoveling out the house and barn. Fortunately Lorene can afford to hire help now. It only took the new farm manager a couple of hours with the snowplow. Ann easily pulls into the drive and up to the house.

Vivian greets her at the door. The woman is smiling sweetly as if her own daughter were paying a visit. The more Ann sees of her, the more she likes her. Still, Vivian's baggage concerns her. Lorene was nearly killed because of the woman's past. She can only hope there are no more Mike Bickels to worry about.

Ann follows Vivian into the living room where her mother sits with her knitting. After exchanging a few niceties, Ann springs her surprise: an all-expenses paid cruise in the Caribbean. The women shriek with delight and "oh mys" and "I can't believe it" and lots of hugs. Afterward, Ann calls Richard. "I'm very proud of you sweetheart." And he means it. This is a first for her. His sincerely comes through the cell's small earpiece with heartfelt clarity. "Thanks," she answers and, surprising herself, adds "I love you".

"I love you too."

****

Empty of all his belongings, the loft seems little more than a vast room. Having to sell it still gnaws at Jack. He loves this place. Bought during his college years, this was the only place in the world where could truly be his own man. He worked out here each morning. He watched multiple Super Bowls with his buds. He brought his tricks --- boys and girls alike --- for long nights of hard fucking. This was Jack's special corner of the universe. It's just real estate now.

"Well, dude, it looks to me like everything's out." Jack's little brother Nick came to help. "Having to sell this place is really shitty."

Jack shrugs. "Got no choice; the old man canned me and doubtful I'll get hired anywhere in the city. Besides, I've got to figure out what to do with my life. The money I've made from the sale should help. The prick has probably changed his will already."

decadence of the 20s. Right now he is reclining on a red velour chaise in the master bedroom that is almost as comfortable as the queen bed.

Joe has been discovering all sorts of cool things about Manchester. Over on Concord Street is a little nonprofit theater company, and an interesting art gallery on West Brook Drive provided some of the apartment's wall décor. There is even a place on Commercial Street that teaches belly dancing.

He is also discovering a fairly active gay community. One of his new neighbors stopped by the other day. An elderly, extremely fey man named Nathanial told him about the bars that cater to GLBT clientele, including a lounge on Elm near Spring Street that he recommends. "They always have things going on, what with drag queens and disc jockeys and karaoke and all. My dear, even the lesbians and straights wander in."

Joe starts to drift off when the phone rings. It's the landline, which surprises him: the only person who calls him is Jack, and he usually calls Joe's cell. Maybe it's some damn telemarketer. He picks it up without bothering to check the Caller ID. "Hello?"

"Jacqueline, dear, is that you?" Joe is surprised by the familiar but rarely heard voice.

"Hello, Mom."

✱✱✱✱

The flight home is quiet. The other seats in First Class are empty, leaving the section to Greg and Julie. It's as if the cabin has been reserved just for the two of them. This allows Julie to stretch out, happy to know that her cast finally comes off today.

"I can't believe he's actually *dating* her," Greg grumbles. Ann showing up on Richard's arm surprised everyone, although Julie is beginning to think that maybe it shouldn't have. "That's what it is, isn't it? First the funeral, now this, what's next."

"My mom was sure pissed."

"Well, it *was* supposed to be your dad's day. Shit, he just got sworn in as a United States Senator and the farm girl spoils the moment by simply walking through the fucking door."

Julie wishes he'd be a little quieter. They may be the only passengers in First Class, but there are still stewardesses who pass by from time to time. "Please don't talk about her like that. Besides, I think they're in love."

"I suppose, although Mom won't talk about it, at least to me. You should really call her." Jack and his mother have barely spoken in the weeks since the big fight. She has never liked confrontation or dealing with life's problems. Her response to any crisis is to ignore it until it goes away.

"I suppose so."

The real estate agent arrives with the papers. Her cheeriness is a little more than Jack can stomach. Fortunately, the process doesn't take very long. Soon the brothers are strolling down the crowded sidewalk. Manhattan's workers are rushing to restaurants and cafes and shops on their lunch break. The two pass a Starbucks, the same one where months earlier Jack learned he is a father. Nick offers to treat him at this little bistro on the corner, one of the newest and trendiest in trendy Soho. "*Your* spending money," Jack teases his little brother. "Dude, what happened, you find a sugar mama?"

"Very funny."

"A sugar daddy?"

"Fuck, you," Nick laughs.

The two of them are seated quickly. The menus are simple, mostly pasta and some sandwiches. "Damn shame about the apartment, Jack; it must have been a great place to party." He wishes Nick would stop talking about the condo. It's tough enough to give it up. Besides, talking about parties makes Jack think his best years are now behind him.

"Hey, Jack, you know that dude? Over there, he's checking you out."

Jack looks up to see Mark Bradley standing at the door. *What the fuck is he doing here?* He hasn't seen the man in months, not since Greg and Julie's wedding. Mark stands at the door, just as surprised at seeing Jack. *Shit, has he been working out? He looks hotter that I remember.* The hostess steps over to greet him, but Mark leaves without saying a word.

"Who is that guy? Did you hook up with him?" *I wish; I'd like to have him on all fours.*

"I can't believe it's him, of all people." He turns back to Nick. "You know Greg's half-sister, the farm girl I told you about?"

"Yeah, the one nobody seems to like."

"That's the dude she married."

"No, shit! The hustler, you mean? Did he see you? Did he recognize you?"

"Definitely." He and Mark met at Greg's wedding. Jack remembers thinking at the time what a pity he was married. It wasn't until Mark's arrest that anyone knew that the guy would drop his pants for the right price.

"Man, what a stupid hick she must be to marry an escort. Think he's doing tricks in New York?"

"The man's gotta make a living," Jack answer with a shrug and a naughty smile.

"Thinking about asking him for career advice?"

Jack and Nick's laughter causes the other patrons to turn and stare at them. "Maybe I should!"

****

Karen St. John is sitting alone on the settee in Greg Halloran's office at the Millyard. She's impeccably dressed and maintains a studied, regal calm. Karen knows that it's important not to look excited. Her plan is coming along nicely. Only one last piece is needed, one opportunity. She just needs to be patient and soon everything will be set right.

This was Lewis' office before his death. Karen remembers when the Hallorans ran the family business out of their mill at Faraway Hill. Those offices were very old school with heavy furniture and paneled walls. The Millyard has a modern, industrial look with big windows and exposed brick. Echoes of the past are reflected in the decor, with historic photos and mementoes scattered about. The Faraway Hill mill is still there and still churns out bolts of cloth every hour. She wonders what became of those beautiful old offices. Probably some mid-level manager uses them now.

Bored with waiting, Karen's eyes wander about the room. She has seen it all before, but one thing --- something new --- piques her curiosity: an open shipping box sitting on the credenza. She is about to rise and see what it is when Greg rushes back in from dealing with some sort of crisis at the Georgia mill.

"I'm sorry," he says. "It seems I spend most of my days putting out fires."

Karen smiles sweetly. It's good that he considers her a friend. "I quite understand. How is Julie?"

"Very happy, she's now out of the cast. We saw the doctor right after coming back from Washington."

"Oh, I'm so glad to hear that. I must call her."

"I'm surprised you didn't go to Ben's swearing in."

"I was invited but I had too many other things to attend to." Actually, Eve warned her sister to "stay the hell away" because "you are too damn unpredictable." So she stayed away.

"Well, Tim will be here any minute with the papers."

"Tim?"

"Our new lawyer; we hired him late last year when Ben decided to close up his firm."

"Yes, that was sad. But when one door closes . . . anyway, I am sure his new career will be far more rewarding."

"I hope so." The two fall into an awkward silence. Karen manages to keep a cool, relaxed veneer. But inside, she is seething. *You have hurt my little girl.* Julie hasn't said anything to her or to anyone, but Karen can sense her pain. A mother knows.

Desperate for something to talk about, Greg remembers the mystery box. "Have you seen this?" He walks over to the credenza, picks up the box, and carries it over to the settee. "The Thai ambassador sent it, as a sign of appreciation for what we are going through with the strike." He pulls out a magnificent teapot, decorated with an intricate leaf pattern. "I'm sure all the U.S. companies got one."

Karen takes it from him. The details are impressive. "It's beautiful." She hands it gingerly back to him.

"He also sent some rare, South Asian tea. I've been showing it to everyone."

The intercom buzzes and Greg's secretary announces the attorney's arrival. She then escorts Timothy Dreyfus in. A handsome young man in his mid-thirties, Karen finds him a delight to look at. He has dark hair and chiseled features and the kind of smile that melts a woman's heart. Tim is also efficient. Within a matter of minutes, Karen St. John becomes the owner of 10% of Halloran Enterprises.

"Thank you Karen," Greg says with a sincerity that almost makes Karen want to forgive him. Almost, but not quite. But she does give him a smile, a genuine smile of happiness and pleasure. Because sitting in that box is the very opportunity Karen has been looking for.

****

He has passed it several times since arrive in Manchester: a funky little store on Elm Street called King's Korner. It has always looked interesting, but, until today, Joe hasn't been able to check it out. He loves it. The place merges a cool boutique with a comfortable coffee shop. The shelves have fun little gift items from all over the state along with a small but eclectic collection of books. The locals seem to enjoy it as much as the tourist trade. Little Jack certainly likes the Korner: right now he is at another table filling in the coloring book that his poppa just bought him. A cute college girl waits on them, giving Jack the kind of special attention that makes the little boy giggle. It's almost enough to make Joe forget about his latest problem. Almost.

His mother's call came as a big surprise. Joe hasn't spoken with her in months. It still angers him that this is a woman who chooses to remain with the man who wants to kill her child. But he avoided saying anything when she announced that Vincent was bringing her to New Hampshire. "I told him I want to work things out with my daughter," she explained. Joe found it impossible to say no. Instead, he immediately called Aaron Tracey. The officer suggested meeting here.

The lieutenant is running late. He's running very late. It makes Joe nervous. After all, it was just a couple of months ago when Vincent's hit man nearly made his son an orphan. When the officer finally arrives, Aaron apologizes. "There was this last minute meeting." The man is so damned hot that Joe finds it easy to forgive him. *Too damn bad he's straight; this is a man built to wear a uniform. I'd take him home this minute.*

Aaron orders a cappuccino and goes right to the heart of the matter. "Okay, so your mother and stepfather are coming to Manchester. I have to tell you --- and my superiors agree --- we can't just arrest him for showing up."

"That's no surprise," Joe has heard that from the authorities before. It's a big part of his frustration in dealing with the bastard. "You can't do anything, even though the man nearly killed me."

"I understand, but we can't prove it."

"What should I do?"

"Well, I've been thinking about that . . . you said your mom wants to talk, that she wants to work things out."

"She says," *and she probably means it.* "I don't know about him."

"This is what I suggest: go ahead and meet them." *Is he kidding? That fucker wants me dead!* "Wait, and hear me out. "Meet them someplace public, someplace where we --- the Manchester Police --- can discretely watch . . . and maybe listen."

"Listen?"

"Look, he's a known criminal. If you are willing to wear a wire, he might say something we can use or at least pass on to the feds."

Joe stops and thinks about this. Vincent can be dangerous, very dangerous. He looks over to his son, who lifts his head up from coloring and gives Poppa a big, happy smile. *Can I really do this? I can't put Jack in any more danger.* Besides, "he's too clever to give himself away like that."

"Under normal circumstances, sure: he'd have his back up. But think about, are these really normal circumstances?"

"Well . . ." the man has a point. A mobster is coming to New England to make amends with his transgender stepchild. What about that is normal? "Can you protect my son?"

Aaron nods confidently. "I'm sure of it. We'll even contact the Feds to get their help. This is your chance Joe, maybe your last chance, to save your family."

"Vincent and his people are good at revenge." Even with Vincent in jail, Joe and his son --- and maybe even Jack --- could end up dead.

"You're not listening to me Joe; there are already things going on. I can't tell you about them, but you're the last piece of the puzzle. You do this and there is a damn good chance that no one in Bologna's operation will be in any position to get revenge."

That's it, isn't it? The Manchester Police have been in touch with the FBI. And my son and I are the bait . . . "I don't know, Aaron."

"This is your last chance Joe; the last chance to save your son --- and maybe save your mother."

✳✳✳✳

A trio of big trucks lumbers down the highway. They are laden with tools and supplies all protected under grey tarps. They make could time until they take the Faraway Hill exit. The trucks must move more slowly now. The town's streets are still a mess from the storm. It takes some creative navigation to get past the snow drifts. People on the sidewalks stop and stare as they past. Soon the trucks arrive at this historic Halloran mansion. With some careful maneuvering the trio drive around the house to get as close to the old servants' quarters as they can.

The garden is back there, covered in a white blanket. Julie, standing in the warm, dry Blue Room --- and relishing in her freedom from the cast --- sees them through a frosty window.

Julie is sorry she laughed at Greg. He did not plan the strange twists and turns of their life together. And, really, who could have predicted that his male lover would have an illegitimate child with a transsexual? *As they say,* she muses, *you can't make this shit up.* Still, it makes her wonder about how people in a small town like Faraway Hill can find themselves intertwined in all sorts of knotty combinations. She and Greg and Ann were all born within a few weeks of each other, grew up not far from each other, led very different lives and never expected to live under the same roof. Yet, here they are. It seems that small town connections are just too strong.

The men start carrying tools into the old, brick building. They are all probably connected in various interesting ways, too. Recognizing connections helped Julie make the decision she made about her marriage. Connections that now include Jack Campbell and Jack's son.

"Mrs. Halloran?"

Julie turns from the window to see Frederick standing just inside the door. This wonderful, elegant, gentlemanly old man is as much a part of the mansion as the marble staircase or the Grand Vestibule. "Frederick, how long have you worked for the Hallorans?"

"Almost 40 years, madam."

"Then you knew Lewis and Lilly Halloran quite well."

"Yes, madam."

"Tell me, how long was it before they had separate bedrooms?"

The butler pauses; this is the kind of personal question a servant is not normally asked. Its obviously one he'd prefer not to answer. "Please, Frederick, it's important. Tell me."

"I am . . . not sure, Mrs. Halloran; perhaps less than a year."

Right after they found out about Lorene's pregnancy. Lilly also got pregnant at about the same time. It happened during her engagement. Just like Julie. *Small towns and their connections.*

"Mrs. Burton is here, madam."

"Please send her in." Agnes Gabler's daughter called earlier today, practically in a panic. She and Greg had just returned from the doctor's office when the call came. Greg is letting her handle it. He's deferring a lot to her these days.

Frederick escorts Scarlet into the room. She looks nervous and a little guilty. "Hello, Julie. Thanks for seeing me right away."

"Of course; Frederick, would you please get us some tea?"

The butler nods and leaves them to sit together on the antique sofa. The Christmas decorations have been removed returning the room --- and the entire mansion--- back to its normal condition. "Scarlet, what's wrong?"

"Well, it's mom's house."

"Is there something wrong with it?"

"Is there something wrong," Scarlet rolls her eyes in frustration. "The county wants my mother out right away. They've just inspected it and say that it's not safe. The place needs a new roof, new wiring, the works. It could take months."

"My God, that's terrible. When did this happen?"

"Just this morning; I suppose that it shouldn't be too big a surprise. After all, the place is just an old sugar house that has been rebuilt and added onto so many times. The result is a crazy hodgepodge."

"A beautiful hodgepodge, you mean." Like everyone in New Hampshire, Julie knows about Agnes Gabler's famous house. The façade is covered with her murals turning an old rambling structure into a remarkable, three-dimensional work of art. "Does she need a place to stay?"

Scarlet smiles a smile of relief. "How did you guess? Mom hates hotels. My place is too small. She really shouldn't be alone . . ."

"Don't worry: Agnes can stay here. We've got plenty of room." *And maybe I'll make a connection of my own choosing.*

✷✷✷✷

The house looks magnificent. All the décor and furnishings are now in place and Karen is showing it off. *New Hampshire Magazine* has sent a photographer to take some pictures, but the really big deal is *Boston Magazine* coming next week for a full-blown photo shoot. Eduardo is ecstatic: he's never had this much press coverage from a single job. The man is so excited that his natural Southie accent occasionally slips out.

Peter arrives just as they are wrapping up. He's out of uniform, but still looking delicious. Karen loves younger men, their hard bodies, abundant energy and willingness to please. Mark was like that. Of course, Mark was paid to be like that. Not Peter. No, Peter is a joy. She just has to keep Denise away from him; the girl has not been discreet about her own interest.

"Hello, sweetheart," Karen greets him in the foyer with a kiss. As for their own discretion, she realizes that they haven't been very good at it. All of Faraway Hill is talking about them. *It's a wonder their families haven't said anything.* "Make yourself comfortable. They are almost finished." Another kiss and Peter heads into the living room while Eduardo leads the photographer into the kitchen.

Discretion is very much on Karen's mind at the moment. Climbing the stairs and into her room, there is something she needs to keep from Peter. From everyone, really. The inspiration came earlier in the day when Greg showed off his gift from the Thai government. Karen has a gift for him, too.

Hidden in her dresser is a little tin. She bought it on one of her many travels. Martin didn't like going anywhere, but Karen always managed to drag him from one interesting place to another. One of these places was Bangkok. A wonderfully colorful city, filled with both the very rich and the very poor. Karen loved exploring the ancient city's little nooks and crannies. It was in a quaint shop on a side street where she stumbled across the tin. Its contents look harmless, just like tea. Exactly like tea.

The plan is so simple and logical. *Daddy would be proud.*

EPISODE NINE

Traditions are important. They provide connections with the past, bridges to the future. Traditions are especially important in very old, very important families. They reflect stability and power. They reflect continuity and prestige. And they are usually unavoidable.

Like tonight.

In a magnificent stone structure west of Boston, a nervous young man is about to do what his father, grandfather and great-grandfather did. He is about to become a full member of the *Sanctus Frater of Thebes.* He is about to become a Brother.

That young man is Patrick Halloran. He is standing alone in a small, richly paneled room deep inside the old building. He is wearing a simple white tunic and nothing else: no shirt, no underwear, nothing. Robert, his cousin, warned him that the final initiation will have a sexual aspect to it. Some of the previous rituals did, too. They are meant to bind the Brothers together in the most intimate way imaginable. But what specifically will happen is unknown. It is the unknown that's making Patrick edgy. He wishes Robert were around. The man is an ass, but he's an ass who has been through this before. Unfortunately, family is not allowed to participate. Patrick must do this alone.

The heavy mahogany door opens with an ominous creak. A lone man enters. He is wearing a white cloak, just like Patrick's but with a hood obscuring his face. The man is about Patrick's height and build and it occurs to him that this could be another plebe, just following orders. He hands Patrick a mug. It is made of silver, very heavy and very old. The warm brew has a sweet aroma, like cinnamon. Patrick knows he is to drink, and he does. With each sip he finds the brew to be soothing, relaxing. His whole body seems to loosen up. So much so that a thought occurs to him: *are they drugging me?*

When he hands back the empty mug, Patrick glances at the bottom to see the silversmith's mark. He recognizes it from the museums he's visited. It was made by Paul Revere.

The man leaves him. Alone again, Patrick feels calmer, less nervous now, even a little woozy. *There was definitely something in that drink.*

The door opens. A pair of cloaked figures enters the room. Patrick cannot see their faces under the white hoods. They are shorter then he and move more slowly. *Probably a couple of old men,* he thinks. The men motion Patrick to follow them into the corridor. The place is quiet. He has always seen members milling about the lodge on past visits. But not tonight; no, tonight it is as quiet as a tomb.

The two old men lead him to a part of the lodge he has never seen before. They open another heavy door to reveal a stone staircase leading down into darkness. Patrick hesitates. *What the hell is going to happen to me?* One of the old men gestures him to keep following, so follow them he does. *I hope this will all be worth it.*

Damp, stale air wafts into his nostrils; the ceremony is obviously happening in the basement. *Maybe it'll just be a lot aging frat guys getting drunk*; he smirks to himself, hoping no one can see him.

Patrick and his guides arrive at the bottom of the stairs. The room before him is dark and small. Blazing torches hanging from the walls offer the only illumination. Standing around the room are a dozen Brothers, all dressed in white hooded tunics, their faces obscured. In the center is a large, wooden table. One of them steps up to the young man. His tunic is a little different; it is trimmed in purple. Robert told him that the Brother leading the ritual would be dressed like this. The man waits for Patrick to begin the ceremony with the ritual greeting, which, like everything else, must be in Latin.

"May ineo frater?" Patrick says, asking permission to enter the august surroundings.

The Purple Man waves his hand toward the assembly. "Vos may penetro frater."

Patrick dutifully walks over to the table. He can barely see faces under the hoods. Some are fairly young, in their 30s and 40s. Others are much older. He thinks he can recognize a few from meetings upstairs, but he can't be sure in this light.

"Est is vir dignus?" Purple Man asks. This is the formal opening, which translates into "is this man worthy?" Each of the Brothers, in turn, asks Patrick a question in Latin. Robert briefed him on what to say and how to say it. The questions are formal ones, to test his knowledge of the Brothers, their history and rules. Patrick answers each one correctly. The men seem pleased.

Purple Man pulls Patrick's tunic up over his head leaving him standing nude before the Brothers. *This is it,* he thinks, *this is what Robert warned me about.* Sex was part of the other rituals at the other levels. One involved jacking off with a group of other plebes. Another had Patrick and a plebe blowing each other. In one unexpected night, Patrick fucked a plebe who then took his anal cherry --- and he's certain that a group of Brothers were discretely watching them. All of this was interwoven into other initiations, like learning Latin and the drinking contest and the footrace a group of plebes ran through the woods behind the lodge. Patrick once asked Robert if women ever played a role in the sexual rituals. "Early on, like a hundred years ago or so" was the man's gruff answer. "But you, know, fucking women doesn't bind your Brothers together in the same way. Besides, women get pregnant. Worse, they talk." Brothers learn early on to keep silent.

With both hands on Patrick's shoulders, Purple Man guides him to his knees. The stone floor is cold and hard. Kneeling on it is a little painful. One by one, each of the Brothers pulls up his tunic and presents his cock to the young man to be licked and sucked to erection. He expected this would happen. *Hell, if this is all I have to do, then it's not too bad.*

But it is not. There is more. Purple Man taps the table, indicating to Patrick that he must climb up and lay out on the top. *Oh, shit, is this what I think it means?* His legs are pushed up. He is blindfolded. *Oh, shit, it is.* He can feel a pair of fingers lube his ass. *No, no, no; I've only done this a couple of times before.* But it's too late. A cock enters him and starts fucking. The thrusts hurt despite the lube. It takes several minutes, but he can feel cum filling his ass. The cock pulls out and another replaces it. And another, and another. Patrick loses track of time as each man cums inside him.

When it's over, the blindfold is removed. Patrick remains on the table, sore and exhausted. *I can't believe they did this.* The Brothers have resumed their position, standing around the table wearing their tunics, hoods concealing their faces. Purple Man raises his arms and again asks the question, "Est is vir dignus?"

"Etiam," one of the Brothers replies, "is vi rest dignus."

Purple Man claps his hands. "Frater supremus totus men, supremus totus families, supremus totus civitas." He steps over to the table and Patrick, his face still hidden. "Exspectata ut brotherhood quod totus suus ebeficium, veneration quod officium."

He is now a Brother. But as the others depart up the stairs, Patrick can't help wondering: *should I feel honored . . . or humiliated?*

****

Faraway Hill, the entire town, seems to sparkle under the brilliant January sun. The drifts of snow reflect light as well as any mirror. Shopkeepers, arriving to open up for the day's business, spread salt on the icy walks. There aren't many people in town. The holiday tourists have shed their tinsel and gone home. Most of the locals have left for their jobs in Manchester. Still, from a distance, the town looks classic, picturesque. Robert Frost knew how to describe this kind of scene. He lived several miles south of Faraway Hill, in a town called Derry where he wrote wonderful poems in the morning and farmed his land in the afternoon. People still gather in Franconia, where Frost later moved, to relish his words. He was a man who could describe any moment, any place in rural New Hampshire and find its beauty.

Well, maybe not. Eve King doubts Frost would know how to characterize this moment in her life.

She is standing outside her sister's new home, the beautiful Victorian with its wrap-around porch. Eve is bundled in her thickest coat, but a chill still runs down her spine. She doesn't want to do this. She'd like to avoid anything and everything involving Karen. But too much is at stake. So Eve is using this opportunity --- with her husband out of town --- to try once again to reason with the woman. This is probably a hopeless task, but Eve needs to try.

Denise Sullivan answers the door. Why Karen hired her remains a mystery. It is early morning in the dead of winter, yet the girl is dressed like she's ready to hit a Boston nightclub or maybe just work a Manchester street corner. Eve smiles to herself, *I wonder if she requires exact change?*

She is escorted inside, through the foyer and into the living room. Karen's pricey Boston decorator certainly earned his fee: the place looks stunning. It can be best described as a sort of contemporary New England country style. No doubt Karen is having the place photographed. Just like when they were girls, Eve's baby sister still insists on being the star.

"Mrs. St. John will be with you in a moment," Denise smiles, her cheap lipstick a little smeared. "Would you care for some tea?" Eve declines that and even having her coat taken. She doesn't plan on staying long. The girl takes the hint and leaves her alone.

Eve paces the room, noticing all of the expensive items scattered about. For years the house was used as a bed and breakfast. It wasn't as successful as some of the others in Faraway Hill, probably because it's a few blocks further from the town square. She has never been inside before. The elderly couple who owned it didn't mingle much. Still, Eve admires what Karen's decorator has done, especially one item. The painting over the fireplace is an incredible portrait of Lake Winnipesaukee as the summer sun sets over the water. It is so remarkable, so detailed and realistic that it almost makes her forget about the cold outside.

"Hello, Eve," she turns to see her sister step into the living room. Karen is wearing a chic, over-the-top designer outfit complete with, of all things, a turban. *A turban? Who the hell does she think she is, Gloria Swanson? She must be deep in Karenland.* "Please, take off you coat and make yourself comfortable."

"No, thank you, I don't intend to stay. In fact, I'll come right to the point."

"As you wish," Karen answers with a royal flourish as she takes to the sofa.

"I know about you and that boy."

"Boy, which boy is that?"

Eve impatiently taps her foot. *She just loves playing these damned games, doesn't she?* "You know who I mean: Peter Brandt. Your . . . 'dating' him, is how I guess I'd put it. The whole damn town is talking about it."

"Sister, dear, he is not my *boyfriend*; he's my lover --- and quite a lover."

"That is so sick! God damn it, Karen, you're old enough to be his mother. He went to grade school, high school with Ann and Julie. Hell, I remember him running around my backyard!"

"That's your real concern, isn't it?" her practiced, gracious smile fading. "It's not what the gossips down at the diner are saying. You are still afraid of my daughter learning the truth."

Eve wants nothing more than to punch her sister in the face for that comment. Instead, she holds her ground --- barely. "Julie is my daughter, Karen, not yours. So, please, leave Faraway Hill . . . *please.*"

"You've asked me that before."

"And you said this house was going to be a part-time home. Faraway Hill is just a little town, a boring place for someone like you. I remember when we were kids how much you hated it here."

"Yes, but the place has grown more . . . charming since then."

"New York is calling you, Karen." *New York,* Eve almost says out loud, *and fucking hustlers like Mark Bradley.* But she keeps the information to herself; it won't help matters if Karen knows what her sister knows --- especially if Ben brings the young man back to town.

"New York is always calling me, Eve. But I like it here. I like having an old, gracious home. I like having a young lover. I like being the center of the town's gossip. And I especially like being so close to my little girl."

"Damn it, Karen, you tell Julie the truth and it will shatter her! You claim to love her and here you are ready to ruin her life."

"That is not true, not at all. I am doing everything I can to help her."

"Help her? Help her, how? She's married to a man who loves her and now has a son of her own. Hell, she's practically the First Lady of New Hampshire! The best way you can help her is to leave town and go back to being that distant, glamorous aunt once again." Eve waits for a response, but Karen just sits there smiling. It suddenly occurs to her: "oh, shit, you did it, didn't you? You bought into the company."

"Yes, I now own 10% of Halloran Enterprises."

Damn, damn, damn. Julie told her mother that the family was opposed to it. Eve hoped that meant Greg wouldn't go through with the deal, that he'd find another way to save the company. But he did anyway. That means Karen is fully invested in Faraway Hill: her house, her lover, her company. She isn't going anywhere.

There is nothing more for Eve to say. She simple turns around and walks out the door.

****

Mark Bradley steps out his shower, relaxed and refreshed. He just finished his morning workout and is getting ready for a day enjoying the quirks of Greenwich Village. Maybe he'll even travel to Chinatown for a late lunch.

This is his life today: working out, servicing his growing client list and making the most of the city, all without worrying about paying the rent. *Thank you Greg Halloran,* he smiles to himself.

It only took a few tricks to raise the money for the really cool furniture, all quality leather he bought from a warehouse dealer in Brooklyn. The sofa and matching chair give the apartment a masculine look he likes and his clients find appealing. They especially go well with the living room's exposed brick walls and large windows.

The front door buzzes. *Who the fuck is that? I didn't schedule anybody for today.* He doubts that it's the cops: one of his regulars is the local desk sergeant. The dude is crazy about him and would definitely give Mark a heads up. Wrapping a towel around his waist, he presses the intercom. "Yeah, who is it?"

"It's . . . its mom." *Shit! How the fuck did the bitch find me?* At first he refuses to see her, telling her "to get lost". But she persists, buzzing him over and over. "Please let me come up, I haven't seen you in so long . . . and I have something important, really important to tell you." He realizes that he can't ignore her when she makes it clear that "I'll sit here all day if I have to." With a grumble, he presses the button to let her in the building. *What the hell does she want?*

Mark doesn't bother to dress; he doesn't see the point. *Just let her in, say what she needs to say, and then kick her out.* When he opens the apartment door, still wearing just the towel, Mark gets another surprise: his mother isn't alone. Standing next to her is one of the last people in the world he ever expected to see again.

"Hello Mark," Ben King says. He has a serious, determined expression on his face. Mark's mother just looks relieved. She gives him an awkward embrace that he doesn't return. "That's enough lady."

"Don't treat your mother that way."

"What the fuck is it to you?"

"Ben, that's okay . . . Mark, maybe you should put something on."

Mark shakes his head. "Nope, I want you both out of here as soon as possible. So say whatever it is you came here to stay."

And they do. Ben, in his calm, lawyerly way, explains everything step by step. He starts with their first date in college, to their break-up and finally meeting again just before Christmas.

Mark's first response is to laugh. It is a cold, cruel laugh, the kind growing up a deep well of anger. Growing up he asked, even begged, to know who his father is, but his mother always dodged the question.

"I couldn't tell you, either of you, until I could find Ben. It would have been wrong otherwise." His parents are not spending the night in New York, so there are things the two needs to know before they leave. When Ben asks his son what kind of relationship he wants, Mark responds "when I know, you'll know."

He kicks them out. The entire meeting last less than half an hour. Thirty shitty minutes that ruined an otherwise terrific day. *Fuck.*

✳✳✳✳

Frederick has alerted the staff to be on their best behavior. The big old house has seen plenty of celebrities come through the Grand Vestibule. These include movie stars and politicians and writers and even royalty. Many have spent the night, but none have come to live. None, that is, until now: the world famous artist Agnes Gabler has arrived to take up residence.

Scarlet Burton's SUV barely fits under the portico. The icy cement makes navigating the walk tricky. Scarlet carefully guides her mother to the door where Ann and Julie Halloran welcome them with warm smiles. A maid helps Agnes' grandson Bobby with the artist's luggage. There is a lot. "Be careful with those paints and easel," the old lady admonishes him.

"Yes, Grandma," the boy answers with the subtle whine of someone who has given the same answer to the same question more than once.

Agnes is escorted up the Grand Staircase ("be careful," Julie warns. "The marble can be slippery") to the first door at the right. These rooms are next to the master suite. "I hope that you'll be comfortable here." To make her more comfortable, some of Agnes' own furniture has been brought to the mansion, including her bed and favorite chair. The bathroom has been "grandmother proofed" with a shower seat and rails on the walls. "I am very impressed," she says looking around her.

Scarlet has made arrangements for a nurse, who will visit daily.

Julie explains that her mother will be coming by later to join them for dinner in the formal dining room. Eve and the artist have become friends over the last several months. "My Aunt Karen will be here too, she lives in Faraway Hill now."

Ann just stands there, smiling. She hasn't been invited to dinner. Even though she and Julie have made-up, Greg's feelings haven't changed much. True, they are getting along better. But that's not the same thing as being brother and sister. Besides, she is spending the night with Richard --- and Ann suspects that a certain question will be asked. She hopes to know what her answer will be.

Feeling ignored, she leaves Julie to entertain their new houseguest and her family. Ann wanders down the second floor hall toward her own suite. It is a long walk, past the master suite on her right and the nursery on her left. A couple of maids are standing next to a laundry cart, whispering. They lower their voices as Ann walks past, but she still manages to pick up something interesting: that Julie and Greg are now sleeping in their own bedrooms.

Reaching her door, Ann knows that those hushed words are her last confirmation: Greg is having an affair with Jack Campbell, and Julie is well aware of it. *Well, I'll be damned.*

✳✳✳✳

"I miss my little girl."

Joe Westbrook grumbles. *I wish she'd stop saying things like that.* He is sitting with his mother in J.D.'s Tavern waiting for Vincent to arrive. She looks sad, deeply sad, as if there has been a death in the family. She often gets like this. It was understandable after the last surgery, when Jackie was finally gone and Joe could finally be Joe. He was even prepared for it then. But now it's just annoying.

"I do, I really do miss her."

It doesn't help that Joe woke up feeling sick. He spent much of the morning in the bathroom with some serious diarrhea. His stomach still feels queasy.

"Mom, most people just try to be happy for their kids."

She's not listening to him. Her thoughts are elsewhere. It's almost like he's not even there. *Where the hell is Vincent? I want to get this over with.* He had some sort of last minute phone call and sent his mother on ahead. *Maybe it's another long-distance hit.* "I miss baking cookies with her and going shopping with her and I miss dressing her in pretty clothes."

Joe rolls his eyes in disbelief. "I hate dresses and you know it." Jacqueline preferred jeans and T-shirts. They were more comfortable and made it easier to play sports or just hang. Besides, all the guys said she was at her sexiest when wearing them. Jeans showed off her ass. "I always felt silly. They weren't me, Mom, they never were."

"Oh, but you were so pretty. I remember buying you a delightful one in pink with those little lace ribbons. You were about ten, I think. You were just adorable." Then, as if wondering what went wrong, adds with a sigh, "until you ruined it roughhousing with the boys." *That's because the boys were more fun, Mom.*

He's glad Little Jack isn't here. Aaron's fiancé volunteered to baby-sit. The officer is currently in civilian attire and discreetly sitting at table just a few steps away. There are also cops outside the hotel in an unmarked car. They are all waiting for Vincent's arrival.

"Mom, it just wasn't me." To make matters worse, Joe's hidden microphone is itching.

She nods and sighs again. In all fairness, it can't be easy for her, having her daughter become her son. It doesn't fit the life she expected. As a young woman, Marjorie Paulson defied her old money family by marrying self-made millionaire James Westbrook. It was the most daring thing a shy, insecure, privileged girl could do. It was also the last daring thing she did. Marjorie then lived the life of a proper California matron: she volunteered with the right charities, wore the right designer clothes and used the right plastic surgeon. The Westbrooks were among the most elegant and popular couples in Bel Air. Few of their friends knew the truth. They wanted a child. They wanted one badly. Years went by and nothing. Not having one was painful. Marjorie especially wanted a daughter, someone to dress up and show off and teach the finer things about being a lady. It took so long that having a girl was the most joyful moment in her life. Given the very feminine name of Jacqueline --- after Jackie Kennedy --- Marjorie doted on her. She saw Jackie as an extension of herself. But Jackie found all that loving and all that hovering stifling. Especially since she felt less and less like a girl with each passing year.

"Mom," he asks impatiently. "When is Vincent supposed to get here?"

"It should be any minute now."

Joe nods, trying to ignore the stabbing pain in his stomach. *It must be some kind of flu,* he thinks, *or maybe its just stress.* He scans the menu but nothing looks appealing. This is odd, because he and Little Jack dined at J.D.'s many times while living in the hotel. Joe particularly likes the Chicken Fontina, yet today the very thought of food makes him feel worse. *I wish I could get this over with.*

Marjorie sips her Tavern-tini, the restaurant's signature drink. Joe is sticking with sparkling water. It's the strongest thing he can keep down.

"So, do you like it here?" Joe isn't sure if she means the restaurant or New Hampshire. "I rather like the décor," he answers. J.D.'s has look of a contemporary western saloon. But his mother shakes her head, "I'm talking about Manchester."

"Yes, Mom; Jack and I are really enjoying it. He thinks snow is way cool."

Her smile is warm, and loving. "I wish you had brought him."

"No, Mom, I can't and you know why."

"Vincent isn't so bad."

"Shit, he tried to murder me! He almost made my son an orphan."

"I'm sure that's not true."

Joe is about to lay into her when his stepfather enters the restaurant. Vincent Bologna is a large man. Not tall, but wide. It's the result of living a life consumed with the perks that come with power. With him are two men, tall and athletic and well tailored. They are always with him; they scope out rooms and drive his car and make sure no one does something they are not supposed to do. Joe notices Aaron trying to look nonchalant.

Vincent instructs his escorts to take a nearby table and then steps over to give Marjorie a kiss. "I am very sorry, but business follows me everywhere."

"Of course, dear."

Joe declines to shake Vincent's hand. There are certain things that are just over the line. The man takes his seat as their server returns with another menu. Vincent orders a vodka tonic. "So," he asks his wife, "what is good here?"

"Jacqueline recommends the turkey wrap, but I'm leaning to this salad they call the Taste of New England. The cranberries and goat cheese sound yummy."

"Mom, I'm not Jacqueline any more. I haven't been for a long time. Besides, I'm not very hungry. Eat what you want."

Vincent's eyes barely look up from the menu. "Oh? If your not hungry then perhaps its stress. I have often heard that wearing a wire can be stressful."

Joe fights the urge to look at Aaron. "What the hell are you talking about?"

"I am no fool, young lady. The car outside, the young man over there: this is a sting."

"Your nuts." *How the hell did he figure it out?*

Vincent chuckles. "I understand of course, but don't expect me to say anything . . . incriminating."

"Well, I'm not wearing a wire. And I don't know why I agreed to have lunch with the man who hired someone to chase me across the country and try to kill me."

His mother remains in denial. "Oh, Jackie, dear, I'm sure you're mistaken."

"Marjorie, the young lady --- sorry, young man --- will believe what he wants. I just hope he'll believe what I am about to say."

I doubt it. "And what is that?"

"A deal, a truce; because I love your mother so very much I have come with an offer."

"What sort of offer?" Joe looks at him suspiciously. Vincent has never been this nice to him, at least not since he learned of Jackie's gender reassignment.

"As long as you stay far away from us in California --- this nice little city would be ideal --- you can consider yourself . . . safe."

"Safe?"

Vincent puts down his menu, leans in the table and looks Joe squarely in the eye. "Safe; you will be too far away to remain an embarrassment. You leave me alone and I'll leave you alone."

"What about Jack?"

"Jack is your son and there is obviously nothing I can do about that. Although I certainly pity the boy; he'll be in quite a shock learning the truth about his mother."

Joe chooses not to take the bait, adding, "What about *my* mother?"

"You are certainly welcome to call each other and email each other. But your life remains here and our life remains there. No visits."

"But will you be good to her?"

"I love her. I realize you have trouble understanding that, but it's true."

He looks so sincere that Joe finds himself wanting to believe the old man. He looks to his mother, whose expression pleads with him to accept. So he does. And he leaves them, feeling too sick. Striding past Aaron, he whispers to him, "I'm sorry dude."

****

Jack's contemporary furnishings look a little out of place in their new, more classical surroundings. The king size bed actually overwhelms the bedroom, leaving precious little space for the dresser and nightstand. But it doesn't matter. Not much does matter right now. At least, not for Greg, who stretches out with a yawn and a smile. He is laying on the bed, nude, his ass pleasantly sore with the memory of his lover. It's not a bad way to start the afternoon: pizza and a quick fuck.

"Now, *this* is my idea of a great day," Jack says as he returns from the bathroom. He is also naked and looking as hot as ever. Greg wishes he did; his sedentary lifestyle has resulted in some flab. Jack always finds time to work out. Of course, being unemployed helps.

"Absolutely," Greg pats the empty space next to him. "It beats the hell out of the business meetings I normally have." Jack crawls over him, grabbing the final slice of pepperoni and mushroom. "By the way, any word from Joe?"

Jack swallows a small bite. "Nope; Little Jack is still with his sitter. It should go okay, I mean, he's got cops all around him." His words are more confident than the expression on his face. "So, you told Julie about him?"

"I had to. She noticed you three walking around Manchester. These days, telling her the truth seems to be the easiest, best thing to do."

"You guys are getting along better," Jack says with the caution of a diplomat.

"Some days are better than others. My life is so fucking complicated. The family is pissed at me, my wife and I are basically roommates, the business is stable for now but things can still go bad. Did I tell you Dad's old secretary is coming back?" Jack shakes his head. "Well, mine's fiancé is moving her to New Haven. Mrs. Stone volunteered to come out of retirement. She starts tomorrow."

"Is that good or bad?"

"Damned if I know; I just felt I couldn't say no. Everyone in the office is in such awe of her." *Or maybe fear, is a better word,* he thinks. There is an unmistakable majesty in that little old woman that could intimidate the most hardened soldier. Mrs. Stone worked for the Hallorans for thirty years and knows the company inside out. She also knew his father better than anyone, especially Lewis' own son.

Jack reaches out to caress Greg's chest. It feels good. This whole afternoon feels good. All the complexity of the real world has been locked outside the door. It reminds him of their college years. Back then, he didn't have to worry about wives or kids or bastard half-sisters. There were no business decisions to be made. All he had to worry about was going to class and having fun. "Your thinking about the old days," Jack smiles at him, as if reading his mind.

"That's the only time in my life I was free, really free." Greg closes his eyes, enjoying the man's touch. "Free to take the classes I wanted, to go the shows I wanted, to hang out at the clubs I wanted, to fuck the people I wanted. No one demanded anything from me, except my professors. Even my parents left me alone. Of course, they pretty much always did."

He can feel Jack's hand gently find its way down to his flabby stomach, wander through his pubic hair and play with soft dick. *Damn that feels good.* "I remember those days, too," Jack whispers into his lover's ear. "They were the best --- especially after we got together."

Greg cock starts to stiffen, the effects of his words and his stroking. He leans back, closes his eyes and enjoys the feel of Jack's hot warm, mouth envelop him.

****

It is late afternoon and halls of the Hart Senate Office Building have fallen silent. Hardly anyone is here, most of the office workers left nearly an hour earlier. Among the very few remaining is Victoria Datillo. Ben arrives to find his chief of staff busy at work, so busy she is oblivious to everything including his own presence. "You need to learn how to take a break."

Victoria looks up, startled. "Oh, wow, what time is it?"

"Almost five," most people leave their offices at four. Its no wonder Washington gets little done. "Maybe you should go home."

"I can't, there's too much to do. What happened in New York?"

"It didn't go well. He laughed at us and kicked us out. I spent the rest of the day with Grace at her apartment." The woman is inconsolable. All she could talk about is what a failure she's been as a mother. It was difficult for Ben to be supportive; despite everything he's learned, it's still hard to think of the arrogant hustler as his son.

Victoria can sense how he feels and opts to change the subject. "Have you checked the news or your messages?"

"No, why?"

"Adam Newman declared his candidacy."

"We expected that. I'm just surprised he took so long."

"Frank is coming by tomorrow morning to brief us on strategy. And I think he's found a professional fundraiser."

Ben nods. He was warned early on that a constant schedule of fundraising events and campaigns stops will consume much of his year. Part of him wonders if it's all worth it, especially since his illegitimate son can easily torpedo it all. "Don't stay too late," he advises Victoria before leaving. There isn't much else for him to do today.

****

Agnes Gabler is holding court in the Blue Room and the big oval parlor is a perfect setting. It allows her to take center stage for an intimate audience of select people, turning an overstuffed chair into a throne. The guests --- including a couple mayors and a few state legislators not to mention representatives from the Currier Museum --- even face her like royal courtiers honoring their queen.

Everyone has donned their finest for the occasion: Greg in his best suit, Julie and Eve bought new dresses. Scarlet is here and Bobby is wearing his grandmother's favorite sweater. The boy hates it --- the thing is heavy and it itches --- but he wears it anyway.

Agnes has just finished telling them a wonderfully bawdy story involving Milton Berle and a nightclub in New York where the comedian tried to pick her up with his wife just three tables away. The punch line is so x-rated, Bobby blushes with embarrassment. Sometimes there are drawbacks to having a famous grandma.

A magnificent door bell chimes. That means Karen has arrived. Eve sits there and wonders just how her baby sister will steal Agnes' moment. *I'll bet it'll be some expensive accessory, a bauble that everyone will be talking about all night long.* Frederick promptly announces Mrs. St. John's arrival. But it isn't diamonds or emeralds or pearls that everyone notices. Instead, wearing a designer suit she obviously bought him, the accessory is Peter Brandt. Eve rolls her eyes in disgust. *How dare she!*

From cocktails through dinner and to dessert, Karen manages to redirect everyone's attention from the guest of honor. Whether she's regaling her own tales, pawing her date or bragging about being Greg's new business partner, Karen is determined to be the night's star. All throughout, Peter tries not to look uncomfortable with the opulent surroundings, and Eve fights the urge not to throttle her sister. Even Julie, who is normally enamored with her aunt, looks unhappy.

But eventually, as they move into the Green Room for coffee, Agnes has had enough. This is a woman who doesn't like having her thunder stolen. At 95, she knows when to be gracious and when to put some youngster in her place. It happens when Karen tells her own bawdy story, one about yet another celebrity. But this time Agnes has the upper hand when she finishes the tale with a clever dig at Karen. Eve's sister is mortified as everyone --- including Mark --- giggle. *Serves her right.*

****

Ann has never been to the Red Blazer before. While in college, lots of people she knew would drive up the interstate every Friday to enjoy live music and a beer special in the restaurant's Peanut Pub. Ann was never invited to tag along. She was kind of surprised when Richard told her they were having dinner here. He seems too old and sophisticated for what she imagined to be a college kid's hang-out. But the restaurant's main dining room turns out to have a cozy and romantic atmosphere with rustic floors and a beautiful, two-story fireplace.

The food is just as good. Ann elects to try the Brazilian Seafood Stew, which mixes lobster, shrimp, scallops and other fish in a garlic broth. She has never had anything like it before and loves it. Richard, who enjoys a sirloin, talks about Ben King and the upcoming election and his chances. "Adam Newman will be a formidable candidate, but Ben has some of the best people in the business working for him. Of course, he needs to make sure to spend a lot of time traveling the state."

"I doubt Mrs. King --- I mean Eve --- will like that." One of the many things Ann has admired about the Kings is how they stick together. She has never known a couple so devoted to one another. The separation, him in Washington and she in Faraway Hill, can't be easy on them. Especially since Eve has a career of her own.

Richard insists that she try one the Red Blazer's famous cheesecakes. The waiter brings her a little plate with a big slice with raspberry swirled through it and studded with white chocolate. But it's the velvet box that comes with the cake that gets her attention. She doesn't even have to open it; the grin on Richard's face says it all. But open it she does and Ann gasps at an incredible diamond ring. "Well," he asks with the anxiousness of a teenager. "Will you marry me, Ann Halloran?"

"Yes," she answers with tear of joy trickling its way down her cheek. "I'll marry you."

****

The next morning Greg Halloran is still chuckling about what happened at dinner. It was fun watching Agnes put Karen in her place. Even Julie loved it; the two of them laughed about it after the party. That was probably the best part of the night. It was like the good old days, less than a year ago, before all the shit came along. But the shit did happen, and when the fun was over they each retired to a different bed.

Greg notices a different world when he arrives at the Millyard. There is a chill in the air, one almost as cold as the temperature outside. People throughout the Halloran offices walk around like high school kids afraid of pissing off the principal. He kind of expected this; after all, this was the atmosphere while he father ran the place. He used to think Lewis was responsible for it. But it was really Millicent Stone.

His new secretary, Mrs. Stone --- and she insists on being called Mrs. Stone --- has the look of an army drill sergeant, from her stern face down to her plain, workman-like shoes. "Good morning, Mr. Halloran."

He feels like saluting her. *Why did I agree to take her back?* "Good morning, Mrs. Stone." Her desk is immaculately organized. This is a woman who doesn't believe in post-its.

"I've booted up your computer and today's schedule appears on the desktop. I also took the liberty of brewing some of that tea the Thai consulate sent you. That should warm you on a cold day and is bound to be better for you than coffee."

Greg thanks her and steps into his office where the tea's aroma greets him. *Damn that smells good.* It reminds him of something, something he can't quite put his finger on. Greg sets down his briefcase and pours himself a cup. A quick sample nearly burns his tongue so he stirs in some cream.

Mrs. Stone buzzes; it's the Atlanta mill with yet another crisis. *Already? Shit, it's just after 9!* The conversation is as frustrating as all the others, but he manages to solve the problem in a matter of minutes. Greg slams the phone down and picks up the cup. The strangely sweet aroma is calming. The taste is soothing.

Then, suddenly, everything goes black.

The Halloran Mansion

The Halloran mansion was constructed between 1801 and 1803 by textile magnate John Halloran (1750-1823), who began his career as a personal aid to Josiah Bartlett (1729-1795), a physician, statesman and New Hampshire's delegate to the Continental Congress.

Halloran was an enthusiastic supporter of the new nation and was present when Bartlett signed the Declaration of Independence. He was also amassing a fortune in textile manufacturing. As the original presidential mansion in Washington DC was nearing completion, Halloran contracted an apprentice to architect James Hoban (1758-1831) to create a nearly identical house in Faraway Hill.

Like the original White House, the Halloran mansion is two stories and was initially built flat to the ground. It has two oval rooms (one, a parlor, on the main floor; the other upstairs as part of the master bedroom suite), a ballroom and other amenities. A portico added in 1820 greets visitors, an especially useful feature on cold or inclement days. Behind the mansion, a large red brick structure was used to house the servants.

The first major renovation occurred in phases between 1898 and 1903, installing electricity and plumbing. By the late 1950s, age had caused serious wear on the

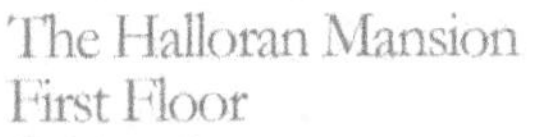

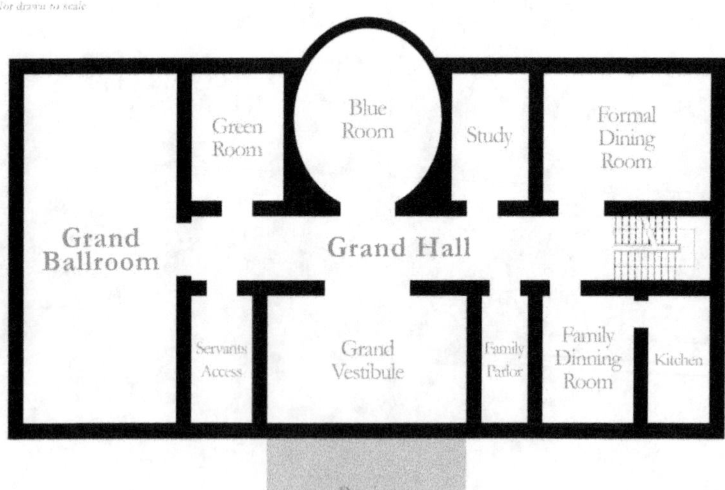

The Halloran Mansion

mansion. Following the lead of President Harry S. Truman's renovation of the White House, the mansion was essentially rebuilt from 1959 to 1962. This involved constructing a proper foundation and basement (which is now used for servants' quarters), new heating, plumbing and the addition of air conditioning.

While the main floor is very similar to the original design, the last renovation introduced two informal spaces: a family room (essentially a den) and a family dining room (in addition to the formal dining room). The kitchen was upgraded (as it would be again in 1996).

The second floor is very different. The master suite, anchored by an oval parlor, has two bedrooms and two bathrooms. The number of bedrooms was reduced to five, each with a private bath and a small parlor (creating small suites). The nursery, located across from the master suite, was upgraded with better plumbing and an adjacent bedroom for a nanny.

Guests to the Halloran mansion are regularly impressed with the wealth and elegant beauty of the Grand Vestibule, the Blue Room, Green Room and Grand Ballroom. The handsome, marble Grand Staircase connects the two floors.

The Halloran Mansion
Second Floor
*Not drawn to scale

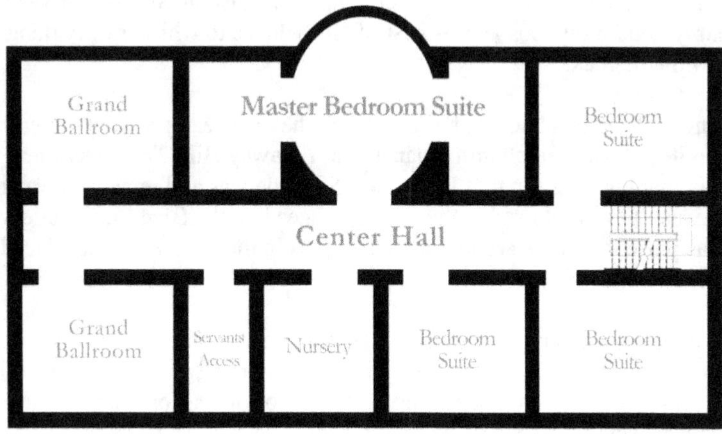

EPISODE TEN

The human mind is an interesting organ. It can be clever. It can be stupid. It can climb to the top of the greatest moral mountain or wallow in the depths of evil. A mind can be equally creative and destructive. The brain can trick an addict into believing that one more hit or one more drink will be okay. A woman can be fooled into believing that the person making love to her is in love with her. Or it can convince a man that the past is the present.

It is that last trick of the mind that is happening to a certain patient, lying quietly in a bed at Elliot Hospital.

Greg Halloran's mind has taken him to another time and another place, back to the happiest period of his life, the period when he was truly free and almost happy: his time at college. In his mind, the past two years have not happened --- or, at least, not happened yet. Greg is not married to Julie King, his parents are still alive and he has never heard of Ann Gale. He is not tied down to a wife or a secret lover or a child or a job. There are no scandals, no hidden agendas and no international strikes. He is simply a junior at New York University where studying and having fun are his only commitments, his only responsibilities.

Greg's life is almost idyllic: his grades are excellent and he is certainly having fun, even if he hasn't many friends.

His mind has taken him back to a chilly January morning. He reaches out to caress the soft, smooth skin of the naked person sharing his bed. Today, it is a woman, and an incredibly sexy one. Susan has a remarkable body, almost no fat and the most perfect breasts he has ever held. She's also great kisser, gives reasonably good blow jobs and --- best of all --- loves to whisper dirty things in his ear while he fucks her.

He has never been this bad. He has never had the chance. As a child, Greg lived in the limited world of the family mansion in Faraway Hill. There were few friends in that big house in that little town. Solitude was and remains a way of life. He wasn't even allowed in the formal spaces like the Blue Room unless an adult was present. "There are too many antiques in there," the pinched-faced nanny would say.

As a teen, he spent nearly all his time at an elite boarding school in Massachusetts. All of the students were boys from privileged families. Hardly any of them were allowed to leave the campus. Boston was only an hour away, but it may as well have been on another planet. This was a strictly male environment. Anything you wanted to do had to be done with another boy. This meant meals, roommates, sports, classes --- and sex. Greg discovered a small group of them who would use each other for relief. They paired off regularly. The older boys clued in the younger ones as to what to do and the safe places to hook-up. Greg fucked another young man for the first and found he liked it. The kid's tight, not-quite-virgin ass was so accommodating, that it made him cum within minutes.

But he knew something was missing because he still thought about girls. He thought about them a lot. All the older boys bragged about the pussy they were (supposedly) getting during summer break. Unfortunately back home, in that big house and that little town, he never had the opportunity. This is why Greg insisted on New York University. He knew that he'd finally be free to do things he wanted, whether it was hanging out in SoHo or going to a Broadway show or getting laid. But to do so meant defying the family. Normally a Halloran attends Yale. A few choose Harvard. Others opted for a different Ivy League school. Not him. This was a rare moment in his quiet life when the young man made a demand and stuck to it.

And it worked. Even when living in the dorms --- first Rubin Hall and then Carlyle Court --- Greg got to live a life of his own choosing.

Ah, the dorms: it was that first semester when he finally fucked a woman. She was a sexy teacher's assistant name Kathy. She was a little drunk after some clubbing when he ran into her but that didn't matter. He also started partying around the same time and they had met at a bar in the Village. Greg took Kathy back to his dorm --- his roommate was home visiting family --- and they spent the whole night together. He never saw her after that. Kathy melted into the vast population of NYU and the city.

No longer in the dorms, he is free and he is alone, living in a comfortable little studio just a few blocks from Washington Square Park. Greg's own family rarely bothers him: as long as he keeps his grades up and stays out of trouble, he parents are satisfied. His aunts, uncles and cousins all have busy lives of their own.

He is still free, but this morning he is not alone. Susan begins to stir. They've been seeing each other on-and-off for about two months. Greg doesn't consider it serious. She is a great fuck and makes him laugh but they have little else in common. Susan is from a working class neighborhood in Newark, the first in her family to go to college. They rarely do dinner or talk much. Mostly they just hook-up a couple of times a week. "Good morning," he wakes her with a gentle nudge.

"Good morning," Susan stretches, yawns and remembers: "Oh, shit, all that fucking work!" Susan has a major group project to work on for one of her engineering classes. It will completely swallow her time for the next few days. "It's going to be a nightmare." She stretches and yawns again. "I really appreciate you keeping Chad company." Chad is Susan's little brother, a high school senior, who is coming into the big city for the weekend.

"No problem, he's a good kid." Three weeks ago, on Chad's last visit, Greg popped the teen's cherry. It had been awhile since he was with a guy, and the handsome, well-built high school jock was at the right place at the right time. He was also eager: the boy hasn't been able to come out to anyone back home and practically threw himself at Greg. As long as Susan doesn't find out, everything will be cool. Greg likes a drama free life.

The two of them shower together, playing and laughing and kissing. Greg would happily fuck her again, but they haven't enough time. Susan isn't the only one with a busy schedule. Greg has a full class load for the rest of the week. They dress, kiss, bundle up for the cold and head off in different directions.

Greg trudges past snow drifts and icy windows toward West 4th Street and Tisch Hall, part of NYU's Stern School of Business. Most of his professors are pretty cool and he gets along just fine with the other students, even though he doesn't socialize much. Having lived such a secluded life has left him uncomfortable in certain situations. To compensate, Greg has joined a couple of the Stern's clubs. But he still feels very much alone. Thankfully, the internet compensates: a lot of college kids across the city use the web for hook-ups. That's how he met Susan.

He passes a lot of people in the busy building, smiling at those he knows. One of the girls, in a very short skirt, gets his attention and she winks back. The next few hours are consumed with dry discussions about branding, inventory methods and accounting. None of it is very difficult for him; Greg easily keeps his GPA up. But they are all needed because some day his father wants him to take over the family's textile business.

The temperature drops at day's end. Greg has to hold his coat close to him. He's really looking forward to spring break. Every year, Stern's entire junior class visits different countries to learn about different companies. Greg is going to Hong Kong. Having grown up in the stifling atmosphere of Faraway Hill and boarding school, the very idea of traveling to the other side of the world is exciting.

Still, tonight, he is walking alone. Greg is often alone. He makes a stop at the Bobst Library. He finds the books he needs, says hello to a couple of people he knows, and returns to his little apartment, alone.

The next day is even busier. There are more classes and he has a meeting with the International Business Association, one of the school's many clubs. He has drinks with a couple of the guys afterward. But they are not friends, not really. Nothing serious is ever discussed, nothing important is ever shared. They are just dudes to hang with.

But there is one dude who never fails to catch Greg's eye. He really stands out among the 2500 "Sternies" who congregate around Washington Square.

Everyone knows him, knows Jack Campbell. The man is beautiful and confident – often cocky --- and people talk about him. They talk about him a lot. Jack can play any sport and often does. He is always the center of attention at any party. He is known for dating the hottest girls on campus and, according to at least one rumor, some of the closeted jocks. But the two have never met. Yet, every time Jack walks by, Greg can't help but notice him.

Friday finally arrives. Susan is meeting Chad at Grand Central and bringing him to the Village. *It's kind of kinky,* Greg realizes *that one of my fuck buddies is delivering another fuck buddy right to my door and she doesn't even realize it.* But deliver him she does, shortly before dinner. The three of them head to one of the many little restaurants in the neighborhood. Chad is really excited; to him, Manhattan is like another world. Greg can understand it. He just wishes the kid would stop staring at him; his sister might catch on.

Dinner is over and Susan kisses Greg goodbye. She needs to meet with her classmates at the Bobst. It's starting to snow as the two men walk back to his apartment. On the way, Chad talks about attending NYU with his sister. "I haven't told the family yet, but I just got the acceptance letter today."

"That's cool, congrats."

"Thanks, dude. Do you think," the boy smiles temptingly, "that we could hook-up a lot next year?"

"Maybe."

"My sister never has to know."

Greg almost laughs. "We're not that serious. Besides, you might find other guys --- and maybe even girls --- to interest you."

They arrive at his apartment building, where navigating the stoop is tricky because of some ice that built up in the afternoon. But ice is on no one's mind when the two men enter Greg's studio. Just as the door closes behind them Chad plants a deep, sensual kiss on him. *Wow, he's really horny.* The kid then steps away and stars a slow, sexy strip. "I've been thinking about you all week," he says bare-chested. He unbuttons his jeans when Greg stops him. "Let me do that." He slides Chad's jeans and brief to the floor, the boy's hard cock sticking out at an impressive 45 degrees.

It doesn't take long until Greg has the kid on his hand and knees on the bed. Chad sighs with each of his thrusts. "Slap my ass dude," he begs Greg, "Just like they do in the porn movies." Greg is happy to oblige. He starts slapping his ass while fucking the boy even harder. "You like that?"

"Yeah, now talk dirty to me, like I'm your bitch."

Shit, this must be some fantasy of his, or maybe he's found a fuck buddy back home who does this to him. "You like this bitch, you like my cock?"

"Yes, sir."

"I'm going to fuck you raw and bloody, bitch-boy."

"Fuck, yes, do it, do it, do it!"

With one last push, Greg fills the boy's ass with his cum. *Holy shit that was quite a fuck.* Exhausted, the two of them collapse on the bed. Greg reaches under Chad when he notices the sheets are sticky. *He came while I fucked him? Wow.*

"So," Chad smiles at him, "am I as a good a fuck as my sister?"

Greg, laughing, realizes at that moment that things are getting too complicated. He'll need to find away to break up with both of them. The two young men spend the rest of the weekend together, exploring the city, fighting the ice and cold and taking in a concert at the Skirball Center. There they run into Denise Sullivan, one of the girls he's hooked-up with in the past. Of course, half of Manhattan has hooked up with her. Greg manages to keep the encounter brief, but her eyes and smile reveal that she knows he's fucking Chad. They find seats far from her and anyone else Greg knows.

On Monday, with Chad gone and Susan still wrapping up her class project, Greg looks for something that will fill in his remaining free time. He scans the university's web site and finds a student-run theater troupe looking for fundraising and publicity help. *That should be perfect.* Greg has done this in the past: being unavailable makes breaking up with someone much easier.

That night he arrives at Marie's Crisis, a popular bar in the Village to meet the girl running the troupe. The place is crowded, which is surprising for a Monday. This is usually the slowest night of the week. He pushes his way past a couple of groups crowding together near the bar until he sees a young woman at the rear making eye contact.

"Are you Greg Halloran?" She asks as he steps up to her.

"Yes, you're Lauren?"

The girl smiles and shakes his hand, "Lauren Thomas, artistic director of Going Nowhere Theatre." Her beauty is striking: auburn hair, immaculately soft skin with just a hint of olive. Her big, bright eyes transmit intelligence and warmth that instantly makes him feel welcome. The two of them spend the next hour talking about her little troupe and its needs --- there are only a dozen members, all NYU students, hoping to rent little places like Stage Left and Manhattan Rep for their plays. "We've got no money, or damned little, so that's an issue, too."

He suggests raising quick cash by doing some improv at local clubs, where the troupe can share in the cover. "What a great idea; I wish I had thought of that."

As the night wears on, the bar's crowd starts thinning out, and they find themselves moving on to other subjects. "My parents own a chain of boutiques in and around Dallas." Lauren tells him. "My father is a died-in-the-wool Texan; my mother grew up in Mexico." That explains her incredible skin, but not her lack of a southern accent. As if sensing his thoughts she explains "I've traveled all over --- so much that my family can barely understand me when I speak. My drawl is gone. It drives them nuts."

Greg surprises himself and starts opening up, too. He describes his childhood, all alone in a big house. "It was like growing up in a museum --- no, make that growing up part-time in a museum. I only spend a couple of months a year there; boarding school since I was seven, or maybe eight. My dad's very . . . distant; my mom always needs to be in charge."

"No brothers or sisters?"

"Nope; I'm an only child."

The rest of the evening is like this, sharing stories of family and youth and life. Greg cautiously steers clear of the more x-rated stories, the ones about school boys and women like Susan and Denise. All through the conversation, he finds himself drawn more and more to Lauren. Yet something keeps him from bringing her back to the apartment. There is something in his heart, his soul, which says she should be more than another hook-up.

Over the next few weeks, meeting Lauren becomes as regular a part of his schedule as classes and club meetings. It's also the most welcome. Greg finds himself looking forward to seeing her, meeting her theatre friends and exploring a part of New York he seldom has in the past. Susan and Chad stop trying to contact him; they seem to have taken the hint.

She introduces him to the Caffe Reggio. Greg has heard about it, but never had a chance to check it out. Opened in 1927, the Reggio is famous for introducing cappuccino to America. Entering the café is like taking a leap over the Atlantic and landing in Paris. Tin ceilings, maroon and green walls, antiques everywhere.

Finally, one Saturday night after rehearsal, Lauren invites Greg to her apartment. She lives in the Village, too, just a few blocks from his place. But the décor is as funky as you'd expect: fabric draping the exposed brick walls, an old carved fireplace, museum posters and found art objects scattered around the cramped studio. That night they make love. It isn't like the past; this isn't mere fucking, at least not for Greg. He isn't trying to cum as quickly as possible. For the first time in his life he is truly making love to another person. The kissing, the caressing and the sweet talk: it is all so much more that anything from his past. When Greg's cock enters her, it is surrounded by a velvety warmth that envelopes him entirely. He stays inside her, not moving, embraced by her sexy legs as they continue to kiss. She cums first, another landmark for him; when he cums, she smiles

From that point on, they are separated only by their conflicting class schedules. Dinners nearly every night; making love at least twice a week; sharing breakfast the next morning. Greg gets to know her friends, who are artists and actors and singers. All of them are colorful and some of them are seriously weird. One is a former marine, as butch and built as any poster, who lives with his boyfriend while auditioning for any role that comes along. Another is a woman from Oakland, California who affects a French accent and dresses in turtlenecks and likes to flirt with him --- or with anyone. Then there is the curly haired woman who seldom says anything but sings more beautifully than anyone he's ever heard.

Lauren's little theater company manages to put on a few shows. None of them make much money or even get written up in the press. But no one involved seems to care. The whole point is the adventure.

Greg loses interest in hooking up with anyone. He finds himself turning away what were his regular lays, including Denise Sullivan, who confidently assures him "you'll be back." The only person who can still distract him is Jack Campbell, who shows up periodically at the Stern or the Kimmel Center surrounded by what can only be described as his posse.

Even though they spend most of their time with her friends, Greg sometimes brings Lauren into his rarefied world. These typically involve business networking and fundraising events that she finds even more boring than he. One of these evenings will stick in his mind for years.

They are at a fundraiser in Brooklyn for a new museum for what is being called "urban art" --- something that Lauren finds fascinating. She comments on works that Greg can't seem to understand, like graffiti painted blocks of concrete and a weird sculpture comprising of a pile of glued beer cans. The most interesting to him is the night's incongruity: street kids (mostly black and Hispanic) in torn jeans and shaved heads mingling with older patrons (mostly white) in tuxedoes and fancy dresses.

Among the guests is a woman that reminds Greg of the classic movie stars. Lauren has recently introduced him to the wonders of TCM, and glamorous ladies of the past like Ava Gardner, Lana Turner and Myrna Loy. The woman is about his mother's age and introduces herself as Karen St. John. "Aren't you Lilly Halloran's son?"

"Yes, ma'am, I am." Karen St. John is a striking beauty, especially for a woman her age. If he were still fucking around, Greg might . . . well, it doesn't matter. Karen is here with her much older husband who keeps a close eye on her.

"This may surprise you, but I used to work for your family."

"Really?"

"Oh, yes, ages ago, before you were born. I was young girl working as a maid. My sister, Eve Scott --- sorry, Eve King --- is even married to your family's lawyer." This elegant lady begins telling him tales of the family mansion, its architecture and its history including stories he's never heard before. It's strange to him, reminding Greg that he is oddly from but not of Faraway Hill. When Lauren joins them she tries to be interested, but he can tell she finds tales of small town New Hampshire to be boring.

It is odd that Greg should meet someone with a hometown connection because contact with Faraway Hill happens rarely. Occasionally his father will call, to ask about his grades or complain about his spending habits. His mother calls even less often. She'll also ask him about grades, along with girls and the current hot show on Broadway. They never call at the same time. It is as if they are living in separate houses. They are clearly living separate lives. Each call reminds Greg of the inherent loneliness in his life. Lauren notices it, and brings it up one night in bed. "Haven't you had many friends?"

Greg's arms are around her, one hand gently caressing a breast. They have just made love and his cock is still a little hard. "No, not really; guys in school I'd hang with but no one really to talk to." He'd fuck some of them, but seldom have a real conversation with them.

"All those people around you, and you never really made a friend?"

"No."

"Why?"

A good question, one that Greg has asked himself over and over. Something deep down makes it tough for him to trust anyone. Maybe because he never learned to trust his parents, the people every child should be able to trust. *Could it be that simple?* "I'm not sure."

As spring approaches, Greg is excited about the class trip. He is also coming to a realization: he has fallen in love with Lauren. This is the one person he can confide in about almost anything including, finally, his experiences with other men. Greg was nervous about telling her, worried about her reaction. *Would she freak? Would she walk out on me?* Lauren does neither. Instead, she laughs. "At least you've had some good times. Besides, that explains a lot."

"It does, like what?"

"Why your so damned good in bed --- practice makes perfect babe!" He soon learns she has experimented with women over the last couple of years. "Hey, it's the thing to do."

Greg feels so good about things with Lauren, he tells Lewis about her in one of their infrequent phone conversations. "That's fine, son," is the only reply.

Then, on the night before he leaves for Hong Kong, it happens. They are in bed, having just made love, Greg's cock still inside her, with his eyes locked on hers, when he declares "I love you."

Lauren doesn't answer; she just smiles and pulls him in for a deep, passionate kiss. *She loves me too. Holy fuck, she loves me too!* He carries this belief with him on the long plane ride to Asia.

Greg has an unforgettable time in Hong Kong. The island city is filled with surprises. One of them is the terrain: he expected the island to be flat but it actually very steep and hilly. The city even has an extensive network of covered escalators.

As to the official reasons for the trip, one of the highlights was visiting a company whose offices are in the impressive International Finance Centre, dual skyscrapers including one that reaches 88 stories into the heavens.

Throughout out it all, he emails and texts Lauren back home, always ending with "luv u". Her messages back are just as loving, or, at least, that's how he reads them.

The trip ends with a dinner party at a quirky restaurant in downtown, housed in a former dairy building that serves the best Mediterranean food he's ever had.

Back in New York, Greg and Lauren start seeing each other as often as before the trip. Her friends are fascinated by his tales of Orient adventure. She seems less so. In fact, as the weeks go on and the weather gets progressively warmer, Greg can sense a change in Lauren.

Then, just before the semester's end, on a surprisingly hot spring day, Lauren meets him outside her apartment. "I'm sorry Greg, but I don't think we should see each other any more."

It's like being hit in the gut. "What are you talking about? I love you! Don't you love me?"

"Well, yes, sort of, but not like you want."

They argue the first real argument they have ever had. It is also their last argument. Lauren insists she doesn't want anything too serious. "That's where things are heading, I can feel it."

"Bullshit! We're in love. It's already serious."

"No, Greg, *you're* in love." That is the last thing Lauren says to him. She enters her apartment, leaving him standing there on the sidewalk all alone. Stunned, he starts walking to nowhere in particular, not paying any attention to the time. *I can't believe it. I can't fucking believe it.*

A few hours after the break-up, he is drowning his loss at a bar in SoHo when --- of all people --- Jack Campbell strolls in. This time he is without his entourage. As always, Greg is impressed with his good looks and air of confidence. Greg was never much for sports, but this unbelievably beautiful man is a naturally gifted athlete and it shows with his every step.

Jack sits on the stool right next to him without any hesitation. "Hey, dude," he greets Greg with a charming smile and strong handshake. He acts as if they've been friends for years and Greg soon learns that Jack has noticed him, too. "What's happened?"

"What makes you thing something's happened?"

"I don't know too many young guys who spend a couple of hours at a bar alone unless something's happened."

"My girlfriend dumped me today."

"Shit."

"It came right out of the blue."

"We've all been there, dude."

It is nice for him to have someone to talk to. The rest of the night they cover anything and everything: school, families, women, careers, politics and so much more. Jack knows something about any topic. There are times when he seems to flirt with Greg, and Greg likes it, and starts hoping it will lead to more. But then he acts like they are just two guys hanging out. It confuses him, but then the whole world seems confusing.

Greg calls to the bartender for a refill, but Jack stops him. "You gotta take it easy, dude. Getting wasted really won't help anything."

"I know, but what else is there?"

"Just relax, relax."

Greg nods and closes his eyes. For a moment, just a moment, he is calm. The noise of the few remaining customers fades away. The scent of spilt beer dissipates. The hot air around him cools off.

Greg opens his eyes. Gone are the bar and the bartender. The dude commiserating with him has disappeared. The smells have changed. He is surprised to find himself not sitting on a barstool, but lying in a bed. *What the fuck happened?* There are wires connected to him and florescent lights buzzing overhead. A woman is sitting in a plastic chair. She looks worn, her own eyes are closed. He can even hear her snore a little.

I'm in a hospital. How the hell did I end up in a hospital? Greg tries to move but finds his muscles stiff from inaction. Finally, he manages to shift a leg. It startles the woman, who jolts awake.

"Uh? What . . . Greg? Greg, you're awake . . ."

She rises, caresses his forehead and gives him a little kiss. "Thank God, your back with us."

EPISODE ELEVEN

"They say you should talk to coma patients. So, I've visited you every day and every day I tell you about what is happening at home, with the family. Do you remember any of it?"

Greg shakes his head. He's still very confused. Less than an hour ago he was sitting in a bar, getting wasted, just thinking about what he it was he did, what it was he said, to make Lauren turn on him. *Why didn't she love me?* He looks at the woman. She seems familiar to him. But it takes a while to figure it out. *Is she a friend? One of my hook-ups?* Then it hits him: of course, *it's Ben King's daughter.* "Why are you here?"

"Where else would I be?" she answers. "Despite everything I <u>have</u> to be here." This makes no sense to him.

"No, I mean, why are you in New York?"

Now she is the one who's confused. "What are you talking about?" *What was her name? Jennifer? Jane? I know that it starts with a J . . .*

"Are you in town with your dad?"

"He's out campaigning with Mom. I'm not sure exactly where. What does he have to do with anything?"

"Don't get me wrong, I appreciate your being here. I just . . ." his head feels woozy. *When will that damned doctor be back?* "Sorry . . . did someone call my parents?"

Suddenly, the woman's expression changes; Greg can almost see a light bulb in her head switching on. She has realized something. "Greg, where do you think you are?"

"New York."

"Why New York?"

"I go to college here. I start my senior year in the fall."

✴✴✴✴

"It must be a side effect."

Julie and Dr. Walter Smythe are standing outside Greg's room. The situation really worries her. There is also a police guard, as there has been every day and night since the poisoning. Only Julie and Joan Lansing have been allowed to visit him. A lot of people, especially Aunt Karen, have asked over and over to come by but the authorities are adamant. Joan is back in Boston, leaving Julie to be her husband's sole visitor. Julie will need to call Joan soon with the news that her nephew is finally awake.

"Does he recognize you?"

"Only as Ben King's daughter; he doesn't seem to know we are married or about Johnny or Ann or anything else. Doctor, he still thinks his parents are alive."

"There is so much about this case we can't predict. It wasn't just the poison, but the concussion he sustained when hitting the floor. The coma was his brain's way of shutting down until he could recover."

"I suppose, but he's been unconscious almost three months --- do you think there is any brain damage?"

The doctor pauses a moment to think, scratching his gray beard. This man has a lot of gray, in his hair, in his skin and even his eyes. "Not according to the latest tests, but we will run more." In the meantime, he suggests consulting a psychologist before anyone tells Greg the truth. "We don't want to shock him."

****

As a girl, growing up on a crumbling farm, Ann Gale would lie on her second hand bed to stare at the cracked ceiling and dream of her wedding. It would be in a garden, surrounded by colorful blooms and rich with fragrance. The most glamorous celebrities would be there. She'd be wearing a designer dress and the guests would dine on imported china. All of the kids from high school, the girls who mocked her and the boys who ignored her, would look on with envy.

The memories of those teen fantasies have been coming back to Ann Halloran, in a way they never did for her first wedding. Things are so very different now; she's not marrying the farmhand. She's marrying a handsome, sophisticated senator who loves her.

"I adore the idea of pale, pink carnations," the wedding planner says, waving her hands as if the flowers could magically appear before them. This woman, Natalie Ramsey, is considered one of Boston's finest. She was recommended by Joan Lansing, who gave her the name even though she clearly did not care much for the family interloper asking for her help.

"That does sound pretty, but do you think they'll look elegant enough?"

"Of course, the ballroom is perfect." The gentle, red haired lady assures her.
They are sitting in the Blue Room going over the final plans. For this wedding,
Ann gets to use the Halloran mansion. Julie gave her permission about a week
after Greg's collapse. She wasn't happy at the request. With her husband fighting
for his life, the last thing she wants to deal with is a party. Ann realized almost as
she asked the question how rude it must have sounded. Julie approved the request
by saying curtly "it's your house, too."

March has been unusually warm and there has been talk of having the ceremony
in the garden, where Greg and Julie wed last year. This would have brought
Ann's childhood fantasy into reality. But not all the flowers have bloomed yet
and, besides, the crew remodeling the old servants quarters is still back there
working on the building. Ann's first inclination was to wait until summer, but
Richard wants to get married right away. So, while the reception will be in the
mansion's ballroom, Ann has reluctantly agreed to have the ceremony at the
Faraway Hill Unitarian Church --- the same place she married Mark. The church
is located right in the town square and a short distance from the mansion. Since
she has to use the church again, Ann is determined to make the site of her
greatest humiliation the place for her most public triumph.

They go over some more details. Richard has left nearly all the planning to her,
but he has some important people who have yet to RSVP. "Don't worry," Mrs.
Ramsey says confidently. "I'll take care of it."

Ann's cell rings. It's her mother. She asks Mrs. Ramsey to give her a moment,
and the woman leaves to revisit the ballroom.

"Hi Mom, how is the trip?"

"Wonderful. Vivian and I are having the best time of our life." She goes on and
on about the places they've been and the people they've met. It's good to hear
how happy she is, especially after all that hell with Munroe and Mike Bickel.
"We are so excited about the wedding . . . and, sweetie, we will have a surprise
for you, too." Ann presses her for more, but she refuses to give any hints. It
doesn't matter; her mother is happy.

****

Julie wants to sit but can't. After three agonizing months, Greg has finally woken
up. Now she is nervously pacing the office of the hospital's psychologist,
who has spent the last hour with her revived husband, anxiously waiting for
an explanation.

It doesn't help that the woman has those silly, inspirational posters hanging on
her walls. One is the famously insipid "hang in there" kitty. Every piece of

furniture but the desk and file cabinets is made of wicker. Julie half expects to find some joints stashed in a drawer.

"I'm sorry, Mrs. Halloran," she says returning. "But I had to take an emergency call." The psychologist is a woman in her early thirties dressed in an overflowing, flowery caftan and her hair in braids. *What the hell does she think this is, the summer of love?*

"That's okay . . . what can you tell me about Greg?"

"It is too early for a final diagnosis, but everything points to a form of retrograde amnesia."

"What's that?"

"It's a condition where the brain has blocked out a period of time in the patient's memory. Usually, it is just a matter of hours or days. But there have been cases where it's been longer."

"But he's lost almost three years!"

"Yes, that is unusual, but not unprecedented." The doctor gently smiles. "May I ask," she says with what sounds like a well-rehearsed Mother Earth voice, "what have the last few years been like for Greg?"

"Well . . . they've been pretty hard on him." *Hard doesn't even begin to describe it.* "I'm sure you've heard all about it: his mother dying, his father being murdered on our wedding night, learning about his half-sister, my giving birth prematurely. All of it covered in the papers and on the web. Do you think all of this has been too much for him?"

"It is possible that his mind, as a defense, decided to take advantage of the coma to block these events."

"Will it be permanent?"

"I doubt it; at some point, the block will fade and his memories return. But there is no way to predict when."

"What should I do?"

"Start bringing him up-to-date. He needs to start living his life again, rejoining the present." The irony of that advice is not lost on Julie, especially when the doctor offers her some herbal tea. "It's organic."

****

Jack calls the Halloran office again and again no one gives him any information. The man he loves has been in a coma for months and no one will tell him anything. Julie won't speak to him. The hospital won't talk to anyone but family. The company has issued few statements. So the *Union Leader* and Patrick Halloran have been the only way to know what is going on. He can't even visit since the police have a 24-hour guard at the door.

Everything about Greg's coma has been a shock. He collapsed after drinking some poisoned imported tea and nearly died. The last news reports had the authorities trying to determine whether someone in Manchester is responsible, or someone overseas.

Joe is another concern. He has been complaining about stomach pains and a weak appetite. Little Jack is getting scared about his papa but his papa refuses to see a doctor. Now, stepping out of the elevator toward Joe's apartment, Jack runs into Nathaniel, the elderly gentleman who lives next door. The man is as fey as they come, right down to the ascot and powder blue blazer. Jack enjoys fucking other men, but doesn't care much for gay men who insist on being walking testaments to faggotry. "Hello my dear, how is our friend doing?"

As far as Jack knows, Nathaniel is the only other person in the building aware of Joe being transsexual. Hopefully the man hasn't told anyone else; Jack can easily picture the old biddy gossiping under a hair dryer at the local beauty salon. "Not well, and I just don't know what to do about it. He won't see a doctor and won't tell me why."

"Well, I may have figured that out."

"Oh?"

"Yes," he motions Jack over as if he's about to tell some deep dark, secret. This is strange since no one else is in the hall. "I have a friend who lives on the north side of Manchester," Nathanial whispers. "She's transsexual too and she tells me that many trans are afraid to go to a new doctor; they are afraid of the prejudice and so forth."

"Okay," Jack whispers back. "So what do we do?"

"There is a town about an hour north called Lebanon. They have a first-rate hospital called the Dartmouth-Hitchcock." Jack recognizes the name from ads the medical center runs across the state. "They have a transgender clinic where they do surgeries and follow-up care."

"It sounds perfect."

Nathaniel has him wait as he steps back into his apartment. He reappears a moment later with a brochure. "The address and everything is on here, including their web site."

"Thank you."

"I hope he'll go."

"He damn well *will go*, even if I have to kidnap him."

****

Greg wants to take a shower. He wants to take one bad. Not that he needs it; he feels clean. But the hot pounding water always relaxes him. Yet, every time he tries to stand up he gets dizzy. Just taking a leak was a chore. An orderly had to assist him. The last time another guy helped him piss, it was after the both of them got wasted at some frat party.

He is back in bed now, bored and confused. *Why the fuck haven't my parents called? Why the hell is there a guard at the door?* No one, not the doctor nor Julie King or the hippie psychologist will give him any answers. Just hours ago he was getting drunk at a Greenwich Village bar with that hunky dude from the Stern, trying to forget the woman who dumped him. Now he lies here in a New Hampshire hospital bed, all alone.

A gentle knock on the door and Julie returns with the retro head shrinker. The doctor has what looks like a folded newspaper. They are both smiling, but it is a nervous smile. *Something is wrong. Something is very wrong.* The two women greet him and move a pair of chairs next to the bed. They sit in the same awkward way they are smiling. *Oh, fuck, what does this mean?*

"Well, Greg, we appreciate your patience," the doctor says. "I know --- we know --- how strange and confusing this situation is."

"I just want to know what's going on. Have my parents been called? What about my girlfriend?"

The doctor hands him the newspaper. "I think you should look at this." Greg takes it from her. Its today's *Union Leader*. And the date is wrong. "What does this mean?"

****

Faraway Hill's little town hall is located just a few steps from the Unitarian Church and in full view of the town's famous statue. Peter Brandt has visited this small wood frame building many times in his young life. Everyone who grows up in Faraway Hill has. It is a simple building. The clerk and mayor and their few aides work on the first floor. The top floor is for archiving and council meetings. When the whole town needs to convene, they do so in the basement.

"Good morning, Peter."

"Hello, Mrs. Oswald."

The woman smiles a little too much. That means she knows something. Harriet Oswald isn't as old as she looks, but the bun and graying hair make her appear to be from an earlier time. As town clerk, she handles nearly every form of paper Faraway Hill issues or receives or processes. This is a job she has held forever. Mrs. Oswald also likes keeping up on all the gossip. She's often more reliable than the *Union Leader*.

"The mayor will be available in a moment, he's on the phone. My you look handsome in that uniform."

"Thanks." Since Sheriff Reynolds' death, Peter has been running the department. He and the mayor have had multiple meetings since. They are typically over little things that get resolved in a matter of minutes.

"And," she leans in with a sly wink, "everyone says that you and Karen Scott make a very nice couple." Some of the older locals still refer to Karen by her maiden name.

"Thank you, ma'am." He's happy that their affair is so well known. It is too hard to keep a secret in Faraway Hill and he'd rather not try. Besides, Peter has been aware for sometime that he is falling in love and has wanted to scream it from the middle of the town square. "But you know, she's Karen St. John now."

"Oh, please! They will always be the Scott girls to me. You two are quite an item. Everyone's is just thrilled, even if she is old enough to be your mother. Does it mean that this Scott girl . . . well, will she become Mrs. Brandt?"

That thought has been crossing his mind lately. "Now, now, Mrs. Oswald, that's between Karen and me."

"Oh, I know young man, I know. Still, an old fashioned wedding would be nice at the church again. They had another same-sex ceremony last weekend."

"I heard." The mention of a wedding has him picturing himself in that very church, standing by the altar, watching a beaming Karen as she walks down the aisle.

"Two women from somewhere in New York. Syracuse, I think. It was very nice but . . . well, it happens so often these days."

"It <u>is</u> the twenty-first century."

"Oh, I'm not judging . . . exactly."

"That's enough, Harriett," a gruff voice interrupts her. "I need to speak to the deputy, alone."

Peter smiles politely at her then follows the mayor into his office where the old man closes the door and gets right down to business.

"Since George Reynolds died last month, the council and I have been meeting with the selectmen from neighboring towns. I am sure you've been hearing about it, what with all the talk that goes around."

"Yes, sir." There are rumors of a merger. If that happens, Peter could be out of a job.

"The stories are true: have decided to merge our police departments. Of course, this will require town-wide meetings and approval from Concord, but I see them as mostly a formality. This will lead to some layoffs, unfortunately, but it will be more cost efficient."

"So, does this mean I'm unemployed?"

"Not at all, Peter. We want you to become the first chief of the Faraway Hill Unified Police Department."

"Me? But, Mr. Fitzgerald, I think I'm a little too young . . ."

The eighty-something mayor waves away his protest. "Yes, yes, I am well aware of that. But don't sell yourself short. You've got a college degree, you've had plenty of administrative experience --- both here in Faraway Hill and overseas with your charity work --- and, to be quite frank, a younger man will cost less that a more seasoned one."

"I suppose that I should be flattered."

"Absolutely," the old man says with a smile. "We are not telling anyone yet, not formally. There are some hoops we much jump through first. But . . . feel free to tell you're your parents --- and that charming woman you've been seeing. It looks like there may be a future there for you as well."

Maybe there is, he thinks.

****

Karen St. John leans back in her chair and flips through a copy of last month's *Boston Magazine*. A six-page spread in the middle showcases her magnificent new house. "A doyenne of New York society for years" reads the article, "Karen St. John has returned to her historic home town in New Hampshire where she has renovated a former bed and breakfast into one of New England's most elegant and magnificent residences." Her decorator gets his own quotes in, but it is Karen and her house that are the focus. *As it should be.* She bought two dozen extra copies for her friends in Manhattan, who all wrote back that they are thrilled for her. *And jealous, no doubt.*

Everything is going well. Maybe not exactly as planned, but no matter: Poisoning Greg's tea was easy. No one suspects her, and why should they? But with Greg out of the way, Karen is getting closer and closer to setting the world right. *Daddy would be so proud.*

Her reverie is disturbed by the annoying squawk of her cell phone. *Who the hell invented such things anyway?* She sees that it is Julie calling. *Good, maybe the ass has finally died. It sure as hell has been taking him long enough.* "Hello, dear, how are things going today?" Like most people, Karen hasn't been allowed in to see Greg. She even tried to bribe someone --- through Denise for safety --- but it didn't work.

"Aunt Karen, I have wonderful news."

"You do?" *No, please, no: don't let this be what I think.*

"Greg woke up today. He is awake and talking and everything." *Shit! Shit! Shit!* It takes Karen every ounce of strength to fake her response.

"I am so happy for you, Julie. Does he . . . does he remember what happened? With the poison, I mean."

"No, and maybe that's a good thing." *Damn right it's a good thing.* "Look, I have to go. I just wanted you to be the first to know. You've been so supportive of me."

"That's because I love you more than you can possibly know."

"Bye".

Karen sets down the phone. *Shit! Shit! Shit! Whoever heard of someone waking up from a coma this long? And what the fuck went wrong with that poison? It should have worked!* Unable to control her anger, she grabs a big, crystal vase from a table and throws it with all her might at the painting of Lake Winnipesauke hanging over the mantel, shattering the vase into thousands of pieces.

Shit! Shit! Shit!

****

Eve King was born in New Hampshire, married here and raised a daughter here. But she has never seen as much of the state as she has in the last few months. There was Stratford, a town of 900 people near the Vermont border popular with ATV enthusiasts. They've been to Albany, home to 600 people not far from Maine who boast of the most photographed mountain in the Northeast. But today is special, because today they are in Keene. Eve and Karen grew up in this city of 23,000 where the memory of their father remains beloved among the older faculty at the college.

It feels good walking these streets again, especially on a sunny spring day. The temperature must be in the mid-50s, brisk but comfortable. Eve is enjoying the sites from childhood, like the Horatio Colony Museum and Miller Brothers where Daddy used to buy his suits to even the hardware store over on Park Avenue.

It's still just the primary season; each party has only one man vying for nominations: Ben for the Democrats and Adam Newman for the Republicans. The last several weeks have been a warm-up for the fall. It sometimes seems like one candidate has been following the other. This morning, Newman gave a live interview to Dan Mitchell on one of the local radio stations. He hit all the right notes, stating positions in just the right way to please Mitchell's conservative audience without alienating anyone else. Ben, in turn, is currently taping an interview with Keene State's radio station. The college's students make up more than a quarter of the city's population.

Right now she is sitting in the Chase Tavern, the restaurant of the E. F. Lane Hotel which itself is a recent change to Keene: it's a former department store renovated into a boutique inn that is becoming increasingly popular with visiting parents and other tourists.

"Excuse me," the waitress says refilling her coffee. "Aren't you Senator King's wife?"

"Yes, I am."

"Oh, good; I _really_ like your husband. He's like a breath of fresh air."

"Thank you."

"Is it true you grew up in Keene?"

"Yes, I did." The two have a friendly chat about all the changes that have happened over the years, most of which the waitress seems to like. "I'm a big fan of the Colony Mill," she says of the former textile mill that was converted into a shopping center in the 1980s. They talk about everything from the Two Arch Stone Bridge to the Wyman Tavern until another customer gestures for service.

Eve can't help but smile. Part of her wishes Mom hadn't moved them to Faraway Hill after Daddy died. The waitress stops by again, to say "I hope your son-in-law gets better." The attempt on Greg's life made news across New England; it even had a big write up in the *Boston Globe*. "Thank you." The scandal over Greg's poisoning reminds Eve of the potential scandal lurking in the shadows. No one has heard anything from Mark since Ben and Grace confronted him in January. But that's no guarantee they won't.

Eve adds a little more cream to the coffee when her cell buzzes. It's a text from Julie with three surprising words: "greg is awake".

****

Greg is crying. He hates crying. It makes him feel weak and childish. But he can't help it. His is lying on the bed, still clad just in that flimsy hospital gown while the psychologist sits patiently at his side. The tears flow and flow until they stop, like a tub than finally drained all its water. He wipes his soaking wet face with a wad of tissues. "I'm sorry."

"That's okay, Greg," the therapist says. "The crying is to be expected." He shakes his head, not believing her. "It is. Your mind has been through a lot, bio-chemically speaking. Being emotional is understandable."

"It just is . . . so much. My parents are gone, I've got a sister and a wife and a son, people I don't even know. On top of all that someone tried to kill me. <u>To kill me</u>. Why the hell would anyone want to kill me?"

"The police are still trying to figure that out."

An idea crosses his mind, something that he has considered before with all the lovers he's had since boarding school. Things did not end well with all of them. "Do you think . . . do you think someone tried to murder me for . . . revenge?"

"What makes you say that?"

"I don't know . . . Julie tells me my dad knocked up some woman and I have sister I've never known. Maybe I was cheating, too. Maybe some husband or boyfriend tried to get me." *Or,* he thinks, *some wife did it because I was fucking her old man.*

The therapist shakes her head sympathetically. "Not likely. You haven't been married a year and no one --- including your wife --- has even hinted any sort of infidelity." Greg isn't so sure: he's always had doubts about his ability to be faithful to anyone. Lauren was the first person he considered committing to. And she dumped him.

"Just give it time, Greg, and everything will work out."

****

Patrick Halloran is exhausted. He is sitting behind Greg's desk at the Millyard, eyes closed, trying to take a break. He spends too much time on the road, shuttling from school in Boston to the company offices in Manchester to visiting his mother in her Concord nursing home and back again. Aunt Joan and Robert insisted that someone from the family be at the company on a regular basis. Patrick was elected because he is the only person available.

What is worse is that he finds himself in the middle of a bizarre love triangle. Two months ago, Julie confided in Patrick his cousin's surprising affair with another man --- confirming what Robert told him last winter at the Brothers' lodge. Now he is fielding calls from Jack Campbell desperate for news of his lover. It's an awkward position. Jack seems like a nice guy and Patrick feels that he shouldn't hide things from him. But he also likes Julie and it feels strange talking to the man who is fucking his married cousin.

There is also the occasional call from a reporter about Greg's condition and Ann's impending marriage. He has given standing orders to not tell the media anything about the former, and refer all queries about the latter to Senator Davis' people.

"Mr. Halloran?"

Patrick opens his eyes. *I wish people would let me sleep.* With the Thailand strike over and the executives handing day-to-day operations there isn't much else to do. Sitting in this chair is often the only rest he gets. "Yes, Mrs. Stone?"

"It's him." *Shit.* Patrick picks up the phone. "Yes, Robert?"

Patrick comes into the office about three days a week and every day Robert calls with questions and instructions. The man makes Patrick feel like nothing more than a glorified intern. They discuss some matters involving the mill in Faraway

Hill and the latest little crisis with the Georgia plant. There are also some real estate projects that need tending. Mercifully, the conversation lasts just a few minutes.

Now armed with his list of chores, Patrick is about to call the necessary people when Mrs. Stone reappears with the news that "Mrs. Halloran is on the phone. She says it's urgent." *Holy fuck, something must have happened to Greg.*

"Patrick, good news: Greg has woken up!"

"Damn, Julie that *is* great news. How is he?"

"Physically he seems okay, but he's having some memory problems."

"What sort of problems?"

"I'll explain that tonight at the house. Frederick is calling everyone in driving distance. It's important."

"Don't worry, I'll be there."

****

They have all gathered together, crowding the usually spacious Blue Room. Julie surveys the assembly: Ben has adjusted his campaign schedule so that he and Eve can be here. Patrick decided to stay the night rather than go back to school. Ann and Richard cancelled their dinner plans in Concord. Even Joan has driven in from Boston, bringing her son Matthew and boy-toy husband Paul along. The little group is waiting for Karen to arrive, which miffs Joan. "I don't see why we need to wait for *her*."

"Because she is Julie's aunt," defends Agnes Gabler who insists on being present. Julie is grateful for the woman's support, especially since even her mother doesn't look happy about Karen coming. When she does arrive, it is with her usual flourish, something that never fails to make Julie smile.

For the next several minutes, Julie briefs them all. "Greg has what they are calling retrograde amnesia. Apparently it's his mind's way of protecting himself after the hellish couple of years --- you know, from his mom's death to the poisoning and all" she glances at Ann, who at least has the good sense not to say anything. "I am slowly bringing him up to speed but he already seems overwhelmed. He's even been crying."

"How sad."

"I know, Aunt Karen, but they say his emotions are all up in the air. The last thing he remembers is breaking up with his college girlfriend --- and then waking up in the hospital."

"When can we see him," Joan asks; actually, she almost demands it. "He needs to be around family."

"In a few days."

"We should have a party, to welcome him back."

"No, Joan, I think it should be quieter than that. He's already got a lot to deal with. Let's not add any, I don't know, hassle."

✴✴✴✴

Some clients are just not worth the hassle. Well, almost not worth it.

Mark Bradley has returned to his apartment, exhausted, angry and frustrated. He just gave an old man in Brooklyn a lap dance followed by a blow job --- all for a measly hundred bucks. This is how far he has sunk, to the level of a go-go boy or a street walker. *I used to fuck the best people for the big envelopes filled with cash.* Now he has to do what he must to earn whatever he can. Greg Halloran's coma has made Mark's blackmail moot --- and his annual rent payment is coming up in just a few weeks.

The old bastard didn't even let me cum. He may have to jack-off to ease the pressure. But Mark hates doing that; it means waiting at least two days before he has a sufficient load built up for another trick.

So, instead, he flops down on the leather sofa and picks up the *New York Times* hoping to take his mind off things. It doesn't help. Flipping page after page, ignoring stories about the economy and the Middle East and a crime spree on Staten Island, Mark's eye catching a small piece, a write-up with a photo. The photo is of his wife, standing next to well-known older man. The brief article begins with "U.S. Senator Richard Davis to marry textile heiress Ann Halloran . . ."

With a howl of laughter, he screams "Fucking A!"

EPISODE TWELVE

It's early in the morning. The sun is just starting its climb into the sky. The little town of Faraway Hill is very quiet. Just off the main square there is a beautifully redecorated old home, nearly perfect save a few pieces of broken glass scattered undiscovered under the living room sofa. Upstairs, Peter Brandt is lying naked in bed admiring the remarkable woman next to him. *She is amazing.* Old enough to be his mother, Karen's body is still as sexy as any of the girls he's known. Nips and tucks and regular exercise --- not to mention good genes --- all pay off. Then there is her skill as a lover. She never fails to get him hard, to discover new things about his own body and make each night together unforgettable.

Everyone in town knows about them; small towns trade on gossip. Fortunately, his ailing parents approve. "We just want you to be happy," said his mother. He also loved telling Karen the news last night of his promotion. They celebrated with a dinner in Manchester followed by hours of slow, sensual love making.

"Good morning, lover," she purrs, her eyes fluttering open.

"Good morning." He kisses her lightly on the cheek.

"Are you staring at me?"

"I only stare at beautiful things."

Karen's hand slides under the covers and slowly strokes his cock. "I like an appreciative man."

He loves her touch, her caress. It won't take much for him to get hard again. But there is something he needs to do first, something that will make the night and morning complete. Peter reaches across the bed to his blazer, which is lying on a chair nearby. He pulls out a little box covered in black felt. "I love you Karen, I love you more than I've loved anyone."

"How sweet."

"Please marry me." Peter opens the little box. Inside is a simple, elegant ring. He bought it yesterday at Pearson's, one the state's best jewelers. The store has been in the same family for nearly a century, and important people like the Hallorans have shopped there for years. What is inside this little box cost him a third of his life savings. But Peter knows that a woman like Karen St. John is accustomed to the finest things and this is the finest thing he has ever purchased.

Peter waits for his answer. He looks at Karen, enjoying the warm smile on her elegant face. But she doesn't say anything. She doesn't say anything for the longest time. "Thank you my darling," she finally answers, "but the answer is no."

He cringes, as if someone just slapped him or punched in the stomach. *She can't be serious.* "But we love each other. If it's about the money, I don't give a damn how rich you are. I'll sign any pre-nup you want. I don't give a fuck about that; I just want to spend my life with you."

Karen shakes her head. "I'm sorry, but as much as I adore you --- and as much fun as we have --- I never plan to marry again. Never. Once was enough."

"But . . ."

"No, Peter, no. Let's just stay as we are."

Now he feels something different. Not the chock of a slap but a deep, internal pain. Like someone has just stabbed him, burying a knife deep into his chest and twisted it. "I don't think that I can do that." With that, Peter rises, nude, dresses in stoic silence and leaves his lover alone.

But outside, on the porch, he allows himself to cry.

✱✱✱✱

Greg is feeling better today. Julie can tell. He is calmer and more like his usual self. He also saw his son for the first time. The way Greg held him and looked into the boy's eyes reminded Julie of those days right after Johnny was born and they felt like a family. *Oh, God,* Julie quietly prayed, *please let us be like this again, be like this from now on.*

Her mother has since taken the baby home so that they can finally meet with the police. But the interview is frustrating; Greg can only tell them so much.

"And that's all you remember, Mr. Halloran?" Victor Romero is a detective with the Manchester Police Department. He is balding, overweight and in a rumpled suit just a little too small for him. The man reminds her of Peter Falk from those old "Columbo" episodes that pop up on late-night cable from time to time.

"Yes, I'm sorry."

Romero nods. All he needs is a trench coat. "The doctors have told me of your amnesia. But if you should remember something, please call us immediately."

"I will."

"As you probably know, the FBI has been very involved in the case. We have been . . . well, sir, frustrated because nothing in our investigation has led anywhere. There appear to be no suspects, you seem to have no enemies, the security cameras at the Millyard have shown nothing unusual. The only fingerprints belong to you and your secretary. For these reasons, the feds are convinced that someone in Bangkok spiked the tea rather than someone locally. No one is sure why but it probably had something to do with that strike over there. According to what I heard this morning, the Thai government --- including the king --- is sending formal apologizes."

Julie eyes him suspiciously. "What does that mean?"

"It means Mrs. Halloran that the investigation has moved overseas and once Mr. Halloran leaves the hospital, we will be ending the police protection. I don't think that there is any more risk."

"No more risk!" *I should kick him in the ass.* "Someone tried to murder my husband and damn near succeeded."

"Ma'am, but I agree with the feds: the tea was tainted overseas."

"Other people received that tea as a gift --- how many of them got sick?"

"No one, at least that we know of."

Julie glances at Greg, who obviously doesn't know what to say. *He's still disoriented.* "Don't you think that's odd?"

"Not necessarily ma'am. The federal investigators think that this was a test, a trial balloon by some terrorists, to see if a broader poisoning would work. Obviously it didn't."

"But won't they try another way?"

"Mrs. Halloran, please, whoever was behind this failed and know they failed. The feds have experts in this area. It was a terror group experimenting for a possible bigger attack, one that is now unlikely since it didn't work."

What bullshit! "I think they'll try again. We're Hallorans, one of the oldest families in the country. Hell, our home was patterned after the White House for God's sake!"

"Ma'am, with all respect, as important as the Hallorans are these people have . . . bigger targets."

That's it: I should definitely kick him in the ass.

****

Ann and Richard are holding hands, waiting in the VIP lounge at the Manchester International Airport. It was in this same room, less than a year ago, when the Hallorans met Greg and Julie coming back from their honeymoon. Ann wasn't present, but heard later how emotional it was.

The two of them sit in overstuffed chairs, looking out the huge window at the planes coming and going, connecting New Hampshire with a wider world. There was a time when Ann dreamed of sitting in this lounge, of taking one of those jets to someplace exotic and different. It would be a glamorous place where she would be special and important.

Richard gently squeezes her hand. He does these little things. She likes it. He may lack the passions of Mark Bradley or the youthful energy of Peter Brandt, but Ann can sense something more, something deeper within this wonderful man. She is certain that *this* is a marriage that will work.

"Hello," a joyful voice calls out. Ann looks up to see her mother, a radiant smile on her face, holding hands with Vivian at the door. Hugs and "I missed you" and laughs are exchanged all around. To Ann, it seems that her mother has finally put the dark period of her life behind her. "Tell us ladies," Richard insists. "What is that news you've been promising us?"

The two women exchange knowing looks. "Think we should tell them?" Lorene asks her lover.

"If you won't, I will. I can't wait any more!"

"Mom, what the hell is going on?"

"Darling, Vivian and I are engaged."

****

Chaos reigns supreme as florists and caterers and decorators all descend on the Halloran mansion. The maids are scurrying about, Frederick the butler is trying to maintain his composure and the wedding planner is panicking about something new every few minutes.

Matthew Newberry has come up from Boston to visit his cousins and be a guest at the great event. And what an event it will be: papers across New England are talking about Lewis Halloran's bastard daughter walking down the aisle with a United States Senator old enough to be her father.

His mother will not be coming. "Why the hell should *I* want to be there? It's too humiliating." No matter how hard Matthew tries, she just won't accept Ann as part of the family. Not that he likes her anymore than anyone else, but the woman isn't going anywhere. "Shouldn't we just make the best of it?" Matthew asked his stepfather the other day. "Don't know dude," was his less than witty reply. It galls him that his mother would marry such a himbo.

Matthew needs to escape the whirl around him. He also needs some advice. His cousin Patrick is upstairs, staying in the suite that was Greg's growing up. He's the only member of the family close to Matthew's age. A quick knock and he opens the door a crack. "Is it okay if I come in?"

Patrick is lying on the sofa, giving himself a break. He needs one. For the last few months he has been burning the candle at both ends, finishing up at Harvard while handling business issues. "Yeah, sure."

"I'm sorry about waking you."

"Nah, I wasn't asleep. I can't seem to sleep. You ever get that way, so tired that no matter how hard you try you just can't nod off? Frustrating as all hell."

Matthew looks around him. The last time he was in here, at Christmas, there was still some of Greg's college mementos scattered about. Most of them are gone now, no doubt moved into the master suite. But a few things remain, like an NYU pendant tacked to a wall. Matthew's own college career starts this fall, at Harvard, just months after Patrick graduates.

"So, what's bothering you, dude? Is it school, your mom, something about Greg? I hear he's doing better." Matthew notices a photo of Patrick's parents on the desk. They look young and attractive and happy. It must have been taken shortly after their marriage.

"Yeah, he'll be coming home soon. It must be weird, losing two years of your life."

Patrick nods. "No, shit. Although I'm starting to feel like I'm in my own limbo. Work, work and work is all I do anymore. I haven't seen my buddies in weeks. There was this girl . . . but that went nowhere."

"Yeah, I guess it all sucks. But weren't you supposed to go into the family business?"

"At some point, sure, but not like this. I spend most of my time driving from school to Mom's nursing home to the office to here and back to Harvard. It's like I'm in hell --- <u>and hell is on wheels</u>." Patrick sits up and looks at him, almost like a guy with his kid brother. "So, dude, out with it: what's bothering you?"

"Well, I . . ." *This is so fucking embarrassing.* "I have another initiation rite coming up."

"And you're scared."

"Yeah, I guess so."

"Where are you in the process? I mean what have you done so far?"

Matthew starts listing them: the classes in the Brothers history, which he finds fascinating and is going well, as are the Latin lessons. He is also learning how to hold his liquor thanks to the drinking contests. "I don't puke as easily as I did." But the athletics are a problem. "I'm not a jock and they have me running through the woods and wrestling and trying to hit a baseball . . . and I suck at all of them."

"You'll get better. The process can take up to four years. But from what I hear, you're doing really well. You'll probably become a full Brother faster than I did."

"That would be cool, I guess. But I am worried about . . . the other stuff." So far he and his tutor have only jerked off together. "It wasn't too bad, but . . . I kind of know what's coming up."

"You've been tested?"

"Yes," Matthew nods. "I'm negative."

"That's not a surprise since you're a virgin --- or have you finally hooked up with some girl at school?" Matthew blushes. There is a girl he's interested in, but she barely notices him. "Don't be embarrassed, besides I found that the stuff we do in the Brothers helps with girls."

"They do?"

"Sure, you gain confidence and you learn what to do. Anyway, your tutor gets tested too. I'll give you some tips. But soon you'll be doing these things with other plebes, which is a lot easier --- especially since there is no pressure to please someone who outranks you." Patrick offers him a wicked smile. "Is there a girl?"

Matthew blushes again. "Yeah, she goes to our sister school a couple of miles away. But she's going to college in Virginia. I'll probably never see her again."

"Too bad."

"Yeah . . . what is that last one like, the final initiation?"

Patrick shakes his head. "I can't tell you." No one can; no one is allowed to and they both know it. Matthew sighs, thanks him, and leaves his cousin alone to get what little rest he can.

****

Jack can't wait any longer. He has been patient for months. Now his lover is awake and he wants --- no, he *needs* --- to see him; his wife be damned. And Jack is determined to make it happen sooner than later. So he is standing outside Elliott Hospital knowing that Julie can't leave without confronting him.

Health crisis have been dominating Jack's life recently. His brother calls every few days with news of their father, who seems determined to torture his family by almost --- but not actually --- dying. Not that it matters much to Jack; he's sure the old man has rewritten his will. But he hates what it's doing to his mother. The woman deserves better.

Then there is Joe, who has finally agreed to see a doctor. They are making a third trip to Dartmouth-Hitchcock later today. The first was for a consultation and the second for some tests. All the while, Joe's pains come and go. He is losing weight and both Jack and their son are getting scared. The boy has started to take care of his papa, almost like <u>he</u> is the parent. It's sweet, but worrisome. He should be enjoying his childhood.

"Oh, shit," Julie grumbles as she emerges. "What the hell are you doing here?"

"I want to see Greg."

"You can't; only immediate family. Fuck buddies are not allowed."

"Damn it all to hell, Julie! I love him and this isn't fair!"

"Fair!" She looks ready to punch him. *Bring it on; I've had enough.* "You want to tell me about fair! Greg is my husband, not yours."

"It won't always be that way. Shit, you agreed to a divorce months ago so that we can be together."

"Well, I've got some news for you pal. There may not be a divorce."

"What the hell are you talking about?"

"Greg woke up with a form of amnesia," she explains with a triumphant smile. "Yeah, that's right. He can't remember the last two years or so --- including you. Isn't that a kick in the ass?"

"Bullshit."

"Nope, it's true. He doesn't remember fucking you or marrying me or his dad's murder --- but I tell you, this is one hell of a guy. He is just stand-up enough to want our marriage to work and I'm seriously thinking about letting him."

"You fucking bitch."

This time she does punch him, in the gut, so hard and so surprising that he stumbles back a few steps. *Wow, she's tougher than I thought.* "Don't you ever, *ever*, call me that! I've been nothing but reasonable and understanding while you humiliated me over and over. Well, Jack, it's done. Even if Greg and I do go ahead and divorce, there is no future for you with him; none at all." She walks over to her car and opens the door. But before getting inside, she turns and makes it clear: "He doesn't remember you and so he doesn't love you. Stay out of our lives, Jack; stay the *fuck* out of our lives."

✱✱✱✱

An hour later and Julie is still pissed at Jack. She spent the time driving around Manchester trying to calm down. *How dare he; how dare that asshole speak to me like that. I'm the one who's been so fucking grownup about everything!* It didn't work. So, instead Julie returns home where she'd slam the front door in frustration if Frederick wasn't holding it for her. Sometimes there is a downside to having a butler.

"Are you okay?" Matthew asks her at the foot of the Grand Staircase. She almost snaps at him, but she stops herself. "Yes, sorry, I'm just dealing with a lot today."

"The wedding and all," he nods, not knowing the truth. The mansion <u>is</u> busy, but right now most of the activity is centered on the ballroom. "I wish everyone would, I don't know, just get over themselves."

"How do you mean?" *He'd damn well better not give me a lecture.*

"About Ann. She's a Halloran whether anyone likes it or not."

He's right; the entire family is still having Ann issues. So am I. But how can we not? Shortly after Greg fell into his coma Ann started planning her wedding as if there was nothing else going on in the world, let alone a major family crisis. "Well, she doesn't make it easy."

"I suppose so."

Julie smiles at him. Talking to Matthew has helped. She climbs the stairs to the second floor to check in on Johnny. The baby is sleeping with the nanny quietly reading nearby. For a brief moment, all is right with the world. She then goes into the master suite. The dress she is to wear at the wedding is hanging on the bedroom door. Julie grudgingly agreed to be Ann's matron of honor --- no one else was willing --- as long as she doesn't have to do anything else.

Frederick has left today's mail on a table. There are a couple of catalogs, her alumni newsletter and a small, elegant envelope. She opens it and finds an invitation to the Currier Museum where "an exciting new acquisition will make its debut." It's a VIP, something only important people like Hallorans receive. It must be a big deal.

Important people; do important people have friends? Do important people have confidants? All through the nightmare of Greg and Jack and the poisoning, Julie has hesitated to talk to anyone. None of her girlfriends would understand. Most of them are intimidated by the big house and her fancy new life. One seemed in awe of her when she and Julie ran into each other at the Mall of New Hampshire last week. Besides, ideally she'd speak to her mother or go to her Aunt Karen for advice. *She would be the best; if anyone is sophisticated enough to get it, it would be Aunt Karen.* But something has always kept her from turning to them. Maybe it was embarrassment or humiliation or maybe, just maybe, something so deep inside her that Julie cannot understand.

"I see you got one, too."

Julie turns to see Agnes, standing with her walker just inside the door. "The Currier invitation; everyone must be getting them."

"Everyone who is anyone, you mean."

"That includes you, Mrs. Halloran."

That includes me. Is it worth it? Is it worth being important? Ann always thought so. Julie never gave it much thought, not until she actually became someone important. *I guess there is no going back.*

"Are you alright dear?" It's interesting how much like a grandmother she can be. This is a woman who has led the most colorful life imaginable. The travels; the famous lovers; the celebrity friends. Yet sometimes Julie can picture her wearing an apron and baking cookies.

"Sure, Agnes, it's just . . . oh, hell it's just everything."

"But you told me that Greg is doing better."

"Yes, but he still doesn't remember anything. The worst part is that the police protection is being pulled."

"Why?"

"Oh, apparently the FBI thinks it was part of some botched terror plot from Asia and doubt they will try again." She still wishes she had kicked that officer. Even punching Jack didn't seem to help.

Agnes closes the door behind her. "That's awful."

"Yeah, well, what can I do about it?" Julie helps her to the comfy, overstuffed settee.

"Is that all that's bother you?"

"Sure," Julie, sitting next to her, answers without even a hint of conviction.

"No, it isn't. I can tell. Ever since I've moved in, something has been bothering you. It's like you have this giant cement block on your shoulders."

"Don't worry, Agnes, its nothing for you to worry about."

"Bullshit!"

"Agnes --- "

"Tell me about it."

"Thank you, but . . ."

"It's no secret around the house that you and your husband have been sleeping apart."

How the hell can she know that? How can anyone?

"Sweetie, you've lived in this mansion for nearly a year and you still haven't learned a crucial fact of life --- that maids gossip? Greg was cheating on you."

The humiliation hits her again, almost as hard as she hit Jack this morning. "Yes."

"Do you know the woman?"

Julie laughs. "Well . . . that's the kicker." To laugh about it feels good. The situation is so damned ridiculous. "It isn't a woman . . . it's the best man from our wedding."

Agnes raises an eyebrow, seeing this as an interesting new twist to an old story. "Oh, dear; well, that sort of thing <u>has</u> been going around for ages. I could tell you a few things about the people I've known! Anyway, this has been going on since the wedding?"

"Not exactly; they were lovers in college who remained friends until last fall, when they hooked up while Greg was out of town."

"I am so very sorry. But . . . you are staying with him."

"Yes . . . no . . . oh shit I don't know! The whole fucking thing is such a mess. I only found out when I saw the two of them kissing. My first inclination was to pack up the baby and leave but . . ."

"But what?"

Damn, it feels good to get this off my chest, to finally have someone to talk to. "My dad is running for office. He does not need to have his daughter caught up in some gay sex scandal. Greg and I agreed to divorce after the election with Johnny and me moving into the old servants' quarters out back."

"So that is why it's being renovated."

"But now . . . but now he doesn't remember anything about Jack and . . . and I feel like I've got my husband back."

"Sweetie," Agnes smiles sympathetically. "Do you think that's realistic? I mean, if he has feelings for this man they could start up again."

"But that's just it; he doesn't even remember Jack. It's part of his amnesia."

"He could still remember. His feelings could still surface."

"Maybe, but there is another interesting twist," Julie starts laughing again, making Agnes curious. "What is it?"

"Well," she takes a deep breath so she can stop laughing long enough to explain. "Jack found out he has a son with this old girlfriend of his."

"That sort of thing happens. Why are you laughing? Are you saying she wants him back?"

This time she can't stop so easily. Agnes looks on, more and more interested as Julie laughs and laughs until finally she gets out the words: "she is now a he!"

****

An hour and half later, Jack is still pissed at Julie. But he manages to put it aside; one of the few good lessons his bastard father tried to instill into him that a true man faces a crisis head-on. Jack hasn't always followed that advice. This time he must.

He and Joe are in the little town of Lebanon. People have told them that it is a pretty place with handsome historic buildings along the Connecticut River. But they barely pay attention to any of it. *Maybe some day,* Jack thinks, *we can spend some time here just exploring the town.* But not today; no, this afternoon the two of them are sitting across from a doctor at the Dartmouth-Hitchcock Medical Center.

"How have you been feeling lately?"

"Well," Joe answers. "I've been bloated and my stomach pains have been more and more severe. It sometimes hurts when I piss and I am seeing some blood."

The doctor nods. He has heard this before, on their previous visits. He doesn't even look up from the file. "And you are still having trouble eating?"

"Yes, and I have diarrhea a couple of times a week."

"Are you in pain, now?"

"No, I'm feeling pretty good today." Joe has enough good days to insist on living his life. He even bought a new car recently, the same one they drove from Manchester.

The doctor nods again, again without looking up from the test results. He closes the file and sets it aside. "I realize that you think of yourself as a man, and in many ways you are a man." He tries to sound sympathetic, but Jack can tell he is one of those types who are more comfortable among test tubes than people. He hooked up with someone like that at college. Unfortunately, the dude developed an embarrassing crush that took weeks to run its course.

"What are you getting at?"

"Part of you will always be a woman."

"Okay . . . what does that mean?"

"I'm sorry to tell you this," the doctor says gently, or at least as gently as he knows. "The CT scan and blood tests have confirmed what we had suspected . . . you have ovarian cancer."

The news is a stunner. Jack and Joe exchange glances. *Holy shit!* Something like this never even occurred to either of them. *I didn't even think Joe still had ovaries.* "How . . . how can . . ."

"We don't know for sure what caused it, but your inconsistent use of testosterone may have been a factor. Testosterone, like all hormone treatments, needs to be monitored." Joe has been on the run for so long he hasn't had any regular doctor visits, and has been refilling his prescription however he can. Jack looks at Joe again. Seeing the tears gently streaming down his face, the man reminds him so much of the woman. Together, holding hands, they hear the doctor speak of "late stage cancer" and how it has "progressed into the upper abdomen" and it becomes increasingly clear that just as the woman has left them, so soon with the man.

****

Life works in patterns. Sometimes they are easy to see; sometimes they are shrouded in fog. But the patterns are always there. Peter, Karen, Ann and so many other people are finding their patterns confusing, even frustrating.

For Peter Brandt, today's pattern leads him to spend the rest of the afternoon walking back and forth on Faraway Hill's few streets. He nods at various people who nod curiously at him. All the while he misses the woman he loves. He misses her smile, her touch, her smell. He misses holding her, kissing her, being inside her. "Let's just stay as we are," she told him. *Why can't we? Isn't it enough?* Maybe it's the age difference or the gossip or the fact she is rich and sophisticated and he's a small town boy. Any of these could be the reasons she said no. But if she's not in love with him and doesn't want to marry him, what does that make Peter? This is the question that roams his mind as he roams the streets.

Karen St. John's life pattern has her thinking very little of her young lover. There have been lovers in the past and there will be lovers in the future. Besides, Peter is no Mark Bradley and Karen begins to realize how much she misses him and his willingness to please --- as long as she pays.

The pattern of Ann's day is one of joy: happiness at her own impending wedding, happiness at her mother's. Richard treats them all to dinner that evening. They talk of how to plans and ceremonies and how terrific their futures are certain to be. But in the back of her mind is the fear that history will repeat itself, that something will come along and ruin it all.

Greg and Julie's patterns are very similar even though they are far apart. Greg is alone in his hospital room, lying in bed eating a bland meal wondering what his life is truly like now, wondering about the things he has missed, wondering about his future. Julie dines alone at the mansion, in her suite, her sleeping baby across the hall and wonders many of the same things.

Ben King is wondering about the future, especially how the patterns of his past will affect it. Eve tries to draw him out, but without success.

The past comes back to Jack as well. The pattern of his afternoon and evening is much like his morning: frustration at his powerlessness. Joe insists on being alone with their son, to spend their own special time together. There is too little left. So, Jack's patterns direct him as they so often have before: to a bar, this time to one on Market Street. There he sits and quietly drinks, ignoring everyone. Everyone, that is, until a certain someone makes a surprising entrance. It isn't long before he and Denise Sullivan are back at his apartment, fucking away the remainder of the evening, just like they did in college.

Some patterns never change.

$$****$$

The wedding planner was right. The pale pink carnations look good in the mansion. They also look good in the little church. It's the kind picture-perfect wedding Ann Gale dreamed of growing up.

Ben King graciously plays father of the bride, escorting Ann down the same aisle in the same church where she married Mark Bradley almost one year ago. But this time it is different; back then hardly anyone came to the ceremony. This year, it seems the entire town has shown up. Her school friends all have seats toward the front where they won't miss a thing. Newspapers and TV stations have cameras crowding the corners, anxious to capture every moment. Ann's mother and Vivian sit proudly in the first pew. Even Richard's daughter, Rebecca, pretends to be happy. She is standing with her father at the altar, as best man.

Unfortunately, the Hallorans are not sharing the joy. Greg and Julie are here. Her half-brother came home from the hospital just this morning. The two haven't had much of a chance to speak. He doesn't recognize her and Ann has been too preoccupied. Besides Greg and Julie, only Patrick and Matthew are present. Joan and Robert refused to come. Joan didn't even bother to RSVP.

Still, with each step, Ann approaches Pastor Elizabeth with a sense of victory. *I've won. I've beaten the bastards who thought I was never good enough.* "Who presents this bride?"

Looking like a proud father, Ben responds "I do, on behalf of her two mothers." Ann glances back at Lorene and Vivian, who are touched. She insisted on this gesture at the last minute, as happy for her mother as she is for herself.

Ann tries to remember every second, but the ceremony is so fleeting, she barely hears anything until Pastor Elizabeth announces, "Ladies and gentlemen, I now present Richard and Ann Davis."

Like a glorious parade, the happy couple leads the wedding party and guests out of the church and into the streets of Faraway Hill. Laughing and talking they pass the famous statue of John Halloran as the warm sun shines from above. TV cameras and reporters follow them recording the joyous march.

Ann is where she loves to be: the center of attention. The dreams of her childhood are coming true: a fancy wedding, celebrity guests, a handsome groom. At one point, she notices her mother speaking to Karen St. John and it occurs to Ann that this is the first time Lorene has been to the mansion since leaving, pregnant and disgraced, almost 25 years ago. *That is so damned cool.*

One of the waiters slips her a note; on it reads "meet me in your room." Ann looks around. The ballroom is crowded with people eating and dancing and having a good time. She can't spot Richard anywhere. *He must want to spend some alone time with me.* She almost giggles at the thought of a quickie with her new husband while their guests wine and dine downstairs.

It takes some doing --- she is the day's star, after all --- but Mrs. Davis manages to extricate herself from the festivities and climb the Grand Stairs. She practically runs down the long hall to her suite. Opening the door, Ann finds her husband sitting on the sofa, sipping some Champaign.

Only, it's the wrong husband.

"It's too bad I missed the ceremony," Mark Bradley, wearing a designer tux and a cocky smile, raises his glass in a toast. "But there wasn't any room in the little church. It sure wasn't like that at <u>our</u> wedding."

Why the fuck is he here? The two of them haven't seen each other since that day at the sheriff's office, when Mark was put under arrest and Ann learned his terrible secret. Clenching her fists, standing her ground, she issues the demand: "Get the hell out of my house, out of my wedding and out of my life!"

"Shit, after everything I went through to see you, babe?" He smiles that sexy smile she used to love. Now she finds it creepy.

"Just how the hell did you get in here, anyway?"

"Well, babe, it's just amazing how a good blow job can open doors."

"I guess that means we fire the security company." *And maybe we'll sue them.*

"Don't be so hard on them," Mark laughs. "It ain't their fault, besides if that waiter didn't let me in there were other ways. I see that a few of the ladies on your guest list used to be clients."

"Ladies? I thought you only bent over for men." It feels good to get a dig at this man.

"Sure it's mostly men; that's just the way the biz works. Men get hornier and they pay better. But I get the occasional woman like . . . well, like Joyce Cassidy. Her name *is* familiar, right?"

It sure is: Joyce handled Ann's divorce before retiring and leaving town. His bringing up her name is . . . weird. "What about her?"

"A hidden web cam can convince even the most scrupulous attorney like her to do all sorts of things."

What the hell is he talking about? "Just get out, before I throw you out."

"You got all those reporters downstairs, babe. I supposed I could call them to --- what's it call --- a press conference? But are you sure you want the scandal? Are you sure you want to do that to Senator Old Man?"

Oh shit, I can't do that to Richard.

"It really is better we talk, just you and me."

"Fine, say your piece and get the fuck out."

Mark takes another sip of his Champaign. "You really should have checked out my stuff --- especially the laptop --- before you dumped everything in the back of my truck."

"I wanted you out of my life. I still do."

"That hurts, babe;" he says faking a pout. "It really does."

"You humiliated me! Between you and Munroe I became a laughing stock across the state. What the fuck did you expect?"

"Yeah, but you're a Halloran now; you've got lots of money."

"Don't expect any of it. We're divorced, remember?"

He laughs so hard he spills Champaign all over his tux. "See, that's what you're not quite getting. We ain't divorced."

"What the hell are you talking about?"

"The papers Joyce had you sign were meaningless, babe. Fake. I mean it got all over the country you being a Halloran. I knew that there was going to be a time when that'll come in handy."

Oh shit, oh shit, oh shit . . . he can't mean . . .

"How's life treating you, Mrs. Bradley?"

"You're lying."

He laughs again, this time a true, deep mocking laughter. *He has to be lying.*

"I have my papers, the divorce decree, all of it. We couldn't get a marriage license without any of them. I had to bring them with me to the clerk's office."

"Fake, babe, all fake; why do you think Joyce retired right away?"

"Bullshit." She motions through the door. "Go, now."

Mark sets down his glass, rises with a smile. Ann can see he's been working out, eating well, generally living the good life. "Check it out. But go on your honeymoon first. Enjoy it; but when you come back, get ready start writing some seriously big checks."

"You are fucking bastard. I'll kill you before I give you a penny."

"Babe, you ain't got the balls."

EPISODE THIRTEEN

Fear is the worst predator, a beast that once it sinks its teeth into you, it won't let go easily. For the rest of the day, her wedding day, Ann faked a smile. She faked it for her fiancé, for her celebrity guests, for the pastor. She faked it for her half-brother and her sister-in-law and her cousins. Her mother was too busy showing Vivian the house to notice anything. All the time, at every moment and with every step, the beast continued biting her, bringing her more pain than she ever thought she could handle. Even now, staring out at Nantucket Bay, feeling a warm spring breeze and watching the setting sun, the fear is so great that she is trembling.

And she can't take it anymore. With tears in streaming from her eyes, Ann is confessing everything to the only man she can.

"Where did you see him?" Richard asks in the type of calm voice used by priests and therapists.

"In my suite; I got this note slipped to me that I thought was from you. But I found Mark sitting in my parlor, with that asinine smile on his face."

They are honeymooning at the Wauwinet, an exclusive inn at the very tip of Nantucket Island. It took them two private jets to get here. Their room, like all the others, is decorated with country pine antiques with hand-stenciled finishes. Everything about the inn --- its look and its feel --- harkens back to a simpler, elegant time when ladies wore gloves and gentlemen escorted them to town on horse drawn carriages. One of the room's few nods to modernity is the plasma TV mounted to a wall.

"How did he get in?"

"By paying off one of the waiters --- he says --- with sex, of course."

"His stock in trade; do you believe him?"

"I don't know," she shrugs. "Maybe he's bluffing, but I doubt it. Something in my gut tells me it's true. I'm so sorry, Richard. I really am."

Richard reaches for his cell. *Oh, shit, he's calling his lawyer. He's leaving me.* "Harold? It's Richard." *Yep, that's his lawyer. We met at the wedding. It's over now. Once more, Mark has humiliated me. The entire state will be laughing at me --- again.* "I'm sorry for calling you at home, but this is important. First thing Monday morning I need you to check the divorce records of Mark and Ann Bradley. Make this your top priority . . . because there is a possibility my wife's divorce didn't come through . . . no, we just learned about it a little while ago."

Ann watches Richard listen to the other man, his face expressionless. "Good, call me Monday night." He slaps the phone shut and looks up at her. Ann steels herself for what will surely be an angry tirade. *I deserve that. I may have ruined his career.* Instead he reaches out and gently takes her hand in his.

"Don't worry; I am not going to let that bastard win."

****

Jack storms out of Joe's apartment. He can't deal with it anymore. The two of them have been fighting for days. "Its no use," Joe sobs over and over. He's been crying like the girl he once was because Jack insists on his going into treatment. But the man refuses. "Face it; I'm going to be dead in a few months!" One more minute and Jack could have punched a wall. So, instead he decides to cool off by taking a walk.

It's a nice, warm spring day; the drifts of snow that were on Manchester's streets have given way to puddles and drying slush. Jack doesn't even bother with a coat. The fresh air should do him good; so he starts walking south down Chestnut Street without any real destination in mind. He just needs to think and burn away his frustration.

Joe is getting more and more depressed. At first, Jack tried to raise the man's spirits but it didn't work and now all they seem to do is fight. Scared and confused, Little Jack has been staying in his room, trying to avoid them. *This can't be good for the kid.* Fortunately, Aaron and his fiancé have started coming by. They took his son to the SEE Science Center this morning for a day of fun. The boy sure needs it. But something needs to be done.

He walks past Myrtle, Orange and Pearl Streets not paying much attention to the houses or the people he passes by. Eventually he comes upon a busy intersection. Looking up he sees that he is standing at the corner of Bridge and Chestnut. *Shit, how far did I walk? Downtown is only a few blocks away. Oh, what the fuck.* He turns left and follows Bridge until reaching Elm where he can see landmarks like the Brady-Sullivan and Verizon Arena.

Jack pulls out his cell and speed dials Greg. He has called over and over and hasn't gotten through even though his lover is out of the hospital. *That fucking Julie must have taken his phone.* After three rings, a surprise: Greg answers.

"Dude, it's you! I'm so damned glad."

"Uh, thanks . . . who is this?"

"Jack, Jack Campbell. I've been trying to reach you for days."

"Oh," the man answers quietly and cautiously. "I got your messages." *Good, then the bitch hasn't been deleting my calls.* As he approaches Mechanic Street, Jack realizes that a truly private conversation is impossible with so many people around. "Look, I know you don't remember much but we've got to meet. It's important." He almost adds *I love and I need you, especially now.*

Greg doesn't respond. *Shit, he's freaked out.* "I'm sorry, Jack . . . but . . ."

"Please, dude: you just name the time and place."

"I'll . . . I'll think about it." Greg hangs up. *Shit! I pushed him too hard. Now what the fuck do I do?*

"Hey there."

Jack turns to see Denise standing at the corner of Elm and Hanover, carry a shopping bag and wearing the tightest blouse in the history of the world.

"I had a lot of fun the other night. It was almost like our college days". *She's not even wearing a bra. I can see her nipples. Damn she looks hot.* But that evening was a mistake. Jack knows he shouldn't be fucking around. But the release was so . . . needed. "That was just," he whispers, so that the other people walking by won't hear him, "you know, a frustration fuck. Don't read too much into it."

Denise chuckles and whispers back, "I know. That's why it was <u>so good</u>."

"Well . . ."

"You walked here, didn't you? I'm parked over at Franklin. Come on, let's have another frustration fuck."

Jack should say no. Jack wants to say no, or at least part of him does. But instead he follows her down the street, admiring her sexy ass with each step.

✱✱✱✱

Karen loves the sight of a sexy ass. Especially on a handsome young man, like the one currently standing outside the Abercrombie & Fitch store. He's lean, athletic about 20 and she finds herself fantasizing about him: running her hands across his hard body, wrapping her legs around him, having him inside her . . .

"Aunt Karen?"

She turns to see Julie coming out of JC Penny. "They are out of his size. Hopefully Macy's will have it." The two of them are out shopping at the Mall of New Hampshire where Julie is trying to find a simple birthday present for the Halloran family's gardener.

"Perhaps clothes are not the right choice, dear."

Julie shrugs. "Maybe not."

"You know, it's not as if he's inside help."

"He's been with the Hallorans for over thirty years. Only Frederick has been with the family longer."

"Yes, I know dear; I remember what he was like thirty years ago. He hasn't changed much." *The gardener was a curmudgeonly old man even when he was a young man,* Karen thinks, grateful that the neither he nor the butler know about her daughter.

"Aunt Karen, what a terrible thing to say!"

"I'm sorry, but I never did understand why the Hallorans kept him on all these years. Anyway, I'm getting a bit hungry. How about some lunch?"

"Sure, there is a nice sandwich place in the food court."

A food court is hardly my style. "Oh, please dear, no: someplace a little nicer."

"Well, let's see . . . Bertucci's is just down there."

"That sounds better."

The restaurant is just a short walk away, located between Macy's and Sears. Karen prefers fancier cuisine in a more exclusive environment. But if eating mere pizza will get her little girl to open up then so be it. They are quickly seated not far from the brick oven that dominates this and every Bertucci in the chain. But the décor is not what interests her: Karen wants to know what, if anything, to do about Greg. *Its time I do a little fishing.*

"Your first anniversary is coming up. Are you two planning something special?"

"I haven't thought about it too much," Julie answers while looking over the menu. "I don't think we'll do anything."

"That would be so sad."

"Well, Greg still can't remember anything much less our wedding. But who knows. He's having a session at the house with the doctor, to see if they can trigger something. I want to be there but, well, the doctor suggests as small a group as possible."

"Your uncle and I had the most romantic first anniversary. He reserved a table at the Rainbow Room. There was music and Champaign . . . oh, it was so special." Actually, Martin was called away to a business meeting. He did that a lot, something that often angered Karen. But the lie serves her purposes.

"It sounds wonderful, but I don't think anything like that will be possible."

"Dear, I know you've had some problems. I wish you would talk to me. Growing up you could tell me anything. You still can."

Julie smiles sweetly, but Karen can tell she's holding back. *Why won't she confide in me? How the hell do I know what to do if she doesn't say anything? Should I try eliminating him again, or is he finally going to be good to my little girl?* "We'll work it out. Actually, the amnesia may be for the best. We have the chance to start over. You know, Lewis' murder was like a curse on us. Everything became tougher and darker after that." *Oh, no, dear you are wrong: getting rid of Lewis was necessary. It's your closeted husband who made things tougher.* "Come to think of it, maybe we <u>will</u> do something. I'll talk to him about it."

Karen hides her frustration behind an elegant smile.

✳✳✳✳

"I hear its warm in Faraway Hill," Eve says wistfully. She and her husband are in Littleton today, a handsome little town not far from the Vermont border. Since Littleton is near the White Mountains the temperatures often get a little lower here. Both are bundled up as Ben's advance team --- three people about Julie's age who are smart, young and enthusiastic --- escort them to a luncheon at Miller's Café & Bakery. Actually, it will be more like an informal town hall meeting. Eve wonders if they'll even get a chance to eat something. She's hungry and has been looking forward to the gourmet soups and homemade desserts that Miller's is known for.

"Don't worry; we'll be home later today."

"And then you'll be off to Washington." Despite her initial concerns, Eve has found one good thing about being a senator's wife: traveling the state has given them more time together than she thought. But that's only while campaigning.

"I'm sorry; that's just the way things are."

"Yes, well, don't forget: we're important people now and I expect you to escort me to the big event at the Currier."

"It would be my honor," Ben smiles.

One of the kids comes out of Miller's to tell them that all is ready. Eve takes her husband's hand and they walk into the lions den together.

****

For the entire weekend, Richard pushes their concerns about Mark aside. "You are Mrs. Davis, from this day forward," he insists. "No one is going to change that, not even that asshole." His words and determination make Ann feel a little better. But she can't help worrying.

They don't make love the first night. They are too physically and emotionally drained. But with sunrise, Richard makes certain they honeymoon. A jitney takes them in to Nantucket Town for some shopping. Later in the day they take a walk, hand-in-hand, along the inn's private beach as the sun sets. The sight is romantic and beautiful and, for a brief period, she forgets all about Mark Bradley. A lobster dinner at Topper's caps the evening. Here Ann can see the other guests for the first time: a best selling author and his wife are at one table, a married movie star sits at another with what must be her lover --- a scene the tabloids would pay a fortune for.

That night, for the first time since the wedding, they make love. Ann is grateful that this wonderful man will still have her. *At least for now*, she thinks.

Sunday is a day of pampering at the inn's spa as well as more romantic walks by the ocean. She starts getting nervous on Monday morning. Ann knows that the truth is just hours away. Richard tries to take her mind off it with a boat ride and another excursion into town. But that evening the call comes in, and it is just as she feared.

"The divorce didn't happen; it wasn't even filed." Richard has the lawyer on speaker so that they can both hear.

"But, Harold, what about the papers? I saw them; Ann and I needed them to get the license."

"A lawyer can fake papers, Richard." Harold has the rough voice of a man accustomed to dealing with matters directly, a man who has little interest in being diplomatic with anyone. Even his closest friend and most important client.

"What does this all mean?"

"For starters Richard, you two are not legally married; but I'm sure you figured that out. But there is more."

"Such as?"

"Well, first of all, Mark Bradley and Ann's attorney --- Joyce Cassidy --- they have both committed fraud. No doubt. They're looking at a fine and maybe a jail sentence. Cassidy will lose her law license, that's certain."

Ann doubts that Joyce will care. "She's retired. I don't even know where she is."

"It doesn't matter, Ann, she's still in trouble. Big trouble. There is another problem: you've committed bigamy."

"That's not fair, Harold. Ann and I never knew about the fake divorce."

"Doesn't matter; technically, you've broken the law. I'm sure most judges will be sympathetic so I wouldn't worry about a fine or jail. Still, it's a serious problem."

"So, what do we do now?"

"Ann files for a real divorce. My people can handle that. You'll need to get married again --- if you want, Richard."

"Of course I do," he answers without hesitation, without even looking at Ann.

"Richard, I hate to say this --- maybe you should take me off speaker."

"I don't give a damn about the politics, Harold."

"Are you sure about that?"

For the first time during the call, Richard turns to Ann. For a mad moment, she expects him to dump her and run from New Hampshire's most scandalous woman. Instead, she can see the love on his weathered face and in his clear, flawless eyes. "Mrs. Davis and I can handle anything that comes up."

****

Greg feels strange.

He is sitting in what was his parents' suite, the three interlocking rooms he seldom saw growing up. Now it belongs to him and his wife. At least, it's <u>supposed</u> to. His clothes are here, his mementos from NYU are here, and his childhood photos are here. Ever since leaving the hospital he has spent most of his time here. Yet, despite all of the hours staring at the oval walls of the parlor, despite being surrounded by familiar objects, Greg still feels like he's trespassing. He expects his mother to walk through the door and insist he leave in her famously curt way.

Since coming home, he has pretty much kept to the master suite. He'll step across the hall to spend time with his son or eat dinner downstairs with Julie. It marvels him, having a son. Just holding the boy makes him smile. But he is as much a stranger to Greg as is his wife. So he spends most of his time alone.

Sitting alone; he did that a lot growing up. At home or in the dorm, it has always been his way. Keeping people at a distance --- be they fuck buddies or girlfriends or relatives --- has been the safest policy. It's harder to get hurt that way.

Something else troubles him. Just like his parents, Greg and his wife are sleeping apart. According to Julie, it happened only six months after their wedding. She won't tell him why. They don't talk much. But it isn't hard to guess: Greg cheated. *Did she catch me with a woman or a man?* It probably doesn't matter; until Lauren he wasn't sure he could be faithful to one person. Now he knows that he can't.

I wonder how long it took Mom and Dad to sleep in separate rooms.

A gentlemanly knock on the door calls his attention. Frederick enters with the news that "Mr. Hoban and Dr. Miles have arrived." Dr. Miles, the hospital therapist suggested that Greg walk through the mansion; it might help restore his memory. It seems worth a try. So, while Julie spends the day in Manchester tending to her little shop, Greg will become a tourist in his family's home --- and hopefully reclaim two lost years.

He follows the aging butler down the marble stairs and through the long Grand Hall to the ballroom at the house's eastern side. Here they find Dr. Miles, an Asian woman somewhere in her 40s with a small frame and short hair and a bemused look her face. While Dr. Miles stands ladylike beside the mantel, she watches a short, rail thin, bald man with thick black rimmed glasses darting around the vast room looking at one thing after another in quick succession like a child in a candy store giddy at each display of treats. *Wow is he weird.*

"Ah, Mr. Halloran, Mr. Halloran," he strides over with surprising speed and grabs his hand, shaking it vigorously. "I am so very excited about this, having another chance to relish this magnificent house."

"Certainly, Mr. Hoban; I just appreciate your help." Greg manages to free his hand to welcome Dr. Miles. Frederick has agreed to be a guide as well, for while Hoban will relate some of the building's history, the butler will add some of Greg's.

They start here, in the ballroom, where so many family events have occurred and where his half-sister celebrated her marriage. *It's odd to think I have a sister.* The staff is efficient; there is nothing left of that party. Hoban regales the general history of the house, about how John Halloran attended the Continental Congress as an aide to New Hampshire's Josiah Bartlett, began the family textile empire with the contacts he made and then --- to celebrate his new nation --- built his home to echo the newly constructed executive mansion in the newly constructed national capital. Dr. Miles seems genuinely interested, but then, so do all visitors to the house. "What a tale that is, what a tale," Hoban enthuses. "It is worthy of a great novel."

He goes on to describe key elements of the room, from the inlaid wood floor to the carved mantel and the antique chandeliers ("these replaced the originals in 1905" Hoban explains "when the house was first electrified"). Frederick adds a few bits about his christening, college graduation party and various other events he attended. Greg remembers much of this, but its history that predates the amnesia and its no help.

"Your wedding reception was also held here," the butler points out. Dr. Miles asks him about this but Greg doesn't recall anything. It is an odd feeling to married to a woman he barely knows.

The four of them reenter Grand Hall. To their right are the stairs that lead to the servants' quarters below. Frederick and the maids live there and Greg has never seen those rooms. They turn left and enter the Green Room. It hasn't changed much in the past two centuries. Hoban goes into details about the silk wallpaper and the fireplace and which pieces of furniture are originals and which were acquired later. Frederick has little to add; this like the oval Blue Room --- the tour's next stop --- is part of the mansion's formal space where kids like he were rarely allowed. But something stirs in the back of his mind, something that sparks a questioning look from Dr. Miles.

"I . . . seem to remember the whole family gathered here for something. Everyone except my dad, but somehow involving my dad . . ."

"Perhaps, sir," Frederick suggests, "you are remembering the meeting with the sheriff last year."

"A meeting," looking around Greg can almost but not quite picture his Aunt Joan sitting in a chair. "Maybe . . . kind of . . . what sort of meeting Frederick?"

"It was here that the sheriff explained the circumstances of your father's death." *That must be it.* He looks over to Dr. Miles who says, "I think this tour was a good idea. Something else you see may remove the memory block."

Across from the Blue Room is the Grand Vestibule, that huge marble space that welcomes guests. Hoban practically drools over the imported material (some from Italy) even as he points out that it doesn't quite fit the mansion's Georgian architecture.

The family parlor and dining room start triggering memories, but they are mostly from childhood. They are few since he spent so much time at boarding schools. They are also not very pleasant: when his parents weren't fighting they shared a cold silence. The formal dining room is no help. They reach one more room: the study.

For every generation of Hallorans, the head of the household calls the study his own. Each adds his own touch to it. Growing up, most of Greg's conversations with his father happened here. These were not warm moments; they were more like business meetings: Greg, in his little monogrammed school blazer, sitting on one side of the desk and his father, sometimes smoking a pipe, on the other. But being in here . . . something doesn't fit. And it hits him: *the chair. That's the wrong chair.* Sitting behind the desk is not the handsome, regal leather chair his father used for over twenty years. The chair Greg awed at as a little boy, the chair from which Lewis lectured his son about one thing or another.

"Greg," Dr. Miles asks concerned. "Are you okay? What's going on?"

This is where my father died. This is where that fucking farmer killed him. So much comes rushing back so fast: getting Ben's call on his wedding night; Jack and Julie standing by him, supporting him throughout the nightmare.

"Mr. Halloran? Mr. Halloran?"

The painting, that painting, behind that is where Jack and I found . . . like water from a burst damn, more images and thoughts and words overwhelm him: being blackmailed by that fucking ass Mark Bradley . . . the shock of Ann moving into the house . . . meeting Jack in Atlanta . . . everything is a jumble and it doesn't all make sense but more and more is coming back . . . *Julie, Julie had to be taken to the hospital . . . Jack telling me about Jackie and Joe and . . . shit, what else , what else?*

Everything goes black.

Greg opens his eyes to find himself back in Grand Hall. He's sitting on an antique chair, Frederick holding a cold cloth to his forehead. *What the fuck am I doing out here?* "Do you think he's okay?" the historian asks nervously.

Images and voices continue to ebb and flow. It takes Greg another moment to ask "what happened?"

"You blacked out," Dr. Miles explains with a confident smile. "I think the trigger we've been waiting for has been tripped. You remember, don't you?"

Greg looks from the serine therapist to the concerned butler to the weird and strangely wired Hoban. Things are still a little jumbled in his head. But he nods, "I . . . I think do."

****

The attorney's office has a very contemporary, industrial feel with the redbrick walls and exposed ductwork running alone the ceiling. The abstract paintings are colorful and interesting. It seems more like a hip ad agency than a small city law firm. But that's what it is because that's what they need.

Jack remembers meeting Tim Dreyfus months ago. Greg introduced them. He had just been hired on as the Halloran's new family lawyer. Still a young man --- Jack guesses in his early 30s --- he has made something of a splash in the state, getting involved in some major cases that helped him snare important clients like the Hallorans. His law firm is in the Millyard, within walking distance to Greg's office. The irony is not lost on Jack, being so close to the man he loves but still far apart.

"Have you spoken to Greg?" Tim asks after Jack introduces him to Joe.

"No, things have been too crazy. He's only been home a few days." *Besides, I have no idea what the fuck to say to him.* Jack wishes he knew another lawyer so that he can avoid this awkwardness. But they haven't the time to shop around.

Joe gets to the point: he explains his sex change, his relationship to Jack and their son. The lawyer is clearly fascinated by everything. "Wow, I mean, please don't be offended --- I know gay people and bisexuals; this is New Hampshire after all --- but you're my first transman and, well, your story is . . . really interesting."

"Yes, I know it's a bit unusual." Joe winces again. Jack can tell he's having another surge of pain. They often come without warning. "But there is more. There is my stepfather. He's . . . well, he's Joseph Bologna."

Tim pauses for a moment, reaches back into his memory to almost but not quite find what he's looking for. "Why is that name familiar to me?"

"The feds have been investigating him on and off for years."

"Oh, yes: I've read about him. The alleged crime boss out in Los Angeles; he was involved in some scandal dealing with a city councilman. It made the *New York Times* last year. He married your mother?"

"Unfortunately; he also doesn't like have a stepson who was once his stepdaughter. I am an embarrassment for him. He . . . he made it clear early on that he wanted me dead and raise our son as his."

"You shouldn't be talking to me. You should be talking to the police."

Joe shakes his head. "No proof; there is nothing they can do. That's why I spent over a year running from him. But it got to be too much for my little boy, so I sought out Jack." Joe reaches out and takes Jack's hand with a grateful smile. This is one of those moments where, in Jack's mind, Joe becomes Jackie again. "He's been great. He even suggested we move here, and we really like it."

Tim's smile is one of understanding and of pride. "I grew up in Sugar Hill --- that's a little town up in the White Mountains --- and really love Manchester. I can't imagine living anywhere but New Hampshire. Believe me, this is a great place to raise a child."

"I think so too . . . anyway, a few months ago Vincent and I reached an understanding. Jack and I --- Little Jack, that is --- will stay here, far from his life and his businesses. In turn, he'll leave us alone."

"Do you think he'll keep his word?"

"The whole situation has been tough on my mother. He loves her, in his own weird way. I think for her sake he will. But there is a new complication, and that's why we need your help."

"Okay, what is it?"

Joe hesitates. This is the tough part. Jack squeezes his hand for support, as if willing his strength through that connection. "I've just been diagnosed with ovarian cancer . . . and its terminal. I need to make arrangements so that Jack can raise our son without any interference from Vincent."

Tim leans back in his chair to consider the situation. *I hope he has answers for us,* Jack quietly pleads, *because we sure as fuck need them.* "Well . . . there are a number of issues that need to be settled. First, we need to prove Jack is the boy's father. The courts are very supportive of keeping families together. A DNA test will do that. Second, you need both a living will and a will. Each should have a clause regarding custody. I can draw those up for you. And . . . and there is one other thing I think you should consider."

"What's that?"

"Well," Tim pauses, obviously trying to find a way to be diplomatic. *I wish he'd come right out and say it.* "You and Jack should consider getting married.

Same-sex marriage is legal in New Hampshire, and considering your past relationship, would make the most sense. Not only regarding your son but your own health issues. It would cement custody and related matters --- like your end of life care and your estate --- in the most complete and efficient way possible."

I never thought about that, Jack thinks. He looks at Joe, who winces again. *He needs his pain meds.* "Can we have a moment please?"

Tim steps out of the office, leaving them alone. Neither man says anything right away. Joe picks up his satchel to find the pill bottle. He winces once more, this time Jack can almost see a tear. *The pain must be awful.* There is a pitcher of water and some glasses on the credenza. Jack pours him some and watches Joe take a pill and ask "what do you think?"

"It sounds to me like getting married would solve almost everything, but . . . but are you sure you want to do it?" *No, the person I really want to marry is already married. And now I'm about to lose you, too.* Then an idea hits: "I'll do it, but on one condition."

"What's that?"

"Get treatment."

"Jack, please . . ."

"I know; I know the odds are against it working, but damn it all, at least try. Promise me that and I'll marry you right away."

Joe doesn't say anything, not right away. But Jack can see the tears well up in his eyes and once again Joe becomes Jackie, the woman he once loved. "Okay," she answers. "If that's the deal, I'll do it."

✱✱✱✱

Like everything else in the Brothers' lodge, the bedroom has an aura of age and stability. The furniture is old and heavy. The floor creaks a little when you walk on it. Hanging over the bed is an expensive painting that must have been nailed to the same place for decades.

Fuck, I hate this. Matthew Newberry is lying on the bed, nervous as to what is about to happen. He has just showered and is stretched out in nothing but a robe staring at the ceiling.

Fuck I hate this. Earlier today he and a group of fellow plebes were out hiking in the woods around the lodge. Its one of the least stressful and most boring activities he has had to endure. The guide was one of the older tutors, a man in his seventies named Gerald Simpson, who spent the hours quizzing each of them on one thing or another. Most of Matthew's days with the Brothers involve lessons and tests.

The walk was casual, and gave Matthew time to spend with the other boys, which apparently was the point. All of them are high school seniors or college freshmen. He has met most of them before, but barely knows their names. Gerald made it clear that this was to be a big day for them. "You will all be spending much more time together," the man explained, "developing a brotherhood that will last your entire lives." He also made it clear that "tonight, the next phase in your road will begin." Everyone knows what that means, and this is why Matthew is so damned nervous. After a dinner of hotdogs around a roaring fire, the boys were instructed to go to their assigned rooms, shower and wait for their tutors.

Fuck I hate this. His cousin Patrick gave him some tips, but Matthew is sure nothing can really prepare him for what is about to happen. So he lies here, waiting anxiously for Justin. That is one consolation: Matthew has come to really like his tutor. For one thing he is not as old as the others; most of the tutors are in their 40s and 50s. Matthew has guessed Justin Wright to be around 30. Spending time in his tutorials is almost like hanging with a big brother.

A knock at the door startles him. *Fuck I hate this.* Justin sticks his head in, "hey dude."

"Hey." *Fuck I hate this.*

Justin, wearing nothing but a robe and a smile, closes the door behind him. Justin is a little taller than Matthew and very handsome. In their tutoring sessions, Justin often breaks up the monotony by telling him about his college years, his career in real estate development and even the girls he's dated. Their time together has made Matthew comfortable around the older man. It occurs to him that this may have been deliberate. Physical intimacy is a big part of the Brothers. "It binds everyone together in a way nothing else can," Patrick has explained. That process has already started; about a month ago Justin and Matthew masturbated together in this same bed. It was the first time he'd ever seen another man's hard cock. It was cool in its way. But tonight . . . tonight will be more.

"Don't be so nervous." Justin brought a mug of something with him, and hands it to Matthew. "Here, try some. This'll relax you. Don't worry; it's herbal."

Matthew sniffs the tea. The aroma is an interesting mix of spices. He takes a sip, likes what he tastes, and drinks a little more.

"Did you like the hike?"

"It was okay." *The tea is relaxing; I feel better already.*

"I like the hikes." Justin slips off his robe and climbs naked onto the bed next to him. "Gets me out of this stuffy old mausoleum and lets me hang with some other dudes." Matthew can't help but stare. Like him, Justin has little interest in sports. But as a swimmer he has a tight, lean, manly body with just a hint of biceps. "Don't worry dude; this has to be done. But once it's over with, a lot of other things get easier."

Matthew says nothing. He just takes another sip. The tea is warm and comforting. His whole body seems to loosen up. Even Matthew's senses start to shift . . . *what is happening to me* . . . and takes another sip. It is as if all hesitation, all fear is dissolving from his mind, from his body. *They must have put something in this.* He sips some more.

"So, Matt, you into kissing or not? Some guys like it but others think it's too faggy. I can go either way."

He shrugs. *How the hell should I know? I've never kissed a guy before. Fuck, I hate this . . . I think.* Justin lifts the mug from his hands and sets it on the nightstand. He then leans in and presses their lips together, gently slipping his tongue into Matthew's mouth. *Wow . . . that's . . . that's not bad.* Matthew leans back, closes his eyes, and enjoys the feel of Justin opening his robe and caresses his chest. *That feels good; that feel really good.* His hardening cock is suddenly enveloped by a warm, wet sensation. Matthew opens his eyes to see Justin sucking him. *Oh, damn . . .* He is about to cum when Justin lets go. The tutor reaches back to the nightstand, opens a drawer, and pulls out a tube. *Oh, shit, its going to happen now.*

"Don't worry dude. Just relax. Let the tea do its thing."

Matthew nods, closes his eyes and takes some deep breaths. He can feel Justin spread his legs, bending them at the knees. He then feels something cool and slick being applied to his ass. *Oh, damn, oh, damn.* Then suddenly something thick and hard pushes its way into him. *Fuck, that hurts, fuck, fuck, fuck.* Another thrust and Matthews eyes open with a jerk and he can see Justin on top of him, completely inside him. "Take it easy, enjoy it." The initial shock is gone and now . . . and now it feels different . . . almost comforting in a way. And as Justin slowly starts to move, the sensation changes again; *it's almost like his cock is massaging me from the inside.* Justin leans over and they kiss again. This time Matthew kisses back, really kisses back. With each thrust forward, a surge goes up his spine. *Damn that feels good.* Faster and faster until Justin stops . . . and Matthew can feel his warm cum fill him. The other man falls on top of him, panting. Finally catching his breath, Justin whispers into his ear, "we are almost there, bro."

Justin pulls out, leaving Matthew feeling empty. *Please stay inside me, please. I can't imagine anything feeling so fucking good.* The tutor lubes up the young man's hard cock and then, with a wicked smile, slides himself down, taking Matthew deep inside, letting the plebe think, *oh shit, I was so wrong . . .* it takes only a minute before Matthew closes his eyes and he cums inside his tutor.

After catching his breath, Matthew looks at Justin, who is lying beside him again, with a smile and a look of accomplishment. *Wow, that was actually pretty cool.* "Now things will be a lot easier with the other plebes," the handsome tutor says, his body glistening with sweat. "Not to mention with girls."

****

Girls or boys, it doesn't matter much to Mark Bradley. If they pay, he will perform. Granted there are still some thing's he'd prefer never to do again. But money is money. And these days, he needs every penny he can earn. So when that insane bitch Karen St. John tracked him down, Mark said he'd come over --- for twice his normal fee. "Oh, wonderful lover," she cooed over the phone. He hates it when she calls him that. Back when she was a regular client in New York he'd repeatedly insist "I am your escort, not your lover" but it doesn't matter. *Crazy is as crazy does*, he mumbles to himself. *At least she gave me the cash upfront.*

Karen was anxious to show him her new home, but he didn't give a flying fuck. He's really interested in getting it up so that he can get out. "Remember, I have you for the whole night." *Damn.*

Still, it's nice to be with a woman again, especially a woman who knows what she's doing in bed. She keeps her body in shape and it doesn't take much effort to get hard. What does take effort is not cumming right away; Karen likes to be fucked and fucked for a good long time. "Not so fast, lover; you always want to go too fast." But the inevitable cannot be put off and soon he is asleep next to her.

Mark wakes up in the morning and finds he is in the bed alone. Karen is gone and so are his clothes. He can see his wallet and keys and the cash she gave him on the dresser. She used to do this back in the New York days; keeping him around longer by needlessly throwing his things in the wash "just to be nice."

Rising naked from the bed, he enters the master bath to relieve himself. After a good long piss, almost therapeutic, he steps out into the hall and is about to go downstairs when he hears an angry voice from below.

"Damn it, Karen, I wish you would stop doing that."

The woman's voice sounds familiar, very familiar, but Mark has trouble placing her. He walks a few steps down but dares not go any further or else whoever it is will see him.

"I don't understand what the problem is. We had a very nice day together. My daughter needed the break. She has been under so much stress lately."

"She is <u>not</u> your daughter. She was <u>never</u> your daughter."

"Strange, how I remember giving birth to her." *Shit, that's interesting. Who the fuck are they talking about?*

"I can't believe I am having this conversation with you again. First you move back here despite the risks, then you take up with Peter Brandt --- a boy young enough to be your son --- and now you insist on spending more time with Julie." *Julie? Julie King? The hot babe Greg Halloran married? Is that who they're fighting about?*

"Eve, dear, I've kept my word. Julie doesn't know anything. As far as she is concerned, you and Ben are her parents. I am just Aunt Karen." Now he recognizes the voice: it's Eve King.

"For how long, Karen? How long before you tell her the truth? I know you are dying to do it. I can see it in your face." *Holy shit, that's it, isn't it: crazy Karen is hot Julie's real mother!*

The news is so incredible that Mark drops naked on the step --- and laughs.

EPISODE FOURTEEN

She's deep in Karenland today, is the first thing Eve King realizes when arriving at her sister's home. *She's in full Gloria Swanson mode, right down to the damned turban!*

Eve is here because of a call she got this morning on her cell. She was driving back on the 293 --- having just dropped Ben off at the airport --- when Julie called to say that Greg's memory is starting to come back. But that good news was ruined by learning that Julie and Karen spent a recent afternoon together. Now, angrier than she can say, Eve King wants to throw something, smash something, do something so that her baby sister will finally see reason. *Maybe, just maybe, if I visit her enough and harass her enough she'll get it and leave town.*

"First you move back here despite the risks, then you take up with Peter Brandt --- a boy young enough to be your son --- and now you insist on spending more time with Julie."

They are face to face in Karen's elegant new living room. The place is picture perfect, like some old time movie set. The ladies of "The View" are debating something on the muted TV.

"Eve, dear, I've kept my word." Her studied, practiced and elegant calm is annoying. "Julie doesn't know anything. As far as she is concerned, I am just wonderful Aunt Karen."

"For how long, Karen? How long before you tell her the truth? I know you are dying to do it. I can see it in your face."

Karen doesn't answer. Instead her attention is diverted by a sound coming from upstairs. It's the sound of a hearty, manly laugh. *Who the hell does she have here? Is it Peter? It doesn't sound like Peter.* Eve studies her sister, who gives her a well-rehearsed plastic smile.

"Who have you got here this time --- maybe some boy from Faraway Hill High School?"

Whoever it is, he's making Karen practically jump. Even her years of practice can't mask it the worry in her eyes. And now the mystery man is laughing harder. "Nope, you got it all wrong lady." *I know that voice.* Eve steps toward the foyer. Karen tries to stop her, but she'll have none of it. Bypassing her sister, she is shocked by something she never expected to see: coming the stairs, completely naked and smiling broadly, is Mark Bradley. "You got to love these small towns," he chuckles, "all the scandals, all the secrets, all the gossip."

Oh, my God, why is he here? What has he heard? She turns to Karen for answers, but she remains silent. It's as if she can read Eve's mind thinking: *you paid him for the night, didn't you?*

"You know, this place shouldn't be called Faraway Hill." He strides over to meet them, eyes twinkling, muscles bulging and long cock swinging from side to side. "This town should really be called --- what was it again? It was a book and a TV show . . . oh, yeah, Peyton Place."

"Uh, Mark, darling, perhaps you should go back upstairs."

"No way, Karen; we are one big happy family." He winks at Eve. "Isn't that right step-mommy?" Disgusted, she looks away. "Put some clothes on."

"No can do, step-mommy, my client here threw my clothes in the wash. Or maybe I should call you Aunt Karen?"

Karen is scared. Eve can't remember the last time her sister looked frightened. She always seems to have a sense of controlled madness. But not now; now she looks like a child caught after doing something so bad she expects a spanking. *No, worse than that: like a wild animal backed into a corner, ready to attack.* "Darling, your clothes will be ready any minute. Please go back to bed."

"Nope," he plops bare ass onto her fancy new sofa. *The prick is really enjoying himself.* "I like this, I like this all very much. It sounds like I have a sister --- well, a sort of sister."

"I think you are a little confused, lover."

"Bull shit Karen, I've just figured out a lot --- and it only took me a couple of minutes. <u>You</u> are Julie King's real mother and not Eve. So, does this mean Ben knocked you up or what?"

"Certainly not," Karen answers, indignant.

"Well, fuck, it would hardly be the first time, right step-mommy?" Eve tries to remain calm, but Mark can read the truth in her eyes. "Oh, wait, Karen doesn't know, does she? What the hell: this is one of those moments of truth, ladies." *Oh, damn, that's just what I don't need, for Karen to have more ammunition.* "You see, Aunt Karen, we found out a few months ago that the good senator knocked up my mother while in college --- and so here I am, naked, semi hard and ready to service another client."

Karen's mood has suddenly changed. She now has a victorious smile on her face. *Bitch.*

"I know your mother wouldn't like you talking that way," Eve begs him, thinking p*lease, please don't say anything more.*

"Like I give a damn. But this, now this is pretty cool. So, if Ben <u>didn't</u> knock up Karen, then someone else got her preggers . . . you and he two took the baby . . . and Julie doesn't know a damn thing." He laughs again. "I love it! I fucking love this!"

Eve is nearly ready to slap him. "Put some damned clothes on!"

But Mark doesn't move. Instead, he leans back, presenting his cock in full view. "Sorry, step-mommy but I like being naked." *I wish to hell he'd stop calling me that.* "I'm here because a dude needs to make living. And it looks like a brand new opportunity has opened up."

The ass wants money. I could kick him in his bare balls. "I'm sure you three want to keep the truth from my baby sister. We just have to figure out the right price."

"Lover," Karen warns coldly, "you don't want to go there." Eve studies her face. Once again, her entire character has changed. As if with the snap of a finger, she is that wild animal again. The sight is so frightening that it sends a shiver of realization up Eve's spine: *my kid sister could kill him, she could actually kill him --- without feeling any guilt.*

Mark rolls his eyes. "Look lady, I've told you a million times: I'm your <u>escort</u> not your lover. I'm in it for the fucks and the bucks. But since I'm a nice guy, I'll give you --- oh, maybe a week, to come up with an offer; a damned good offer." Then, with his arrogant smile returning, he rises and strides naked back to the foyer an up the stairs, his tight ass rising and falling with each confident stride.

The two sisters say nothing more. Karen just glares at the staircase. Eve, her body shaking from top to bottom, picks up her purse and heads out the door thinking, *Good God . . .*

✱✱✱✱

"Welcome to Four Corners."

Ann smiles proudly at her mother and Vivian, who have just arrived in Concord to see her new home. There are boxes everywhere. While on their honeymoon, Frederick arranged to have her things delivered. It will take Ann a few more days to finish unpacking.

She introduces them to the housekeeper, Gertrude, who sweetly greets the ladies with a casual acceptance, as if lesbian couples often visit the farmhouse. Ann leads them on a brief tour, telling them what she knows about its history.

Richard's grandfather built the place. It was the center piece of a working farm back then. The barn and animals and fields are all gone now. So is her husband, who is in Washington.

Her husband. Richard still insists that, despite Mark, they *are* married. She loves him for it, but continues to feel that her new life is built on quicksand.

Over lunch they talk about weddings and Nantucket. Lorene and her future wife are just starting to plan everything. "No, I don't want to hire someone. This should be about <u>us</u>." They know they want it to be a small affair, at the church in Faraway Hill. "After all," Vivian teases, "it's not like your mother is marrying a senator."

Ann is a little uncomfortable talking about weddings. Her own marriage --- *my illegal, bigamist marriage* --- is so tenuous. She tries to redirect the conversation. "Greg's memory is starting to come back."

"Is it?" Lorene seems genuinely pleased.

"Apparently it's all a jumble. He's mixing things from his college days and his marriage and so forth. He's still putting it all together and I guess it's pretty frustrating."

"Still, that's good news. Everything seems to be going well everyone these days. Vivian and I have found each other again. Greg is getting better. Ben has an exciting new career. And you've have married a wonderful man."

Ann smiles and says nothing. Lorene looks at her curiously. "Ann, you should be so happy."

"Well, Mom," she answers with a sigh. "I am. I really am. But . . ."

"But what?"

She considers whether to say anything. Richard surely wants as few people to know as possible. But after everything they've been through --- Munroe's crime, the revelation about Lewis, Vivian's husband --- it only seems right to tell them. "But you can't breathe a word to anyone."

"We promise."

As simply as possible, Ann describes the situation: Mark surprising her at the reception with his claims, the shocking discovery that she is still legally Mrs. Bradley and Richard's determination to set things straight. The ladies sit and stare for a moment of stunned silence until Vivian speaks up. "Mark wants money, doesn't he?"

"Yes; he hasn't set a price yet but I'm sure we'll hear from him soon."

"Will you pay it?"

"I don't know, Vivian, all I know is that Richard refuses to let Mark bully him."

Lorene smiles, "He loves you that much."

"He really does, Mom, he really does."

"Then don't worry; everything will work out."

****

It's just before Noon, and Jack Campbell is admiring himself in the mirror. He's managed to start working out again. He can see the improvement, but what he really missing is being on a team. Those were great days: at prep school and college, playing basketball and football. Getting sweaty, hearing the roar of the crowds, the hot cheerleaders and the camaraderie of his buddies --- and the discrete hook-ups with both.

I actually look damned good today. Joe insisted that they each buy a new tuxedo. But as he starts to adjust his tie, his thoughts go back not to college but to another time . . . the day he did this for Greg, at Greg's own wedding.

Odd, how that memory flashes back. And in such detail: Jack coming into Greg's room, seeing him struggle with his bow tie just as he has always struggled with his bow tie. He can remember the feel, the warmth and even the smells of that moment. Jack had his lover face this big mirror and he positioned the tie just right. It was that moment, for the first time in a long time, that both men said "I love you" to the other. He remembers talking about their regrets, about how Greg had to "suck it up" and marry the mother of his child.

Now it's my turn to suck it up.

Jack's cell rings. *Oh, fuck, not another problem.* Throwing together this impromptu wedding has had more than a few twists and turns. He's sure there is another complication, another fire to put out, but the name of the phone's screen tells him otherwise. He grabs it and answers anxiously "Hey Greg."

"Hey," Jack can still hear the quiet uncertainty in his voice. So he very gently asks, "Are you okay?"

"I just . . . I just wanted to call and tell you that, well that some things are coming back to me." *Thank God.* "And . . . I've kind of figured out what you mean to me."

"I'm glad, dude, more than you know."

"We should get together soon and talk."

"Sure, but . . . do you remember . . . I mean does you memory include
Joe Westbrook?"

"Yeah, well, kinda . . . I think I remember you telling me about someone called
Westbrook, but I don't quite remember a Joe."

"Then let me bring you up to speed."

****

It only takes a few minutes to drive from Karen's house through Faraway Hill's
main square and arrive at the Halloran's. All the way Eve kept thinking again and
again *she can kill, she can actually kill . . . and maybe she _has_ killed.*

The butler greets her with a smile. Neither Greg nor Julie is here, but that's okay:
she's not here to see Greg and Julie. She's not even here to see her grandson ---
whom Fredrick tells her, is out with the nanny. She's here to speak to the one
person in the world she can speak to. The only one.

Eve climbs the marble stairs up to the second floor. She knocks on the door and a
gentle voice invites her inside. Eve find Agnes Gabler, wearing her smock and
sitting in front of blank canvas. The suite's parlor is cluttered with knickknacks
and keepsakes from a long and full life: photos of famous people, odd little
objects, a few of her recent paintings hanging from the walls. It's like an
encapsulated version of the artist's famed sugar house.

"Am I glad to see you, dear," Agnes says with relief.

"Why is that?"

"I keep worrying about my house. I can't concentrate. They are having so many
problems trying to, well, trying to fix all those problems. First it's the electrical,
and then it's the roof now there is some nonsense about the plumbing.
Sometimes I think it'll take forever."

"That's a shame."

"And, look at this: nothing frustrates me more than an empty canvas . . . what's
wrong? You're actually shaking!"

Eve has had trouble keeping calm ever since leaving Karen's house. She's surprised Frederick didn't say anything. She thought she was doing a good job pretending to be calm, but maybe he was just trying to be polite. The little lady with big bright eyes and charmingly wrinkled face studies Eve and quickly assess, "something's wrong, isn't it? Something very serious."

"Yes, and scary. I just . . . just don't know who to talk to about."

"Not even Ben?"

"I can't get through to him. He's flying back to DC. He won't be back until this evening."

"Then tell me."

"It's about Mark Bradley."

"Is he causing trouble?"

"Oh, hell, yes . . . more than I ever imagined."

"Is he threatening to tell the world he's Ben's father? Surely a good PR person can manage that."

"Agnes, it's much worse. Much worse."

"How so?"

"He spent last night with Karen. She paid him for his services. I didn't know about it. I went over there because . . . because I'm worried about all the time she's spending with Julie. He heard us arguing. He <u>heard</u> us, Agnes. He knows everything!"

"Oh, dear."

"The bastard plans to blackmail us. We're supposed to come up with an offer within a week. But that's not the scary part."

"<u>That's</u> not the scary part?"

"No, believe it or not . . . it's Karen. It's like I saw, I don't know, a new and frightening ride in Karenland today. I'm convinced of it . . . my baby sister is capable of killing someone."

"Are you sure it's not the stress of the moment?"

"No, no . . . I know my sister. I'm sure of it. I think she may have <u>actually done it</u>."

"This is your intuition."

"Yes; am I being ridiculous?"

"Maybe, but I doubt it. I've always put a great deal of stock in intuition."

"What should I do?"

"About what, Mark or Karen?"

"I don't know. Either; both."

"Well, you won't know what to do with Mark until you know for sure what he wants, what he'll accept. If he wants money that badly he's not about to let all the secrets out; He doesn't gain anything that way."

"True."

"As for Karen . . . intuition isn't evidence."

"Yes."

"And there is only one sure way of neutralizing Mark. Remember, several months ago, I told you my Jack Nicholson story?"

Eve nods. Before Agnes moved in with the Hallorans, she told Eve the story of Jack Nicholson being raised by his grandmother, thinking she was his real mother. In reality, his "sister" gave birth to him. "I don't know Agnes . . . I don't know how I can tell Julie the truth . . . and I don't know if she'll be able to handle it."

"Only you and Ben can decide that. But don't underestimate Julie. I've been living here for some time and believe me, she is capable of more than you realize."

"Maybe . . . but Karen, she really scares me. I've always known that there is something off with her. She's been like that since we were children. But today . . . good God, today, I'm beginning to truly understand. She is dangerous, Agnes, dangerous in ways I never considered before."

****

It's a warm spring afternoon in Manchester; the sun is shining bright, the flowers are starting to bloom and birds can be heard overhead. The perfect day for a wedding.

Jack, Joe and Little Jack are all dressed for the occasion; their son giddy with excitement. Aaron and Chloe arrive just as they are finishing up. Strangely, it's Nathaniel who is running late even though he lives next door.

Chloe and Joe have spent the last few days making all the necessary arrangements; this is another instance where Joe seems more like Jackie, at least to Jack. The two gleefully dealt with every little detail. *Even when girls become boys,* Jack thinks, *they still dream about their wedding.*

The biggest challenge was finding a place to hold the ceremony and a dinner afterward. Joe insisted that it be someplace special. So he and Chloe scoured Manchester and the surrounding area looking for the right spot. Joe was really hoping for a church. Several often hold same-sex weddings
--- the Congregational churches in Concord and, of course, Grace Episcopal in Manchester --- but only after a period of couples counseling sessions. There is not time for that.

Another problem was that none of the banquet rooms they like were available on such short notice. Every time Joe and Chloe returned to the apartment all they could do was talk about what was wrong with one place and how frustrating it is that they can't book some other place.

That left Jack to focus on his son. To him, spending time with his son was the best part of the chaos. It brought a sense of serenity, almost normalcy to the weirdness of the situation. Little Jack marveled at the statutes in Veterans Park. They told each other silly jokes over ice cream at the Ben & Jerry's on Elm Street (carefully avoiding King's Korner). An afternoon bumming around the Mall of New Hampshire turned into a mini shopping spree with Jack buying his son storybooks and toys and munching on pretzels from Auntie Ann's. Along the way, Jack comes to learn how naturally smart and sweet the boy is. It isn't weird for him to see his poppa marry another man and Jack realized that his son wants what all kids want a home with his own bedroom and his own family and all that they mean.

But Jack's thoughts often went back to Greg. So it was good that the two men spoke this morning. They agreed to meet in a few days. *I'm so glad he's being cool about this.* His own family is less so. When he spoke to baby brother, all Nick could say was "dude that is way, way beyond weird." None of the Campbells are coming.

Finally, Joe settled on the Hanover Street Chophouse. The choice surprised Jack. *A steak house for a wedding?* "Don't worry," Chloe assured him last night. "It's much classier than it sounds." They are especially lucky, she explained, because the restaurant had a last-minute cancellation. "Besides, the Hanover is close to the hotel for your honeymoon."

The honeymoon: another issue. Jack still isn't sure he can be intimate with Joe. But the transman has been too wrapped up in wedding preparations to talk about it.

Taking two cars, the wedding party makes its way to One City Hall Plaza. The clerk's office isn't very busy. Joe and Jack are third in line. It takes several minutes to complete the paperwork and a marriage license is granted. Tim Dreyfus has arranged for a judge he knows to perform the ceremony, so the small caravan moves on to the restaurant.

The remaining afternoon is spent celebrating the event at the Hanover Street Chophouse. Chloe was right: this restaurant is impressive in its service and sophisticated décor. It reminds Jack of some of the better restaurants he used to frequent in New York. They've reserved the intimate Merrimack Room, which doesn't seem so intimate with only eight people. The staff has arranged for a beautiful centerpiece of white roses. They contrast nicely with the rich paneling on the walls.

For this brief moment in time, there is no cancer and no Bologna family threat. Jack's old man and his self-righteousness are miles away. All there is in the world are good friends, good food and a beaming little boy.

****

Sparks fly, wood crackles, the flames are almost hypnotic. Ben King is sitting in his living room, staring at the fireplace. The temperature outside has dropped considerably, going from a comfortable 60s to a chilly 40s; It's all part of a normal spring in New Hampshire.

Eve has just finished telling him what happened this morning. Confiding in Agnes Gabler has helped to calm her, and even see things a little more clearly. "Personally, I think our best bet is to come up with some sort of dollar figure --- Karen will probably kick-in most of it --- and that should put an end to all of this."

He doesn't say anything, not for a long time. At least to Eve it seems like a long time. Finally, Ben looks up at her. "I can't believe that boy is my son."

"I know."

"I didn't raise him. This is not a man I can call my son. And now . . . he won't stop you know."

"What do you mean?"

"He won't stop, not with just one payment no matter how big. He'll come back for more."

"Maybe not; Karen was so scary this morning. I bet she can frighten the shit out of him."

"Did he seem frightened this morning?"

Eve shakes her head. *No he didn't.*

"And he didn't seem frightened when I met him in New York. I don't know what we're going to do about him, but I can't let him go on torturing us forever."

****

Carefully, very carefully, Frederick lights each candle. There are dozens of tapers big and small scattered throughout the formal dining room. Julie Halloran watches the old butler move from one to another; his quivering hand and shaking legs make progress slow. Eventually, with a triumphant smile, he lights the last one.

"If you will excuse me, Mrs. Halloran, I must check on how dinner is progressing.

"Thank you."

As the butler gingerly steps back into Great Hall and walks toward the kitchen, Julie realizes how that frail but dignified old man --- who never married, never had children --- has devoted his life to this family and to this house.

Julie takes in the scene: the formal dining room is seldom used. It is one of the many spaces on the first floor that is more museum than home. Still, the tapers add a romantic glow; and the table is set with the mansion's finest china. Hanging on the wall across from her is a portrait of Abigail Halloran, from the 1890s. She is in full Victorian regalia, sitting in a chair with a somber expression. The portrait has been hanging on that same nail in that same spot for decades. Julie has heard stories about her. But, of course, anyone who grows up in Faraway Hill hears all sorts of stories about the Hallorans. Legend has it Abigail never married, never left Faraway Hill, was ruled over by her older brother, his wife and their kids, and died a virgin. *No wonder she looks so unhappy.*

Voices start coming from Grand Hall; its Greg and Patrick returning from a day at the Millyard. Patrick is still technically running things, but in reality he's just been office sitting. He finally admitted to Julie that Robert --- famously known in the family as The Quiet Halloran --- has been calling the shots from California. "He's really starting to piss me off" he complained last week. It was easy for him to find some time today to give his cousin a tour of the offices. The psychologist was right about exposing Greg to familiar surroundings. More and more of his memory is coming back.

The two young men stop at the dining room's threshold. Patrick lets out a low whistle, "now that's nice. See you later, dude." Patrick and Julie exchange smiles and he leaves them, climbing up the stairs to have dinner with Agnes.

Greg also smiles, but it's a nervous smile. Almost a first date smile, and Julie realizes that in a sense, this _is_ their first date. "Hi."

"Hi."

He steps over and gives Julie a nice, but not very passionate kiss. "Happy anniversary."

"Thanks, and to you."

"The room looks great."

Greg reaches into his pocket and pulls out a little box. It has PEARSON'S printed in gold on the lid. He hands it to her. Opening it, Julie discovers a beautiful diamond bracelet, trimmed in platinum. _It's gorgeous._ "Thank you." _He must have put some thought into this._

They spend the rest of the meal exchanging little pleasantries. Greg describes his day with Patrick and how certain memories are coming back. They also discuss upcoming graduations: Patrick from Harvard, Matthew from prep school. Little is said about Ann, which tells Julie that her husband's recovered memories include the unhappy ones of his half-sister. She reminds him that they are expected at the big event coming up at the Currier Museum. Mostly they talk about the baby: what John did yesterday, how he smiled this morning, how much he looks like his dad. "He really does," Julie insists when Greg waves away the comparison. "I've seen your baby pictures, the two of you could be twins."

Of all the things they talk about, the one thing they avoid is the one thing Julie knows they must face. So she decides to bring it up herself: "Have you heard anything from Jack Campbell? I know you are starting to remember him."

"Are . . . are you sure you want to talk about him?"

"No, I don't. I don't want to talk about my husband's gay lover on our first wedding anniversary. But . . . I am a realist, Greg. I also know that this is our last anniversary. Have you spoken with him?"

"Yes, this morning."

"And?"

"It's . . . kind of weird."

Julie chuckles. "Greg, as you remember more you will remember that our whole marriage has been weird. What is it this time?"

"He got married this afternoon, to Joe Westbrook."

Now _that_ was news Julie never expected. She isn't sure whether this good news or bad news. Still, she can't help but say, with a laugh, "is Joe pregnant again?"

"Joe is dying." _Oh shit._

"What do you mean?"

"He has cancer. The doctors say he's got less than a year. Jack agreed to marry him for Little Jack's sake."

What the hell do I say to that? Instead, she simply looks into his eyes and sees a lost little boy who barely remembers his past and has no clue to his future.

****

Jack has no clue what to expect. It's his honeymoon and all he can think about is _what the hell is going to happen tonight?_

Aaron and Chloe have just dropped him and Joe off at the Radisson. They've kissed their son goodbye --- he'll be staying with their new friends --- and are now standing in the hotel's lobby nervous and awkward.

This is where they stayed when first arriving in Manchester more than six months ago. So much of his life has changed since then. Yet, oddly, the hotel seems just as it was. Now as then, guests are mingling around the lobby. A pianist is playing some light jazz. Young couples arrive for a steak dinner at JD's Tavern.

He and Joe exchange uncomfortable smiles and they walk over to the desk to register. The familiar clerk recognizes them. Her face is radiant. "Congratulations, guys. I had a feeling about you two!"

The elevator ride up to the ninth floor is almost excruciating. They've never discussed what will happen on their wedding night. Jack has never been with a transsexual before. He has no idea what to think, what to expect or even what to say. Neither man looks at each other. They simply stand side-by-side, holding their respective luggage and staring at the closed doors. Joe eventually breaks the silence by asking, "Have you spoken to Greg?"

"This morning."

"You tell him . . . you tell him about us?"

"Yeah, everything."

Joe nods and says nothing more. Jack continues to wonder how this night will play out. He tries to think about Joe as the man he's become, comparing him with the other men he's had. Jack has always been particular about his lovers: the women need to be playful, curved and sexy; the men have to be buds he could play ball with as well as fuck. Jackie was always an interesting, attractive mixture of the two. He remembers the softness of her skin, the fullness of her breasts, her squirming with please as his tongue played with her pussy. He especially remembers the feel of being inside her. Jack knows her body is different now, but isn't sure if he can handle seeing it . . . much less having sex with him.

They've taken a one bedroom suite. It's decorated in warm, welcoming earth tones. The windows provide a panoramic view of Manchester, the city's lights twinkling and the Verizon Arena ablaze for a concert. There is a parlor. There is also a king size bed --- the only bed.

"I really haven't put much thought into this," Joe admits. "I mean, you know, with all the wedding stuff and all."

"Yeah, me too."

"Chloe actually arraigned for this part."

Joe unzips his bag and pulls out a small plastic bottle. "We don't . . . I mean, we can just spend the night watching old movies." He pours himself a glass of water and opens the bottle. These are the new pain pills the doctor proscribed and so far they seem to be working.

"Is that how you dreamed of your wedding night?"

Joe smiles ruefully. "No, but I bet you didn't either. Besides, I'm sure your thinking about Greg."

"Yeah. His memory is coming back. Little by little. He's being pretty cool about this. I mean, after I reminded him about Vincent and all."

Joe sits on the bed and watches his husband stand before him, shifting nervously from one foot to the other. "I have an idea. Come here, Jack. Let me show you how we can do this."

****

The Union Oyster House is teeming with people, filling booths and tables to enjoy the restaurant's famous seafood. When she was a young woman struggling to succeed in Boston, Karen Scott would sit at the famous circular oyster bar savoring whatever she could afford, just for the sake of being here. But tonight, she has driven out here for a purpose, a very special purpose. Karen St. John needs help. And only one man can provide it.

The hostess seats her not far from the famous Kennedy Booth, so named in honor of the president who was among the restaurant's many famous patrons. Her own booth isn't all that different: the seats' high backs cut off much of the noise, creating a little cocoon of privacy.

Karen has barely looked at her menu when the man arrives. He slides into the seat across from here. She has not seen him in many years. His dark hair has turned gray, his face has wrinkles. But otherwise the man hasn't changed.

The man doesn't bother to greet her. He simply says, "I was surprised to hear from you."

"I need your special services, your special skills."

"Tell me what you need."

Karen briefly lays out her plan. It is very simple, very logical. Her daddy often reminded her that true logic is always simple. The man nods. "I can do that."

"How soon?"

"You set the date. Just make sure I can get in well enough in advance. Payment upfront."

"Of course," she smiles. "Shall we order now?"

EPISODE FIFTEEN

Jack spent the night drifting in and out of sleep. He kept coming back to the experience of making love to a man who was once a woman, a woman he often made love to. It was an odd mixture of similarities and strangeness. Joe, like Jackie, knew how to get him hard. Joe remembered how Jack likes to be kissed and how he likes his cock sucked. But Jack found it strange to no longer have Jackie's well formed breasts, to enter Joe's ass rather than Jackie's pussy. And he found it odd how Joe's cock looked like every other but didn't entirely function like any other.

Joe, on the other hand, fell right to sleep and softly snored through night.

It was the shower that finally woke Jack. He stirred beneath the thick, soft sheets, nude save for the wedding band on his left finger. In the distance, under the water, he can hear Joe sing. It was something Jackie did every morning after they made love. The water stops and he can hear a muffled voice say, "good morning."

Jack doesn't move.

"I know you're awake."

Jack pulls back the covers and turns to face him. Joe is standing there with a towel wrapped around his waist. Again, it is odd to him how similar and different he is from Jackie. "Good morning."

"You okay?"

"Sure."

Joe sits on the bed next to him and gently brushes some hair away from his eyes. "I was afraid you might freak this morning."

"No, it's cool. Really."

Joe smiles and gives him a little kiss. He rises and steps over to the desk where he takes a pain pill. "Oh, by the way, the doctor called yesterday. Everything was so crazed I didn't get to tell you. He wants to see us again."

"Why?"

"I guess to plan out my treatment. I'll call him this afternoon and set things up."

"Okay, no problem."

Joe winks at him, drops his towel on the floor and saunters bare assed back to the bathroom, knowing full well that Jack is watching him.

Just as Jackie used to do.

****

Greg has come to realize that getting your memory back is the kind of mind trip every drug addict dreams of. This morning is a good example. While getting dressed, he came across an old photo of his mother. It must have been taken about two years ago and somehow ended up at the bottom of a drawer. Seeing it gives him such a rush he has to sit on the bed for a few minutes.

The picture takes him back to their last conversation. He had just graduated from NYU. She was throwing a big party at the mansion. That made little sense to him. Hallorans usually attend Harvard or Yale, and his choice caused a minor scandal in the family. Besides, he was in no mood to celebrate. Greg and Jack had just broken up. Losing him was even harder than losing Lauren. But no one said no to Lilly Halloran. She never allowed it.

They fought, mother and son. The two were never close. Lilly never allowed that, either. She was less like a mother then a stern aunt who seldom saw her nephew except at holidays and family events. But this time they went at it. Greg had realized that she was throwing the party not to celebrate his accomplishment, but to hurt his father. Greg was never close to Lewis, either. But at least _he_ never played these little games with his son. Lilly won, as she always did, and Greg made the best of an awkward evening.

She would be dead two weeks later.

The photo also reminds him of her funeral. Everyone commented on how brave he was. He wasn't being stoic. She just didn't mean that much to him. But that is how things have been lately: something comes back to remind him of his father's death or his son's birth or meeting Jack in Atlanta or being blackmailed by that prick Mark Bradley.

It's such a rush.

The dizziness passes, as it always does, so Greg walks downstairs. The family dining room is crowded with Patrick, Julie and Agnes along with the servants. Even Johnny and the nanny are here. She sits with the baby at the far end of the table, feeding him from the bottle of milk that Julie regularly expresses. With the craziness of taking care of him, running her shop and supervising the house, she is often too tired to breastfeed.

Everyone exchanges pleasant "mornings" all around. Greg kisses his wife and his son. A maid brings him a plate with scrambled eggs, toast and bacon. A hearty breakfast, although it occurs to him that he's put on a few pounds. That thought has brought another rush of memory: jogging in the town square, around the John Halloran statute. Fortunately he's sitting down for this one and no one notices.

A pair of conversations happens at once: he and Patrick are to meet with some of the execs today as well as the accountants. Greg finds himself getting into the groove of the company. That's good news for his cousin, who needs to concentrate on finals and his upcoming graduation.

The other conversation is between Julie and Agnes. They are going shopping today with Julie's mother and aunt in Portsmouth to buy gowns for the big event happening at the Currier Museum. "I can't believe we waited this long," Julie sighs. "The reception is tomorrow night."

"Well, dear, they are just unveiling some painting. That's not quite the same has the queen opening parliament."

The mood is light and happy and very . . . very family. It's something Greg didn't have much of growing up and it makes him realizing something else.

This is a rush, too.

****

Denise marvels at Karen St. John. Even early in the morning, when most people are struggling to face the day, the lady is cool and elegant. She even butters a croissant with class.

"I really appreciate your giving me the extra days off."

"You are very welcome, dear. I hope your family is doing well." Denise had to make a last-minute trip home for her grandfather's funeral. Everyone expected his passing to come, but no one thought it would happen so quickly.

"Yes, ma'am, thank you."

"By the way, I need you to call my lawyer this morning. He should be in his office in little more than an hour."

"Certainly.

"I need him to overnight to me the special package."

"The special package?"

"He'll know what I mean."

****

Lorene takes a deep breath, inhaling the fresh spring air. She loves this time of year. The bitter cold of winter has past and the simmering heat of summer has yet to arrive. All she needs is a comfy sweater and someone to share the day with.

That someone used to be her husband. Now it's her wife; or, at least, the woman who will soon be her wife.

She and Vivian are holding hands as they stroll through Faraway Hill's main square, watching the little shops open for the day. The flowers around John Halloran's statute are starting to bloom. A few birds are chirping overhead. It's as if the world is waking up from a long slumber.

The couple makes their stops. Mr. Shutlz at the bakery offers them fresh rolls and some of the best chocolate chip cookies Lorene has ever had. The deli has their order ready. The antique store around the corner is ready to deliver the new chair Vivian discovered the other day.

Everyone welcomes the pair as naturally as they do the sunrise. It makes Lorene feel especially happy. Things weren't always this way with Munroe. Whenever he was drinking --- and sometimes when he wasn't --- getting him out of the house or off the farm was a challenge. And people weren't always happy to see him. But Vivian likes the town almost as much as she does. Leaving the little dollar store, she turns to Lorene and says "for the wedding, let's Invite <u>everybody</u>."

****

Mark is just stepping out of the shower when he hears the knock. "Housekeeping," says a muffled voice. Mark chuckles; he really enjoys these visits by the hot little maid. He wraps a towel around his waist, walks over to the door and opens it with his best client smile. "Hey."

The hot little maid is a girl around 19 or 20, wearing a pale blue uniform and standing next to a supply cart. She blushes. "Hello, sir. I'm here to service the room."

I like that; we all need to service our customers. "Knock yourself out, babe."

The girl blushes again. He steps aside to let her work. Mark is staying in Room 204 of a little highway motel. It's the most discreet place he could find. It's also a cheap place, with the shag carpet, old TV and worn bed. Still, it's been a lot of fun watching the girl as she makes her regular visits. She is always careful not to look directly at him. Mark knows this routine; he's experienced it before. It comes from having the kind of well-defined body that's difficult to ignore. When she disappears into the bathroom, Mark picks up his cell and sends Greg Halloran a quick text. With the word out that his memory is returning he needs to meet with the dude. *It's time to pay the rent.*

The girl emerges from the bathroom carrying used towels and a trash bag. She actually giggles while stuffing them into her service cart.

"You know, you've never told me your name."

"Meryl," she answers with a timid smile.

"Meryl?"

"My mom was a big fan of Meryl Streep."

"Cool."

He starts getting hard at the sight of her tight little ass as she bends over the bed to pull off the sheets. "Work here long?"

"About a year." Meryl bags the old sheets and brings out a clean, neatly folded set from her cart. Mark can tell she's thrilled with the attention.

"Like it?"

"Not really."

"How come?"

Meryl bends over again, this time to put the fitted sheet in place. *Gotta love that ass.* "Most of the guests are kind of weird."

"Weird?"

"Yeah, like last fall. There was this guy, an old guy, who stayed right here in this room for the longest time. But he wasn't nice, like you. And he never left the room."

"Never?"

"Nope and it was creepy --- real creepy." She slips the pillows into new cases. "The room was always a sty. Half-eaten food, dirty clothes everywhere. He'd have the TV blaring at all hours."

"Sounds like some sicko."

Meryl carefully keeps her eyes on her task. "Yeah, well, that's not the weirdest part."

"What was?"

"He just up and disappeared. Right after Thanksgiving."

"I'm sure lots of people ditch the motel without paying."

"Oh, no, the room was paid up. But he was gone."

"What's so weird about that?"

"I came in that morning and the place was perfect. I mean, totally cleaned up. I was the only one on duty but the bed, the bathroom; everything was like he'd never been here."

"That _is_ weird."

Finished with the bed, Meryl looks up at him again. She takes a deep breath and notices the bulge in his towel. "Well, that's everything, sir."

"Are you sure about that, Meryl?"

The girl blushes yet again. _It's been a long time since I've fucked for fun._ He drops his towel to the floor.

"Well, sir . . . I guess I can stay for a few more minutes."

✱✱✱✱

The hour drive to Portsmouth is more like a traveling party than a shopping trip. Karen rents a black Lincoln Navigator limo for the day, riding around Faraway Hill to pick-up Julie and Agnes (who chuckle at the car), then Eve (who shakes her head) and finally to Concord to get Ann (who squeals at the sight). The interior seems particularly roomy with only five passengers. Ann marvels at all the little amenities like the fiber optic lights and LCD TVs.

The ladies sip sparkling cider on the ride east (the Champaign being saved for the trip home). Ann talks about her honeymoon in Nantucket, Julie about the baby and Karen relates the colorful tale of meeting Liza Minnelli at a Manhattan party ("the poor girl had gained so much weight I could barely recognize her").

They arrive at Madeline's Daughter, a specialty boutique in Lafayette Plaza, just in time for their appointment. The staff has pre-selected some suggestions and the women begin acting like schoolgirls preparing for the prom, laughing and acting silly. Karen and Eve select simple, elegant gowns. Julie chooses a blue dress with a little sparkle along the sleeves. Agnes decides not to buy anything, insisting that she has just the right outfit at home.

Ann turns her shopping into a mini fashion show, with her the star. Or at least she tries to. Each dress is more flashy than the first causing everyone's eyes to roll. Groans are occasionally heard. Julie realizes that this is her first real shopping trip. So, she takes her sister-in-law aside, whispers something, and the next dress turns out to be the last. It's fairly tame and Ann quiets down.

They have lunch next door at Margarita's Restaurant while the gowns are altered ("we are happy to put a rush on this for you, Mrs. St. John.").

On the way home, all five enjoy the Champaign but are otherwise more subdued. Ann is particularly quiet after Julie's little talk. But mostly the ladies are just tired. One by one, Karen drops them off at home: first Ann then Julie and Agnes until finally it's just she and her big sister. Eve takes a sip from her glass and asks, "Have you heard from Mark?"

"No, but I've already spoken to Ben."

"When did that happen?"

"During lunch; I got a call when I was in the ladies room. You needn't worry; we've worked out what to give the boy. Everything will be fine."

The limo pulls up to Eve's house. "They'd better be."

✳✳✳✳

Jack has walked past Shaskeen Pub several times since moving to Manchester. He's often thought about stopping in but the place usually gets jammed in the evening. It's across from City Hall Plaza and he happened to notice yesterday while getting his marriage license that the place is relatively quiet during the afternoon. It should make a good, private place for him and Greg to meet.

He is sitting at the bar, admiring its workmanship. The bartender told him that the wood came from a church in Ireland and was custom built for the place. Jack found himself ordering bourbon-on-the-rocks, his dad's favorite drink. He doesn't know why. Maybe it's because he is now a married father, too. *Or maybe I need something a little grown up.*

Grown up? Jack Campbell? He glances at his reflection in the bar's mirror and smiles at the irony. *Maybe I am grown up now.* He's married; he has a son. But this is not the way he wanted it. Jack seldom thought about marriage before, always content to party and hook-up. But Jackie was always the exception; Jackie made him wonder about having a wife and kids. Now he has a son who doesn't know Jack's his dad and a husband rather than a wife --- and who will be dead in a few months.

Joe will be dead. Jack has been so busy being the hero he hasn't really thought about what this will mean. *Holy shit, how can I handle losing him? How can Little Jack? What the fuck do I say to him about his papa?*

"Hey."

Jack looks up to see Greg Halloran standing there with a cautious smile. Without caring about what anyone sees or thinks, Jack jumps up and gives his lover a bear hug. It's been nearly four months since the men last saw each other, making love in Jack's apartment. "God, how I missed you, dude!"

"I've missed you, too," Greg answers returning the hug.

"You remember?"

"Yeah, almost everything."

The two sit at the otherwise empty bar. Jack wonders how their meeting looked to the bartender, who doesn't seem at all phased. Greg orders a Diet Coke ("I'm still on meds" he explains) and begins to hear Jack describe his brief but odd wedding. Greg listens to everything politely, nodding when appropriate, but doesn't ask him about the wedding night. *Good; I don't want to talk about that.* Jack lied to Joe. He *is* freaked about what happened. It was an experience he never wanted and never expected to enjoy.

He also wonders if he's cheating on someone. *Is it on Joe or on Greg?*

Greg sips his Diet Coke. "I guess that means we're . . . what are we? I mean, what do we do now?"

"Keep going, I guess. Both Joe and Julie know about us and they seem pretty cool about it."

Jack can see how torn he still is, the internal conflict is written on the man's face. "Maybe, but Julie . . . Julie has been there for me. She's my wife, the mother of my son."

Holy shit, is he backing out on me? He can't! "And Jackie's my wife --- sort of --- and Julie is the one who came up with the plan."

"I know . . . but I like having a family. It feels good."

"Man, I'm going to need you. I can't handle what's going to happen to Joe and Jack, not alone."

Greg looks Jack firmly in the eyes. "You won't be alone. I promise. But, before anything else, there is a mess I need to clean-up first." *What the hell is he talking about?* "You remember Ann's first husband?"

"The hustler." Jack remembers seeing him briefly in Manhattan months ago.

"Yeah, well, I was one of his clients. Don't look at me like that. He's got me on tape. I've been paying his rent since he left. But I got a text from him this morning. He's in town and wants more money."

"Shit. What are you going to do?"

"Well, for one thing, I'm not going to let this fucker blackmail me forever. I'm going to offer him one big pile of cash --- but only if he turns over every copy to me."

"Are you sure you can trust him?"

"No, but I've got to try."

****

"Give yourself a little time, son." Peter Brandt's ailing father told him. "You'll be fine."

That has been the old man's advice since Peter was a child. It is his variation of "time heals all wounds" and Peter is tired of it. Time can be as much a torture as a healer. Every day has been that way since Karen St. John dumped him.

Tomorrow he is to be sworn in as the first chief of the newly formed Faraway Hill United Police Department, a merged entity policing Faraway Hill and neighboring towns. But tonight he is sitting in Hugh's Bar, a dark little place a block from the square and drinking away the afternoon.

"You don't want to overdo it," Hugh warns Peter. "You got a big day tomorrow."

"Just give me another."

Hugh nods and refills his beer mug. Actually, this is Hugh Jr. Father and son have owned the bar for decades. Little of it has changed. The bar itself dates to 1930s, an aging relic of dark mahogany. The red vinyl booths were installed in the 1960s. The tin ceiling is painted black. The windows are made of glass block. Even the seldom played jukebox has nothing but 70s tunes. Coming inside here is like entering a different Faraway Hill. This Faraway Hill no longer exists. When Hugh Sr. ran it, workers from the Halloran Mill crowded the place between shifts. No one was divorced or gay or had a college education. No one drank mineral water or logged on to get their news.

Even Hugh Jr. looks like he's from another time. Approaching 80 and completely bald, the old man wears the kind of rough shirt Peter remembers his own father wearing to work at the mill.

"You should feel good about yourself," Hugh says shaking his head.

"Why the fuck should I?"

"Boy, I've known you your whole life. And as smart as you are, you're still clueless."

"About what?"

"You got everything. Great parents, college, working overseas helping people. Your young, getting a terrific job."

"And alone."

"Look around you, we are all alone." Peter doesn't have to look around him; there are only three other people in the bar and they are sitting far from each other. "This is your time, Peter. Enjoy it."

****

Richard Davis has been craving a scotch since this morning. He has had one stressful meeting after another, and all about the same problem. So the moment he arrives home that evening he immediately walks into the living, stands at the bar and pours himself a Dewar's on the rocks.

It's been that kind of a day.

The first meeting was with his lawyer. Richard has known Harold Greene since prep school. They've double dated together, gone to college together, married and raised kids at about the same time and have even gone grey together. But today was one of the rare times they've ever fought. Harold had the divorce papers all ready for Ann and Mark to sign. He also felt the need to say something that nearly got him a punch in the face. "You can get out of this, you know."

Richard spent an hour defending the woman he loves to his best friend even as his best friend's concerns raised doubts in his own mind. And he longed for a smooth scotch.

The next meeting occurred during lunch at the Common Man, where Richard sat with some key campaign contributors. He would've ordered a drink then, but needed to stay sober. Too much of the discussion was been about the wrong things. Even though none of these men know about the bigamy or the blackmail, they all seemed more fascinated with the senator's wife than with the senator. It surprised him. No matter what Richard did to steer the conversation toward an issue or a donation, it kept coming back to Ann and Lewis Halloran's murder; Ann and the male hooker; and Ann's months-long fight with the Hallorans for her inheritance.

Through it all his craving for a scotch grew.

After lunch came the meeting with his chief of staff. Richard hadn't told Jerry Miller much about the situation. Jerry had never been keen on the marriage, worried that Ann came with too much baggage. But now, with the risk of people finding out about the blackmail, Richard had no choice. They stood alone, in his Concord office, and argued. Richard isn't sure how long they fought, but it was even worse than what he went through that morning with Harold. Jerry is much younger, more politically attune and has his own ambitions. "I was afraid something like this would happen. That girl just brings trouble with her."

Even meeting with his banker, to make the necessary withdraw, was stressful. The woman found it odd that the senator would need $50,000 in cash. But she was careful enough not to ask.

The final meeting was, oddly, the easiest. Richard drove south to meet with Bradley at some tacky motel off the highway. He greeted the senator wearing nothing but a cocky smile and a pair of tight, white boxer briefs. "I though I should dress up for this, dude." The whole thing was over in twenty minutes. The man signed the papers and got his money. "Give my best to the Mrs." was all he said as Richard left.

Now, finally, he gets to have his scotch. One of the worst days of his life is over. Ann will be home soon and he can tell her that Bradley is out of their lives forever. But as Richard savors the soothing alcohol, a voice in the back of his head whispers the question: *is she worth it?*

✱✱✱✱

Mark lays back on his bed, nude, stretching out with a satisfied grin. It has been a good day.

It began by fucking that cute young maid this morning. She was really into it. And it was nice being with a woman again, especially one with a young, hot body. *What was her name again? Mary, Marie? Something like that.*

Just before lunch he heard from Ben King and started negotiating his fee. That afternoon Ann's new husband stopped by to wrap up there deal. Now, there is just one more pigeon to pluck and he can go back to his life in New York.

As if on cue, his cell rings. Mark picks it up. His pigeon is calling. "Hey dude, how's my favorite client?"

"Never mind that shit. I've got a deal for you."

"Shoot."

"I'll pay your next two years' rent in advance on two conditions: you give me every copy of that video, including the master, and you stay the fuck out of my life forever."

"Dude, that video is gold."

"That's my offer."

"Well, here's my counter: two years' rent and ten grand in cash."

He can hear Greg mumble a curse. "Fuck you."

"Is that a yes?"

"Fine. When and where do we do this?"

"I'll get back to you."

****

The following morning feels more like summer than spring. Denise has just emerged from her little apartment, a cozy second floor walk-up in downtown Faraway Hill. It has hard wood floors and decorative fireplaces and a bay window overlooking the square. Such an apartment would cost a fortune in Manhattan. Here, though, it costs Denise less than a week's pay.

She stops off at the corner coffee shop for her usual latte. Today's gossip includes people seeing the town's new police commissioner, the hot young Peter Brandt, boozing it up at the pub down the street. "He seems so sad," one little old lady tells another.

Denise sips her latte as she strolls toward Mrs. St.John's house. She lived with her boss for a short time until the lady suggested they both need their privacy. Denise is fine with that; she has even been able to hook-up with a couple of guys since moving in.

She arrives at the same time as the UPS man. *He really knows how to fill out that brown uniform.* She signs for the thick overnight envelope --- clearly Mrs. J's "special package" --- and enters the house. Her boss, as elegant as always, smiles at Denise while on her cell explaining to someone that "you should do it at King's Korner. That's the best place."

****

Greg slowly, cautiously, opens the door. He has not been in this room since the day of the tour, the day his memories began coming back to him. But it's time for him to do what every generation of Halloran men has done and claim the mansion's study for his own.

This room, in many ways, is more about family legacy than almost any other in the house. Along the walls are echoes of the past, portraits of Hallorans who have come and gone. The locked mahogany gun cabinet holds John Halloran's bayonet from the Revolution and another belonging to Theodore Halloran from World War I.

A pocket watch carried by Greg's grandfather sits proudly under glass. Next to it on the bureau is a photo of a dignified William Halloran standing next to Herbert Hoover taken somewhere in Europe. There is also much of his father still here: the pictures on the desk, the little notes taped to the computer monitor.

Greg's eyes wander about the room until they come to a framed, antique document hanging from a wall. It's beautifully inscribed in a worn Latin script that he can barely read. Seeing it causes him to have another memory flash, something about someone speaking to him in Latin. But the dizziness doesn't last long and the image is gone. *That was weird.* Normally when he has a flash, the memory is clear.

Looking at all of these mementos of husbands and fathers has him thinking about his own roles. Greg likes being married and having a son. The daily rituals of mealtime and holding the baby and seeing his wife smile feel good and comfortable and right.

Greg sits in the big leather chair behind the desk. He starts to open drawers to peer inside. There are some outdated company memos and an album from his dad's college years. Flipping through it Greg can't help but think how much they, father and son, look alike. One photo has Lewis and another handsome young man, arm-in-arm, at a beach somewhere. They both look tan and fit and happy. A scrawled notation beside it reads, "me and Alex Mundy, summer of 1988."

In one drawer he comes across a folder. On it is written in his father's hand, "Greg & the Brothers". Curious, he opens it to find lined yellow sheets with comments by Lewis such as "ask about initiation process for older plebes" and "get Robert to help lobby the elders." None of this makes any sense to him.

A knock at the door; Patrick opens it and steps inside. They are supposed to go into the office together today. But since their meetings aren't until the afternoon the two cousins allowed themselves the luxury of sleeping late. "Hey, dude, can we talk?"

"Sure, come in." The young man looks both serious and uncomfortable. Greg closes the folder as Patrick takes the chair opposite him. They sit silent for an awkward moment. Greg tries to break the tension with his own personal family joke. "I've been thinking about how being a Halloran comes with two hundred years of baggage."

Patrick grins but still seems uneasy. He clearly feels the need to say something and that something suddenly occurs to Greg: "you know about me and Jack, don't you?"

Relieved, the young man sighs. "Yeah, I do. I'm pretty sure Ann knows too."

"You seem cool about it."

Patrick shrugs. "Dude, who am I to judge? Anyway, is that why you and Julie aren't sleeping in the same room?"

"You know about that?"

"Servants gossip."

Fuck. "I don't know what to say."

"You don't have to say anything, but, really, don't you have to make a choice?"

"Actually, Julie already made it."

"She did?"

"She decided months ago. After her father wins the election, we're getting divorced. That's why the old servants' quarters out back have been renovated. She and Johnny will move in there."

"Is that what you want?"

That's a good question. "I'm not sure anymore."

****

Mark Bradley loves to shock people. Ever since he was a little boy, when he'd do something to his mother or a teacher or anyone, it always gives him a good laugh. Like the other day, sitting naked in Karen St. John's living room and making the two sisters squirm.

This is why he is spending the afternoon in Faraway Hill.

Strolling through the town square, he smiles at familiar faces, each surprised to see him. Those in pairs and groups point and whisper; he responds with a wave. Mark is sure to be the focus of gossip once again. He stops by Shutlz's Bakery, where the owner looks him over warily. Mark peruses the fresh muffins, gives the man a wink and steps outside.

The town looks pretty good, he thinks, noticing the flowers blooming around the Halloran statute. The site reminds him of tonight, when he meets Ben King and Greg Halloran at King's Korner. Neither man knows the other is coming. Neither man knows the other is bringing a big payoff. *It should be a lot of fun; I can't to tell the old man that his son-in-law used to fuck his little boy.* He chuckles at the thought.

Strolling along the sidewalk, Mark welcomes the gawking. Eventually he comes to Hugh's Bar. He misses this place; it is quiet and dark and was always a good place to unwind --- and an even better place to meet clients.

From the moment Mark steps inside, Hugh grimaces. Mark takes it all in stride, sits at the bar and orders a beer. Hugh pours him a draught, leans in and says simply, "I don't know why the hell your back, but don't cause any trouble."

"No problem, dude". The old man doesn't look convinced. Mark takes a sip and looks around. The place hasn't changed in the year he's been gone. The red vinyl booths, black tin ceiling, glass block windows. All of it is just as it was.

Seated quietly in a corner is another familiar face. It's Ed Connor, a local feed supplier, and one of Mark's old clients. *Old is right, the fucker's sixty if he's a day.* Back then Conner serviced Munroe Gale's farm and Mark serviced Conner. It was never easy. Pale, wrinkled, graying, Mark always had trouble getting it up.

Now Conner is sitting alone, nursing his beer, a scene that reminds Mark of the first time they met here. Only this time, the old man just stares at him, surprised and scared of an old scandal coming back to haunt him.

Mark smiles and raises his mug in salute.

****

As the sun starts its slow decent for the night, guests begin arriving at the Currier Museum of Art. They are all important people, arriving in town cars or limos or expensive hybrids through the landscaped plaza past an impressive steel sculpture. They enter the stately Henry Melville Fuller Winter Garden to discover a buffet of treats, a little stage and, most importantly, an open bar.

"Where's Greg?"

Julie turns from the buffet to see Ann and Richard standing together, smiling. Over their shoulders she can see people point and whisper at the senator and his infamous wife. *I'm sure she loves that.* "He had a last minute call at the office." Julie excuses herself to bring a plate to Agnes, who is in her wheelchair admiring the view through the gallery's huge windows. "I just love this place," the old artist says with a sigh. "Especially those," she adds indicating the pair of colorful Sol LeWitt murals.

"Then we should come here more often."

Julie looks across the room. The crowd is getting larger. She sees many familiar faces, some of people she's met and others she's seen on television. Several of them come over to introduce themselves. Agnes knows almost all of them, and, of course, they all know her.

Eventually, she begins scanning the crowd for her husband or her parents. None are here yet, not even Aunt Karen. *That's strange.* Eventually, her mother appears. Alone. Julie leaves Agnes to chat with some admirers to ask her mother, "where's Dad?"

"He had a last minute call. Where's Greg?"

"The same." Julie instantly knows something is wrong. *Could they talking to each other? What could it be about?*

Before they can discuss it, the museum's president calls the audience to the stage. "We are very honored tonight to have been presented, through the efforts of one of New Hampshire's most illustrious daughters, something very rare, something very historic. The original illustrations of an artist and author named Willem Arondeus." The president describes the Dutchman's involvement in the anti-Nazi movement and how he illustrated his own novels. Just as he begins describing how the Nazis destroyed most of his works before executing him, Julie's cell vibrates. She steps away from the presentation to take the call. It's Mary Armstrong, the girl who works for her at King's Korner. "I'm sorry, Mrs. Halloran, but the store is on fire."

"What! How? What's happening?"

"I'm not sure. I closed up as normal and went out to dinner with friends. But all of downtown now is tied up. You'd better get out here." Julie thanks her, briefs Agnes (who agrees to get a ride with Ann) and rush out the door with her mother.

As they are leaving, Julie glances behind her to see the museum's benefactor take the stage --- her Aunt Karen.

****

By rights it should only take a few minutes to get from the museum to the shop. All Julie has to do is drive down Ash Street, turn right onto Bridge Street and that takes her directly to Elm. But the moment they pass the Chestnut Street intersection --- only a few blocks from Elm Street --- they are stopped. Police are out directing people north and away from the scene. *Holy shit, is it really that bad?*

Julie rolls down the window to call one of the officers over. "We think the fire is at our store. Is there anyway we can get there or talk to someone?"

The officer, a woman, steps away and pulls out her walkie talkie to talk to what Julie suspects is her superior. She turns to her mother, who is just finishing a call on her cell. "Mary says that all of the employees are safe."

"Thank God for that."

The officer returns to the car. "Ma'am, if you park over there on Church Street, another officer will meet you. You'll have to walk, but he'll take you to speak to the fire marshal." Julie thanks her and follows her instructions. Within a moment, another officer, a handsome young man, greets them. "Are you ladies the owners of King's Korner?"

"Yes, I'm Julie Halloran; this is my mother, Eve King."

"I'm Lieutenant Aaron Tracey. Please follow me." He leads them down Nutfield Lane --- a little street one block east of Elm --- until they reach Amherst and walk up to Manchester's main drag. A huge section of Elm is blocked off with fire trucks, ambulance and police cars. WMUR-TV has a mobile van on the scene. People crowd the sidewalks to watch the firefighters at work. *Oh my God,*

Julie thinks. *It looks like an entire block was hit.* She glances at her mother, who appears calm and controlled even though their little business is now a black char.

Lt. Tracey advises them to wait here, until he can get someone to answer their questions. Julie takes her mother's hand in hers, and gives it a supportive squeeze. The crowds seem to be getting bigger when she sees a familiar face. *Is that Mark Bradley? What the hell is he doing here?*

The fire chief walks over and introduces himself. "Mrs. King, Mrs. Halloran, I'm sorry to say that it's totaled."

"Any idea what caused it?"

"We won't know until the investigation is complete, but we think it may be electrical."

That makes no sense, Julie thinks; *we had the place rewired before opening the shop.* Another fireman motions the chief who excuses himself.

"Don't worry mom, we're insured."

"I know, but . . . it still hurts."

The chief returns, this time with a grim look on his face. Something else is wrong, very wrong. "Ladies, I'm sorry again, but . . . we found a body inside."

"Oh my God! Any idea who it is?"

"We found his ID." With a great deal of genuine sympathy he looks directly at one of the women and says, "It's your husband."

TO BE CONTINUED IN BOOK THREE

Book Two Discussion Guide

This guide has been created to facilitate book clubs and their members in discussing *Faraway Hill: Book Two.*

- The first chapter resolves the cliffhanger of *Faraway Hill: Book One.* Did you have your own theory as to who pulled the trigger and who was hit? Were you right or wrong?
- Much like a flashback sequence in a television soap opera, Karen spends some time reflecting on her past. Does knowing her history make her more or less sympathetic?
- How do you feel about the way Julie handles her husband's affair with another man? Does this reflect inner strength or her lack thereof? What would you have done in the same situation?
- Jack's response to a dramatic moment with his family is to go to New York, hit some bars and spend the night with strangers. What does this say about him? Have you ever used sex as an escape valve or for comfort?
- How has Ann's relationship with her mother changed since Vivian's arrival?
- Karen is becoming increasingly frustrated that, no matter how logical or carefully executed, her plans are not working out as well as in the past. What must she do to change this?
- Did you expect the connection between Ben King and Mark Bradley?
- Right now, the Kings suspect that Lewis, not his son, was Mark's client. Do you think the truth will ever come out? What do you think the repercussions will be if it does?
- Joe makes a bargain with his criminal stepfather. Do you think that this deal will hold? Why or why not?
- Karen becomes frustrated when Julie won't confide in her anymore. What do you think is holding Julie back?
- In this book, the reader starts learning about the Frater of Thebes, something that the author only hinted at in *Faraway Hill: Book One.* Had you heard the Thebes story before? What do you know about sexuality in the ancient world? Do you think there is a sexual component in organizations like college fraternities?
- Patrick's final initiation ceremony culminates in something even he didn't expect. Did it shock you or did it titillate you? Why or why not?
- Ann thinks she has finally found the right man in her whirlwind romance with Richard Davis. How do you think Mark's blackmail has complicated their relationship? Do they have a future?

- *Faraway Hill: Book Two* introduces three elements common in soap operas: the coma, amnesia and a trip (of sorts) to the past. How does learning about Greg's college years affect your opinion of him? Was Julie being realistic when she thought his amnesia gave them a fresh start?
- Joe's health becomes an issue. Did you know transsexual men sometimes have ovarian cancer? What do you know about the unique health issues of transsexuals?
- This installment of the trilogy ends with a death. One of two major characters --- Ben or Greg --- is dead. Which do you think it is? Why or why not?